Praise

"Ian Healy's *Just Cause* is a slam-bang good superhero story: part *JLA*, part *Young Romance*, with some splashes of *Our Army at War* to keep you on your toes. I thoroughly enjoyed Mustang Sally's adventure and look forward to reading more of Healy's work."

—Rob Rogers, author of *Devil's Cape*

~ ~ ~

"Ian Healy's *Just Cause* is solid, serious superhero action in the classic tradition, with tons of interesting characters, extremely well-crafted action scenes, and real depth. Highly recommended."

—Van Allen Plexico, author of *The Sentinels*

~ ~ ~

"The best thing about Ian Healy's books is the accessibility of their worlds and characters. He welcomes us in and takes us for a fun and memorable ride, and unlike other superhero universes, we never feel like the understanding of an entire mythology is out of our grasp—or would take thousands of reading hours to accomplish."

—Allison M. Dickson, author of *The Last Supper*

"Mr. Healy once again manages to fully embrace the more fantastic aspects of superhero fiction (magic guitars, amazing powers, giant robots, colorful costumes) while grounding the story with characters you care about and serious consequences for them."
Corey L. Bishop, *Creative Commoners* podcast

~~~

"Ian Healy's *Just Cause* is a great superhero book because it creates a world that is so close to our own we almost think that maybe these things did/are really happening, it's just that we don't live in the right city, and don't maybe have that special brick touch pattern to get us to Diagon Alley."

—Jenn Zuko, *Nerds in Babeland*

~~~

"It almost feels like you're watching a movie instead of reading a book when the superheroes are battling the villains."

—Megan Bostic, author of *Never Eighteen*

More books by Ian Thomas Healy

The Just Cause Universe

Just Cause: Revised & Expanded Edition

The Archmage

Day of the Destroyer

Deep Six (Coming Fall 2013)

Novels

Blood on the Ice

Hope and Undead Elvis

Pariah's Moon

Rooftops

*Starf*cker*

The Guitarist

The Milkman: SuperSekrit Extra Cheesy Edition

Troubleshooters

Collections

Tales of the Weird Wild West, Vol. 1

The Bulletproof Badge

Nonfiction

Action! Writing Better Action Using Cinematic Techniques

Titles available at Local Hero Press
(localheropress.ianthealy.com), Amazon.com,
BarnesandNoble.com, and other online retailers.

DAY OF THE DESTROYER

A *Just Cause Universe* Novel

IAN THOMAS HEALY

Local Hero Press

ISBN: **0615749844**
ISBN-13: **978-0615749846**

Printed in the United States of America

First Printing March 2013

As always, the *Just Cause Universe* novels require a lot of behind-the-scenes work. First and foremost, I must thank my chief editor, Allison M. Dickson, for her tireless work on my behalf. She surprised me with the full edit on this one for my birthday! A huge shout-out goes to Jeff Hebert for his fantastic cover art. This guy has a feel for my characters like nobody I've ever met. Much love and many thanks to my family for their support, and to my fans for giving me a reason to continue this bad habit.

Introduction

Making it Real

When I was growing up, Spider-Man was my favorite hero. It wasn't just because I'd seen him from my early days watching *The Electric Company* (ah, Spidey, how I remember you and your dialog balloons). And it wasn't because of his awesome 1970s animated series ("...does whatever a spider can..."). It was because to me, Spider-Man was real.

Oh, I knew he was a fictional character. But he didn't come across as *just* a hero; there was always more to him than that. He had girl troubles (whether they were Gwen or M.J.). He had to deal with bullies, both at school (hey there, Flash) and, when he was older, at work (J.J.J., you sly dog). He had to have a day job, not as a cover for his secret identity but to pay the rent. There were times when he'd have doughnuts for dinner. And he experienced grief, whether it was the death of his beloved uncle, or of the girl he loved, or of a colleague: When Mar-Vell was dying of cancer in *The Death of Captain Marvel*, Spider-Man was overwhelmed and said that superheroes are supposed to go in battle, while taking down a villain or saving the world; they aren't supposed to die from cancer.

He was real.

That's what makes the most interesting—and the best —superheroes and supervillains: they have to be real. We have to be able to relate to them, not just understand them but sympathize with them. Under their masks, they should be people, just people—people we want to know better. Yes, these people have fantastic powers and use them to save (or possibly attempt to take over) the world. But despite the costumes, they're just like you and me. They have dreams. And they have pain. That pain can take many shapes. It can be as subtle as temptation, or as blatant as a punishment. It can be the sting of unrequited love. It can be the horror of abuse. All of these things turn characters from two-dimensional notions of good and evil and transform them into characters with depth.

And that's what the heroes of Just Cause—and the villains they fight—bring to the table: depth. It's their human flaws that make them real, and make them so much more than their parahuman powers—which, admittedly, are very cool. It's what makes us want not just to be them but to hang out with them (whether or not it's a Wednesday night). It's what makes us root for them during the fight scenes, or when they're trapped in a burning building. And it's what makes us care about the bad guys too.

Because let's face it: it's not as simple as good versus evil. The best stories never are.

—Jackie Kessler, co-author of *Black And White*
January, 2013

ONE

July 13, 1977, 9:00 AM

Faith smiled as she awoke, despite the jangling alarm clock on her bedside table. She had been dreaming of Rick, his soft fur caressing her skin, a rumbling purr emanating from his thick chest. The clock drove away the last remnants of golden mane and liquid amber eyes from her mind, leaving only warm fuzzy feelings lingering inside her as she opened her eyes. The lion-faced superhero had starred in many of her dreams of late, and more often than not, she found herself watching him when they were together in headquarters, careful never to let anyone notice her attentiveness. Especially not Bobby.

Bobby rolled over and mumbled something in his sleep before his snores filled the air once again. She watched the rise and fall of his chest beside her, smooth and hairless, unlike the wild-maned torso of her crush.

Faith loved her husband, but he was so… tame.

She and Bobby had been together since '69, and the last exciting thing he'd done was to steal his father's car so they could go to Woodstock together. Since then, he'd been a comfortable but mundane husband. Even his parahuman ability of enhanced hearing could never be considered the least bit flamboyant. They'd been married since '72 and he was the only man she'd ever slept with. It made her feel both old-fashioned and at times, disappointed. At twenty-three, she wasn't the oldest member of the Just Cause superhero team, but she'd been with them since she was sixteen—much longer than anyone else—and some days she felt like the only adult surrounded by petulant teens.

She didn't want to stay in bed any longer. Superheroes didn't punch a time clock, but it bothered her to lounge around instead of being responsible. The least she could do would be to honor the heroic tradition set by her parents, the founders of Just Cause, and drag her sorry self into headquarters, at least to give the illusion that she was doing something to better the city and state of New York.

The morning had already grown hot. New Yorkers could expect more triple-degree temperatures with no relief in sight, the radio announcer warned. Bobby had been talking about installing central air conditioning in their brownstone, but until that actually came about, they slept in the miserable heat and humidity, windows open and fans fighting a losing battle against the merciless daytime sun and stagnant nighttime air.

Faith took a fast shower, not bothering to wait for warm water. She soaped away the night sweat and the smell of Bobby on her skin. The metaphor wasn't lost on her, as she remembered snippets of her dream, the feel of Rick's claws gently pricking against her skin. She shivered, and not from the cool spray.

Wrapped in one towel and another around her blonde hair, cut in the feathered style Farrah Fawcett had made famous, she headed for the kitchen to brew a pot of coffee. Halfway down the short hall, she stopped to gaze upon the photo montage of her fellow heroes and friends. Her eyes lingered longest on the picture of Rick, dressed as Lionheart, mugging for the camera next to a real lion that day the team had gone to the circus. In comparison to the great cat, he looked much more human than feral, but the similarities were unmistakable. If King Richard from Disney's furry-animal version of *Robin Hood* had been real, he'd have been the spitting image of Rick Lyons. Faith reached up to touch the picture.

Bobby stirred in the bedroom and Faith drew her hand back in a guilty blur as if the picture had scalded her.

She retreated into the kitchen. Although she had little skill in the art of cooking, she did lay in a supply of expensive African coffee. Bobby drank the stuff like it was water.

Rick had likewise acquired a taste for it after Faith brought him some to try one day. Ever since then, she made a point to bring him fresh coffee when she could.

While the coffee percolated, Faith returned to the bedroom to dress. She kept three complete costumes in rotation, so while one was at the Chinese laundry up the street, she still had a spare in case the one she wore got torn or dirty enough to necessitate a change. She pulled on the cropped crimson t-shirt with the yellow horse-head logo emblazoned across the front. Her mother had worn the same logo as Colt, one of the founders of Just Cause. Faith's own take was far more revealing than her mother Judy had ever dared to be in the Forties and Fifties. Where her mother's outfit had been demure and conservatively cut, Faith as Pony Girl was a symbol for the sexy, liberated women of modern times. Her low-cut red stretch-denim jeans with the yellow piping showed off her legs all the way down, as her mother liked to say.

She debated whether or not it was too hot to leave her lightweight fringed leather jacket behind, but common sense won out. It wasn't so much for protection from criminals, because there weren't any who would dare take on a parahuman anymore. One slip-up at super-speed and she'd give herself a nasty case of road rash without the jacket to protect her. She pulled on her soft leather boots with the heavy steel-belted dual-ply radial soles. They were weighty, but her legs were fast and strong enough that it didn't matter.

She tucked her fingerless yellow gloves into her sash, shook out her hair, and rested her goggles on her forehead. The former were a quirky affectation and the latter a necessity, for nothing felt worse than to have a piece of road grit or a bug hit an eye at well over a hundred miles per hour. A quick check in the full-length closet door mirror and she was satisfied with her appearance. She wondered if Rick checked her out as much as she watched him.

She turned around and found Bobby sitting up in bed, watching her.

"Oh!" She jumped in spite of herself.

He smiled. "I'm sorry, I didn't mean to startle you. You look great, babe."

"Thanks." Faith's heart pounded. After all the dreaming and then daydreaming about Rick, she now felt guilty, like she'd been caught stealing. "Was I too loud? I tried not to wake you."

He flicked one of his ears and grinned. "I can hear what they're saying across the street, babe. Don't worry about it. I'm used to the noise by now."

"Do you want me to wait for you?"

"Nah, you're already ready to hit the road. I'll grab a bite and catch a cab into the city."

"Okay." Faith turned to go.

"Love you, babe," said Bobby in a soft voice.

Faith crossed the room to him. "I love you too," she said, determined to mean it with all her heart. She kissed him, morning breath and all.

She skipped to the kitchen and filled a thermos full of coffee, and then stepped out the door. In a couple steps, she accelerated to a nice and easy sixty miles per hour. She could have gone much faster, but Rick had asked her to keep her speeds down except on emergency calls. Drivers tended to panic when a pedestrian blew past them like a jet on two legs, even if those legs were as nice as hers.

Faith hurried for Manhattan; she wanted Rick's coffee to still be hot when she arrived.

~~~

"Boy, you best get your lazy butt out of that bed!"

Thirteen-year-old Harlan Washington didn't move. He laid in his bed in the Harlem tenement with his hands folded behind his head and stared up at the ceiling, not seeing the water stains in the old corkboard. Instead, he was inventing things in his mind. His teachers had called him *creative*, *inattentive*, and *prone to daydreaming* and that was why he was stuck in summer school for the second year in a row.

He hated school. It was so boring, the way he had to learn bunches of facts and numbers and formulas and dates about stuff that didn't make any difference to him. He'd rather be tinkering in his workshop. He could learn more in an hour in a mechanic's garage than he could in a month in that school with the busted old ceiling fans and the crabby teachers who seemed to delight in humiliating him. The desk where he was supposed to do his homework in his room was cluttered with tools, pieces of Erector sets, and miscellaneous mechanical and electrical parts that he tinkered with instead of playing outside.

He closed his eyes again, imagining a giant, like *Mechagodzilla* from the movies. He dreamed of seeing neighbor kids flee in terror before it instead of going out of their way to tease and belittle him because he was a little smaller, a little dirtier than the rest of them. In his mind, he rode within the behemoth, safe within its armor, surrounded by the switches and levers of control. It followed his directions to the letter, spreading forth destruction at his whim. Like a king surveying the destruction wrought by his armies, Harlan smiled.

His mother flew into the room like a football linebacker. She was a large woman who worked two jobs to keep food on a table and a roof over the heads of Harlan and his two sisters, and she had no patience for layabouts like him. In one fell swoop, she closed a meaty hand around Harlan's ankle and yanked him right off his mattress. "If I told you once, I told you a thousand times to get a move on."

"Ow, Momma." Harlan rubbed his head where it had bounced off the floor.

"Get your clothes on and come have breakfast before you leave." His mother flounced out of the room.

"Bitch," Harlan muttered. He lay on the floor for a moment, trying to recapture the vision of gears and shafts he'd been imagining when he felt eyes on him. He turned to see Reggie staring at him. His younger sister wore her hair in two poofy pigtails on either side of her head. She held a dirty stuffed elephant clutched against her t-shirt.

"What?" growled Harlan.

"You done said a bad word. I'm gonna tell." Reggie's voice was full of glee as she skipped off toward the kitchen.

Harlan said another forbidden word under his breath, and then threw on a clean t-shirt and some grubby jeans. He jammed his feet into his Keds without bothering to tie them and trotted into the kitchen where Reggie was regaling their mother with half-truths about Harlan's language. Momma wasn't really listening; instead, she was fawning over Irlene, much to Harlan's disgust. Beautiful Irlene. Brilliant Irlene.

Irlene the parahuman, who'd just become a member of Just Cause.

If Harlan disliked his mother and tolerated Reggie, he detested his older sister Irlene. She was eighteen and could shrink herself and other objects or people down to ten percent of their original size. Harlan still remembered the night in March when she'd announced to the family over the dinner table, tears streaming down her cheeks, that she had parahuman powers. Instead of being upset, Momma had been ecstatic. From then on, Irlene could do no wrong in her eyes. She'd flown about the apartment in her shrunken state and zapped dust bunnies down to the size of dust motes to Momma's and Reggie's great amusement. Harlan had looked on with disgust. He perpetually heard "why can't you be more like Irlene?" from Momma and here was yet one more thing he could never aspire to.

Momma and Irlene ignored Harlan as he slipped into his chair at the stained Formica table, and that was just fine with him. They were busy making last minute adjustments to the hero costume Momma had spent all week sewing in between her day job at the bakery and her evening job cleaning up a dentist's office. Momma had described the colors as *berry* and *dove*, but to Harlan it was just a pink and gray bodysuit with a stylized *I* on the chest and a domino mask. Irlene had teased her hair into a large stylish afro and put on lipstick and face makeup.

"I swear, you look as good as Pony Girl or that trollop Sundancer," said Momma with conviction.

"Oh, Momma, do you really think so?" Irlene floated into the air and twirled about.

Harlan bent forward and shoveled cereal into his mouth, hoping the crackle of his corn flakes would drown out the coos of his mother and sisters.

"I think you look real pretty, Leenie." Reggie stuck her tongue out at Harlan.

"Thanks, sweetie," said Irlene. "What do you think, Harlan?"

Harlan glanced up and shot his older sister his most withering look. It infuriated him that as much as he couldn't stand her, she was friendly and even kind to him. Just once, he wished she'd get angry, call him a name, scream at him. Such a display of real, human hate from her would give them common ground from where they could forge a real sibling relationship. But no, she always smiled pleasantly at him and spoke to him with love. He knew he was supposed to reciprocate, but he felt nothing, and that made him hate her even more. "You look like a strawberry slush with whipped cream," he said in a weak attempt to be mean.

Irlene laughed it off. "That's wonderful, Harlan. Thanks. I feel that sweet. Hey, maybe you can come with me to visit Just Cause Headquarters sometime. I bet they've got some really cool equipment there that you could look at."

"For God's sake, Irlene, don't encourage him," said Momma. "The fool boy spends all his time playing in repair shops and junkyards instead of learning what he ought to be in school."

"School's stupid," mumbled Harlan.

Momma sighed in exasperation and turned back to Irlene. "You better be off, sweetie. You don't want to be late on your first day."

Irlene laughed. "Momma, I'm not punching a time clock with them. I'm a superhero, not a line worker."

"But they are paying you?"

"Yes, Momma. The Devereaux Foundation—they're the folks that run Just Cause—they pay us all a salary."

Momma's eyes glistened with tears. "I'm so proud of you, Irlene. If only your father could see you now."

Harlan only had faint memories of his father, who'd disappeared when Harlan was only two. Most days he wore the old man's army jacket from when he served in Korea. He often laid awake at night wondering whatever had happened him. Momma wouldn't ever speak of it. In his active imagination, he fantasized about his father doing some kind of great work in secret, and that someday he would return to take Harlan away to a life full of adventure and excitement instead of his current miserable existence.

"You best be on your way, sweetie," said Momma at last. She stopped fussing with Irlene's costume and stepped back.

"Guess so. Don't wait up, Momma. They might want me to do a night patrol or something."

"Make me proud, Irlene." Momma picked up a dishcloth and commenced her assault upon the prior evening's dinner dishes that she'd been too tired to clean after her second job.

"I will, Momma." She shrank down to the size of a pigeon, flitted around the kitchen once, and then sped out the window to head south toward the ritzy part of Manhattan.

Harlan growled deep in the pit of his throat. Momma must have heard him, and a wooden spoon cracked across the back of his hand. "Boy," she said, "you best rethink your attitude before you leave this house today, or there will be hell to pay by the time you get home."

Harlan hung his head just a little lower.

~~~

The lazy smoke from his clove cigarette curled in the breeze from the ceiling fan as Tommy lay naked amid mussed sheets in his Greenwich Village apartment. A couple of pigeons perched on the fire escape outside his window and cooed to each other over the noise of the morning commuters below. The closed bathroom door muted the hiss of the shower. André was nothing if not considerate. Tommy had met the French Canadian at the beginning of the man's vacation, but it was ending today and André would have to return home. The thought made Tommy feel a little wistful; André had soft and delicious skin, but like so many other relationships, this one had been doomed to fail from the start.

Tommy didn't try to sabotage his relationships on purpose. They just seemed to fall apart after a month or two, or a night or two. Sometimes he felt all he ever did was jump from the arms of one man to another. "Perpetually rebounding," Pony Girl said to him. He supposed it was a good description. He took a long drag on the cigarette and let the fragrant blend assail his lungs from the inside. The time with André had been good. He was thoughtful, kind, generous—everything Tommy could hope to find in a long-term partner. But of course, when he did find someone who exhibited those traits, circumstances demanded it be only short-term.

The shower stopped and a moment later André stepped into the bedroom, one towel wrapped around his waist as he dried his hair with another. "*Bonjour, mon cher,*" he said in his soft tenor.

Tommy smiled. "Good morning to you too."

André raised a finger. "Ah ah, *en français, s'il vous plaît.*"

Tommy's smile faltered as he tried to recall some of the French André had taught him. "Uh, *bonjour. Comment ça va?* Is that right?"

André took the cigarette from Tommy and took a drag. "*Ça va bien.* Very good. You have paid attention." He sighed. "It is a shame I must return home today."

"You can't stay another day?"

"*Mon cher...*" André traced a finger down Tommy's jawline. "Truly I would love to. You have been a gracious, accommodating host, and I have enjoyed this past week. But I would never fit into your lifestyle for a long-term commitment."

"What do you mean, my lifestyle?" Tommy gestured around at his apartment, full of Quaker-built furnishings, tasteful artwork, and track lighting.

"Please," said André. "Do you think I was born yesterday? I know who you are. Him. *La Tornade.* Tornado. The hero of the Just Cause team."

Tommy looked away. "So what if I am?"

André gave a sad smile. "You are a superhero. I am only a florist."

"What does that have to do with anything?"

"Ah, Tommy. You are a sweet man, full of love and life, but it is not for me to share. Your heart belongs to another. I could see this from the moment I met you."

Tommy pulled away from André and slipped out of the bed, the sheet wrapped around him like a robe. He went to the window and looked out at the city beyond the fire escape. How many hours had he spent flying between those towers? How many miles had he logged with his cape flapping behind him as he tried to outrun his own feelings? "You're wrong," he said at last. "I'm just another swinger, André. That's all. I'm not in love with anyone."

André embraced him from behind, resting his cheek against Tommy's shoulder. "*Tu es un pauvre menteur.*"

"What does that mean?"

"It means you're a bad liar, *mon cher*. Who is it, dare I ask? Whose face do you imagine when you make love with me?"

Unbidden images of a stone-cold, chiseled face came to Tommy's mind. Angry at himself, he thrust the thoughts away.

Tommy brushed away André's hand with a sharper motion than necessary. "Nobody," he said. "But I think you should leave."

André was silent for several seconds. Tommy could sense the man wanted to say something helpful. Instead, the Canadian returned to the bathroom and shut the door.

A profound sadness took hold of Tommy. He wasn't the sort who cried at the drop of a hat, but his eyes got a little watery and he sniffled once or twice. Once again, he'd managed to sabotage a budding relationship, and this time he hadn't even done anything. He sat in the windowsill and watched the world pass by on the streets of Greenwich Village below until André left the bathroom.

André bent down and brushed Tommy's lips with his own, his dark stubble scraping gently against Tommy's smooth chin. "*Au revoir, mon cher.* May you find peace with yourself."

A moment later, he was gone, and Tommy watched as André walked up the street without a look back.

The black emptiness threatened to overwhelm him. He couldn't stay in his loft any longer. The sky called to him. He yanked open his closet and grabbed the garment bag containing his Tornado costume. He drew on the blue and white bodysuit, the gray boots and cape, and clasped the sparkling faux-gold bracers around his wrists. He shook out his shoulder-length hair, which a reporter had once compared to the best of both Cassidy brothers.

A photo taped to the back of his closet wall caught his eye. The Just Cause team smiled back at him from the grand opening of their new headquarters in the World Trade Center, completed just two years ago. Lionheart showed his sharp canines and leonine features, his mane carefully brushed out for the occasion. Pony Girl looked pert and pretty as ever beside her husband Audio. Javelin stood with the Steel Soldier, both resplendent in their polished armor, burnished bronze and shining steel. Beneath his armor, Javelin was a wisecracking Puerto Rican, whereas the Soldier's armor protected only the circuitry and mechanical linkages of the advanced combat android. Beautiful Sundancer stood with Tommy, and John Stone hulked behind them both, eight feet of solid granite. Tommy stared at the man who looked like a living statue. John was his best friend. He couldn't be in love with his best friend, could he?

Ludicrous.

Nevertheless, he kissed his fingertip and brushed it against the photo anyway, obscuring John for a moment with his blue-gloved hand. Then Tommy spun on his heel and went to the window. If anyone looked up as he climbed onto his fire escape, they'd know where Tornado of Just Cause lived, but at the moment, Tommy didn't care.

He called to the winds, and they swirled to do his bidding. His cape filled with capricious breezes like some great parachute, and he flew skyward to heal his soul from gravity's clutches.

~~~

Since graduating in June, Gretchen had been working at Joe's Diner as a carhop. It was a fun job. She got to see all her friends on Friday nights and even got to wear roller skates to deliver the food to the strapping farmers' sons in their pickup trucks and muscle cars. They flirted with her and she gave back as good as she got and even made decent money in tips.

Then one night there was Donny Milbrook.

He'd spent all evening parked at the diner, smoking and drinking and occasionally ordering some fries or a corndog. By closing time, his Trans-Am was the only car left in the lot besides Gordie the cook's. Gretchen discovered he'd fallen asleep at the wheel. She gently shook him awake. "Donny, it's time to go home. We're closing up for the night."

He grunted and opened his bleary eyes to look at her. "'Zat time already?"

"I'm afraid so, Donny."

He yawned and dry-scrubbed his face. "Can I give you a lift home, Gretchen?"

Her bicycle sat alone on the rack at the side of the diner. She lived two miles away and didn't mind riding it home even late at night; Dyersville didn't have serial killers lurking in the bushes like big cities did. But it was a nice night, and Gretchen felt a bit lonely and Donny looked really handsome in his shiny Trans-Am with the Firebird decals on the hood. "Okay," she said.

The inside of his car smelled like cigarettes, beer, aftershave, and pot. She squealed with laughter as he floored the accelerator and the car fishtailed out of the lot in a cloud of stinking smoke. He took a bottle of Stroh's from between his legs and took a swig. "You wanna beer? I got another one here."

"Sure." She fumbled with the bottle opener hanging from his rear view mirror and shrieked as foam shot out of the neck.

"Oh shit," he said. "Drink it, quick! Don't get it all over my car!"

Gretchen laughed and wrapped her lips around the cool glass until the eruption subsided. Donny kept the pedal mashed down, ran through the flashing stoplight in the center of town, and blasted around a corner. Beer bubbled out of her nose as Gretchen slid across the vinyl bench seat into Donny. The car fishtailed as he reacted to her sudden, unexpected impact. She clutched at him in surprise and he responded by throwing one hand around her shoulders.

It felt nice, so she let him hold her as he guided the car past the edge of town. "Uh, Donny?" she said. "You passed my house."

"Oops." He grinned. "Guess I'll have to find a place to turn around."

She looked out at the dark rows of cornfields as they gleamed in the moonlight. They were on Olde Stage Road, famous among the local youth for the numerous places to pull off the road and fool around. She glanced sidelong at Donny, who squinted into the darkness as they passed occasional turnouts occupied by other cars that rocked with the rhythmic motion of their inhabitants. He kept going, well past the last parked vehicle.

"Donny," said Gretchen. "Why don't you turn around?"

"Jus' looking for a place. There, that oughtta do it." He slowed and pulled the Trans-Am onto a gravel lane beside a small grove of trees and shut off the engine.

"Donny?" Gretchen felt a little spark of fear.

Donny leered at her, his teeth gleaming in the moonlight. "You're a really nice girl, Gretchen. I like you. I been watchin' you."

Gretchen slid back across the seat, putting some space between them. "You're nice too, Donny, but I think you ought to take me home now."

"Oh, I will. Eventually." He scooted over next to her and put one hand around her shoulders and the other on her thigh. "I said you're a nice girl. Show me how nice you are."

"You're drunk, Donny. Cut it out."

"Come on, Gretchen, be a sport. All the other girls do it." His hand slid up her thigh toward her crotch.

"I'm not the other girls, Donny. Get off!" She squeezed her legs together and tried to push him away. He growled in the pit of his throat, took a handful of her hair, and yanked her head back. She cried out at the shock of pain. He gnashed his teeth against her neck and sucked, giving her a hickey she'd have to explain to her parents. She slapped at him and he drove a hard fist into her face. Bright stars flashed in her eyes and the world spun around her. Her flailing hand found the door handle and a moment later, she spilled out into the shallow ditch beside the lane.

Before she could get her bearings, Donny jumped onto her. He slapped her twice across the face. Gretchen couldn't see, couldn't breathe from all the blood and snot in her nose. Somewhere above her, Donny was laughing. She felt the cool night air in places she shouldn't have as Donny yanked off her shorts and underwear. Her hands fluttered, helpless against him. She wanted to scream, but she couldn't seem to draw breath. He leaned forward and forced himself into her.

"Shit," he gasped. "Fucking whore. You fucking bitch. You're a fucking virgin. I love that shit." He thrust again and again. "Nothing like—" *pant* "—a cherry pie—" *pant* "—for dessert—" *pant*.

Out of her dizzy, murky brain, a single thought bubbled up. She wished he would just stop breathing on her. Her entire body had gone numb except for where she could feel his hot beery breath on her cheek. She just wished he would stop.

Thunder crashed all around her...

...A hand on her wrist awakened Gretchen. She started and stared around at the interior of the Greyhound bus before she remembered where she was.

"I'm sorry, I didn't mean to startle you," said the matronly woman seated beside her. "We're almost there."

Gretchen leaned over to peer out through the glass at the Manhattan skyline. The buildings rose up farther than she'd ever even imagined in her tiny hometown of Dyersville, Iowa. She'd left home two days ago, without telling anyone but her best friend Elizabeth. After what had happened, she couldn't possibly stay in town.

"Honey, I don't mean to pry, but did a man do that to you?" asked the woman.

"What? Oh." For a moment Gretchen had forgotten her black eye, tender nose, and bruised cheekbone. She'd covered it as best she could with makeup and put on some large sunglasses to hide the rest. "No, uh, I just fell."

"Hmph," sniffed the woman. "Well, I hope you're on this bus to get away from him, honey. Men are pigs."

"I'm not..." began Gretchen. Then she sighed and smiled. "Yeah, I am getting away from him. And he was a pig." A flash of blue and white caught her eye and she saw Tornado flit between two buildings. That brief glimpse more than anything helped to solidify that she'd finally gotten away from Donny and Dyersville.

TWO

July 13, 1977, 10:00 AM

Faith stepped off the elevator onto the 95th floor, which contained Just Cause Headquarters and the related support offices. She nodded to Holly, the receptionist, and headed left into the team's side of the floor.

Two years ago, when the World Trade Center had opened, Just Cause's founder and benefactor Lane Devereaux had made a strong case to both building management and the Mayor of New York to let the team move its headquarters there. With their approval, the team had packed up everything in the Lower East Side warehouse they'd been using as a headquarters and moved into brand-new facilities near the top of the city. After a year, the carpet still looked new except for some unexplained stains the cleaning staff hadn't ever been able to completely eradicate. Faith was certain they were party-related.

All the Just Cause traditions had likewise transferred to the new headquarters. The most important of these was Wednesday Night Poker. The weekly poker match had started a few years ago between Javelin, Lionheart, and John Stone on a slow night. As time passed, more heroes joined the game, and even crime rates dipped on

Wednesdays, because nothing brought down the full wrath of Just Cause like being called away from a high-stakes hand.

Eventually, Wednesday Night Poker became more than just a gambling night. Nowadays, it was an excuse for wild parties. Just Cause heroes, their friends, their friends' friends, acquaintances, other celebrities—all made regular appearances on Wednesday nights. Sometimes the place was so packed full of people drinking and dancing that Faith couldn't navigate through headquarters without getting elbowed, bumped, and groped.

She hated those parties and all of the drinking and drugs. Both men and women had propositioned her numerous times, even though her marriage to Bobby was public record. And if she hated the parties, it must have been a thousand times worse for him with his parahuman hearing. Bobby's powers weren't nearly as flashy as Faith's, but extremely useful in their own way. He could hear clearly at great distances, like a shotgun microphone, and could pick out distinct details from auditory mishmash. He didn't like to deploy with the rest of the team; he didn't have a costume and only accepted the code-name Audio at Devereaux's insistence. Bobby preferred to work behind the scenes as the team's administrator.

The team didn't have much in the way of training facilities on the premises of the World Trade Center. Building management had balked at the idea of parapowered people blasting each other with lasers or energy darts and shaking the entire building with enhanced strength. Devereaux had been happy to oblige and spent a small fortune refitting the Lower East Side warehouse from a full headquarters to a large training facility. With multiple combat rooms, obstacle courses, target ranges, it was now considered one of the best places for parahumans to train anywhere in the world, and heroes came from all over to test their skills against the facility's combat drones and each other.

In spite of regulations, the team managed to finagle a few training amenities on-site, and it was in the dojo where Faith found Lionheart doing his morning forms. Richard Lyons looked like he was frozen halfway through a transformation between man and lion. Tawny fur covered his dense, powerful muscles, and a magnificent golden mane framed his leonine features as both hair and beard. His nose and jaw protruded forward slightly to give him an even more bestial appearance. Instead of finger and toenails, he had razor-sharp claws, and his teeth were best suited for tearing flesh. In an earlier age, he might have been hunted as a demon or worshiped as a god, but now he was the leader of Just Cause. He was one of very few bona-fide mutants in a world where most parahumans could pass as normal. Like John Stone, the living granite statue, Rick had been born with his catlike appearance. It had forced him to grow up early, learning to fight the hordes of bullies that came after him in school before his parents finally admitted defeat and had him study with private tutors for the remainder of his education.

He'd developed his own style of Kung Fu after studying for years with some of the best Chinese masters. He called it, naturally, Lion Style. It complemented his greater-than-human strength and toughness, and incorporated many of the moves that lions themselves used when taking down prey. Faith watched the play of his muscles under his fur as he sprang and spun through the air, carving furrows in the wooden combat dummies around him, which the support staff had to replace weekly because he wore them out every few days.

He wound down his routine. The training room air was heavy with the musky scent of his sweat as he swiped a towel from a hook, worked it through his prodigious mane, and then hung it over his shoulders. He smiled at Faith with a mouthful of sharp fangs. "Early as always, I see."

She held up a thermos. "I brought you coffee, Rick."

"My hero." He took it and unscrewed the top to inhale the fragrant steam.

She grinned up at him; he towered over her by a foot. "Always in the right place at the right time. That's me."

Lionheart laughed. "So you are, Faith. That new girl will be here today. Think you could show her the ropes?"

"Sure," said Faith. "Make the old lady do the grunt work."

"You're like our House Mother. Hey!" Lionheart wasn't fast enough to avoid Faith's playful punch at his bicep.

"This fraternity ought to be closed down for pledge violations," said Faith.

"What fraternity?" Sundancer strode into the dojo. Her white and yellow leotard with the triangle-shaped opening over her navel offset her dark tan. The Hispanic beauty was like a ray of sunshine in both a figurative and literal sense. A faint glow suffused the air around her, and occasional motes of brilliance spun away to burn out in the air like sparks from a campfire. She was a cross-continental transplant, having grown up in the surf country of southern California.

"The fraternity of stupid boys on this team." Faith smiled. "It's like a high school boys' locker room."

"How do you know about boys' locker rooms?" Sundancer giggled. "You must not be quite as good a girl as you've led us all to believe."

Faith and Sudancer followed Lionheart out of the dojo. As they did, Javier staggered out of one of the overnight quarters the team maintained for those heroes who needed to stay on site. The Puerto Rican hero stumbled across the hall into a bathroom. The sounds of vomiting emerged from behind the door a moment later.

Faith raised an eyebrow at Lionheart, whose nose wrinkled in distaste; with his enhanced sense of smell, he was probably getting a bad whiff of stomach acid and bile.

"Maybe we do need to review some house rules," said Lionheart.

Javier came out of the bathroom all smiles, despite the pallor under his natural skin tone. "Rules were made to be broken, *amigos*. Or at least, bent."

"What did you take, Javi?" asked Sundancer. "Pills? Coke?"

"No pills," said Javier. "Too much tequila. I was doing shots with these twins. Twins, Ricky! They're still sacked out in my room. Hope you don't mind."

"Pig," said Sundancer.

"Says the centerfold," said Javier. "Miss February had bigger tits, but you were a hell of a lot more a looker than Miss April."

Sundancer's glow brightened and sparks of fury shot from her eyes. She'd done a photo shoot with Devereaux's permission; the first parahuman ever to appear in *Playboy*. She was proud of her pictorial, but Javier delighted in cheapening it.

Faith stepped between the two bickering heroes. She hadn't minded so much that Sundancer did the glossy spread, and had even been approached numerous times to do one herself. But having to deal with Javier's chauvinism day in and day out would grow even more tiresome if he had that extra ammunition.

"Knock it off, you two," said Lionheart. "Save it for the bad guys."

"What bad guys?" Javier asked.

He had a good point, admitted Faith to herself. It had been years since any parahuman criminal had dared to rear their heads and risk the wrath of the greatest superhero team in the world.

And like a muscle that didn't get used with sufficient frequency, the team was getting soft.

~ ~ ~

Harlan decided to ditch summer school for the day. Again. He'd catch hell for it later from his mother, but he had a project at the junkyard that was nearing completion and felt his time was better spent there turning wrenches than learning to diagram sentences or whatever foolishness would be covered in class. Where most people saw trashed vehicles and garbage, Harlan saw opportunity. He spent as much time as possible—really, far more than was prudent —working on his fanciful projects there amid the rusting hulks of Chryslers and Pontiacs.

Harlan loved science fiction books and movies. He was a slow reader, but he struggled through a few pages every night, marking the words with his finger and sounding them out under his breath. When he could, he sneaked into movies and watched them. He had a special love for the Japanese giant monster movies, and one of them had inspired his latest project.

The massive hulking machine that would walk like an elephant and was strong enough to tear a building apart was nearly ready. Harlan imagined sitting inside it at the controls and laughing at everyone who'd ever teased him or talked down to him as he turned them into human jelly.

The first thing he had done with the abandoned junkyard was to secure it as much as he could. His gift for mechanical engineering helped him rig a crane to move heavy parts and even entire vehicles. He blocked and barred every possible way in, leaving himself only one secret entrance under a fence and through the trunk of a rusted-out Buick.

He wriggled through this tight space, pausing to disarm his security systems with a switch hidden inside the Buick. He'd installed the autonomous security devices after having problems with rats, both of the four-legged and two-legged varieties. They sensed motion and heat signatures and delivered a suitable warning: recorded sounds of dogs barking and men shouting and waving flashlights. Normally that was sufficient to scare off any stray animals or juvenile delinquents looking for cheap thrills.

And if those weren't sufficient, well, Harlan had thought of more severe consequences.

The sentry turrets looked innocuous, placed around the junkyard in locations where they could cover significant areas. They were tied into the same systems that detected motion and heat, and if the offending intruder didn't leave the area after a certain number of seconds, the turrets would go into action.

He called them Eggbreakers, because he'd once heard someone say *you can't make an omelet without breaking a few eggs.*

Every so often, he'd find a dead dog or cat out in the open spaces of the junkyard, the victim of an Eggbreaker turret. The cleverly-designed devices fired engine block bolts like deadly projectiles, using a propellant that he mixed himself with a half dozen different ingredients including gasoline and talcum powder. It had never occurred to him that what he was doing was wrong. They were trespassers, and he didn't even bat an eye when he cleaned up the bloody remains of a furry interloper. To the contrary, he rather enjoyed the vindication of his design.

As he crawled out of the Buick's trunk, he found a new victim awaiting him. A man laid face down amid a large bloodstain with one hand outstretched and snagged in the tarpaulin covering the giant robot. The thick cloud of flies around the body resembled a moving shadow, obscuring the man's tattered and shabby clothing.

Harlan froze as he took in the grisly scene laid out before him. The man might have been a hobo or vagrant. He might have come in over the fence, or even found the secret entrance by accident. Maybe he was looking for something to steal or sell for a few pennies. He'd ignored the warning sounds and gotten a little too curious for his own good. The buzzing of the flies matched the humming in Harlan's brain. This wasn't an accident. This was on purpose. This man was dead because Harlan had intended it. Yet he didn't feel remorse. Instead, it made him feel powerful.

"Got you," whispered Harlan. He pointed at the body, his arm moving as slowly as if it were underwater. "I got you, you fucker." His extended finger drew a circle around the dead man's head. It wasn't enough, though. He had to see it up close.

He felt lightheaded and giddy with success as he tiptoed toward the body. Just because the man lay motionless in a bloody, muddy mess in the dirt didn't mean he was really dead. Flies lined the edges of the congealing blood like pigs at a feeding trough. Close up, the coppery smell of death overcame even the odors of rusting metal, rotting plastic, and petroleum byproducts.

Harlan's whole body shook as he stuck out a toe and kicked at the man. His poke elicited no response. He kicked harder. The shock of the impact of his toes against the man's side ran all the way up his leg through his spine to explode in the pleasure centers of his brain. He kicked harder, over and over, and giggled with glee like a toddler.

"I got you, you motherfucker!" he shrieked as landed one blow after another, his foot making sounds like a sledgehammer might against a side of beef. "You thought you could just come in here and do whatever you want. Well, I sure showed you, dirtbag!" With his last word, he kicked the man hard enough to roll the corpse over.

The man's eyes were wide open and his face frozen in a permanent mask of surprise. The hexagonal head of an engine bolt protruded from the center of his forehead.

Harlan's breakfast launched itself out of his stomach and he vomited his corn flakes onto the ground beside the corpse. With a shaking hand, he wiped his mouth. The flies swarmed around his puke with new excitement as he backed away from the dead man before him. Harlan took a deep, shuddering breath. He felt empty, not just from vomiting, but as if someone had taken a fire hose to him and rinsed him out, leaving only an empty shell waiting to be filled anew. He wasn't disgusted at his handiwork; he was awed. His Momma had dragged him to church regularly, but he had never had any sort of religious experience until he looked upon the face of a man he'd slain by his own hand.

Sticky wetness flooded his groin.

He'd attend to that later.

Right now, he just wanted to gaze upon his works and feel the world tremble beneath his feet. A bit of poetry that he must have read in school at some point bubbled up in his buzzing brain. *Look on my works, ye mighty, and despair.* Yes, that was fitting.

"Despair, motherfuckers," whispered Harlan to the world.

~~~

Tommy sat with John Stone in the team's conference room when the others entered. He felt at ease beside the huge man of stone. Indeed, he longed to be even closer, but settled for leaning in to share a joke André had told him. John had brought a bag full of bagels and was demolishing one between his quartzite teeth.

"All here, I see," said Lionheart. "Where's the Soldier?"

The air in one corner of the room shimmered and the seven-foot tall combat android became visible. "I AM PRESENT. I HAVE BEEN TESTING MY OPTICAL CAMOUFLAGE SYSTEM."

"You can turn invisible?" asked Sundancer in surprise. "That's a new modification?"

"AFFIRMATIVE," rumbled the Steel Soldier from his basso vocoder. The android was technically sexless, but when the U.S. Supreme Court declared him a sentient being with the same rights afforded to humans back in 1974, he chose to represent himself as male. Just Cause had found the Soldier in the midst of a destroyed building, the victim of unexplainable circumstances. His memory had been erased and his armored body showed signs of combat. Javelin theorized the Soldier was an involuntary time traveler, for the android's construction was advanced beyond the capabilities of present-day technology.

"That's cool, man. I didn't know you could do that." Javier eyed the bagels, but he still looked a little green around the gills. Unlike Tommy or anyone else in Just Cause, Javier had no native parahuman powers. A brilliant physicist, he'd used his extensive understanding of magnetism to develop a prototype flying suit of armor. He'd been thrown out of MIT before he could do anything with it, because his womanizing ways had led him to his Department Head's wife. He could have taken his suit design and privatized it, or gone to the military, but instead he'd joined Just Cause as the hero Javelin.

"It is a function I have recently repaired. Unfortunately the camouflage is only effective against visual reconnaissance. I can still be easily detected through infrared or audible means."

"Somebody say my name?" Bobby walked into the conference room. "Sorry I'm late. Cabbie didn't speak a word of English."

"New York. What a town." Tommy laughed. John chuckled beside him and it made Tommy feel like a balloon was lifting him right out of his seat.

Bobby kissed Faith and then sat in the chair beside her. "Since we're all here, I call the meeting to order." Side conversations died down as the Just Cause heroes turned their attention to the team administrator. Lionheart led the team in the field, but behind the walls of headquarters, Bobby ran the show. "For those of you who weren't paying attention, we have a new member joining us today.

Her name is Irlene Washington and goes by the moniker Imp. She can fly and shrink herself, objects, and people."

"Shrinking? What good would that be?" Javier wrinkled his nose at the coffee.

"I can think of a half dozen useful applications offhand," said Lionheart. "Crowd control, reducing collateral damage, insurgence and stealth."

"She's in the offices, getting her paperwork all in order. Devereaux will bring her in a little while to meet everyone. Faith is going to show her what we do here in Just Cause."

"Besides partying, you mean?" asked Faith.

Bobby's brow wrinkled in consternation. "Yes, there's that. Maybe we should tone things down a little. Make a good first impression."

Javier's snort carried across the room. "It's *Wednesday*," he said as if that explained everything.

"Oh, that reminds me," said Sundancer. "I've got extra tickets to the Mets game tonight. Anybody want to join me?"

"Count me in," said John Stone. "I love baseball."

"I'll join you," said Tommy.

Sundancer smiled. "That's handled, then. Count us out for poker tonight."

"May as well have a party, then," said Javier. "They introduce eligible young ladies at parties, don't they? We ought to introduce Imp to our adoring public."

"Fine," said Bobby. "Let's just try to keep it from getting out of hand. Devereaux's spending a fortune on us here."

"I am indeed," said a cultured Bostonian voice. Lane Devereaux was tall and spare like a scarecrow, with a shock of carefully styled graying hair and eyes surrounded by laughter lines. Pushing fifty, he looked far too friendly and approachable to be the CEO of the multi-million dollar foundation that supported Just Cause and parahuman research around the world. Unlike many executives, Devereaux was a hands-on man, and made his center of business operations in Just Cause headquarters where he was often the first one into the office and the last one to leave on any given day. Behind him strode a slender black girl in a homemade pink and white costume and a large afro. She smiled nervously at the others, as if expecting to be judged. "Ladies and gentlemen of Just Cause, I'm pleased to introduce to you Ms. Irlene Washington, also known as Imp."

Devereaux made introductions around the team for Irlene, who looked overwhelmed at meeting so many new parahumans.

"Don't worry, Irlene," said Faith. "There's not going to be a test or anything. Tell us a little about yourself and your powers."

Irlene tucked one foot behind the other ankle as if embarrassed. She looked at the floor as she spoke. "There's not much to tell. I live with my Momma, little brother and sister. I went to Renaissance High. Um, I can shrink stuff and people down to doll-size. And fly." She smiled at that. "Flying is very cool."

Tommy smiled. "I have to agree with you there. Maybe we can patrol together sometime. It'd be nice to have someone to fly with besides Javelin here."

Javier gave him a sour smile.

"Oh, really?" Irlene looked as if her heart had skipped a beat from the sudden attention of the golden-haired heartthrob.

"What does that shrinking look like? How small can you make things?" asked Lionheart.

Irlene shrank herself down to the size of a Barbie doll and flitted about the room. "This is as small as I can make myself," she shouted in a curiously high-pitched voice. "Everything else scales like this."

"We'll be sure to let you know if we run across any vicious gerbils or sparrows." Javier laughed.

Tommy could see the look of dismay cross Irlene's tiny face. "He's joking with you," he said quickly. "He's like that. Don't pay him any mind." He glared across the table with such ferocity that Javier sat back and looked away.

"Well, on that note, does anybody have any new business to bring up?" said Bobby. "No?" Nobody spoke. "Well then, morning briefing's adjourned. Let's go protect the city."

~~~

The bus squeaked to a stop in a canyon of steel and concrete. Gretchen pressed her face against the glass and stared at the bustle of Manhattan. The stink of exhaust wafted in through the open windows and made her nose wrinkle. Around her, passengers pushed their way toward the front exit as the driver opened the luggage bays on the side.

"You got somebody meeting you, honey? You have someplace to go?" asked the woman who'd sat beside her since Chicago.

"Yeah, I think so," said Gretchen.

Her best friend Elizabeth had promised to call her cousin in New York. "He's real responsible," she'd said. "He works for Con Ed. That's the power company. He's twenty-three. I'll tell him you're coming out to New York. He'll help you find a place to stay while you go talk to the Just Cause people."

Gretchen still couldn't wrap her mind around the notion that she was a parahuman. She'd left Donny lying in the ditch, dead, his lungs full of his own blood. She didn't know what had happened to him, except that somehow she had done it. Elizabeth had figured it out though. "You must be a parahuman," she'd said in awe after a tear-stained Gretchen told her what happened. "The trauma must have activated it."

"Trauma?" Gretchen had nearly shrieked. "He ruh… ruh…" She hadn't been able to say the word.

"Shush, you'll wake my folks. Boys do that," Elizabeth said. "All of them do it sooner or later. Even the ones you think are nice. You just learn to live with it. For me it was Eddie Rogers." She'd grabbed a bag from a shelf and started filling it with clothes. She and Gretchen were the same size and swapped outfits so often they didn't really know whose were whose originally. "You can't stay here, though. Not after what you did, I mean, what happened to Donny. There are laws about using parahuman powers against people."

Gretchen felt like her world was crashing down around her in splinters. "What can I do? Where can I go?"

"Go to New York. Go to Just Cause. Tell them what happened. They can help you."

"New York?" Gretchen's jaw dropped. "I can't go to New York! I've never even been further away than Des Moines."

But Elizabeth had raided her parents' emergency money in the cookie jar in the kitchen, and along with Gretchen's tip money for the night they had enough for a one-way bus ticket to New York City. Then she drove Gretchen to the bus stop just outside of town in Donny's car. "I'll hide it somewhere," she said. "Hopefully nobody will notice he's gone for a day or so. By then you'll be on your way. I'll call my cousin in the morning and tell him to meet you."

Gretchen had really broken down then. "Oh, Lizzie," she cried, "what will I do? I wish you could come with me. You're so much smarter about stuff like this."

Elizabeth held her tight. "You'll be fine. I wish I could go with you, but somebody's got to stay behind and give you time to get away." Her eyes were also bright with tears. "I wish I could go with you. When you're a big superhero with Just Cause, I'll come visit you. Make sure you wear the blue shirt, because I'm going to tell Shane to look for it."

It had seemed like the only option at the time, but now as Gretchen stared wide-eyed at the titanic skyscrapers and bustling streets, she felt more lost than ever before.

She bent to pick up her bag and another hand closed on the handle beside hers. She gasped as she saw a man with greasy black hair flowing out from under a fedora grinning at her. A toothpick rested in the corner of his mouth and a gold tooth gleamed in the morning sunlight.

"*Buenas dias, señorita.* New in town?" He had an accent kind of like some of the Mexicans who came to work in the fields in Dyersville, but looked both cleaner and, well, slimier than they did.

"That's my bag," said Gretchen. Fear arose in her as if someone had turned a spigot. She tugged meekly at it.

"Easy, *chica.* I didn't mean nothing by it. You need a ride somewhere? Someplace to stay?" He looked her up and down like a prospective buyer taking in the lines of a new car. "Something to eat?"

"I'm fine, really. Will you please let go of my bag?" Gretchen tried to keep the terrified shudder out of her voice but didn't quite succeed.

"Everything okay here, miss?" The bus driver lit a new cigarette from the butt of the one he'd just finished, then flicked the smoldering dog-end into the dry gutter.

"We're just talkin'," said the man in the hat. "Ain't no law against talkin'."

The bus driver looked at Gretchen, looked at the man with his hand still on her bag, and apparently decided not to get involved further. He shrugged and walked away, a dark line of sweat marking the outline of the bus seat on the back of his uniform shirt.

"Please," whispered Gretchen. "Please let go."

"What you so afraid of, sweetmeat? I ain't gonna hurt you. I'm just tryin' to be nice. Now why don't you come with me and we'll get a sandwich and talk about it." He lifted the bag.

"Please don't." Tears spilled down Gretchen's face. She hadn't been in New York a minute and here she was already about to get mugged. This was the kind of thing that her parents had shaken their heads at over the dinner table. Big cities were full of people like this man here, always looking to prey on the helpless. Pimps, muggers, serial killers.

The power leaped out of Gretchen, unbidden. "No!" she yelled as it sought a target and centered on the greasy-haired man. She wouldn't kill again. She steered it aside at the last moment. Each tire along the side of the bus facing her crumpled and imploded in sequence. The Greyhound bus shuddered and lurched as it lost its support. The power wasn't finished yet, and Gretchen gasped as a softball-sized sphere of air somewhere inside the bus cabin vanished into nothingness. The resultant blast of thunder shattered every window in the bus. People yelled in surprise and clapped their hands to their ears too late to block the sound.

The man with the hat dropped Gretchen's bag.

Despite the sudden outburst of her mysterious power and the disorienting crash of thunder, Gretchen kept enough presence of mind to take her bag and hurry away from the damaged bus. Maybe she could find some place to hide from the greasy-haired man, but when she looked back, he had already disappeared into the crowd. She realized with growing terror that she was completely alone in the biggest city in the world, and had nowhere to—

"Gretchen? Gretchen Gumm?"

At the sound of her name, Gretchen whirled around. The power rose up again, eager to spring free once again, but she quashed it as deep as she could. A slender man in Con Ed coveralls stood before her. He had shaggy brown hair brushing his collar, a pathetically thin mustache, and a friendly smile. He had to be Elizabeth's cousin.

"Yes, that's me."

Relief flooded his features. "I thought it might be. Elizabeth said you were pretty, blonde, and wearing a blue t-shirt. I'm Shane. Shane Clemens. Pleased to meet you." He held out his hand. "Can I carry your bag for you?"

"N-no, that's okay," said Gretchen. "I'll carry it. Can we get out of here?"

"Sure thing. I'm on my way to work, anyway. I'm double-parked, but I'm in a truck so it's probably okay. Do you mind riding with me until my shift's over? Then we can see about getting you someplace to stay."

Gretchen looked behind her at the bus half a block away. It had drawn a sizable crowd of interested onlookers as the bus driver regarded the state of his bus in profanity-laced dismay. "Yeah, I can ride with you," she said. "Let's go. I don't want you to be late for work."

THREE

July 13, 1977, 11:00 AM

Faith smiled at Irlene. "Ready for your first patrol?"

Irlene smiled back, a little nervous. "I think so. What do I do?"

"Stick with me. Mostly patrolling is just about being seen out there in the city. Hey, how high can you fly?"

"I don't know," said Irlene. "I never tried to find out."

"Well, if you can get up to it, we've got an aerial-only access on this floor. Tornado and Javelin use it all the time. It's a lot less hassle than the elevator."

Irlene shuddered. "Javelin ain't a very nice man."

Faith nodded. "He's an asshole. Keep your distance from him, especially at parties."

"Do I call you all by your names or your superhero names or what?"

"You can just call us by our names. Superhero names are for when we're in public."

The elevator bell dinged and the doors slid open. A few people looked up at the costumed heroes with interest. "Hi, everyone," said Faith. "Ground floor, please." They rode downward in silence until one hesitant woman asked if she could have their autographs. Before the elevator finished its descent, Faith and Irlene had both signed several autographs.

"Is it always like this?" Irlene whispered as they crossed the lobby.

"Sometimes. Being in Just Cause makes you a celebrity, like if you were in a band."

"Wow." Irlene sounded thoroughly starstruck to Faith. "I never thought that being a superhero would make me famous. Will I get to be on TV and in the papers?"

"Probably," said Faith. She worked hard to keep her private life out of the media. At the end of the day, she wanted to be able to enjoy a quiet dinner with Bobby in a restaurant somewhere. They stepped out into the bright sunshine that peeked down between the other skyscrapers to illuminate the plaza.

"So what do we do?"

"Mostly we just make ourselves visible," said Faith. "We're a visual deterrent to street crime."

"Street crime? We don't go after parahuman villains?" Irlene stared at the passing New Yorkers who took in the colorfully attired women with typical aplomb.

Faith laughed. "I hate to burst your bubble, Irlene, but Just Cause hasn't run across any parapowered criminals since early '75." She bent in and whispered, "We think we might have got them all."

Irlene's eyes widened behind her pink mask. "Really?"

Faith shrugged. "No way to tell for sure until someone new surfaces, but we've tracked down all the parahuman offenders we know of."

"Does it happen often, someone new showing up?"

"You did. Lucky you chose to be one of the good guys."

"Lucky?"

"Lucky for you." Faith winked at her. "Come on, let's head over to Times Square. Maybe we can catch a purse snatcher or something."

"Do we take a cab or something?"

Faith grinned. "Something. I'll run. You fly. Try and keep up."

Irlene bowed her head, no blush apparent behind her dusky skin. "I'm sorry, I still ain't used to—"

But Faith winked and took off at—for her—an easy lope of forty miles per hour. She glanced back over her shoulder and saw Irlene flying ten feet over the ground, a few yards behind her and catching up. "You meanie," called the teen over the sound of wind whipping past them. "I wasn't ready."

"You're in Just Cause now, kiddo. You have to be ready all the time. You never know when you'll have to respond to something at a moment's notice." Faith dodged around a bicycle messenger and hurdled a sawhorse blocking an open manhole cover with a bored-looking Con Ed crew standing around it drinking coffee.

Times Square was bustling, even so early in the day. People hurried through on their way to work, early lunch, or loitered and transacted shady business deals. A man selling watches out of a briefcase closed it up and hurried away when he saw the Just Cause heroes arrive. Faith watched him go. She'd spoken to him once and knew he was harmless, but just the same she appreciated the gesture on his part. The flesh trade was already underway. People —mostly men—slipped into theaters and other houses of ill repute. Others talked to prostitutes, negotiating terms and leaving together. Pimps loitered in doorways and solicited business with passersby. Most people gave only token respect to the heroes' authority. Despite having police powers specifically in New York City granted by the governor, lawbreakers knew that for the most part, they were well beneath the attention of the superheroes.

"I can't believe this," Irlene said. "Doesn't anyone care who we are, or what we are?"

"Not really," said Faith. She glared at a beat cop as he walked out of a peepshow, adjusting his Sam Browne belt.

"Let's make the rounds. It isn't very hot yet. Maybe everyone will behave themselves today."

Faith knew she'd spoken too soon, for they heard a woman shriek near the bus station. She and Irlene glanced at each other, and then hurried toward the sound of the commotion.

Faith arrived first, zig-zagging through curious onlookers to find an elderly black woman sprawled on the cement. She knelt down to carefully help the woman to her feet. "Ma'am, are you all right?"

"That young son of a bitch stole my purse." The woman rubbed her hip. "Knocked me down."

"What he look like?" Irlene dropped out of the sky to land next to Faith and the elderly woman.

"Spic with greasy hair and a hat. Oh my, I did take a tumble."

Irlene flew upward and scanned the area. "I got him," she said. "He's running."

"Go after him, Imp. I'll catch up."

"Okay, uh, Pony Girl." Irlene shrank down to the size of a Barbie doll and sped away; she could fly faster when small.

Faith turned her attention back to the woman. "Ma'am, do you need a doctor or anything?"

"You just catch that son of a bitch and bring back my purse, young lady, and God bless you."

Faith nodded and ran after Irlene. The cityscape blurred around her with her speed. She overtook Irlene in a matter of seconds and spotted the fleeing purse snatcher. Faith poured on the speed to pass by him, then skidded to a halt, turned, and braced herself with her arm outstretched.

The purse-snatcher clothes-lined himself right across her forearm. The shock of impact jarred her senses, but not as much as it must have his. His feet flew up into the air and he crashed to the cement.

Faith grinned. Sometimes it felt good to do the right thing. "Mister, you are under arrest."

~~~

Harlan hid the vagrant's body in the trunk of a crushed Ford. He looked askance at the trail of blood that remained along the path where he'd dragged the carcass. It hadn't rained in days and didn't look like there would be much relief coming anytime soon. It didn't matter so much, though, because anyone who came into the junkyard and didn't disarm the security systems would suffer the same fate. That thought gave Harlan a cheerful shiver.

He ambled across the clearing to his makeshift workshop, a disused Volkswagen bus with the side door ripped away. It hunched on rusting, naked rims. The broken headlights gave it a somber, almost wistful expression. He'd tacked canvas sheeting to the van's roof and stretched it out to poles hammered into engine blocks for a makeshift roof. It flapped in the warming breeze. Various half-done tinkering projects littered the dirt around his workshop. Many were pieces he'd started without really understanding what they were or even their intended purpose. Others had been begun, ripped apart, and rebuilt in different ways many times over. Trial and error was Harlan's format of creation. Sometimes he worked on a component for months until he understood that it was ready and installed it. Often it was at the installation that he realized what it was he'd built. It was like a teacher lived in his head. Not one of the cranky old ladies at the school Momma made him attend, but like a scientist and engineer and chemist all rolled into one. Harlan listened to that voice, and it taught him how to make things.

He was pretty sure that none of his work had been disturbed, but went on to check his masterpiece, to make sure the unscheduled visitor hadn't damaged it in any way. It hulked in a back corner of the yard, surrounded by numerous wrecks that Harlan had moved with the ingenious crane arrangement he'd built from scrap parts.

Anyone who didn't know what it was would have only seen what looked like two semi truck cabs stacked on top of each other with some parts sticking out at random. But Harlan knew better.

He'd built a suit; his own *Mechagodzilla*.

Not just any suit, either. This one was *big*. It crouched on four heavy hydraulic legs powered by the Diesel engine in the lower truck cab. When he powered them up, the rig would raise itself up to a fearsome height, nearly twenty feet tall. Numerous layers of rubber, cut from rotting tires, padded the suit's feet. The upper cab boasted four arms, designed for no other purpose than destruction. Two housed mobile versions of the belt-fed Eggbreaker guns, one of which had killed the vagrant. Another carried a powerful flamethrower with a large tank of pressurized fuel. The last held a huge circular saw blade. Harlan had found it in a disused corner of the junkyard. It must have belonged to a timber mill at some point, but now it ran on Diesel power from the upper cab. Heavy armor plating protected the engines and hydraulics, and the pilot's cabin at the very top of the suit was armored like a pillbox.

He had no name for the suit. He didn't even know for certain why he'd built it, except he was compelled to. When he dreamed, gears and pistons and hoses filled his thoughts. The only time he truly felt good about himself—happy, even—was when he was working on the suit. It was an extension of himself, like he was building a second skin to go outside of his own; something to make his dreams a reality. Nobody who saw it would tease him, or tell him to do chores. They'd scream in terror and run away.

He longed to instill that fear in others.

He'd never switched it on, but when that day finally came, he'd crawl into the machine's belly and become a part of it, and he would feel complete for the first time in his life.

His father would have been so proud of him.

He checked connections, fuel levels, hydraulics. Everything seemed to be in order; he could find no sign that the suit had been disturbed in any way. The last thing he checked was the heavy insulated cables running from a nearby power pole. Making that connection had come close to killing him, late one night when he'd sneaked away from the apartment to work under cover of darkness. He'd brushed against a live power lead and caught a minor jolt of electricity which made him slip and fall from a precarious perch fifteen feet above the ground. When he hit the ground, it had felt like the current still ran back and forth throughout his body, seeking an exit but finding none. He'd lain in agony without moving or breathing, knowing his spark of life was fading away like a candle flame under a glass jar. And as he sprawled on the pavement, damp from Fall rains, staring without seeing up at the murky clouds overhead, something had arisen within him. It shocked him with bright pain and hate, startling his autonomic nervous system into action once more. He drew a ragged, shuddering breath as his heart thudded behind bruised ribs, and groaned out his agony. For the better part of that night almost a year ago, Harlan had lain helpless on the ground, full of pain and hate and blaming the world for it. As the sky began to lighten over the Atlantic, he'd found he could move once more, and staggered home in an exhausted, hateful fugue.

The next day he'd gone back, his head still spinning, and connected the line to the bank of car batteries ensconced deep inside one of the semi truck cabs. The tired old batteries needed a constant charge either from the grid or the onboard engines or else they'd simply die, and then Harlan's suit would lose everything that didn't run via direct drive or hydraulics.

Satisfied the vagrant hadn't disturbed his masterwork,

he pulled the tarpaulins down again around the suit.

He frowned at his current project. It needed something that he didn't have. He screwed up his face in deep concentration. He knew there was a word for it. If he could only remember it. Harlan's blood pounded in his ears and he felt faint and realized he'd been holding his breath. He blew out a lungful of stale air and as he inhaled, it came to him. *Thermocouple*. He needed some thermocouples. He grinned in relief.

Gonsalvo would have some. Gonsalvo always had what Harlan needed.

~~~

Sundancer grabbed the Steel Soldier and made for the air-access balcony, leaving Tommy stuck with Javier once again. Tommy sighed as he watched John Stone and Lionheart walk out of the conference room, bound for the elevator. Just Cause protocols dictated that whenever possible, the heroes would operate in teams of two. With four fliers, it meant Tommy wasn't ever paired up with one of the ground-pounders, although he figured that would change with the addition of Imp to the mix.

Bobby clapped him on the shoulder. "Sorry, man," he said quietly. "Really."

Tommy put on his bravest smile. "It's all right. Into every life a little rain must fall."

Bobby chuckled. "We could use a little rain in all our lives. This weather is ridiculous. It's making people crazy. As if we didn't already have Son of Sam out there looking for his next victims." The serial killer had wrapped up the city in a grip of fear and paranoia.

"We'll catch him," said Tornado with confidence. "It's only a matter of time."

"Time for what?" Javier re-entered the conference room in his burnished bronze armor. "I hope you meant time for a smoke. I'm dying for a cigarette here."

"I'll catch you guys later," said Bobby. "I'll be in the monitor room. I'll call you if anything comes up." The monitor room was where Just Cause scanned police and emergency radio bands and the coordinator, normally Bobby, would dispatch the heroes around the city to where they needed to be.

"Yeah, yeah," said Javier. "You ready to go, pretty boy?"

"I suppose so," said Tommy.

They went to the airlock balcony, an open-air entrance designed for the flying heroes to enter and leave headquarters. Tommy punched in the code on the electronic lock. They'd installed it after a drunken civilian at a party had wandered out onto the windowless room and would have fallen to his death had Tornado not been alert enough to see him tumble out.

Sundancer and the Steel Soldier had left the louvers open so the wind whipped through the chamber as Tommy and Javier entered it. It smelled of dust and faint automobile exhaust from nearly a hundred stories below. Tommy let the wind billow out his cape as Javier swung his half-helmet up over his face and latched it.

"Where do you want to head first?" asked Tommy.

"Central Park," said Javier without hesitation. "After that, I don't care." He whooped and leaped between the steel louvers into the open air beyond. A moment later, his boot rockets flared and he began a spiraling descent toward a more reasonable altitude. Tommy followed him out, letting the winds buoy him after his patrol partner.

Javier flew fast enough that Tommy had to summon a minor gale to catch up to him. The Puerto Rican man headed for Central Park as if possessed.

"Did we get a call already?" Tommy shouted over the rushing wind. Most of the team had to use walkie-talkies, something Tommy found awkward and distracting while airborne, but Javier's radio was built right into his helmet.

Javier didn't reply. They cruised lengthwise along the

southern edge of the giant park. People on the paths looked up as the heroes flew past. Many of them smiled and waved. Tommy waved back; Just Cause was as popular as ever.

"There!" called Javier and pointed. Tommy saw a small group of four young black men turn to flee toward some trees. "Cut 'em off, Tommy!"

The winds blew fierce around Tommy as he swooped in to block the four men. One of them pulled a cheap pistol from his waistband. A concentrated burst of air sent it flying into the underbrush and left the man wringing his hand in pain. They turned to flee from Tommy and Javier dropped down in front of them. He fired a particle beam blast into the ground, creating an ugly scar of ashes and charred dirt.

"Easy there, Stope. Hands in the air," said Javier.

"*Shee*-it," grumbled one of the men, who wore a shapeless floppy hat and a lightweight leather jacket over a t-shirt.

"Be cool," said Tommy. "We don't want to hurt anyone." Whatever Javier was doing, he had to back him up.

"Why you hasslin' me, superhero?" mumbled the man in the hat. "Ain't you got no real crimes to stop? We wasn't doin' nothin'."

"Come on, Stope, it's me. You see me and start running, what the hell do you think I'm going to do?" Javier held out one hand. Electricity arced between the fingertips of his gauntlet. "You holding?"

"Naw, man."

"We can do this at a cop shop, or five hundred feet straight up, or right here," said Javier. "What's it going to be?"

Stope grimaced. "Yeah, okay, I got a little blow is all. Ain't no thing."

"Hand it over."

"*Shee*-it."

Tommy kept his attention on the other three men, who glared back at him. Little dust devils swirled in front of each one, a gentle reminder that Tornado was more than just a name.

Javier stepped back from Stope with a small vial clutched in his hand. His grin was just visible under the edge of his visor. "Stope, I'm going to do you a huge favor. I'm not going to take you in for dealing."

"I wasn't doin' nothin'!" Stope protested.

"Intent to deal, then. Get going. Beat your feet. Scram, *pendejo*."

Tommy watched as the four men scrambled away, making sure none of them turned around for a parting shot. Once he was satisfied there would be no further trouble, he turned back to Javier. "Why did you let them go?"

Javier shrugged. "I hate doing paperwork. You want to spend all day in a police station with no air conditioning? Not me."

"So you just turn them back out onto the street?"

Javier raised his visor to gaze evenly at Tommy. "Look at it like this. Coke's expensive, and this guy's not going to have any cash to show for it. That means he'll be accountable to his supplier. If he can't come up with the money or the coke, well, those guys tend to police their own. I sure ain't going to shed a tear if he turns up on the Hudson with a couple of new holes in him. And neither are you."

"No, I guess not," said Tommy. "It just doesn't seem very heroic."

Javier burst out in laughter. "You want heroic, you're in the wrong business."

~~~

"So," began Shane as he threaded the oversized service truck through the congested traffic, "Elizabeth didn't say a whole lot about you except that you needed help here in New York. Are you in some kind of trouble?"

"No," lied Gretchen. "I just decided to move here, find a job, that kind of thing." She stared out the window at the Big Apple. So many cars, so many people. How could anyone live like this? To her small-town upbringing, everything seemed loud and smelly and busy, and yet there was a certain underlying energy that she did find appealing. Maybe that was what made people want to live on such a congested, overbuilt island of concrete and steel.

"That's cool. What kind of work? Are you an actress? Lots of people come here for that, but I haven't ever heard of anyone making it big."

"No, I'm just looking for any job. I'd even be a waitress."

"Well, I'm sure you'll find something. There's this diner not too far from my building. Great blue plates. I have breakfast there a lot because I can't cook. I can start a fire trying to boil water."

Gretchen smiled a little at that. "I can make pancakes."

"If it wasn't for my roommate I'd probably starve to death. He's in culinary school."

"You have a roommate?"

"Mostly everyone in New York does. It's too expensive to live alone."

"Oh. I don't know what to do about that."

"You can always find someone needing a roommate if you look around. We can check into it tonight after my shift is done."

"I'm going to need a job first," said Gretchen after a long pause. "I don't really have much money." She wasn't ready to tell him she didn't have any money at all.

Shane glanced at her as he changed lanes to avoid a stalled box truck. Horns and some angry shouts filtered into the cab. "You could always crash at my place. I mean, you know, on the couch," he added quickly as she stiffened.

"Your roommate won't mind?" She felt her cheeks grow hot. Her hidden power growled inside her like a living thing, begging to come out and play awhile. She concentrated controlling it by telling herself that this man was not trying to hurt her the way Donny had.

"I barely see him. When he's not in school, he's working. He won't mind."

"I'll think about it."

He smiled for a moment before leaning on the horn at a lady in a big Dodge station wagon who wouldn't be denied her lane change. "Learn how to drive, you fucking asshole!" he yelled out the window. She shook her fist at him.

It was such a cliché New York moment that Gretchen broke out in giggles.

Shane chuckled and took a crumpled cigarette pack from the clutter on his dashboard. "Smoke?" he asked as he thumbed out a Camel and stuck it between his lips.

"No thanks, I don't smoke."

He paused with a battered Zippo lighter halfway to his mouth. "Oh. Uh, do you mind if I do?"

She shrugged. "There's so much gunk in the air here, I don't think I'd notice."

He flicked open the metal lighter and spun the flint. "You're from Iowa, right? Elizabeth's town? I forget what it's called."

"Dyersville."

"Oh sure. Nice place? I've never been that far west."

"It's okay, I guess."

Shane blew a lungful of smoke out the window, trying to be considerate of Gretchen's lungs. The Con Ed truck had no air conditioning and Gretchen could already feel beads of sweat forming on her neck and between her breasts. "So why did you leave, if you don't mind me asking?"

"You ask a lot of questions, Shane."

He smiled. "It's not every day I get to talk to a pretty

girl like you."

Despite the heat in the truck, a shiver ran through Gretchen. The memory of Donny forcing himself upon her was still fresh like a raw wound. She couldn't imagine ever doing that with anyone else. It was like Elizabeth said; all boys wanted the same thing. Even Shane, who was far nicer to her than anyone had been back home. She turned away from him and gazed stone-faced at the city as they crawled through it. "It's a long story why I left."

"Maybe you can tell it to me sometime when you feel like talking." He took another long drag.

"I'm sorry, Shane. I'm still trying to adjust to this. I had to come here. I need..." Unbidden, tears spilled down Gretchen's cheeks.

"Aw, hell. I didn't mean to make you cry. Shit. I don't have a hanky or anything in here."

She wiped her eyes. "It's okay. I'm sorry."

"Something bad happened to you back there, didn't it? I mean, you've got those bruises and you're jumpy as all get out."

Gretchen sighed. She felt like she owed something to him just for being such a nice guy, but she couldn't bring herself to talk about it. "I fell." She knew it sounded as lame as it felt.

"Okay. I get that you don't want to talk about yourself. That's cool. Anyway, here we are."

Gretchen looked up from where she'd been knotting her fingers together. Shane had turned the truck off the main avenue onto a street filled with more black people than she'd ever seen in her life.

"Welcome to Harlem," he said with a smile.

FOUR

July 13, 1977, 12:00 PM

Faith pulled her radio from the inside pocket of her jacket. "Bobby, are you there?"

"Go ahead, babe."

She smiled at Irlene, who held a struggling, nine-inch-tall would-be felon in one hand. "Imp and I collared a purse snatcher in Times Square. We're going to book him in."

"Congratulations on making New York a safer place." Bobby chuckled. "I'll dispatch Sundancer to cover for you until you're clear. Love you, babe."

"I love you, too." Faith tucked away the radio again.

"You guys are so sweet together." Irlene sighed. "I hope I meet somebody like him someday."

"I'm sure you will," said Faith. "You got a good grip on the perp?"

Irlene looked down at the doll-sized man in her grasp. He struggled against her fingers but to no avail. "No problem."

Faith led the flying Irlene across the square to the nearby police station. Officers whooped and elbowed one another as the two costumed women entered the building.

"Pony Girl, always a pleasure," said the desk sergeant. "Who's your friend?"

"Boys, this is Imp. She's our newest team member. Please make her feel welcome."

"I'll make her feel welcome," hooted a plainclothes detective.

"A little fellow like you?" Faith winked at Irlene.

"Little?" The detective drew himself up to his full height of... four feet tall. "Hey, what the hell?" Raucous guffaws echoed through the station.

"All right, knock that shit off," hollered the sergeant. "Can we please try to act like professionals?" He turned to Faith and smiled. "What have you got for us today?"

"Purse snatcher," said Faith. Irlene displayed the perpetrator, who looked a little green from being slung around like a doll.

The sergeant adjusted his glasses. "Whose purse did he steal, Barbie's?"

"Imp, if you'd be so kind." Faith gestured at Irlene, who was staring around the police station at the cops, perpetrators, and the intricate ballet of organized chaos.

Irlene raised a hand and pointed at the purse-snatcher. He grew slowly until he was back to his original size.

"Now that's more like it." The sergeant fed a fresh form into a typewriter.

As the sergeant began interviewing the man they'd arrested, Faith turned away to where Irlene was fielding questions from a cluster of officers. The pretty young girl reveled in the attention, much like Sundancer did when anyone pointed a camera in her direction. That kind of openness could get a naïve, young superhero into a lot of trouble, considering some of the hangers-on who showed up at Just Cause parties. Faith resolved to take Irlene aside when they had a moment and speak to her about it.

"Hey, Pony Girl," called an officer. "Something just came in on the teletype you might be interested in."

"Oh? What have you got?"

"Murder in someplace called Dyersville, Iowa. The coroner believes the victim had parahuman powers used against him."

"What? Let me see that." Faith snatched the printout from the man's hand. Irlene floated up into the air to better read over her shoulder. The details were sketchy at best. According to the coroner's report, the victim had "localized trauma to the thoracic cavity consistent with instantaneous implosion. Cause of death attributed to asphyxiation."

"What's that mean?" Irlene asked.

"I guess it means his lungs collapsed so bad they ripped apart." Faith read through the teletype again.

"That sounds horrible!"

"And impossible, which means it may have been a parahuman ability. This is bad."

"Why's that?"

"If a parahuman murdered someone, it reflects badly upon all of us. It means the FBI will be involved. *Parahuman powers used in the commission of an index crime violate federal statutes.*" Faith quoted what she remembered from the Just Cause rulebook. She looked up at Irlene. "It says here the top suspect left town and they believe she came to New York on a bus. Photo sent by fax."

"The fax is coming through now," reported an officer. The machine wheezed and chattered with agonizing slowness. Finally, the officer tore away the sheet and brought it over for Faith.

"Gretchen Gumm, 19 years old, suspected of the murder of Donald Milbrook," read Faith. "Suspect may be parahuman; approach with extreme caution." She turned to the sergeant. "Can I have a copy of this?"

The sergeant nodded and snapped his fingers. "Mac, run these through the copier."

A plucking at her elbow made Faith look behind her. The purse-snatcher stood there looking nervous and guilty. "What?"

"Hey, uh," he said, nervous. "I seen that chick."

The sergeant snorted. "You'd say anything to get out of here, skell."

"No, man, I seen her at the Greyhound station. I, uh, offered to carry her bag but she got pissed off."

Faith raised an eyebrow. "I can't imagine why," she said. "You're the very picture of chivalry. So what happened?"

"There was thunder and the bus windows broke. Freaked me out, so I left."

"Did you see where she went?" asked Faith.

"No, man. I had other pressing engagements."

Faith took Irlene and the sergeant aside. "What do you think?"

"He's a lying sack of shit," said the sergeant. "He's saying what we want to hear."

"We can check out his story easily enough. If there's a damaged bus, then at least that much holds up," said Faith.

"I think he's telling the truth," said Irlene. "He's scared of us, of parahumans."

"Tell you what," said Faith. "Hold him here until we check out his story. If it holds up, just cite him and let him go. If not, throw the book at him."

The sergeant grinned. "With pleasure."

"Come on, Imp," said Faith, "let's go catch a bus."

~ ~ ~

Harlan pedaled his mongrel bicycle into East Harlem. He'd built it from scrap parts of several junked Schwinns. It wasn't much to look at—merciless kids teased him about it whenever he rode it into his own neighborhood—but he'd outfitted it with several gadgets, which made it cooler than any of the retards on his block could even imagine. His pedals didn't crank the sprocket, but instead charged a powerful, lightweight generator which in turn drove a motor that kept him tooling along at a steady fourteen miles per hour. A gyroscope kept him upright even when he braked to a stop. He imagined it must look odd to anyone who actually noticed him sitting at an intersection, pedaling hard without ever putting a foot down.

Gonsalvo Ramirez was a mechanic and tinkerer, much like an older, crustier version of Harlan. Harlan had been searching for someone to help him acquire parts he couldn't find in the scrapyard, and had found a kindred soul in the old Hispanic who spent his days fixing carburetors and changing oil on other peoples' cars and his nights rebuilding a '51 Mercury he'd named Carmella. In return for Gonsalvo's help, Harlan brought the man parts for Carmella whenever he could.

Harlan pulled his bike up at the front of Gonsalvo's Auto Repair. All three bays were open to let in what little breeze forced its way through the heat of the morning. The stench of ancient oil and fresh welding spilled outward onto the street.

Gonsalvo was welding a patch over some sheet metal when Harlan walked in. He tipped his welding mask back to reveal a pockmarked face with black stubble and sparkling eyes. "*Buenas dias*, Harlan."

"Hi, Gonsalvo," he said.

"No school today?"

"It's summer. No school."

"Mm hmm." Gonsalvo wiped his face with a rag only a little cleaner than the shop's floor. "What can I do for you today?"

"I need some thermocouples. Do you have any?"

Gonsalvo leaned back on his stool and looked at the ceiling deep in thought. "I might have one or two. I'll have to check the Parts Room."

Harlan loved the Parts Room. It held some thirty or forty years' worth of tools, gadgets, gizmos, devices, and parts that Gonsalvo thought he might need for something someday. For Harlan, it was like Wonderland and a candy store all mixed into one. He'd whiled away many hours amid Gonsalvo's trinkets, helping to organize and catalogue them, and occasionally helping himself to items he figured he might need.

"Oh, I brought you something." Harlan dug in his pocket and pulled out a bent metal implement. He thrust it at Gonsalvo, eager to see the man's reaction.

The aged mechanic dug his glasses from his breast pocket and squinted at the piece. "Outside door handle," he murmured. "'51 Mercury. Passenger side." He smiled at Harlan. "Carmella's been asking for one of these for a long time. *Gracias*, my friend. She'll be very happy. Where did you find this?"

"I saw one in a junkyard up north. I knew you needed a handle and took it." That wasn't precisely true. He'd seen a Mercury, but it was parked on a street. With the small tools he carried in his pockets out of habit, Harlan had popped off the handle and run away before anyone saw him. "And the thermocouples?"

"I have work to do. If you can find any in the Parts Room, they're yours."

Harlan leaped to his feet and hurried toward the rear of the shop, eager to begin the hunt. He slipped into the Parts Room. A naked bulb hung from the ceiling and bits of sun leaked in through a window encrusted with decades of grease and dust. He closed his eyes and took a deep breath. Stale lubricants provided a sharp tang to the air, balanced by the bright accents of copper and steel, the sweetness of plastic, the subtle cool of ceramics, and the persistent thrum of rust and dust underneath it all. With the scents of industry flooding his head and making his mind whirl with possibilities, Harlan dove into the drawers, piles, and stacks of parts in search of the elusive thermocouples. Minutes stretched as he sorted through mysterious pieces, pocketing those he thought he'd need for his own work. He didn't consider it stealing; that was why he brought Gonsalvo parts for Carmella. The old mechanic understood Harlan like nobody else in the world.

Given a chance, Harlan thought he might like to come and work for Gonsalvo and maybe someday the garage would be his.

"Hey, Harlan, come out here a minute," called Gonsalvo.

Just then, Harlan saw the parts he'd sought. He must have looked right at them four or five times and not seen them. He grinned and tucked them into his bulging pockets before sauntering back into the shop.

Gonsalvo had his welder apart and was wrestling to reconnect something within the framework. Sweat poured off the man, its odor enough to overpower the normal miasma of the repair bay. "I need your help," said the mechanic. "My hands are too big to fit in here and reconnect this stupid plug that came loose."

Harlan took a step toward the welder, but a loud pop and unmistakable hum and hiss of freed electricity made him freeze in his tracks. He felt the hair on his arms and neck stand on end. "Gonsalvo?" Fear danced across his shoulders, making them twitch.

The mechanic sniffed the air. Harlan did likewise and caught the reek of sharp sourness and smoke. "Blown transformer," said Gonsalvo. "I bet there's a cable hanging loose on the roof. We better get out of here, *amigo*."

They left the garage and crossed the street. Harlan looked back and saw a spitting wire dangling down from a smoking transformer. It sparked every time it brushed against the roof of the shop. Up and down the block, people were peeking out windows or stepping out of buildings. Gonsalvo pushed a couple of dimes into Harlan's hand. "Here, go find a pay phone and call Con Ed. Tell them that if they don't get somebody out here soon there's going to be a fire."

~ ~ ~

"Hey, I gotta take a leak," announced Javier as he and Tommy flew along the Hudson. He pointed toward an innocuous warehouse. "Those guys don't mind me using their can. I busted up some kids who were looting stuff from there and reselling it last year. They said swing by anytime. Besides, it takes a few minutes for me to get out of this armor."

"I can't believe you haven't redesigned it yet," said Tommy. This was an ongoing issue with Javier.

"I'll get around to it one of these days when we have some down time."

"All we have anymore is down time," Tommy said, but Javier was already diving down toward the warehouse's concrete apron. Tommy sighed and followed him.

Javier landed with a heavy thud, but the shock absorbers in his lower legs easily soaked up the impact. *"Buenas dias, amigos!"*

Warehouse workers whistled and shouted *"Hola, Javelin!"*

"Necesito los baños." Javier strode into the warehouse like he owned the place, leaving Tommy standing alone in front of the building and feeling foolish. He didn't feel like dealing with curious fans, so he sprang back into the air and circled high over the warehouse for several minutes. Eventually, Javier strolled out and ignited his boot jets without paying any attention to his surroundings, setting some barrels on fire.

Before any of the warehouse workers could respond, Tommy created a whirling vortex over the barrels to draw the flames up and away from them.

Javier whooped and laughed as he did a loop-the-loop. He had his lips pulled back in a snarling grin behind his visor as he flew up to circle Tommy. "Man, I feel so much better!" he said. "My back teeth were floating."

"Your nose is bleeding," said Tommy. Streaks of blood flecked the inside of Javier's visor.

"It is? Oh, shit, it is." Javier reached inside the visor and swiped the blood from his upper lip. "Hey, man, I need to go take care of this." He raised his visor, sniffled, and then blew out a glob of bloody snot, which spun away in the breeze.

"Do what you have to," said Tommy. He knew very well that Javier had snorted the coke they'd just confiscated. It suited him fine; he'd rather be alone with his thoughts today.

"I'll catch up with you later. Cover for me?"

"Of course."

Javier heeled over and headed back inland, in the general direction of his bachelor pad.

Tommy's radio beeped. He pulled it from his belt. "Tornado," he said.

"Tommy, it's Bobby. I can't reach Javier."

"He had to head back to his place. For repairs."

"Ah," said Bobby in a voice that implied he knew Tommy was lying. "Anyway, there's a potential jumper on the GWB. Are you close enough to intervene?"

Tommy turned to look toward the George Washington Bridge. He could see flashing lights on the distant deck. "Affirmative. I'm on my way."

He summoned up gale-force winds to carry him over the water at blistering speed, his eyes locked on a white speck where none should be—against one of the towers. As he barreled onward, the speck resolved itself into a young woman who perched on a narrow ledge just out of reach of the NYPD officers trying to reach her. Tommy poured on the speed because he could see the woman was distressed. As he approached, she either slipped or jumped.

He had only moments to react. He created a powerful updraft beneath the tumbling woman. The swirling air mass sucked up water from the Hudson into a powerful miniature waterspout that slowed her fall. Without hesitation, Tommy dove into the spinning vortex and gathered up the shrieking woman in his arms. Air buoyed them both to safety on the far bank. Tommy pushed his sopping hair out of his face. They were both drenched from his waterspout.

"Are you all right?" He took the woman by her shaking shoulders as sobs racked her. She collapsed into him and bawled like a child. He felt awkward but held her as she clung to him.

"I'm sorry, I'm sorry," she repeated like a refrain.

"It's all right," he said.

Over several minutes, her tears wound down until she only had occasional hitches of her shoulders and a case of the hiccups.

"What's your name?" asked Tommy.

"M-Miranda. Miranda Kovnesky," said the young woman. She was pretty in a way that Tommy would have found appealing if he were into women. Honey blonde hair, dark eyes, full lips. In her white button-down and pencil skirt, she looked kind of like a secretary, although she had execrable taste in shoes.

"I'm Tommy. Nice to meet you, Miranda."

Miranda shivered a little. Tommy called up a warm, drying wind to wick away the last of the Hudson from their skin, hair, and clothing.

"I feel so stupid," said Miranda. "Right after I jumped, I realized I'd made a terrible mistake."

"Why did you think about jumping at all?" Tommy laid his hand on her arm. "What's so terrible about being Miranda?"

She shook her head. "It was about a man. God, it sounds so stupid when I say it like that."

Tommy spread out his cape across the dirt riverbank, sat down, and patted it. "Want to talk about it?"

Miranda blushed. "Oh, no, I couldn't. I've already wasted your time today."

"Saving a life is never a waste of my time. It's not every day you get a second chance to be alive."

"No, I guess not." Miranda started to sit, but then paused. "I'm going to get your cape all dirty."

"It's machine-washable." Tommy grinned. "Now what's on your mind?"

Miranda sat and drew her knees up to her chin. "Have you ever loved someone you knew would never love you back?"

Words caught in Tommy's throat and he could almost see the granite face of John Stone reflected in the water. The great pylons holding up the bridge over their heads were exactly the same shade of gray as John's skin. He coughed. "Yes," he said at last. "I believe I know exactly what you mean."

~~~

Shane smoked cigarette after cigarette as he drove the service truck through the streets of Harlem. He'd explained that if he didn't have specific job duties, he was supposed to monitor the local power grid for any trouble or potential repairs. "They train us to watch for loose power lines or to recognize the sound of a transformer blowing or whatever."

"I always thought power guys just hung around drinking coffee and eating donuts until something went wrong," said Gretchen.

Shane laughed. "When we can. But I'm trying to give you a better impression of New Yorkers. How am I doing so far?"

"Not bad."

"Hey, you hear that? Under the sound of the traffic?"

Gretchen cocked her head and listened. Just barely, she could hear a humming, hissing sound. It reminded her of something from a mad scientist's lab in an old black and white movie. "I think so," she said.

"That's a dying transformer." Shane checked his mirrors and then cut across two lanes of traffic onto a side street. "Any second now…" Gretchen heard a loud bang like a gunshot and saw a puff of black smoke rise a block away. "There it goes," said Shane. "Now I get to play hero, because I'll be Johnny-on-the-spot."

"Shane on the spot," said Gretchen.

He got on his radio and called in the blown transformer, repeating a bunch of numbers and information to the Con Ed dispatcher. Shane parked the truck in front of a small auto mechanic's shop. "You want to get out or wait here?" he asked.

Gretchen looked out at the street full of unfamiliar dark faces. She didn't think of herself as racist, but she felt completely out of her element. "I'll wait."

"No problem," said Shane. "I've got a thermos of Coke under the dash. You're welcome to it. We'll grab some lunch after I'm done here."

The word *lunch* made Gretchen's stomach growl. She hadn't eaten since the day before. Her stomach grumbled again, this time loud enough to make Shane look back at her as he climbed out of the cab. She bent her head forward to let her hair fall across her face, obscuring the blush she could feel crawling up her cheeks.

She watched in the side mirror as Shane pulled tools and equipment from the side of the truck and then jammed a hardhat on his head.

"It just hummed and then blew," said an old Hispanic man with oil-stained hands. "You got here just in time."

"I'll take care of it, mister." Shane grinned from ear to ear. "I'll need access to your back lot. You don't have a dog back there, do you?"

"No, no dogs." The man led Shane behind the shop.

Gretchen reached down, found the thermos, and poured herself a cup of soda. A few people glanced at her riding shotgun in the Con Ed truck, but most of them went about their business or watched as Shane climbed up the telephone pole toward the now-quiet transformer. She sipped at the Coke and then heard the sound of parts and tools rustling around. She looked in the mirror and saw a kid was rummaging through the side-mounted toolbox on the truck. Shane was already up the pole, and nobody else seemed to notice. She'd have to be the one to do something.

She leaned out the window and looked back at the kid. He was scrawny, in his early teens, and filthy. He had the furtive, haunted look about him of someone who'd been persecuted pretty much every day of his life. In his own way, he was as much a victim as Gretchen was. She felt a little sorry for him, but she couldn't let him steal something from Shane's truck. She cleared her throat. "Can I help you?"

He jumped back from the truck as if he'd been scalded by a hot stove. His eyes widened as he realized he'd been caught red-handed. His face betrayed the terror of someone who knew a far worse fate lay ahead.

"Easy, kid. I'm not going to do anything. Just leave the tools and stuff alone, okay? My friend needs them to fix the power."

The kid narrowed his eyes. "You're not going to turn me in?"

Gretchen smiled at him. "No, you're not hurting anything. Just leave the stuff alone and we'll call it even, okay?"

He wavered, uncertain what to do. Maybe he wasn't used to anyone being nice to him, Gretchen thought. She knew a couple kids like him back in Dyersville; kids whose fathers liked to drink and got violent when they did; kids who showed up to school with bruises and haunted expressions.

"What's your name?" asked Gretchen.

The boy looked around as if seeking an escape, and Gretchen had just decided he was probably going to run away when he replied, "Harlan."

"Hi, Harlan. I'm Gretchen." She stepped from the truck and extended her hand in greeting.

Harlan looked her up and down, from her Keds to jean cutoffs to blue t-shirt. His eyes lingered on her chest before he shook her proffered hand. "Nice to meet you," he mumbled, as if the words were unfamiliar.

"Harlan, are you messing with that truck?" The older Hispanic man who'd first talked to Shane hurried up. Harlan's face tensed up.

"No, it's fine," said Gretchen. "We were just talking."

"If you say so." The man turned to watch Shane work atop the telephone pole.

"What were you looking for?" Gretchen asked Harlan.

"Just stuff," he said. "I build stuff, and I need parts sometimes." He bowed his head like he was embarrassed.

"What kind of stuff do you build?"

"Maybe I can show you sometime." Harlan glanced up at her to see if she was looking.

Gretchen realized in surprise that the boy had developed a sudden crush on her. She felt flattered and a little embarrassed—she was much too old for him, but she didn't see any harm in letting him imagine.

It was refreshing to have innocent attention for once.

FIVE

July 13, 1977, 1:00 PM

"At first we thought a bomb went off in it," said the fleet service manager at the bus station, whose embroidered name tag read *Dwayne*. The air inside the shop was smoky and made Faith's throat sore. A fine black film of sooty grime covered everything in the building, and Faith made every effort not to brush against any of it. Dwayne's hands and face were smudged with it, and decades-old oil was ground into his pores, giving all his exposed skin a stippled appearance. He gave Faith and Irlene a tour of the bus in question. "But there's no sign of fire or explosion. The seats aren't even damaged. Whatever it was just blew in the windows."

"Excuse me," interrupted Faith. "Blew them *in?*"

"Yeah. We didn't find any glass on the street at all. I'd have suspected kids with rocks, except there isn't anything inside that looks like it was thrown." He shrugged. "I heard when it happened. Sounded like thunder. I thought maybe the heat was going to break and we'd finally get a little rain."

"Maybe it was like those Memorex commercials," said Irlene. "Some kind of loud noise busted all the windows."

"The problem with that is that it affected the bus on both sides," said Faith, deep in thought. "A loud noise would have only caught one side of the bus, and probably damaged other things on the street too."

Dwayne motioned for Faith and Irlene to look inside the bus. Irlene shrank herself back down to doll-sized and zipped in past Faith's head like an eager sparrow. The manager jerked in surprise but then managed to keep his cool. "We already started to clean it up. We didn't know Just Cause would want to see it."

Faith saw a pile of broken glass swept into the middle of the aisle. She marveled that every single side window was shattered. Cracks marred the windshield in a radial pattern, which intrigued her. The way the safety glass had cracked made it look like someone had hurled a bowling ball at it from outside. "Everything was pulled inside," she said. "What could do that?"

"And 'phyx-u-ate someone's lungs, if it's the same person," said Irlene.

Faith snapped her fingers. "Vacuum!"

"What?" Irlene landed as softly as a butterfly on Faith's shoulder and perched there.

"This girl can create vacuums. She created one in that boy's lungs and killed him. She created one inside this bus and blew in all the windows." Faith turned to Dwayne. "You said all the tires on one side were flat?"

"Yeah. That made me think it was pranksters or something, but when we filled them back up we didn't find any signs of leaks."

"Like the air inside them had just vanished," said Faith. "Is the driver who brought it in still here?" She felt growing concern nipping at her heels. A new, unknown parahuman was always a danger, and this one seemed powerful and had already killed someone. "We need to see if we can get any more information about this girl."

Dwayne shook his head. "He's deadheading back to Chicago. Law says he can't drive for at least eight hours.

They're a good hour away already. Want me to call the bus and hold it somewhere?" He looked eager at the idea of getting to do the kind of thing reserved for prime time cop dramas.

He'd have to play *Starsky & Hutch* some other time. "No, I don't want to inconvenience any other passengers," said Faith. "But do tell him we're on our way. We'll catch him en route."

"But they're thirty or forty miles away!"

Faith grinned. "Fastest girl in the world here, remember? I'll be there in no time." She turned her head to look at Irlene, perched on her shoulder. "How fast can you fly?"

Irlene shrugged. "Fast enough. If I can't keep up, I'll shrink myself down enough to ride in your pocket."

"Better do that now," said Faith. "I'm planning on hitting three hundred."

"Three hundred miles per hour?" spluttered Dwayne as Irlene slipped into the pouch beside Faith's radio. "What's that like?"

Faith winked at him. "It's fast."

~ ~ ~

Harlan stared wide-eyed at the pretty girl beside the Con Ed truck. She was a real fox, as some of the older boys in the neighborhood would have said. He could see a fading bruise beside one of her eyes that she'd tried to cover by makeup and sunglasses. Harlan felt they must have a lot in common; he'd been punched in the face lots of times.

At thirteen, he'd never spent any time with girls. Other boys his age, or even younger, had girlfriends in the neighborhood, but Harlan didn't like being around other people to learn what they really did with each other. He just knew what he'd seen on the television, which struck him as odd and contrived. One thing was certain, though, and that was he wanted to impress Gretchen.

"Want to see my bike? I built a bunch of things onto it."

"Sure," said Gretchen, not really looking at Harlan. She seemed distracted, like something was bothering her. He figured that at the very least he could give her something else to think about.

"I'll go get it." He scampered across the street and ducked back into Gonsalvo's shop.

As Harlan entered the darkened shop, a glint of stray sunlight from a shelf caught his eye. Curious, he went to see what was there; perhaps it would interest Gretchen so she would talk to him more.

It was a tin box with a fine patina of rust on its surface. A shiny stainless steel crank emerged from one side. That was what had gleamed at him in such an enticing way. Harlan picked it up in wonder, and memories flooded into him.

When he was only eight, he'd stolen Reggie's wind-up jack-in-the-box toy and taken it apart to see how it worked. He'd found the clever spring-powered mechanism fascinating and decided to build something else with it. He'd felt a little bad about taking one of Reggie's favorite toys, so he built a replacement for her. When he turned the crank, the box unfolded like a flower opening to display an intricate carousel that spun, with horses that went up and down on their wire-thin poles. He'd been so proud of it that he couldn't give it away. Reggie wouldn't have been impressed by Harlan's arrangement of gears, springs, hinges, and pushrods. She'd probably just have broken it playing with it.

So Harlan had kept it, and showed it to Gonsalvo, who'd delighted in the craftsmanship. Now he was beyond such primitive engineering; instead of springs, he used motors and hydraulics, electricity and combustion to power his creations. He turned the crank. The box squeaked and clattered, but still unfolded the way he'd designed it to. Surely, Gretchen would be impressed.

Surely, she'd stick around to talk more with him. He set it in his bike basket and wheeled it back outside.

The Con Ed man was down from the pole and rummaging through the back of his truck when Harlan came out of the shop. Gretchen was chatting with him about lunch of all things. Harlan's stomach rumbled to remind him he was also due for a meal. As he had many times before, he pushed thoughts of food out of his head to focus on the task at hand. "This is my bike, Gretchen." He raised his voice so she'd be sure to hear. "I built it myself. It has a lot of cool features."

"Does it? That's nice, Harold."

"Harlan. I'm Harlan."

"I'm sorry." Gretchen looked at the Con Ed man, who shrugged and said he needed probably another ten or fifteen minutes.

"So do you want to see it?" pressed Harlan.

"Sure, I'd love to see your bicycle," said Gretchen.

Harlan showed off the gyroscope that kept it balanced even at a standstill, and the electric generator and motor. It even had a headlight he'd salvaged from a Volkswagen Bug.

"You don't ride it at night, do you? Don't you have to stay home and do homework or chores or spend time with your family?"

Harlan shrugged. "Sometimes."

"Well, it's a very lovely bicycle," said Gretchen. "Thank you for showing it to me."

Harlan felt his ears burn. She was talking to him like he was a little kid, not a scientific genius! He'd show her something she couldn't ignore. "Here, look at this." He pushed the box into her hands.

"What is it?" Marginal interest flared in her face as she looked at the tin box.

"It's a surprise." Harlan gave her a shy smile. "Turn the crank."

Gretchen shrugged and began to turn it. A cheerful

little tune emerged from the box. She jumped when it split open and the carousel unfolded. "Oh!"

"Keep turning it," urged Harlan. "There's more."

Her bemusement turned to joy. The device clacked and whirred as hinges opened and rods moved into place. The tune changed once the carousel had completed unfolding. Gretchen's eyes shone and she laughed as the carousel rotated with its tiny horses going up and down. The tune finished and the box folded itself back up once more. "You made this?" She sounded incredulous. "It's wonderful!"

Harlan felt like his heart might explode. He knew, deep down, Gretchen would fall in love with him and they'd get married and live together forever. "You can have it if you want."

"Oh no, I couldn't. This is something really special."

"No, I want you to have it. I can always build another one. A better one, with motors and batteries." Harlan already had a design in his tireless mind.

Scattered applause sounded on the street as the power came back on. Harlan turned to see the Con Ed man walking back toward the truck and stripping off his gloves, a big grin plastered across his face. Harlan realized Gretchen was about to be taken away from him. He thought hard, desperate for something that he could say to keep her there with him.

Then he had an idea.

~ ~ ~

"Tell you what," said Tommy to Miranda. "Are you feeling a little like lunch? My treat."

"Oh, no. I couldn't," she protested. "I've wasted so much of your time already."

"You haven't wasted any of my time," said Tommy. "Besides, I get to take a lunch break. I'd love if you joined me."

"Well…" Miranda wavered.

"I know a lovely little cafe in the Village. Outstanding sandwiches and fresh coffee."

Her last shreds of resistance blew away like so many scraps of paper in one of Tommy's gales. "All right, I guess that's okay."

Tommy flew her back to his neighborhood and landed on the roof of his building. "I'm just going to change. I hate eating in my costume."

"What, right here?" Miranda blushed.

"No, I live downstairs."

Her jaw dropped open. "You live here? But you just told me that! You don't even know me. What if I was a criminal or something?"

Tommy shrugged. "I don't have anything to hide. I don't wear a mask. My identity is public record. Anyone who wants to can find me. I want to be an accessible hero."

"I thought you were supposed to worry about protecting your loved ones."

"Not an issue for me." Tommy smiled. "I'll just change. Be right back."

He scampered down the fire escape and into his apartment, where he replaced his blue and white costume with a gray Mets t-shirt, khaki shorts, and tennis shoes without socks. He called Bobby to say he was dealing with the potential suicide and would be off the air for a little while. Then he pulled his flowing locks back with a rubber band and returned to the roof.

Miranda did a double-take when she saw him. "Oh my God, you look so different without your costume! You look so ordinary."

"That's what I'm shooting for," he said. He led Miranda to the rooftop access to the main stairwell and down to the street below.

Geno's was only a block away. Tommy frequented the place both for lunch and in the evenings, when it turned from a bohemian-style cafe into a full-blown meat market. Geno, a butch Italian with a chest full of hair and an ass like two hams side by side, waved at Tommy and bade him sit anywhere. Miranda deferred to him to order, so Tommy requested two Monte Cristos and cappuccinos, which Geno produced with a flourish.

"So..." Tommy blew on the steaming coffee. "Who's this man who drove you to jump off a bridge?"

Miranda looked scandalized for a moment, until she realized that was exactly what had happened, and she folded in on herself, looking glum.

"I'm sorry. That was insensitive of me." He reached out and touched Miranda's hand on the tabletop. "I'm not very good at this kind of thing."

She shook her head. "No, you're doing fine. It's just me being stupid. He's my boss. I'm his secretary. It's a really small brokerage. Just the two of us, really, except for an occasional temp. I've been there for two years."

"And somewhere along the way, you fell in love with him?"

"Yes." She sniffled and stared down at her sandwich. "But we can't ever be together."

"Is he married?"

Miranda raised her eyes up to meet Tommy's. "No. He's gay. Tommy, I fell in love with a gay man and didn't know it."

Tommy didn't mean to laugh; it just slipped out between bites of his sandwich. It started in his belly like an explosion of fireflies and built into a burst of guffaws that made Miranda's cheeks turn bright red. Geno came over to see if he was all right but all Tommy could do was wave him away. "I'm sorry, I'm so sorry," he gasped to Miranda. "Honey, you and I are more alike than you know. You're in love with a gay man, and I'm in love with a straight man. There, I said it." Tommy's laughter abated as quickly as it had begun. "I've been lying to myself for so long, it feels good to stop."

Realization washed over Miranda's face. "Wait, you're gay too?"

That set Tommy off in another gale of laughter. "Oh my," was all he could manage for a couple of minutes.

"I mean, after that feature in Life magazine, I thought you and Sundancer were an item." Miranda looked like she was ready to sink right into the floor.

"Sundancer is a dear friend of mine," said Tommy. "But she doesn't do a thing for me, if you know what I mean."

"Well, maybe you haven't met the right woman yet. Or you were abused as a child. Or whatever makes you gay."

Tommy smiled. "Nothing makes me gay. I just am, like you're not. I had a wonderful childhood and was very close to my parents before they died. Car crash. I was nineteen and had just joined Just Cause. They were so proud." He finished his cappuccino and signaled Geno for another. "They didn't really get that I was gay, but other than that we got on famously."

"Oh, I didn't know that. I'm sorry."

"Thank you. I still miss them. But here I took you to lunch to talk with you about your problems and I'm talking about mine."

"No, please do," said Miranda. "It helps to know I'm not the only one stuck like this. Is it someone on the team? I bet it's Lionheart." She sighed. "With all those muscles and that mane. He's so fab."

Tommy shook his head. "It's John Stone."

Miranda crinkled up her face. "John Stone? But he looks so lumpy. Like a statue or something."

"Love looks deeper than skin," said Geno. Tommy hadn't realized the man was standing behind him. He looked up and Geno smiled at him from behind his stubbly jaw. "Even if that skin is made of stone. I'm so happy for you, Tommy. You've been miserable for so long. It warms my heart to see you really smile. Lunch is on me."

"Wisdom from behind the counter, Geno?"

The hefty Italian man winked at him. "All we restaurateurs are wise beyond our years, Tommy. It's why I make such good sandwiches." He shot a pointed glare at Tommy's untouched plate. "You really ought to eat that before it gets cold. Free or not, I hate to see it go to waste."

Tommy picked up the Monte Cristo and took a gargantuan bite. Cranberry sauce ran down his chin. Miranda giggled.

"That's more like it." Geno danced off toward the counter to a beat only he could hear.

~~~

"My sister's in Just Cause," said Harlan in a voice tinged with desperation.

Gretchen's mild pleasure at the boy's crush had lasted several minutes, but it became apparent that he wasn't going to leave her alone. Everything he did and said seemed intended to entice her further, and it had grown tiresome. His statement about Just Cause brought her attention back upon him in full. "Really?" She searched for any trace of dishonesty or guile in his face.

"Yes," he said. "Her name is Imp. She can shrink herself and other things."

"I never heard of Imp," said Gretchen.

"She just started today," said Harlan. "Honest!"

"Just Cause is the reason I came to New York," murmured Gretchen.

"I bet I can get you in to meet them!"

"Meet who?" Shane wiped sweat from his face with a dirty bandana.

"Just Cause," Gretchen said.

"Well, it's Wednesday, so they should all be at their headquarters tonight."

"Why? What happens on Wednesdays?"

"Wednesday Night Poker," said Shane. "At least, they used to play poker. Now they mostly just have big parties. Crime rates dropped on Wednesdays because they got mad about their games being interrupted."

"So they'll all be there tonight?"

"Most likely."

"How do I get in to see them?"

Shane scratched his jaw. "It's a pretty exclusive scene from what I hear. Like getting in to Studio 54."

"I don't know what that is," said Gretchen.

"I can get you in," said Harlan. "I'm sure of it. I just have to call my sister."

"You're sure?" Gretchen clasped her hand around his shoulder.

"Yes, definitely."

"Can we meet you back here after lunch?" Gretchen turned to Shane. "Can we come back here?"

"I guess so. Unless I get a service call," he said.

"I'll go call her now!" Harlan leaped onto his bike and sped away, presumably in search of a pay phone.

"That kid has a crush on you," said Shane.

"I think it's kind of sweet." Her voice dropped to a whisper. "Although he smells."

Shane laughed and lit a cigarette. "So, you hungry?"

"Starving!" Gretchen's excitement waned quickly as the reality of her situation set in. "But I'm kind of on a budget since I don't have work yet."

"You're in Harlem. Best soul food in the world right here. Lunch is on me. You're nice company. That's worth a plate of chicken and waffles." He started the truck and pulled it back out onto the street.

"Chicken and waffles?"

"You'll love it. Trust me."

Shane drove to what Gretchen thought looked like a seedy part of town and parked the truck outside a small restaurant. The smells emanating from the greasy wooden building made Gretchen's stomach tie itself in knots.

Shane led her inside. She noticed they were the only two white people in the joint, but the hefty woman behind the counter called out, "Hi, Shane, who's the pretty girl?"

"Myrna, this is my cousin's friend. She's visiting the Big Apple and I wanted to be sure she got the best food in town."

"Why'd you bring her here then?" cracked the short order cook.

"Willy, I ought to take a spoon to your knuckles," called Myrna. She turned to Gretchen and smiled. "I'm Myrna, honey. The jerk in the back is my husband, Willy. Any friend of Shane's is a friend of ours. Welcome!"

"I'm Gretchen, and thank you." She looked around the small restaurant, packed with people. It felt homey, like somewhere in a small town. "It smells wonderful."

"Two specials, please, Myrna." Shane found a small, empty table and motioned for Gretchen to join him. The smell of rich, flavorful food had Gretchen's head spinning in olfactory delirium. She'd never heard of eating waffles and fried chicken together, but she was too famished to give it much thought.

A few minutes later, Myrna set in front of her a plate stacked with three thick waffles loaded with butter and syrup, and two pieces of fried chicken stacked artfully on top. "You want a Coke or root beer, hon?"

"Root beer, please." Gretchen could barely speak around all the saliva in her mouth.

"Don't be bashful," said Shane. "Dig in."

Gretchen tried to be prim and proper but she was so hungry that she was soon shoveling creamy waffles and crispy chicken in as fast as she could and not choke.

Shane ate at a much slower pace and was only half done by the time Gretchen was sopping up the last of her syrup. "So, you're looking for Just Cause. Why is that?"

Gretchen wiped her fingers and lips with a paper napkin before answering. "It's complicated."

"Are you a parahuman or something?"

Hot blood rushed into Gretchen's cheeks. The power longed to lunge out and protect her from a perceived threat, but she forced it back into submission again. She bent her head forward to hide her face with her hair, but it was too late.

"Oh my God." Shane lowered his voice and looked around. "You are, aren't you? That's so cool! What can you do?"

"Shane, I don't want to talk about it." Gretchen's feelings were spiraling into misery again.

"I can dig it," he said. "I'm not going to pry. But if you want to talk about it, I'll listen."

His easygoing attitude and smile gave Gretchen an unexpected level of comfort, and she returned his smile. "Maybe later, okay?"

SIX

July 13, 1977, 2:00 PM

Cars and trucks blurred past as Faith tore along the shoulder in the breakdown lane. A rooster-tail of dust roiled in her wake. Her special boots thundered on the pavement in rapid staccato.

She slowed to check the number on a bus, but it wasn't the one she sought. No matter. It just meant the driver was a bit further than she thought. She poured on the speed until the lane dividers blurred into a solid white line. She was so inured to the rhythm of putting one foot in front of the other that she almost blew past her target bus. At the last moment, she caught a glimpse of it between two semis and skidded to a more manageable sixty miles per hour.

Faith used standard hand signals and then merged into traffic. She'd begun the practice years ago and made every effort to let it be known publicly that was how she moved among vehicles on the roads to try to reduce panic braking among drivers. She hoped Dwayne had at least warned the bus driver that she'd be intercepting him as she pulled in alongside the bus and rapped on the door. The driver's eyes widened but he pulled the lever to slide the door open. Faith took hold of the rail and climbed aboard.

"Let me use your intercom," said Faith. She felt movement at her hip as Irlene clambered out of the pouch and flew up to perch on her shoulder.

"Damn, that was fast!" exclaimed the girl.

"Do you need me to pull it over?" The driver, a heavyset black man with graying hair, mopped his face with a kerchief.

"No, sir," said Faith with a smile. "We'll try to disrupt things as little as possible for your passengers." She took the intercom and held it up to her mouth. "Ladies and gentlemen, we're Pony Girl and Imp of Just Cause. You are in no danger. We're just here to speak to a passenger." She consulted a small notebook in which she'd recorded what she learned from Dwayne. "Harry McMurtry?"

The nervous passengers relaxed at her placation. A man in a rumpled Greyhound uniform shirt at the back of the bus raised a tentative hand. Faith smiled at the other passengers as she moved down the aisle. She knelt down beside McMurtry.

"Mr. McMurtry, you drove a bus from Chicago to New York last night?"

"Y-yes."

"Relax, sir. You aren't in any kind of trouble. We need to ask about one of your passengers." Faith produced the faxed image of Gretchen Gumm. "Was this girl on your bus?"

McMurtry stared at the picture and scrunched up his face in concentration. "Yeah. Yeah, I'm sure of it. Blonde chippie. Nice rack. Oh, uh. I'm sorry. Long night."

"That's all right, sir. Give me as much description of her as you can, please."

McMurtry shrugged. "Blue tee-shirt, jean shorts, sandals. Straight blonde hair. That's about it. She slept the whole way."

Faith nodded. "Go on."

"Can't really think of anything else. Oh, wait. I think she had a black eye. She wore sunglasses, but you could still kind of see a shiner, you know?"

"Somebody hit her?" asked Irlene.

McMurtry jumped a little at the tiny hero. "Jesus, I didn't even see you. Look at that, you look like a doll!"

Irlene smiled. "Thanks, you're real sweet to say so."

"Yeah, anyway, I been driving a bus for ten years. You get so you recognize people, you know? Not like individual people, but types. I've seen plenty of girls like her in my time. Girls whose husbands or boyfriends get a little free with their fists. Sure, they might say they walked into a door or fell down the stairs, but they ain't fooling anyone. They all have a certain look about them. Like they're afraid of everyone." He leaned back in his seat. "She had that look."

"Do you have anything else?" asked Faith.

McMurtry shook his head.

"You've been very helpful, Mr. McMurtry. If you think of anything else, please call Just Cause and leave a message for me. We're in the phone book."

Faith's radio beeped as she headed back to the front of the bus. "Pony Girl, go ahead."

"This is the switchboard," said the voice. "We have a caller holding who claims to be Imp's brother."

"Hang on, let us get someplace quiet. Give me a minute." Faith took the intercom once more. "Ladies and gentlemen, thanks for your cooperation. Enjoy your trip."

The two heroes ducked out of the bus, one on foot and one in the air. Faith crossed the lanes of traffic, careful to check behind her for inattentive drivers, and then skidded to a halt on the grassy shoulder. Irlene grew herself back to her full size as Faith retrieved her radio. "Go ahead, switchboard." She passed the unit to the younger girl.

"Hello? Harlan, is that you?"

"Yeah it is. Hi."

Irlene covered the mouthpiece. "It's my little brother. He hates me." She turned back to the radio. "What's shakin'?"

"There's this girl. Um, she's in my class. I was wondering if maybe I could bring her to your headquarters sometime?"

Irlene's eyes widened. "A girl, Harlan? You? That's great news!"

"So I was wondering, uh, if you could get me a couple of passes to come in."

"I guess so," said Irlene. "Or you could just come when I'm there and I'll show you around."

"No, that's no good. She'll be more impressed if it's just me."

"That makes sense," said Irlene. She turned to Faith. "Is there some kind of entry pass?"

Faith nodded. She always carried a few with her. It was good public relations to pass them out. Everyone on the team did, although most of those passes wound up in the hands of party guests. She pulled two passes out of her pouch and handed them to Irlene. "Give him these."

"Okay, Harlan, I've got a pair for you."

"Could you give them to me now? I'm, uh, at school."

Irlene glanced over at Faith. "He's in Harlem. I can be there and back in less than an hour."

Faith shrugged. "Why not?"

Irlene grinned. "Thanks. This is a pretty cool gig, being a superhero." She tucked the passes into her own pocket and shrank back down to the size of a bird.

"Since you don't have a radio yet, meet me back at headquarters."

"Roger wilco." Irlene laughed and zipped off into the summer sky like a pink and white hummingbird.

Faith's radio beeped again. "Pony Girl."

"Babe, it's me," said Bobby. "You better get back here on the double. The Feds are here about your mystery parahuman killer."

Faith couldn't even see where Irlene had gone anymore. She made a mental note to make sure Lionheart issued her a radio as soon as possible. "I'm on my way. Irlene's taking care of a family thing, then she'll meet us back at headquarters."

She lit out for Manhattan.

~~~

Harlan lurked by the pay phones outside the school, keeping one eye out for truancy officers and the other for any of the kids who liked to bully him. Most of the worst offenders were also in summer school like him—no great surprise there. During the school year, he'd gotten used to the humiliation. However, fantasies about getting his revenge kept him warm on cold nights.

As he waited, Harlan's thoughts turned to Gretchen. He needed to get her away from the Con Ed jerk. Because of how excited she'd been to see his wind-up carousel, he knew she'd be beyond words when he showed her his giant robot. He wondered if he could hold the passes at his junkyard, so she'd have to come there to pick them up. Then he frowned. A beautiful, small-town girl like her wouldn't want to come to an inner-city junkyard in Harlem of all places. It occurred to him that the only way he could get her there would be through a trick of some sort. He would have to stall. Gretchen was tied to the Con Ed truck. If he could keep it around, she'd have to stay too. He knew he could keep the Con Ed guy working in the area. All he needed was a few minutes in Gonsalvo's Parts Room to build the device, which formed in his mind.

"Hi, Harlan."

He turned to see a pigeon-sized Irlene perched atop the phone. The sight startled him enough that he jumped back and uttered one of the words his mother had forbidden him ever to let pass his lips. "Shit, Irlene! How long have you been there?"

She pirouetted neatly in midair. "I just got here. Traffic is pretty light twenty feet over the ground."

"Oh. Hey, don't tell Momma I just said *you-know-what*."

Irlene smiled from behind her raspberry-colored mask. "I won't. I promise." She looked around at the empty grounds around the school. "Where is everybody?"

"Half-day today," said Harlan.

Irlene shook her head. "You didn't get that filthy in class today. Harlan, when are you going to stop lying to us and ditching school?"

"I ain't lying." He felt blood rushing to his cheeks and ears.

"Oh, Harlan. You're such a bright kid. I really hate to see you wasting yourself this way. You ought to be getting straight As so you can go to college. A real college, like M.I.T. or something. Someplace that's for people like you who design and build things."

Harlan kicked the bottom of the pay phone post. "School is stupid. Everyone hates me. Even the teachers."

"Except your girlfriend?"

"She ain't my girlfriend. Well, not exactly."

"It's okay, Harlan. I understand. I brought you two passes to come visit headquarters. Do you know when you want to come? I'll see if I can show you around, even though I'm still brand new myself."

"I'm not sure," he said. "I'll have to see when Momma will let me go."

"She's going to want to know about your grades," said Irlene.

"This is for extra credit. It'll bring my grades up."

Irlene didn't look convinced, but she said, "All right, Harlan. Just a moment." She flew from the top of the pay phone and grew downward until she was her normal size. She fished two cards from her pocket and handed them to him. He seized them and looked carefully at the neat block printing. Just Cause Visitor Pass. Beneath that was a blank space for a name and at the bottom was Pony Girl's signature. Harlan tucked both passes into his deepest pocket. These were treasures, worth more than gold or diamonds to him.

They would make Gretchen like him.

"Thanks, Irlene."

Irlene reached out and ruffled his hair. "You're family, Harlan, and I love you. I'd do anything to help you that I could."

He ducked away from her touch. She lowered her hand, knowing she'd crossed a line somewhere. A hint of tears glistened in her eyes. He wouldn't meet her gaze. "Thanks for the passes, Irlene."

"You're welcome, Harlan." She looked like she wanted to say more, but he started to glance around, hoping she'd get the message that he didn't want to be seen with her. "I'd better get going. I might not be home tonight. Tell Momma for me."

"Okay."

Irlene shrank back down, circled Harlan once like a moth around a light bulb, and then flew off into the broiling sun.

"So… Greasy thinks he's good enough for superheroes, huh?" A voice like a crow cawing jarred Harlan out of his thoughts. He spun around to see four boys from the school approaching from across the street. They must have been lurking around the record store there and seen the whole thing with Irlene. They called him *Greasy* and *Pig Pen* when they felt like picking on him. They must have felt they needed some afternoon entertainment. He started to edge toward his bicycle.

"What's the matter, Greasy? Too good to hang out with us anymore?"

"Maybe he's gonna run home to his mommy," teased another boy.

"She ought to teach him how to take a bath."

One of the boys wrested the bicycle out of Harlan's hands and hopped onto it. "Hey, look at me!" he called.

"I'm Greasy Washington. I'm too cool for school because I know a superhero." He leaped off the bike and swung it viciously against the curb. The old frame folded. The other boys' raucous laughter echoed around Harlan. "Oh no, I done broke my bike! Good thing I'm Greasy, because I can just slide on home."

Rough hands shoved Harlan from behind. Another boy caught him, spun him around, and shoved back. "So you know a superhero, boy? You got parapowers too, boy? Can you fly? Fly, Greasy, fly!" A hard push knocked him to the ground and Harlan yelped as his wrist banged painfully off the cement.

"Guess he can't fly," said the boy who'd shoved him, eliciting more laughter from the others. The one who'd trashed his bicycle kicked it until something broke loose.

The sight of the piece whirling away into the street sent Harlan into a murderous rage. "I'll kill you!" he shrieked, and struggled to get up.

The four boys, done with their taunting, turned to outright brutality and commenced punching and kicking him in earnest, until all he could do was huddle and whimper and wait for the end.

~~~

"Thanks so much for lunch and for talking with me," said Miranda. "I feel a lot better."

"You're not going to go find something else to jump off of once I'm gone, are you?" asked Tommy.

Miranda laughed. "No, I promise." They strolled up the street towards his apartment.

"I just hope you find some peace with yourself," said Tommy. "You'll meet someone else. It's a big city."

"Even though I don't want to," said Miranda. "Any more than you want to look past John Stone."

"Touché," said Tommy with a laugh. "Listen, do you want to come inside?" Miranda raised an eyebrow. "Not for that," said Tommy quickly. "It's just that, well, I don't really know anyone who's not a superhero, and it's nice to talk to you."

"It's nice to talk to you too, Tommy, and I'd love to."

Tommy led her up the flight of stairs and unlocked his apartment. She looked around at the high ceilings, the tasteful wall art, the track lighting. Quiet ceiling fans circulated the hot midday air enough to make the apartment's temperature at least tolerable. Diaphanous white curtains billowed gently in the breeze.

"It's lovely," said Miranda. "You live here alone?"

"Yes." Tommy saw the flashing light on his radio, which meant someone had tried to reach him. He picked it up from the table and told Miranda, "I'll be right back. Make yourself at home. *Mi casa es su casa*."

"So cultured." Miranda laughed.

Tommy stepped into his bedroom and pulled the door shut. He called headquarters. "Tornado, checking in."

"Tommy," said Bobby. "About time. Listen, I need you to go check on Javier. He's not answering his radio and we've got the Feds here. Apparently there's a rogue para loose here in town who killed a guy in Iowa."

"Oh shit," said Tommy.

"My thoughts exactly. This could blow up bigger than the Son of Sam."

"Javier was having an equipment malfunction," said Tommy through clenched teeth.

"His malfunction is in his goddamn head. One of these days we're going to find him dead."

"Don't even joke about that."

"I wish I was."

"Okay, I'm on my way."

Tommy pulled on a spare costume, still clean and fresh from the Chinese laundry he used. He walked out of his room, clasping his cape around his neck.

Miranda was examining the photos and news clippings in Tommy's small Just Cause shrine. "You must lead such a fascinating life," she said as he approached her. "All these strange and wonderful people you've met, and the things you've done."

He shrugged. "I'm still just a regular guy. It's just a job, like being a cop or an actor."

Miranda sighed. "Still a lot more interesting than what I do for a job."

An idea popped into Tommy's head. "Listen, do you like baseball?"

Miranda wrinkled up her nose. "Baseball? What has that got to do with anything?"

"John Stone, Sundancer, and I are all going to the Mets game later. Would you like to join us?"

"Are you serious?" Miranda's jaw dropped in surprise. "You guys do that?"

Tommy smiled. "It's that or another party at Headquarters tonight, and as fun as they are, I could use the change of pace."

"I'd love to go to a game with you. If you're sure it's okay, that is."

"Positive. Do you want to meet us there?"

"Sure. I live in Queens, so I'm not far away." They worked out details of where and when to meet at the stadium, and then Tommy offered to call her a cab. "No thank you," she said. "It's such a lovely day, I couldn't stand being in the back of a stuffy cab."

Tommy raised an eyebrow. "It's hot and humid and you think it's lovely?"

She winked. "It's a lovely day to be alive. You're a real sweetheart, Tommy Tornado." Miranda stood on her tiptoes and kissed his cheek. "I'll see you tonight."

~~~

"So that's how I wound up out here in the Big Apple," said Shane. He'd spent most of the past half hour regaling Gretchen with the tale of his journey from Des Moines to New York City. It wasn't a very interesting story, but she didn't mind listening to his cheerful chatter. It kept her from thinking about her own problems. Besides, they'd needed something to do while sitting outside Gonsalvo's repair shop, waiting for Harlan's return.

"Do you ever miss it?" asked Gretchen. "Small towns? Fields of corn and wheat? Clean air?"

"Sure." Shane stabbed out his cigarette. "I get back a couple of times a year to visit my folks, but this city has a way of getting in your blood. Once you call New York home, everyplace else you're just visiting."

"I wonder if I'll ever feel at home here." Gretchen stared out the window without really seeing anything. She could feel Shane's eyes on her as he appraised her from his seat.

"I'm sure you'll do just fine," he said. "You got a strength about you. Plus you're a para."

She gave him a tight smile. "Yes, there's that." She'd thought a lot about telling him about her power. He didn't seem the type to do anything threatening with information about her. She opened her mouth to divulge a little more about herself but the radio interrupted her.

"Shane, come back."

"Go ahead," said Shane.

The dispatcher told him a police substation was suffering intermittent power failures and asked him to check it out.

"Copy," Shane said and turned to Gretchen. "I can't stay here any longer. Duty calls. Do you want to wait for your friend?"

"No, I'll go with you," she said. "Let me leave him a message here." She slipped out of the truck and dashed into Gonsalvo's where she borrowed a pen and wrote Harlan a quick note on a service request form. She asked him to leave the passes with Gonsalvo if he couldn't wait for her and she'd stop by after Shane's shift was done. She looked up and down the street once more but saw no sign of Harlan in any direction.

"Okay, let's go." She climbed into the truck.

Shane took the truck around the block and headed for the highway. "I'm not looking forward to this," he grumbled. "That's a really old station building. You should see what passes for wiring in some of these places."

"Maybe I should," said Gretchen.

"What?" Shane glanced sidelong at her as he nosed the truck up an on-ramp to merge with early afternoon traffic. Heat waves poured off the blacktop with almost audible force, making everything blurry.

"I feel like such a jerk, riding around with you all day and wasting your time. Can I help you with your work somehow?"

"Hmmm." He steered the truck around a stalled taxicab, oblivious to the angry horns behind him. "It's not really allowed in regulations. You have to be an apprentice first."

"So I'll be your apprentice. I'll hand you tools and put my finger on knots so you can tie them tighter."

He laughed. "We don't use knots."

She poked him in the side. "You know what I mean. How about it, huh? Time I started earning my keep. Maybe I'll go work for Con Ed."

"All right, I guess so. I think there's a spare set of coveralls behind the seat, although I don't know how clean they'll be."

Gretchen turned around and rummaged through the accumulated junk and trash behind the truck's seat and crowed with success when she discovered the lightweight denim coveralls. They stank of stale cigarette smoke, but were otherwise tolerable. She kicked off her tennis shoes and slid her legs into the lower half. The legs and sleeves were too long, but she could roll them up. She zipped the coveralls halfway up her chest and then grabbed Shane's hardhat from the seat beside him. She set it rakishly on her head. "How do I look?"

"Like you should be on a calendar," he said.

Surprise washed over her like the heat boiling off the pavement. She couldn't speak for a few minutes and just watched as Shane took the truck down an exit ramp into a different part of Harlem.

He parked the truck and looked down with skepticism at Gretchen's feet. "This is going to be pretty hard on your shoes," he said. "Do you have any others to change into later?"

"I've got some sandals in my bag," she said.

"Okay. I've got an extra hardhat and gloves in the back. Let me give you a quick rundown on tools."

Gretchen rolled up the pant cuffs and sleeves on the coveralls and then climbed out of the truck. Shane proceeded to show her clamps, voltage meters, screwdrivers and wrenches. "I know what those are," she laughed. "I'm not a complete rube."

Shane smiled back at her and Gretchen realized in surprise that she was developing genuine feelings for him, that she wouldn't mind going on a date with him or even letting him kiss her good night. But then she remembered the feel of Donny's breath on her neck and she repressed a shudder.

"Ready to go get dirty?" he asked.

She smiled back at him. "Sounds like fun."

"Good, because we're probably going to have to go into the sewer."

Gretchen's smile faded.

SEVEN

July 13, 1977, 3:00 PM

Lionheart was waiting at the elevator when the doors opened. "No Imp?" he asked as he sniffed the air. "She had to go meet her brother," Faith said. "She'll be along as soon as she's done."

"Government suits," growled Lionheart under his breath. "I hate the Feds. They reek of corruption and cheap bourbon."

"Is everyone else here?"

"No. We can't raise Javier on the radio. Bobby sent Tommy to track him down." Lionheart looked angry enough to tear a building down with his teeth. "The man's addictions make him a disgrace to this team. He thinks I don't know, but I can smell every pill he takes, every line of blow, every woman leaching out of his pores."

"Easy, Rick." Faith curbed her urge to scratch him on the back of his head to calm him. "First things first. Let's listen to the Feds and do what we can to help them and then look to our own internal problems."

Lionheart sighed. "You're right, of course. I may lead this motley bunch in name, but you're far wiser than me. I'd be lost without you."

Suddenly Faith realized they stood very near each other. His natural musky scent filled the air and made her head spin. She loved her husband Bobby, and had for many years, but she felt an undeniable attraction toward Lionheart and had almost from the day they'd first met. She knew he felt a similar draw to her. So far they'd never acted on those feelings.

Some days it was harder to resist than others.

"No," she murmured, more to convince herself than him.

He backed away, not wanting to cause either of them further embarrassment, and the moment passed.

Three empty seats in the conference room bore mute testimony to the fragmentation of the team. Sundancer toyed with a lock of her hair. Bobby sipped coffee. The Steel Soldier gave off regular ticks in the corner, sounding like oil dropping into the pan of a hot engine as he idled. John Stone sat at attention, looking at the two men in ill-fitting, off-the-rack suits at the far end of the conference room. They glanced up as Faith and Lionheart sat down.

"Everyone who's going to be here is here," said Lionheart.

"Good," said one of the men. "Ladies and gentlemen, this is Special Agent Stull and I'm Special Agent Simmons of the New York office of the FBI." Stull handed him some folders from a briefcase and Simmons passed them out to the heroes. "As I'm sure you're aware, we're investigating a murder we believe was committed using parahuman powers, which is automatically a federal crime. Everything we know about this case is in these folders."

Stull stood up and brushed a hand across his clean-shaven scalp. "The victim, nineteen-year old Donald Milbrook, died of internal thoracic trauma consistent with violent, immediate change in air pressure. The lack of external injuries implies he was killed using parahuman abilities."

"We already know all this," Faith pointed out. "It was in the initial police report from Dyersville."

Simmons ignored the interruption. "Our top suspect is Gretchen Gumm, also nineteen. A witness at the diner where she works confirmed she left with Milbrook at the end of her shift. They apparently drove to a secluded area to have intercourse."

Lionheart raised an eyebrow. "What led you to that conclusion, Agent Simmons?"

Simmons tapped the folder with his finger. "Stains and residue found in the course of the autopsy."

"Was it consensual?" asked Sundancer.

Simmons gave her a blank stare.

"As opposed to rape," she added. Stull winced at the term, as if hearing it brought him physical discomfort.

"Look," began Simmons. "We're not here to discuss potential moral failings of an otherwise upstanding young citizen. Whatever happened, let's not forget he's the victim here, and his killer is on the loose."

Faith glanced over at Sundancer. Sparks of barely-restrained fury danced in the young woman's eyes. "Let me propose a scenario, Agent Simmons. Suppose your all-American farmboy here decided to get a little drunk, which I see was included in the autopsy report, and got a little too free with his hands. He takes Gumm out to his secluded area and forces himself on her. But he doesn't know she's a parahuman, and she exacts fatal revenge on him for his act. Does that fit into your world view?"

Simmons sniffed in disdain. "I'm not going to be lectured by a *Playboy* bunny. This is a Federal murder investigation and I won't have you making a mockery of it."

"Be that as it may," growled Lionheart, trying to restore order to the meeting. "She's your primary suspect. Why is that, and what's she doing in New York?"

"I'll take this one," said Stull. "Her parents were concerned when she never came home after work two days ago, and called the police. By then, Milbrook's body had been found and we were looking for suspects. We questioned several of Gumm's friends, but none of them had any idea where she'd gone. We checked local bus and train schedules and found a potential match. Further questioning of the driver and ticket agent in Des Moines confirmed that she bought a one-way ticket to New York City."

"All right, it certainly sounds like she's a good suspect," said Faith. "But here's the thing. Imp and I interviewed the driver of the bus she was on, and he said she had a bruised eye. Maybe she was acting in self defense."

Stull made a dismissive wave. "I don't care. That doesn't excuse the fact that she used parahuman powers to kill. That much is clear-cut. If she was defending herself, that's something for the lawyers to determine."

"That's why we're enlisting your help," said Simmons. "As parahumans yourselves, you may have insights about where she might have gone or who she might have talked to. And if we have to take her down, it would be good to have you for backup."

"Nobody's taking anybody down until we know what's going on," said Lionheart.

"Maybe if we talked to her friends," said Sundancer.

"We've already interviewed her friends," grumbled Stull.

"They may be protecting her. You guys do come across as pretty heavy-handed," said Faith. "I think Sundancer's right."

"I CAN FLY YOU AND SUNDANCER TO DYERSVILLE TO CONTINUE THE INVESTIGATION AS YOU ARE THE TWO LIGHTEST TEAM MEMBERS CURRENTLY PRESENT," said the Steel Soldier.

"I can fly myself," Sundancer said.

"AT SUPERSONIC SPEEDS, I CAN TRAVEL THERE IN APPROXIMATELY NINETY MINUTES, EVEN BURDENED WITH TWO PASSENGERS."

Faith turned to Lionheart. "It would make sense for us to get some feet on the ground there. Maybe we can find out something that the kids won't tell the Feds."

He nodded. "Do it."

The Steel Soldier whirred into a higher level of activity. "I POSSESS TWO CASES IN WHICH YOU WILL BE PROTECTED FROM WIND AND FRICTION. THEY WILL BE CRAMPED, BUT I UNDERSTAND HUMANS CAN ENDURE DISCOMFORT FOR CERTAIN AMOUNTS OF TIME."

Faith sighed. "Steel, I'm sure glad you're not a doctor, because if you were, you'd have a lousy bedside manner."

~~~

Harlan trudged into Gonsalvo's shop, pushing his bent bicycle. His stomach churned from the blood he'd swallowed and his ribs ached from repeated kicks.

"*Madre de dios*! What happened to you?" A surprised Gonsalvo dropped the wrench he was holding when he saw Harlan.

"I fell off my bike," said Harlan. "And then it got hit by a car."

Gonsalvo looked from the twisted frame of the bike to the bruises on Harlan's face and shook his head sadly. "The girl from Con Ed left you a note. They got another service call and had to leave."

Harlan sniffled a little and tasted blood. "I'd have come back sooner if I could." He took the note and read through it twice to make sure he didn't miss any hidden meaning. All it said was that Gretchen was sorry she'd missed him. If he'd leave her a pass and his phone number, she'd pick it up later from Gonsalvo and call Harlan to work out a time to visit Just Cause. That way he wouldn't have to wait around for her.

Harlan closed his eyes. He felt like he was being kicked in the head all over again. Didn't Gretchen understand how important she was to him? Obviously not. He'd have to take steps to show her, to prove himself to her. First, he'd have to get the Con Ed truck back out to the neighborhood, and he knew exactly what that would take. He folded the note with care and tucked it into a grimy pocket. "Can I use your tools and the Parts Room to fix my bike?" he asked Gonsalvo.

"Go ahead." The mechanic leaned under the hood of a Datsun. "You need me, I'm out here."

Harlan wheeled his battered bicycle into the back of the shop. He did not intend to repair it until later. He needed parts from it to make the creation that kept battering the inside of his skull, begging him to build it.

A broken power drill became a handle and trigger mechanism. The rails from adjustable bucket seats transformed into a framework. Harlan cannibalized the battery pack from his bike and installed it where the drill's original battery had been. His would be much more powerful for this application. He set about wrapping coils of wire around some flat pieces of metal to make magnets.

Filtered sunlight crawled across the Parts Room floor as Harlan's device took shape. He mounted the magnets in a series along the frame rails and connected them through the trigger to the battery. He thumbed off the safety, pulled the trigger, and was rewarded with a humming sound. The magnetic field made his skin feel funny and his vision blurred for a moment. If he was going to use this device more than a couple times, he'd want to install some shielding around it. But for now, this was a quick, jerry-rigged invention. He'd make it better in later designs.

Harlan took up Gonsalvo's grinder and a flat metal disc. He shaped it into a crescent moon and sharpened the inner edge to a razor's thickness. Using solder, he thickened it just behind the blade edge so it'd fly like an airfoil and then tack-welded a length of copper welding rod to the outside. The whole affair looked like a toy magic wand when he was finished.

A few minutes of additional work and he had a small windshield-wiper motor installed as a quick-release clip to hold the blade-wand in place. Time to test his invention. He slid the wand into the device's barrel where it snapped into place, held tight by the washer motor clip. The crescent-shaped blade airfoil poked out of the snout. He shook the weapon to test it but the wand didn't fall out. So far, so good. He raised the weapon, sighted down the rails toward a discolored spot on the cinder block wall, released the muzzle catch, and pulled the trigger.

The magnets hummed, his ears popped, and the wand disappeared from Harlan's view with a sound like paper tearing. A loud bang resounded through the Parts Room as cinder block chips exploded outward.

"Harlan? You all right in there?" called Gonsalvo from out front.

"Yeah. I dropped something." Harlan lowered his weapon and hurried to look at the wall.

He'd blown a fist-sized hole through the cinderblocks, and dusty sunlight shone through it. The hole sat at the center of a crater the size of a trashcan lid. Harlan gaped in astonishment at the effectiveness of his weapon. A world of possibilities opened up to him as he cradled his new toy like a proud father. He could see so many uses for it, so many things he could do with it to impress Gretchen.

First, he had to get her back into the area. Harlan shuffled some shelves and boxes around to hide the hole in the Parts Room wall as best he could so Gonsalvo wouldn't notice. He shoved his battered bike far under a table. He had time to make more of the blade-wand projectiles, and ideas for improvements to the gun flooded his brain thick and fast. A strap. A quick reload mechanism. A targeting sight. All those things could wait until later, for he had far more urgent tasks.

Destruction whispered its seductive poetry into his ear.

~ ~ ~

Javier lived in a high-rise apartment in Manhattan. Tommy flew to the building's roof, which was a maze of flower and vegetable gardens and bird coops. A few of the building's tenants were on the roof, enjoying the sun and slight breeze of the higher altitude. They stared as the winds deposited Tommy in their midst.

"Good afternoon," he said. "Has Javelin been by here?"

An older man with a salt and pepper beard nodded and spoke with a mild German accent. "I saw him this morning when I was feeding my birds."

Tommy thanked him, signed a few autographs, and headed down a flight of steps to the elevator lobby. Javier lived two floors down in a large apartment. Tommy had never been inside, but he'd seen enough through the door before to recognize it was a typical bachelor pad.

The door to the apartment hung open several inches.

Tommy's heart started to pound harder. Had something happened to Javier? Out of his armor, he wasn't anything more than a man, and crime could strike at any time in New York. Tommy stepped into the apartment, gathering up whirling spheres of air in his hands, just in case. He became aware of a sour stink in the air, like rancid milk. The heat was stifling with no air conditioning. The ceiling fans hung still in the quiet air.

"Javier?" Tommy looked around. The large, overstuffed couch had a large puddle of drying puke spread across a cushion and running onto the shag carpet. A half-empty bottle of Scotch sat on the coffee table amid some lipstick-stained glasses and a mirror to which clung a few random flakes of cocaine. Javier's armor lay in a haphazard pile in a corner of the room near the minibar.

Tommy glanced into the kitchen area but saw nothing but some cartons of old Chinese food congealing onto the counter. He hurried into the back bedroom area of the apartment, fearing the worst.

He found Javier sprawled across the hall. Foamy, pinkish vomit leaked from his mouth and nose and his complexion had gone ashen underneath his normal olive skin tone.

Tommy cursed and yanked off his gloves to check for life signs. Javier's pulse was weak and seemed too slow to be safe, and his breathing bordered on catatonic.

Using his fine control of air currents, Tommy raised Javier up on a cushion of air, face down, and tilted so his head was lower than his torso. He used a gentle stream of air pressure to force Javier's lungs clear, inflating them to push out syrupy hunks of bloodstained phlegm. He wished he could keep Javier breathing, but Tommy didn't have enough control to maintain Javier's breath and perform the intricate procedure he was about to attempt. Javier would have to breathe on his own for a few minutes, because the next part would be even more unpleasant. While maintaining the air cushion under his teammate, Tommy forced another stream of air in through Javier's mouth, pushing it past his throat and esophagus into the man's stomach. He couldn't see what he was doing and had to estimate distances. If he guessed wrong, he could rupture an intestine.

Air flowed into Javier's belly and pushed out the slurry of alcohol, bile, undigested pills, and other foulness onto the rug. The odor made Tommy gag. It took all his strength to keep down his Monte Cristo as he blew Javier into the bathroom. He set the man into the bathtub and stripped him down to his underwear. Under ordinary circumstances, Tommy would have taken a moment to appreciate Javier's well-defined body, but nausea threatened to overwhelm him. He turned on the shower full blast. Javier jerked a little as the cold stream hit him. He groaned, coughed, and dry-heaved, but he had nothing left to throw up.

Now that the immediate emergency was past, Tommy

realized he was boiling mad. "You stupid son of a bitch," he yelled over the hiss of the shower. "What did you take? How much? You almost died, you shithead!" Tears of fury ran down his cheeks. "This isn't how we're supposed to be!" He sank down on the toilet and put his head in his hands. "This isn't how we're supposed to be," he repeated in a whisper.

"T-Tommy?" Javier's voice barely carried across the bathroom. "What're you doin' here?"

"Saving your life, you asshole."

"'M all wet," Javier mumbled. "'N' sleepy."

Tommy fled the bathroom, unable to look at his teammate. He retreated to the kitchen in search of cleaning supplies. He found some spray cleaner and set about dealing with the stains. Every few minutes he checked on Javier. The man had passed out, but was breathing on his own as the shower beat down on him.

The worst of the vomit cleaned up, Tommy dumped the whole mass of sodden paper towels and linens down the garbage chute. Javier could buy himself new ones. Using his powers, Tommy dried the carpet in seconds, and then collected Javier from the shower. .He stripped Javier's dripping underwear off and used his powers to blow the man dry.

"Don' touch me, you fag," mumbled Javier.

"I'm going to pretend you didn't say that." Tommy wrapped a towel around Javier's waist. "You're out of your head."

Javier retched once but nothing came up. "I'm sorry," he said. "Don' feel so good."

Tommy half-led, half-carried Javier to the bedroom. "You're lucky to be alive, you asshole." He laid Javier down on top of the covers.

"Tommy?" Javier shut his eyes. "Thanks. You're a good friend." He hiccuped once. "Ev'n for a fag."

Tommy sighed and called back to headquarters to report in.

~~~

It's one thing to talk about the sewers, thought Gretchen, and another to actually be under the city streets with flashlights and rats and God-knows-what flowing past in the trough next to the narrow ledge where she stood. Shane had a junction box open and was checking connections as Gretchen held a flashlight over his shoulder. She kept jumping at noises.

"I'm sorry," she said after the fourth time. "It's just that I've never…"

"It's okay," said Shane. "It's a different world down here." He grunted as he stretched to check another connection.

"Is it true that there are alligators down here? Or snakes?"

"Oh, I don't know," he said. "Everybody's heard that, but I never saw anything worse than some big goddamn rats, cockroaches, and spiders."

"*Spiders?*"

Shane laughed. "Once in awhile." He shut the junction box. "Not a damn thing in there. Problem must be in the wiring."

He shone his light upward, following electrical conduits up the wall. Cockroaches skittered away from the beam. Then the yellow beam illuminated a furry body with glowing crimson eyes and sharp teeth. The rat perched high up, screamed at him and jumped for his face. "Whoa!" he yelled and slipped on the slick stone. His circuit tester plunked into the flowing water.

The power leaped from Gretchen to protect her friend. A muffled thump and a wet sound came from the attacking rat.

"Shit," said Shane as he stood up. "I lost my tester. Did you see that fucking rat? I was going to be its Meals on Wheels." With shaking hands, he lit a cigarette. "Are you okay?"

Gretchen wasn't okay; she was shaking like a leaf in a gale and biting her knuckles in dismay, hyperventilating.

"Gretchen? It's okay. The rat's gone. Don't be upset." He patted her shoulder awkwardly, as if he didn't know how to console someone.

"I'm sorry," she said as tears welled in earnest. "I was so scared and it jumped at you and I didn't know what else to do because I thought it would kill you down here and then I'd be all alone." She turned into him, buried her face against his grimy shirt, and sobbed.

His arms encircled her and he held her as she cried, making hushing sounds and stroking her hair until she calmed down. "Hey, uh, it's okay. It was just a sewer rat. No harm done."

She sniffled. "I'm sorry."

"It's okay." He paused. "What exactly did you do?"

"What do you mean?"

"You said you didn't know what else to do, so you must have done something."

Wordlessly, she stepped back and swung the flashlight beam down until it centered on a bloody mass of bone, meat, and fur that might have once been a rat.

"Shit," said Shane slowly, drawling it out like a Southerner. "What happened to it? It looks like it was torn apart."

"It was me," whispered Gretchen. "It was going to bite you. I stopped it."

"How? You didn't even move."

"I made all the air inside it disappear."

"The *air?*"

She shrugged. "Air in its lungs, its intestines, its stomach."

"And you made it all just go away?"

"Yes. That's my parapower. I just discovered it."

"What's left when you destroy the air?"

"Nothing."

Shane scratched under the edge of his hard hat.

"Nothing? You mean like a vacuum?"

"I think so."

"And that's what tore the rat apart." He hunched down to get a better look. "That's crazy, man. You could really mess someone up if you did that."

"Shane, I kind of did."

He took a step back. "You what?"

"He was hurting me. I just wanted him to stop. That was all. I n-never wanted t-to…" Fresh tears tracked clean lines down the grime on her face.

"Oh, shit. Shit. I'm sorry."

"And you've been so decent to me when you barely even know me," said Gretchen.

Shane smiled at her. "That's just how I am. And you've been good company today." He looked down at the rat carcass. "And there was this guy. He might have bit me if not for you. That makes you a hero in my book."

Gretchen smiled up at him. "Me, a hero?"

"Sure. Hey, shine that light back up there again."

Gretchen did so and gasped as she saw a gnawed rat carcass beside a broken conduit sprouting frayed wiring like rust-colored weeds. Shane crowed with success. "There's the bastard. I thought I saw something right before that other fellow jumped at me. There's something about the wire insulation the rats love. They chewed on it until one of them hit the jackpot."

"So we can fix it?" asked Gretchen.

"We sure can." Shane looked down at her and she up at him for a long moment that she was sorry had to end.

EIGHT

July 13, 1977, 4:00 PM

The shriek of the Steel Soldier's afterburners was only partially muffled by the sealed evacuation stretcher tube in which she rode. When the Soldier rescued injured victims, he had two of the aerodynamic units, which he could lock onto his arms. They were better than a helicopter for rapid transport of victims to the hospital.

They made for lousy air travel, though. Faith winced at the pounding in her temples from the roar of the jets. She wished she hadn't been so eager to pursue the investigation lead, but she'd seen how the Feds were handling the case. They'd already made up their minds on what had happened in Dyersville, and moved onto their manhunt in New York. Faith hoped to gain some insight into Gretchen Gumm's personality and perhaps learn something to find her before the short-sighted and trigger-happy Feds did.

"How you holding up?" called Faith into her radio.

Sundancer rode in the tube carried in the Soldier's opposite arm. The two women were the lightest members of Just Cause, which allowed the Soldier to maximize his thrust. "I'm just great," she complained. "This was a lovely idea."

"It's better than babysitting Javier," Faith said.

"True. God, I can't stand that man. And I use the term loosely."

"Did you ever, you know, sleep with him?"

"God, no. There isn't enough booze in the world for me to give it up to him. Not for lack of effort on his part."

Faith laughed. "We'd better make sure Irlene stays away from him. He'll have her out of that costume faster than even I could do it."

That made Sundancer laugh.

"Did you ever sleep with anyone else on the team?" asked Faith. "There's not a lot to choose from. Javier's an asshole. Tommy's gay. I hope you never slept with Bobby. Steel's a robot—no offense, buddy."

"NONE TAKEN. THIS IS AN INTERESTING CONVERSATION," rumbled the Soldier over the speakers.

"Hey, speaking of that," said Faith, "I don't mind you listening in, but this is a private conversation, so don't repeat any of it, all right?"

"OF COURSE."

"Which leaves John and Rick," said Sundancer. "John doesn't seem to have any libido. Not that he's my type. But Rick... Yeah, we slept together once. How about you?"

Faith spluttered. She hadn't expected to be asked that. "I'm married," she said at last.

"That never stopped anyone. I've seen how you and Rick look at each other."

"We don't... I mean, we haven't... I mean, what was he like, in bed?"

"Furry," said Sundancer with a giggle. "That tawny fur covers every inch—and I do mean every inch. It's very soft. And his tongue is raspy, like a cat's. If he's careful, it's lovely."

"Oh my." Faith felt herself blush.

"He's pretty aggressive, but I don't mind that." Sundancer sounded wistful over the speaker.

"How come you didn't stay together?"

"Oh, Faith, it wouldn't have worked with us being on the same team, and we both know it. It was fun once, but it's better in every way that we find our partners elsewhere."

"Do you think it's bad that Bobby and I are married?"

"No. You guys were together long before you joined Just Cause. Didn't you meet at Woodstock or something?"

"Close. We stole his father's car to go to the concert," said Faith. "I was fifteen. He was seventeen and the most handsome boy I'd ever seen."

"He's still a fox," said Sundancer. "Not that I'd ever sleep with him. I respect you more than that."

"I ESTIMATE OUR TIME OF ARRIVAL IN DYERSVILLE TO BE TEN MINUTES," reported the Soldier.

"Thank God," said Faith. "I need to pee!"

"URINE WILL NOT HARM THE INTERIOR OF THE STRETCHER PODS," said the Soldier.

"You're not helping, Steel."

The Soldier dropped down in altitude, cruising in over fields of wheat, corn, and soybeans. Sparse clumps of trees huddled together, hiding farmhouses and barns. The hiss of the pods' air conditioning stopped as the Soldier shed speed. Exterior vents opened and Faith could smell the sweet scent of the fields tinged with the tang of fertilizer and silage.

"How are your power levels after that flight, Steel?" asked Faith. "You've got to be running on fumes."

"MY ENGINES ARE CADMIUM-POWERED ION DRIVES AND DO NOT EVER RUN ON FUMES, BUT I AM UTILIZING RESERVE POWER. I WILL REQUIRE TIME TO RECHARGE FROM THE LOCAL GRID."

"Then you better set us down here," said Faith. "We can get into town on our own power and you can plug into one of those transmission lines. We'll keep our radios on open transmit so you can monitor us in case we need you."

"That is a sound plan." The Soldier deployed braking flaps and touched down beside a road as lightly as a bird. He popped open the pods and the two women gladly tumbled out.

"Holy smokes!" cried a voice. Faith looked and saw a middle-aged man in overalls and a straw hat astride a horse. "Martians!" He spat a glob of brown spittle. "Or Russkies, mebbe?"

"No, sir. We're the good guys." Faith crossed her knees. "Can we please use your bathroom?"

The farmer scratched his head under his hat. "Well," he said slowly. "I s'ppose."

"You are a wonderful man," said Sundancer with a radiant smile that glowed even in the afternoon sunlight. "Is it okay if we plug in our robot here?"

"Well," said the farmer again. "I s'ppose."

~~~

His pocket full of half a dozen blade-wands, Harlan collected what he'd begun to refer to as his magnetic crossbow and slipped out of the Parts Room. Gonsalvo had his entire torso buried in the Datsun's engine compartment as he tried to loosen a recalcitrant spark plug. Harlan didn't disturb him and instead headed out to the vacant lot behind the shop. At various times over the years, the lot had been used as a dump, a vagrants' campground, a garden, and a burial ground for dead pets. Gonsalvo didn't own the land, but a lot of larger pieces which he didn't have space for in the Parts Room sat out in the dry weeds, slowly rusting into oblivion.

Harlan didn't go into the back lot very often. Most of the parts there were ruined and useless to him compared to the treasure trove of the Parts Room. He wouldn't touch the twisted, stunted vegetables that grew wild amid the weeds and oil slicks, and the corner with its little pet headstones freaked him out. The back lot bordered a pawnshop on one side and on the other a *taquería*, which Harlan had never felt brave enough to try. The high fence around most of the lot should give him ample privacy for his work.

He scouted around the terrain until he found the best angle to hit the nearby overhead power lines. The magnetic crossbow had a small kick when it fired, so he sought a spot where he could brace himself. A rusting hulk from the front end of a De Soto proved to be a suitable location. He hunched down, laid the barrel across the hood, and took careful aim.

Harlan's first shot whistled high, arching up and out until he couldn't see it sparkling in the mid-afternoon sun any longer. He wondered where it would come down and what it might do when it did, but not enough to care who it might hit. He reloaded the weapon and aimed once more, taking into account the blade-wands' tendency to waver mid-flight. With the next press of the trigger, he was rewarded with a blue flash as the wand severed one of the overhead lines.

Harlan crowed his success. He'd hit the first line with his second shot, which left him four tries to hit the second. Perhaps he'd have a couple left over to rework with vertical stabilizers. He ignored the spitting wire as it twisted among the dirt and weeds of the back lot and took aim once again.

He missed with his third and fourth shots, and began to think he'd had beginner's luck. The problem with the gun's effectiveness was that he couldn't pick up missed shots to reuse them. As aerodynamic as the blade-wands were, they could fly as far as several blocks and he'd have no way to find them again. He considered ways to track down misses as he squinted along the barrel, trying to place the sight right over the power line.

"Harlan, what the hell are you doing?"

Harlan whirled, ready to berate someone for interrupting his work. Gonsalvo stood by the shop door, gaping at him, his mouth moving without voice. He braced himself with one hand against the door frame and with the other felt at the length of copper welding wire, which emerged from his throat.

Harlan gasped and looked down at his magnetic crossbow. There was no blade-wand in the tube. He didn't even remember pulling the trigger but he must have. Blood sluiced from the neat four-inch-wide cut across Gonsalvo's throat. The old mechanic sank to his knees, making unintelligible grunting sounds. He looked confused as to what happened. His eyes met Harlan's, and then he pitched forward into the dust. The bloody mouth of the blade-wand pushed higher out of Gonsalvo's neck when the man's face hit the ground, like some bizarre monster being born.

Harlan shoved his fist into his mouth and screamed against it. Gonsalvo had surprised him. He should have seen what Harlan was doing and not interrupted. If the old man had been a little more patient and a little cooler, he'd still be alive right now. Instead, he'd gotten himself killed, and that threatened to ruin all of Harlan's meticulous plans.

"Old fool," grunted Harlan. Now he'd have to hurry. He loaded his last blade-wand and shot it, missing by a country mile because his hands were shaking. He'd have to hurry and make more so he could sever that second line and cut power once more.

Wait. There was one more he could use.

Harlan reached for the blade-wand poking from Gonsalvo's neck. It was streaked with gore and sinew, but he needed it.

One good yank and the blade-wand came free. Harlan brushed the blade dry against Gonsalvo's shirt and checked it for imperfections. There was one notch, probably from when the crescent-shaped airfoil had cut through the man's spine. Harlan didn't think it would interfere with the missile's flight. He loaded it into the magnetic crossbow and sighted down the barrel once more. This was his last chance. He took a slow, deep breath, held it, and pulled the trigger.

With a shower of sparks, the second power line parted. Over the sound of passing traffic, Harlan could hear the groans and shouts of the locals as their power flow was interrupted for the second time that day. He smiled; his luck was holding. But now he had to really hustle to clean up the mess Gonsalvo had made.

Grunting and sweating in the heat of the shop, Harlan dragged Gonsalvo's body back to the Parts Room, where he hid it under a pile of burlap bags. He looked at the bloody trail he'd left. That wouldn't do. An idea struck him, and he grabbed a couple quarts of automatic transmission fluid from Gonsalvo's supplies. He poured the reddish fluid all along the bloodstains, and then sprinkled the mess with absorbent clay cat litter. He swept up the resultant slurry and deposited it all into a trash bin.

Then he took up a sledgehammer and shattered his magnetic crossbow. He didn't need the prototype any longer; he could rebuild a better one later when he had more time and materials to work with. Satisfied that he'd covered his tracks sufficiently until he could disappear into the morass of Harlem with Gretchen, he picked up the phone and dialed the operator to report a downed power line in the back lot of his friend's building.

Harlan set the two Just Cause passes on the workbench and then sat to wait for Gretchen to return to him. He'd already dealt with Gonsalvo's death in his mind. When he'd hidden the body, that was the end of it. It wasn't his fault that Gonsalvo had died; it was Gonsalvo's. Served him right, thought Harlan. But it didn't matter. The Con Ed man would come back, and Gretchen would be with him.

He couldn't stop grinning.

~~~

A heavy knock on Javier's door startled Tommy out of a light sleep. After cleaning up the drug and alcohol mess in the apartment and using his powers to dry the carpet, he'd sat in an easy chair and put his feet up. Just for a minute, he'd told himself. A glance at the wall clock showed he'd been dozing for about half an hour.

He rubbed sleep out of his eyes and went to the door. Through the peephole he saw a stony expanse that could only belong to one man. He threw open the door and smiled at John Stone.

"How's he doing?" rumbled the gentle giant. He took slow, careful steps into the room in case his heavy weight might overstress the floor. He moved to the couch and arranged himself across it to distribute his heft over a larger surface area.

Tommy yawned and stretched. "He's been in and out of consciousness, and when he's awake he's not very coherent. From what I can tell, he came back here on a coke high, and must have called a couple of his girlfriends who brought him some quaaludes. All that plus booze…" Tommy shook his head. "I pumped his stomach. At least, I think I did. He's lucky to be alive."

John shook his head. "He's lucky you cared enough to come and check on him. You're far more decent a fellow than he deserves."

Tommy toyed idly with his cape clasp. He felt drained. "What happened to us, John?" he asked. "When did we stop being superheroes and start being this way? Hell, I don't even know what we are now."

"Celebrities?" asked John. "More than anything, that seems to be our job these days. Being famous. The Greatest Superheroes in the World."

"That used to actually mean something. When was the last time Just Cause actually helped anybody? How long since we were needed because we were superheroes, not because we were famous?"

John scratched his jaw, stone dragging across cement. "When did we finally put down the Malice Group? Must have been about '74. Right after you joined."

"I remember," said Tommy with a wistful smile. "I was nineteen. Those were good times, taking them down. It felt like we were really doing some good."

"We did do some good," said John. "We got some dangerous parahumans off the streets and saved a lot of lives and property."

"Sure, and what have we done since then? Nothing. We play poker and have parties. We appear at department store grand openings and in parades. We're modeling nude and we're addicted to drugs and alcohol." A miniature twister formed in the middle of the floor, matching Tommy's turbulent thoughts.

He realized he'd been pacing as he spoke and whirled to face John. "We've become superfluous in modern society. Who in their right mind would challenge Just Cause? Nobody, because we're the best, the Greatest Superheroes in the World. Why should Joe Blow use his super-strength to rob banks when he can join the team and have fame and fortune handed to him on a damned silver platter?"

"What are you suggesting, Tommy? That you need to fight supervillains to feel useful?" John sounded amused.

"No, of course not." Tommy paused in his pacing. "But maybe Just Cause does."

"The organization does exist for that type of purpose," rumbled John. "From its origins with parapowered commandos in World War Two to the American Justice team of old, Just Cause has always existed to battle against foes that normal law enforcement couldn't handle."

"And we got so good at it that there's nobody left to challenge us," said Tommy. "No wonder we've sunk so far. Nobody needs us anymore." Sudden angry tears threatened to overflow.

"That's not true and you know it," said John. "Bobby said you saved a potential suicide's life earlier today. She needed you. Every time we help people, they needed us, whether or not they realized it. And more importantly, we need each other. Javier needed you today. Maybe you'll need him tomorrow."

"Maybe I'll need you," said Tommy with a ghost of a smile. "Maybe I do now." There was so much more he wanted to say, but he couldn't overcome the dark lump of fear crouching in his belly like a serpent ready to strike. He was terrified what would happen to his and John's friendship if he dared clutter it up with an admission of love. In all the years he'd known John, Tommy had never heard the stone man speak of love or romance. That didn't mean he didn't crave it; inside that cold granite torso of his beat a heart as warm as anybody's.

Tommy dreamed that he might one day find the key to unlock John's heart. Perhaps not today, he thought, as he heard Javier groan and retch from the bedroom.

"Stay," ordered John. "I'll take a turn. You've earned it."

"John?"

The stony figure turned to look back at Tommy. "Yes?"

"I'm glad you're here."

John smiled. "All things being equal, I'd rather I wasn't."

~~~

Shane wrestled with the broken conduit, splicing in fresh wire and coating the whole thing with a vile-smelling chemical paste. "It keeps the rats away," he said. "But it only lasts a few days." He was grimy from head to toe. Gretchen was certain she matched him stain for stain. Between the sewer slime and the soot from Shane soldering in a new section of conduit, she thought she might be the filthiest she'd ever been in her entire life.

Shane checked his work once more and then stepped back, looking pleased. "Pop on up the ladder for me and yell down if the station power goes on."

"You got it," Gretchen said. She scampered up the slick ladder and poked her head out the manhole. "Okay, go for broke," she called back to Shane. Without fanfare, the overhead fluorescents turned on. She could see them through the open station windows. Whistles and sarcastic applause echoed within the police station as the officers realized they had to get back to work. "That did it," she said.

"Cool." He grinned and closed the junction box. "Let's close up the shop." They climbed out of the manhole and Shane sealed it.

A plainclothes officer approached them as they gathered up the orange cones. "Nice job, you two. It's good that somebody in Con Ed gives a shit about Harlem."

Shane smiled at him. "I'm just glad we got it fixed so quickly."

The officer winked. "Your helper's damn cute." He signed a stack of papers on a clipboard thrust at him by Shane, but kept his eyes on Gretchen. "I don't think I've ever seen a girl working for Con Ed. You been with them long?"

She shook her head. "I'm new."

"Doesn't really seem like the kind of work most women would go into."

"My dad was an electrician back home. I worked with him." The lie rolled off her tongue with such glib ease that she almost believed it herself.

It must have satisfied the officer's curiosity for he nodded and smiled. "What time do you get off tonight?"

"We're just starting our shift. Swings, you know," said Shane. "In fact, we just got a hot call so we'd better be on our way."

The officer glared at him for a moment before smiling at Gretchen in an almost predatory way. "Pity, that." He passed her a business card. "Listen, if you're ever of a mind to have a late dinner, I'd love to take you out to one."

"Oh." She slid the card into a pocket of her grimy coveralls. "Uh, thanks."

She and Shane retreated into the truck. She sat rigid in her seat and didn't look at him until the truck was well away from the station and crawling up an on-ramp into rush hour traffic. Then she reached over and touched his arm. "Thank you," she whispered. "He really caught me by surprise."

"I'd think you'd be used to it." Shane checked his mirrors, a cigarette dangling from the corner of his mouth, and didn't look at her. "Pretty girl like you."

"What? Oh, no, I'm not," she said. "I must be a real mess right now."

Shane bullied a smaller car until the driver braked to let the service truck over. "Remember, I saw you this morning before you had sewer slime and imploded rat all over you." He finally glanced over at her. "Caught my eye."

"Oh."

"Listen, um…" He stabbed out the cigarette in the overflowing ashtray and lit another. "I was kind of hoping that maybe I could take you out to dinner. You know, on account of you saving me from getting rat-bit and all."

Gretchen turned away and stared stonily out of the window. All of them do it sooner or later. Even the ones you think are nice, Elizabeth had said. Shane had been nothing but sweet and polite to her, and hadn't made a single move toward her the entire day. He'd listened when she'd told him about her power, and hadn't recoiled in disgust or fear the way people in her hometown would have. And there was no denying the moment in the sewer when she'd felt like kissing him. She peeked over at him as he smoked and drove in the awkward silence. A muscle twitched high up in his cheek. Maybe dinner could just be dinner, she thought. Time would tell.

And if he tried anything, she had the power to protect herself, and she'd kill again if she had to.

"I'd like that," she said at last.

Shane relaxed and his easygoing grin returned. "That's great. Do you like Greek?"

"I don't know. I've never had it."

"If you feel adventurous, there's a nice little café walking distance from my apartment. Otherwise there's Italian, burgers, whatever. It's Manhattan."

"Greek sounds fine to me." Gretchen felt hungry enough to eat almost anything. "I'll need to find someplace to clean up."

"Well, there's a shower at the Con Ed station where I have to take the truck, but it's not really co-ed. If you want to—and I totally understand if you say no—you could freshen up at my place. Me and my roommate keep it pretty clean. We've got extra towels and stuff. You can lock yourself in the bathroom and I'll be a perfect gentleman and wait." He smirked. "Besides, I don't want you to do that implosion thing to me."

Gretchen gasped. It was like he could almost read her mind. She wondered suddenly if he was a parahuman too, but then dismissed that as a ludicrous notion. If he could read minds, he'd be on Just Cause. She couldn't detect any trace of ulterior motives in his simple words. He was so sincere, she found herself almost trusting him.

Almost, she reminded herself.

"Okay, I guess that would be all right. But no funny stuff or *kapow*." She pointed at him for emphasis.

He jumped a little at that. "It's cool. I'll just chill out. Let me check and see if someone else can take this call. You know that place we were at this morning? They've got lines down now." He checked his watch. "Swing shift guys are out now. Maybe one of them can pick it up."

"Shane, I need to go back there to see if that kid came through with those Just Cause passes," said Gretchen. "That's the whole reason I came to New York."

"Oh, right, right," said Shane. "That's cool. We'll stop by and see if he brought them, and then go turn in the truck and grab a shower before dinner. Uh, separately, that is."

Gretchen laughed.

NINE

July 13, 1977, 5:00 PM

"So as you see, it's pretty cut and dried as far as we're concerned," said Dyersville's Chief of Police, a sweaty, rotund man named Swensen. "Don't know why you ladies felt like comin' all the way out here to hear it, but we're satisfied with our interpretation of events."

Sundancer grumbled something offensive under her breath. Faith agreed with her. Chief Swensen had been condescending and smarmy under his veneer of polite helpfulness. If it wouldn't have gotten her in a world of trouble, Faith would have dumped him on his copious ass hard enough to make a point. "Nevertheless, Chief, this is a federal murder investigation, and we'd like to question the friends and family of the suspect and victim."

Swensen smiled without the slightest trace of humor. "Of course. Here's the list of everyone we questioned." He slid a sheet of paper across the desk. "Good luck, ladies."

Faith and Sundancer fled the small police station like it was on fire. "God, I'd love to give that man a sunburn on his lily-white ass," muttered Sundancer.

"Amen to that, sister," said Faith. She looked at the list. Only six names. She folded it, then tore it in half and handed part to Sundancer. "Stay in touch," she said. "Steel's listening in. He'll come if we need him."

Sundancer's aura brightened even in the afternoon sun and she flew off in search of the first name on her list.

Faith looked at her own list. The first name was Robert Milbrook, the victim's father. He worked at the corn mill by the railroad tracks. After a quick foray across town and a brief conversation with a hero-dazzled foreman, Faith learned Milbrook's shift was already over, but he might be found at a bar in town. Another jaunt down Main Street brought her to Harryhausen's Tavern.

The tavern stank of sour beer and old whiskey and sweat. A film of dust coated the windows and the mirror behind the bar. Faded posters of Western movies decorated the walls and a jukebox in one corner struggled with the crackling strains of country music. The bar's interior was darkened against the late afternoon sun, and a large, loud man was holding court against a well-varnished counter. He held up a glass brimming with beer and with tears in his eyes, shouted, "to Donny!"

"To Donny," repeated the other men in the bar with reverence. They slammed their empty glasses down on the bar and someone called for a subsequent round.

Conversations died out as Faith walked across the bar. The only sound was the jukebox belting out a Conway Twitty tune. She could feel the men's eyes on her as she strode toward Milbrook. "Mr. Milbrook?"

He looked her up and down, undressing her lithe form with his eyes, unconsciously licking his lips. "Yes?"

"I'm Pony Girl from Just Cause. May I speak to you about your son?"

He shrugged and slammed down another glass of whiskey. "Sure," he mumbled. He nearly fell as he slid off the barstool. Faith reached out a steadying hand but he brushed her off. "C'mon, too noisy in here fer a fella to hear hisself think." In spite of his complaint, nobody in the bar spoke a word as Faith and Milbrook made for the door. She sensed strong antipathy in the room. She could understand why; one of their own had been murdered by a parahuman like her. In their eyes, she was the enemy.

Milbrook led Faith behind the bar where crates of empty bottles towered in a neat stack. He lit an unfiltered Pall Mall and glared at her. "What do you want to know? I already talked to the police."

"Tell me about Donny. What kind of boy was he?"

"He was a real good boy. The kind what grows up to make his father proud. He played football in high school, ya know. Could have gone pro if he hadn't tore up his knee."

"What was he doing? Working?"

"He was doing carpentry work around town to pay for stuff on his car. He loved that car. I'm sure that bitch took it."

"She took his car? What was it?"

"A '73 Camaro. Cops haven't been able to find it. He was driving it the night he …"

"Easy, Mr. Milbrook. I know your loss is still fresh. Can you think of any reason someone would want to harm your son?"

Milbrook dashed his arm across his face to hide his unmanly tears. "He was a popular boy. Everyone liked him. Sure, he'd go out and raise a bit of a ruckus on the weekends, but we all did that. Boys will be boys. I can't imagine why anyone would hurt him." His face grew hard. "You catch that little whore and you bring her back here, Pony Girl. I'll see to it she gets what's comin' to her."

Faith was taken aback at the venom and underlying violence in the man's words. Nevertheless, she handed him a card. "I promise you, we'll do everything in our power to track down your son's killer, Mr. Milbrook."

"You better," he grunted. "Shouldn't be too hard. He was killed by a freak like you."

Faith shut her mouth with a snap before she uttered a cutting remark that wouldn't help the local situation at all. The man was distraught at the death of his son. Surely he couldn't hate her just because she was a parahuman, could he?

Maybe he could. The thought was a bitter pill to swallow. Racism was alive and well in America, and some people would always feel that way, whether about Asians, blacks, or parahumans. She spun on her heel and walked away, leaving Milbrook behind to stew in his juices. As she did so, she caught a glimpse of movement from the corner of the bar. Someone without super speed might have missed it, but Faith saw the young woman's face peeking around the edge of the building. The young woman ducked out of sight but not before Faith had a chance to commit her face to memory. It could have been simple hero worship or curiosity, or it could have been something more.

Either way, Faith had more questions to ask. She picked up her radio. "Pony Girl, moving on to the next name on my list. Steel, you listening in?"

"AFFIRMATIVE."

"Think you could find a missing 1973 Chevrolet Camaro in the area with your super-duper sensor thingies?"

"I SHALL IMPLEMENT SEARCH PROTOCOLS IMMEDIATELY."

"Groovy. Pony Girl out." With one last look in the direction she'd seen the mysterious watcher, Faith headed across town.

~~~

The first Con Ed truck pulled up, but it had some strange man in it. Harlan chewed on his lip. They couldn't have sent somebody else, could they? But then he saw another Con Ed truck round the corner and stood so fast that he knocked over the stool. Gretchen was returning to him!

He hurried out to the street as the truck stopped. Through the windshield, he could see the surprise in Gretchen's face as she noticed the cuts and bruises on his face. He shrugged it off but before he could call to her, a Plymouth screeched to a halt in front of him.

"Boy, you are in a world of trouble." His Momma stepped out of the driver's seat and slammed her door. "Get your sorry ass in the car." She marched around the front, and with each step Harlan knew she was getting angrier and angrier.

"No, Momma!" He wanted to run, but knew that would only get him into worse trouble.

"Don't you *no, Momma* me," hollered the woman. "The school done called me at work, said you hadn't been in today. I had a hunch you might be here, wasting time."

"Momma, I'm not—" started Harlan, only to be silenced by a cuff upside his head. Fingers like a steel vise closed on his ear and she began to drag him to the car. In spite of wanting to appear grown-up and macho for Gretchen, he squealed in pain. "Please, Momma, I need to —ow!—get something inside!"

"Boy, the only thing you need right now is a good whipping," hissed his mother. "Now you get into that car this instant or as God is my witness I will beat you right here on the street."

Harlan looked around, desperate for a way to escape or someone to intervene on his behalf. People along the street were staring at the spectacle Momma had created, but he only sought one sympathetic pair of eyes. At last, he saw Gretchen staring at him, her face a mixture of sympathy and dismay. "They're on the workbench," he shrieked at her just before Momma slammed the door shut.

Momma weaved through the streets of Harlem in her sweltering car, lecturing and screaming at Harlan until she wedged her big Plymouth into a parking space by their tenement building. "Now get your sorry ass inside and think real hard whether or not you want to keep living under my roof."

Harlan stomped off to his room, threw open his window, and sat on the sill. Outside on the street below, children played in the hot sun with kickballs and double-dutch jump ropes. He watched them without really seeing. Instead, he replayed the scene of Gonsalvo's death in his mind over and over again. The man's death had been an accident, and Harlan absolved himself of any responsibility because Gonsalvo could have prevented it with more caution on his part. It comforted Harlan to know that despite the loss of his friend, it wasn't really his fault.

As the scene repeated, Gonsalvo's face transformed into that of Harlan's mother. He imagined the blade-wand splitting her throat and a slow smile crept across his face. Pulling the trigger on her wouldn't be an accident. Like the man who'd broken into his junkyard the night before, his mother's death would be on purpose. The thought cheered Harlan like a suit of armor against the upcoming tongue-lashing he'd get at the dinner table.

"What's so funny, Harlan?"

Startled, he whirled in the window, coming close to falling out. Reggie stood in the door, cuddling her stuffed elephant.

"You little brat, you almost made me fall," said Harlan.

She sniffled a little and hugged her elephant tighter. "I'm sorry. I didn't mean to."

"What do you want, Reggie? I'm busy."

"I was just wonderin' what was so funny. You was sittin' there laughin'."

"Oh. One of those kids down there fell down. I thought it was funny. That's all."

"I wish I'd'a seen it." The little girl's expression grew wistful.

"Reggie, I'm on punishment. You ain't supposed to be talking to me."

"I know. Momma said not to." She rocked the elephant like a baby. "Harlan? How come you hate us so much?"

He looked at her. "I don't hate you, Reggie. You and Momma and Irlene just don't understand me. That's all."

She thought about that, struggling to understand concepts that Harlan knew were far above her. "Okay," she said. "I don't hate you neither. I'm a-scared of you when you get mad though."

Harlan shrugged. "Sometimes I get mad. You don't have to be scared of me. Unless you're the reason I'm mad," he said in a low voice. "Then you better look out."

Reggie's eyes grew wide. Before she could say anything else, Momma called from the kitchen. "Regina Washington, you best not be talking to that no-account brother of yours!"

"No, Momma," called Reggie. "Bye, Harlan," she whispered, and then skipped down the hall.

He reflected on his relationship with Reggie, which was different than the one he had with Momma and Irlene. She was always curious about him and his ideas. He could tell her about an invention, and she'd listen with honest interest, even if she didn't understand a word he said. That was why he'd made her that wind-up carousel, even though he never gave it to her. Sometimes he felt bad about that, and even felt sorry for her growing up in the shadow of their overbearing mother and superhero sister. He wouldn't go so far as to say he cared for Reggie, but he tolerated her.

That goodwill did not extend to the other members of his immediate family, and Harlan amused himself by imagining them at the mercy of his giant robot.

~~~

"Are you going to be okay, Javier?" Tommy and John stood over the Puerto Rican man as he lay amid pillows and rumpled sheets on his circular bed.

Javier nodded, wincing at the pain that must have shot through his skull. An ice bag sat atop his head, covering his eyes. "I'll live," he grunted. "I might wish otherwise later."

"I'm borrowing some clothes," said Tommy. "Two costumes in one day. The laundry's going to love me."

"If it fits, it's yours," said Javier. He was four inches shorter than Tommy and of a slenderer build.

Tommy grimaced at the outfits hanging in the closet. "You got anything that won't make me look like a male prostitute?"

John burst out laughing and even Javier managed a weak chuckle. "Listen," Javier gasped. "Clothes make the man."

Tommy held up a shirt as evidence. "This pattern looks like somebody threw up all over it." He found a pair of shorts and a t-shirt he could stomach, and selected some sandals that were too small but would serve until he got home.

"I drove," said John. "Do you want a lift?" With his heavy, oversized frame, John found it difficult to get around town. The team administrators had responded by purchasing an International Scout and paid a shop to outfit it with a heavy-duty suspension, reinforced frame, and oversized controls. John loved it and drove it everywhere. He called it the Stonemobile.

"I'd love it," said Tommy. "Let me just change." He ducked into the bathroom. As he dressed, he could hear the low overtones of John's voice as he lectured Javier some more.

Tommy finished changing and left the bathroom in time to hear John say, "Now knock that shit off before I sit on every piece of your armor until it looks like a manhole cover."

"Okay, okay," grumbled Javier. "I'm hip."

"Ready to go?" asked Tommy, his costume tucked into a plastic garbage bag.

"Yes, for sure." John clomped over to the door. "I don't trust the regular elevators in this building. I'll take the freight elevator down and meet you in the lobby, Tommy."

Tommy rode the elevator down to the main floor, said hello to a pleasant young couple waiting at the bottom to go up, and walked over to the freight elevator just as John stepped out. "So I know there was a big meeting," said Tommy. "What'd I miss?"

"A boy in Iowa was killed, apparently by a parahuman," said John. "The Feds believe she is here in New York now. Faith, Gloria, and Steel flew out to question the locals."

Tommy shook his head. "It's a sad world we live in, my friend."

"Well what about you? You saved a life today." They headed through the lobby. John took careful steps to avoid breaking the tile floor.

"Yeah, that's true," said Tommy. "She and I had a long talk afterward. She was distraught because she'd fallen in love with her boss, and he couldn't love her back."

John shook his head. "That's sad." He showed his ticket to the parking garage attendant and said he'd get the car himself instead of calling a valet to bring it around. The attendant got John to sign an autograph while Tommy stood in the background.

"Anyway, she got me to thinking," said Tommy as they crossed the concrete expanse of the garage toward John's car. "Maybe it's better to just have those feelings out in the open, instead of just letting them twist and turn in your heart until they make you crazy."

"Makes sense to me." John climbed into his Scout, which sagged despite its heavy suspension.

Tommy hopped into the passenger seat. He touched John's arm. "John, wait. I need to tell you something."

"What is it, Tommy?"

Tommy took a deep breath. His heart raced and his palms were wet with nervous perspiration, and when he spoke, the words came out like bullets in some kind of linguistic Gatling gun. "John… I'm in love with you. I have been for years. You're in my thoughts constantly. You're the most important person in my life, and I thought you should know that." He finished and realized he had his shoulders hunched up as if to brace himself for a blow.

John was silent. He wouldn't turn to look at Tommy. His huge hands grasped the oversized steering wheel and squeezed until the steel rang.

Tommy could feel his heart beating somewhere in the vicinity of his Adam's apple. Tears threatened to spill as the deafening silence hung over the men like a guillotine on a frayed wire. "John…"

John bowed his head until the brim of his fedora obscured his face.

"John, please say something." Tommy felt panic start to rear its ugly head at him and wanted to fill the empty void with words. "You can't have me tell you something like that and then just sit there. Please, John, for the love of God, say something!"

"Tommy." John's voice was so low it was almost subsonic. Tommy strained to hear. "I wish it could be different, but I can't love you back."

~~~

"They're on the workbench," cried Harlan as the woman who must have been his mother shoved him into the car. Gretchen watched the Plymouth roll away in a cloud of blue smoke. She felt bad for Harlan; he'd had a really rough day from what she could tell, and now he was in trouble at home on top of everything else.

She turned to Shane, who was discussing the downed line with another Con Ed technician who'd arrived right before they did. "Hey, I'm going inside for a minute. Be right back."

Shane smiled. "Okay. Oh, Glenn? This is Gretchen."

Glenn, an older man with a sizable paunch and a bushy mustache, shook her hand with bemused politeness. "Pleased ta meet'cha," he said with a thick accent. "I didn't know we had any dames workin' for us."

Shane brushed off the question to explain what work he'd done earlier in the day, so Gretchen slipped inside the auto shop.

"Mr. Gonsalvo?" she asked.. She heard no reply. Maybe he was in the bathroom, she thought. She went over to the workbench, gasping a little at the stifling heat. Sitting atop the greasy surface, she found two cards with the words Just Cause printed upon them and signed by none other than Pony Girl.

"Wow," Gretchen breathed in surprise. Harlan had really come through for her. She tucked the passes into a pocket and almost skipped out of the shop to find Shane.

He stood by his truck, chatting with Glenn and smoking. "Get what you needed?" he asked.

"Yes." She couldn't keep a wide grin from spreading across her face.

"See you later, Glenn. We're going to go clean up."

They got into Shane's truck. "Check these out." Gretchen pressed one of the passes into Shane's hand. "That's Pony Girl's signature there."

"Sure is." Shane turned the card over to look at the official Just Cause logo on the back. He passed it back to her and started the truck.

Gretchen yawned and leaned back in her seat. The day had worn her out. She closed her eyes, telling herself it was just for a minute.

The next thing she knew, Shane was shaking her awake. "Hey, Gretchen, wake up. We're here."

She looked around, bleary-eyed. "At your apartment?"

"No, at the Con Ed shop. I just signed the truck back in. I was thinking I'd run in and take a shower here in the locker room so I don't have to once we're home. To my home, I mean."

Gretchen yawned. "Oh, okay. What should I do? Wait here?"

"There's a ladies' room up by the customer service counter. They're closed, but I have a key. You could at least change and wash your face and hands there."

The ladies' room was small, but at least it was clean. Gretchen shucked out of the coveralls and the sweaty t-shirt she had on under them. Her shoes were a total loss; she tossed them in the trashcan. After splashing water on her face and shaking out her hair, she felt at least clean enough not to repulse anyone nearby. She pulled on a clean t-shirt, slipped her feet into her sandals, and went back out to the customer service lobby to wait for Shane.

He arrived after only a few minutes, wearing blue jeans and a clean white t-shirt. "Ready to go?"

Gretchen smiled and twirled around once. "How do I look?"

He laughed. "Better than when you were covered in sewer muck."

"Do you have a car?"

He shook his head. "It's subway and hoofing it from here."

"I've never been on a subway." Gretchen picked up her suitcase.

"Don't stand with your back to any creepy old men in raincoats," advised Shane. "Keep one hand on your valuables at all times. And assume any puddle is piss."

"God, is it really that bad?"

"Afraid so."

In fact, the subway wasn't as terrible as Shane had proclaimed. Nevertheless, Gretchen didn't realize she was staring at a woman wearing a short leopard-skin dress until the woman said, "See anything you like, honey?" and spread her legs apart to show a lack of underwear. "Thirty bucks for you. Forty if your boyfriend wants to watch." Gretchen blushed and bowed her head as the woman let out a derisive cackle.

As they got off the car at Shane's stop, Gretchen took his hand so she wouldn't lose him in the press of commuters. They moved along with the flow of people. She clutched her bag tight lest someone grab it away from her. Gretchen had never in her life seen this many people in one place.

They ascended the stairs to street level and the crowd thinned out somewhat, but Gretchen kept hold of Shane's hand. The feel of his rough, tobacco-stained hand felt comforting. She found herself craning her neck wide-eyed at the skyscrapers. The tallest thing back home was the corn mill. "You live in one of those?" she asked.

"No, those are all commercial buildings," explained Shane. "I live on the seventh floor of an eight-story building six blocks from here."

"Eight stories!" It seemed like a tremendous height to her.

Shane led her four blocks in one direction and two in another to a red brick building with granite edifices decorating the roof and the space between the fourth and fifth floor. When she saw it, she gasped. "It's beautiful." The building might have been fifty years old or more, and it felt like a magical place to her.

Shane looked up at it, as if really seeing it for the first time. "I guess it does look good. I'm used to seeing buildings like it all over town. It's not that special."

"It's where you live. Maybe where I can live too. That's special enough for me."

A man with flowing blond hair and clothes too small smiled at them as he got off the elevator. "Shane," whispered Gretchen after the doors closed. "I think that was Tornado."

"Who?" Shane pushed the button for his floor.

"Tornado, from Just Cause," said Gretchen. "Does he live here?"

"That's crazy. What would he be doing here, anyway? He probably lives in their headquarters in the Trade

Center. I bet they all do. I doubt they'd even try to live among us little people."

The elevator bell rang and the doors slid open. "I guess you're right," said Gretchen. "Still, can you imagine having a superhero living next door?"

Shane grinned. "That's some imagination. Come on, I'm right down the hall here."

TEN

July 13, 1977, 6:00 PM

Faith's remaining interviews were brief and didn't disclose anything the Feds hadn't already told her. The dishwasher at the diner had seen Gretchen leave in Donny's car. No, he didn't know if they were involved with each other. No, he couldn't think of any reason she might have to harm him. The other waitress working that night remembered that Donny had been drinking but otherwise had nothing to share. She didn't think Gretchen was dating him, but Donny changed girlfriends the way some guys changed their shirts.

"He was kind of a jerk, though," said the waitress as Faith prepared to leave.

"How's that?"

The waitress shrugged a plump shoulder. "Sometimes he got a little fresh. Wandering hands, you know? He'd lay a girl and then move on."

Faith lowered her voice. "Off the record… Did you ever sleep with him?"

The waitress nodded, causing a stray lock of mousy brown hair to fall across her face. She pushed the errant strand back behind her ear.

"How did he treat you?"

She shrugged. "Rough. Like I said, he was a jerk."

"Thanks for your help," said Faith. She'd seen the girl she'd glimpsed watching her earlier and decided some questions were in order. She zipped around the diner and skidded to a halt beside the lanky brunette. "Hi there."

The girl jumped as if she'd been scalded.

"It's clear you want to talk to me," said Faith. "Well here I am. No time like the present. What's your name?"

"Elizabeth. Elizabeth Hague." She glanced about to see if anyone was watching. "Gretchen is my best friend. Can we talk in private?"

"Of course," said Faith, excited by the apparent secrecy. This might be the lead she needed.

Elizabeth led her to an old Dodge pickup and coaxed it to life. "Keep down," she told Faith. "I'm not supposed to talk to you."

"Who told you that?" Faith hunkered down in the seat.

"My dad. The police chief. They know Gretchen and I were friends. They all want to see her fry because she killed their golden boy, but I know the truth and I didn't want to tell anybody but Just Cause." She paused as she passed by the police station and headed to the western edge of town.

"Why us?" asked Faith.

Elizabeth glanced sidelong at her as she pulled the truck off along a dirt road until the tall rows of corn and wheat hid them from the main part of town. "Look, uh, Pony Girl. Gretchen is one of you. A parahuman. You guys take care of your own, right? That's why I sent her to New York. To find you."

"You sent her?"

Elizabeth killed the motor and turned to look at Faith. Her intense gaze burned as bright as the sun shining through the windshield. "Donny raped her. He raped my best friend and she killed him with a power she didn't know she had."

"Jesus," whispered Faith. She'd feared that might have been the case but had hoped for something better.

"She came to me afterward. She was a wreck. When I realized what had happened, I knew she had to leave right away." Elizabeth's voice took on a hard edge. "Dyersville is a small town, and we're pretty backwards in a lot of ways. Women are pretty much second-class citizens. We do what we're told, put out for the boys, get married and be barefoot and pregnant. That's the way it's always been. The town elders wouldn't stand for a woman being uppity with one of the popular boys. And as far as killing him with parapowers?" She shuddered. "She'd never even make it to a trial."

"They'd kill her?" Faith was incredulous. She never realized this kind of thinking still existed. Living in a modern city like New York had colored her view of the world in a much broader palette than in America's Heartland, she realized.

Elizabeth nodded and sniffled. "They don't like folks who are different around here. More than one long-haired hippie or Negro has gotten himself beaten up here. Or worse."

"Jesus," Faith repeated. "Can you prove this?"

"I gave Gretchen my folks' emergency cash to buy her bus ticket."

Faith shook her head. "That's not good enough. I believe you, but that's not going to wash with the Feds on the case."

"The Feds?"

"Using parahuman abilities against someone mundane is a federal crime. Your friend is in an awful lot of trouble and a lot of people are looking for her right now. You better hope it's the right people who find her, and that's Just Cause. Now you've got to give me something tangible."

"How about Donny's car? I can tell you where I hid it. It's under a big pile of hay in Mrs. Wickersham's barn. Her husband died last year and she's giving up the farm so nobody would notice it."

Faith pulled out her radio. "Steel, did you copy that?"

"AFFIRMATIVE," said the Steel Soldier over her radio. "MOVING TO CONFIRM THAT REPORT NOW."

Faith sighed. "The car will help. But that's still not enough. Gretchen arrived in New York this morning and disappeared. If she tried to get to us, she never made it. Where would she go? What would she do?"

"I don't know," cried Elizabeth. "I called my cousin and asked him to meet her. I don't know if he did or not. I haven't heard from either one of them and I'm worried sick about it. I've heard stories about New York, about the bad things people do to each other there."

Faith shrugged. "Sounds like they do bad things to each other here too, Elizabeth. What's your cousin's name?"

"Shane. Shane Clemens. He works for that power company with the funny name."

"Con Ed?"

"Yeah. That's it."

Faith grabbed her radio. "Sundancer, Steel, meet me at the western edge of town. We've got our lead."

~ ~ ~

"Harlan, Momma says to come out for dinner." Reggie's voice piped down the hall in a tone that set Harlan's teeth on edge. He trudged down the hall, knowing he was in for another round of tongue-lashing.

It began before he even reached the table. "Boy, you better not sit down at my table with hands and face looking like that. Get your butt into the bathroom and wash up."

Harlan sighed and headed to the small quarter bath off the kitchen. He scrubbed grease and dirt off his hands. For the first time that day, he saw just how badly the boys had beaten him up earlier. His lower lip was swollen and cut.

He had caked blood around his nose. One of his eyes had bruised so that it looked like someone had colored it with a Magic Marker. He splashed water onto his face until the smudges and dried blood were gone.

Thus presentable, he returned to the table. Momma had baked a ham casserole and cooked some greens on the side. It smelled delicious, but Harlan felt a little nauseated and knew it wouldn't take much to make him ill.

"Momma, can I say grace?" asked Reggie.

"Yes, baby," said Momma. She shot a significant glare at Harlan that implied if he didn't behave himself that she would knock the black right off him.

"Thank you Lord for our food and our house," Reggie intoned. "And bless Momma and Irlene and Harlan and me. In Jesus' name we pray. Amen."

Harlan muttered "Amen" along with her to avoid any unpleasantness. His God was Science, with angels named Tesla, Einstein, and Edison, but no one else needed to know that.

Momma dished up and passed plates to Reggie and Harlan. Reggie dove in with gusto but Harlan could only push the food around his plate with a fork.

"Momma, isn't Leenie going to eat with us?" Reggie asked between bites.

"Not tonight, baby. She's working on a case with her teammates," said Momma. She turned to Harlan. "She called me earlier to say so. She also said she gave you some passes to visit Just Cause after you gave her a song and dance about impressing a girl."

"That was true, Momma."

"Then where are they?"

Harlan's ears burned. "I don't have them now."

Momma's face tightened, as if her skin shrank as her temper rose. "It's bad enough that you lie to me, but now you got to drag your sister into this."

Here it comes, thought Harlan.

"I don't know why you can't be more like Irlene," said Momma, launching into one of her favorite tirades. "She never cut classes. She graduated at the top of her class. Top of her class! Don't you know what that means for a young black woman today? She could go to college. Nobody in our family ever went."

"Momma, may I have some more, please?" Reggie held up her empty plate.

"Land sakes, Reggie, I don't know where you put it all. You certainly may." Momma spooned more casserole onto her plate, and then returned her attention to Harlan. "You're a smart boy, Harlan. But you need to buckle down and study so you might get the chance to get out of this neighborhood too. I won't let you skip school anymore. From here on, either Irlene or I will take you to school every day."

"But, Momma," began Harlan.

"I'm not finished," said Momma. "No more going to that horrid garage. I won't have you wasting your time in all that dirt and filth when you should be learning."

Harlan sighed. "I promise I won't ever go back there again," he said. "Gonsalvo retired today. I don't know what will happen to his shop."

Momma sniffed. "Well, that's something. But your obsession with tools and things ends now. Your one focus in life is to be school, and nothing but school until your grades come up."

"That ain't fair!"

"You gonna tell me about *fair*? Of course it ain't fair. It ain't fair that I have to work two jobs to feed, clothe, and house you. It ain't fair that you got no father to whip you when you mouth off." Momma's face darkened. "And it ain't fair that I've got an ungrateful little bastard of a son like you!"

Reggie knocked over her milk glass and shrieked in surprise. "I'm sorry, Momma! It was an accident!"

Exasperated, Momma went to the sink for some rags. "I know, Reggie. Try to be more careful."

"I will." Reggie took a rag and carefully sopped up spilled milk. She smiled at Harlan as she cleaned up her mess. He blinked at her. It had looked to him like she'd knocked it over on purpose, but he couldn't understand why.

Momma grumbled about the waste as she wiped up the table to get what Reggie had missed and went to the sink to rinse the rag.

"Ain't you going to eat, Harlan?" whispered Reggie.

"I'm not hungry," he said.

"Give me some of your food."

Keeping one eye on Momma's back, Harlan scraped half of his food onto Reggie's plate. Their mother returned to the table and sat down.

"Momma, I'm sorry. My eyes was bigger than my tummy," said Reggie.

"That's all right, baby. We'll have leftovers for tomorrow." Momma took Reggie's food and put it back into the casserole dish.

"May I be excused?" asked Reggie.

"Yes, sweetie. Go get ready for bed."

"May I be excused too, Momma?" Harlan figured that maybe he could salvage something of the evening if he got off her bad side.

She grunted but took his plate and scooped the remains back into the dish as well. "You aren't out of the woods yet, mister. I don't want any more trouble from you tonight. You get your filthy butt into the tub."

"Yes, Momma." Harlan ran away to avoid any further wrath. He stopped at Reggie's door. "Hey, I know what you did, and I just wanted to say thanks." The word felt strange in his mouth.

Reggie smiled at him. "It's okay. I don't like when Momma yells at you. She yells at me, but not as bad as you."

"Someday…" Harlan stopped, not knowing what he'd been about to say, except that it had an air of finality about it.

~~~

Tommy wanted to run, to scream, to hit something. He didn't know whether to cry or die. Outside, dust swirled through the parking garage as miniature zephyrs twisted around John's car in a reflection of Tommy's inner turmoil.

"Is it because you're straight? I know you probably are. Most guys are."

"No, it's not that," said John.

"Is it me? Something wrong with me?"

"No, of course not."

"Then what? What is it? Why can't you love me?" Tommy's voice rose in an accusation. Dust pelted the side of the car like a sandblaster.

"Tommy, listen to yourself. Do you even know what you're asking?"

"For you to love me!"

"Which means what?"

Tommy sighed. The swirling wind in the garage died down as he tried to put his thoughts into words. "It means you love someone, John. Love, you know?"

"Tommy, I don't know."

Tommy's head spun. It was like trying to describe the color red, or the sound of a flute. "When you care about someone, more than anything in the world. When their well-being and happiness is more important than yours is. When you'd die so they might live."

"Tommy, you are a good friend, and I care about you, but what you're describing are feelings I'm not capable of experiencing."

"Bullshit." The wind whistled with vehemence in agreement. "Everybody is capable of that."

John sighed. "I'm not like everybody else. I don't have any strong feelings." He smiled wryly. "I'm very much like a rock in that regard. I don't suffer hate, or incapacitating grief. Joy is beyond me. And so is love."

Dust pattered against the windows. "That's terrible," said Tommy at last. "I feel sorry for you."

"You don't need to, any more than you need to feel sorry for someone who can't fly. Just because someone can't experience something doesn't mean their lives are less fulfilling."

"Still," said Tommy. "I wish I could... I don't know, teach you or something. Being around you, being with you, it makes my heart cry out for you."

For a long moment, the only sound in the car was the wind whistling around the antenna. John snorted and then put his hand over his mouth. His shoulders quaked, making the car rock on its springs. John's barely-restrained mirth set off Tommy into helpless giggles.

Soon both men were guffawing with the kind of laughter that only two close friends could share. "My heart cries for you," said John in the most simpering voice he could manage with his stentorian baritone.

Tommy shrieked with fresh peals of laughter. "I could teach you, you know." They crumpled into each other, cold stone and hot flesh leaning together for support. The laughter slowed until Tommy wiped his eyes. "Christ," he said. "I needed that."

"It felt good," said John.

"Hey, I thought you didn't feel strong emotions," said Tommy.

"Humor is humor." John smiled at him. "And it was very funny."

"Yeah, I guess it was," admitted Tommy. "Thanks for not freaking out at me."

"You're too good a friend for that. I just hope you understand."

"I'll try. It won't be easy."

"Nothing ever is. That's why they call it life."

"I thought that was a magazine."

"Funny." John started up his car. "Shall we go?"

"Yeah, I need to get into my own clothes. I feel slimy in Javier's." Tommy noticed the manila folder on the seat between them. "Is this the file from the meeting?"

"Yes."

The Scout groaned as it climbed out of the underground garage. Like everything else he did, John drove with slow, deliberate care, keeping plenty of safe distance between him and the car in front. Tommy put his feet up and out the window to read the folder. "Comfortable?" asked John with a smile.

Tommy laughed. "I could use a cold drink if you've got one. Preferably with a lot of strong alcohol in it."

"Well, there's always the watered-down beer at the field."

"Jesus," muttered Tommy as he read. "Nineteen years old and killed a guy. What a way to start out. She should be going to parties and making out with boys."

"What were you doing at nineteen?"

Tommy grinned with fond memories. "Going to parties and making out with boys." He looked at the faxed picture of her. "She's pretty. At least, I think she is. This is a lousy picture."

"I thought you were gay." John chuckled.

"Doesn't mean I can't appreciate beauty. I mean, I wouldn't sleep with her." He glanced sidelong at John. "You, on the other hand…"

John shook his head.

"I'm kidding. Well, I'm not, but you know what I mean."

"Yes, but don't get your hopes up."

"Why? Are you going to say you can't have sex either?"

"Well… I can't."

And that set them off into more laughter.

~~~

In all her life, Gretchen couldn't remember enjoying a shower more than when she was at Shane's.

He'd dashed into the apartment ahead of her, she presumed so he could hide dirty underwear, dirty socks, dirty magazines, or whatever bachelors kept lying around their homes when nobody was around. The apartment was a modest two-bedroom with a small but well-apportioned kitchen. A large couch, television, and a wall of vinyl records from bands such as The Beatles, the Rolling Stones, and Steppenwolf dominated the living area. Even with the windows open, no breeze found its way inside to clear the stuffy air, which carried the scent of something spicy cooked in hot oil. Gretchen couldn't tell whether it was the remains of something Shane's roommate might have cooked or if the smell was wafting up from a lower apartment.

Shane had pushed a stack of clean towels at her after checking his bathroom for any embarrassing items or messes. Gretchen had found a bottle of Elizabeth's shampoo in her bag and with a smile at Shane, shut and locked the door.

And now, finally, she felt clean.

She luxuriated in the hot spray, in spite of the day's heat. Her muscles relaxed and she found herself feeling optimistic about her future. She experimented with her power, creating marble-sized pockets of vacuum in the spray. They made popping noises like champagne corks, and each time she made one, the water within it flash-froze into icy flakes that melted in the spray.

With regret, she shut off the faucet and wrapped a towel around her hair the way her mother had taught her. She'd have loved some lotion, but that wasn't the sort of thing to find in a bachelor's apartment. She took a moment to look herself over in the mirror. Her bruises had already faded to a dull yellow and her eyes weren't so shadowed anymore. Satisfied with herself, she turned to get some clean clothes from her bag.

Then she realized her bag still sat on the floor in Shane's living room. Had she left it open? She couldn't remember. She hoped she didn't have underwear and bras hanging out of it for Shane to see. She could wear the clothes she'd changed into at Con Ed, but they weren't really nice enough to wear to a restaurant. Besides, she hadn't been really clean when she'd changed before and didn't want to stink herself up again so soon.

Gretchen wrapped the biggest towel she could find around her chest and checked in the mirror. It hung down low enough to cover everything, as long as she was careful about bending over. Shane had been a gentleman so far, and she felt safer around him than she had since leaving Dyersville. She closed her hand around the doorknob, hesitating. *All of them do it sooner or later. Even the ones you think are nice.*

"No, not Shane," she muttered aloud. She unlocked the door and tiptoed out into the short hallway.

Shane was asleep on the couch, his arm over his eyes and his sock feet up on the side. Gretchen saw her bag sitting at the end of the couch and tiptoed over to retrieve it, keeping one hand clutched on her towel.

Then her toe mashed into the corner of the coffee table. She let out an inadvertent squeak and Shane's eyes flew open just as she overbalanced and fell, the towel fluttering to the floor ahead of her.

His eyes widened as she sprawled spread-eagled in front of him. Then his cheeks burned crimson and he covered his eyes. "I'm sorry, I'm not staring."

Gretchen scrambled to retrieve her towel and at least cover the most strategic areas. "It's okay, I just stubbed my toe."

"Are you okay?" he asked.

"I'm fine. It's okay, I'm covered up now. I didn't mean to, uh, startle you." She forced a laugh. "I know I'm not much to look at."

"I think you're real pretty," said Shane.

Gretchen's own face burned, but in spite of the embarrassing predicament, she felt unexpected heat elsewhere. She looked down at Shane huddled on the couch, still hiding his eyes out of miserable deference to her, and she realized she very much wanted him to kiss her.

Instead of ducking back into the bathroom with her bag, she sat down beside him. "Shane…" She pulled his arm down. "It's okay."

And then they were kissing, devouring each others' lips with hungry urgency. He tasted like cigarettes but she didn't care. The feeling in her grew and she knew deep down that Elizabeth was wrong; not all boys were like the ones back home. Shane was different, and this was how she was supposed to feel. Her heart hammered with mad desire. She followed each passionate kiss with a light peck, like the punctuation of a sentence. She could feel herself wanting to open as if she were a flower bud first touched by the morning sun.

With one decisive motion, she pulled aside her towel. Shane's eyes grew to the size of saucers. She took hold of his wrists and guided his hands to her breasts, his touch setting off fireworks under her skin. "I want you to make love to me," she said.

"Are you sure?" he asked.

She pulled him close. "Yes. Please." To help convince him, she pulled his t-shirt off and planted a kiss against the hollow of his throat.

He leaned her back against the arm of the couch and nuzzled against her neck. She shivered with the sensation as he brushed his lips down her breasts and belly. "What are you doing?" she gasped in delight.

Her head was humming so much, she missed his muffled reply. But then she felt the touch of lips and tongue where she'd never dreamed such a thing, and she threw her head back and gave herself over to the pleasure.

ELEVEN

July 13, 1977, 7:00 PM

Faith finished recounting her information to Sundancer and the Steel Soldier. Sundancer shook her head at the rape story. "That's a horrible thing to happen to anyone," she said, "but especially to a young girl like that. No wonder she freaked out."

"But it implies she isn't fully in control of her powers," said Faith. "And I can't think of any way to counteract someone who can destroy air."

"I LOCATED THE MISSING VEHICLE BASED UPON YOUR INFORMATION," reported the Steel Soldier. "THAT SEEMS TO CORROBORATE YOUR WITNESS' STORY."

"The bottom line is that we've got a very scared young girl back home, and she's got a dangerous ability. We've got to find her before the Feds do, and we have a starting point," said Faith. "Steel, can you radio Headquarters?"

"NEGATIVE. THERE ARE LARGE STORMS AMASSING BETWEEN HERE AND NEW YORK, AND THEY ARE INTERFERING WITH RADIO SIGNALS. DO YOU WISH ME TO LOCATE A LAND LINE?"

"No," said Faith. "I think we're done with this hick town."

"Me too," said Sundancer. "Besides, I've still got that game tonight. I hate for the boys to go without me along to tell them what's going on down on the field."

Faith and Sundancer climbed back into the Soldier's stretcher pods. "I HAVE SUFFICIENT POWER FOR A BALLISTIC TRAJECTORY COURSE," said the Soldier. "THIS WILL SAFELY CARRY US ABOVE THE DANGEROUS WEATHER PATTERNS. FOR YOUR SAFETY IN THIS TRANSIT, I AM FLOODING YOUR TUBES WITH A MILD ANESTHETIC GAS."

"Wait—" began Faith, but then her vision blurred and she felt like she was falling into a deep, dark tunnel.

She awoke with a jarring bump. For a moment, she didn't know where she was, except that she was trapped in a tight, enclosed space. Then, with a hiss, the tube split apart and she remembered she had been in the Steel Soldier's stretcher pod. "That was a dirty trick, Steel," she said. The anesthetic had given her a pounding headache. They had landed on the platform for Just Cause Headquarters in the World Trade Center.

"MY APOLOGIES," said the Soldier. "I ANTICIPATED YOU WOULD FIND SUBORBITAL FLIGHT DISTURBING. IT WAS MY ERROR. I HAVE SAVED THIS INFORMATION FOR FUTURE REFERENCE. I BELIEVED SPEED WAS OF THE ESSENCE."

"It was," said Faith, "but you can't go around knocking people out without their permission. Save it for the bad guys, not your teammates."

"UNDERSTOOD. I REQUIRE SIGNIFICANT RECHARGING AND REFUELING. I SHALL TAKE MY LEAVE OF YOU TO RETURN TO MY MAINTENANCE FACILITIES." The Soldier clomped over to the edge of the deck and rocketed away.

"You want me to stay?" asked Sundancer.

"No, go on and enjoy your game. I'll call you guys if I need you. Hopefully I can track down this Shane Clemens fellow and find our fugitive before she gets herself into worse trouble." Faith knew how much Sundancer adored her Mets team and that the poor girl would pine away all night if she missed the game.

Sundancer squeezed her arm. "Thanks, Faith. I owe you." She trotted off toward the locker rooms to change into her civilian clothing.

Faith went to the team's coordination center to talk to Bobby; however, when she got there, her husband was gone and a frustrated Lionheart was pecking out something on a typewriter with the tips of his index finger claws and growling under his breath. "Hi, Rick. Where is everyone?"

He leaned back from the typewriter and pinched the bridge of his broad, feline nose. "Our friends the Feds were distinctly uncomfortable with my nonhuman appearance, and it was suggested that perhaps Bobby and Irlene should accompany them in their investigation so as not to frighten the public."

"What?" Faith was aghast. Lionheart was as highly regarded as anyone on the team, and even more so as the field leader.

"Bobby defused things by saying he'd go and asked me to stay. So here I am, trying to type a goddamned report with fingers too big to hit the keys."

"Oh, man, that's the worst," said Faith. "Want me to type it for you?"

"My hero," he said, and her heart jumped a little. To distract herself from the fibrillation, she recapped what they'd learned about the fugitive Gretchen Gumm. Lionheart shook his head in disgust. "What is this world coming to?"

"I could go track down this Con Ed guy." Faith didn't feel very enthusiastic about it; her head still throbbed from the Soldier's anesthetic.

"No, Bobby and Irlene are already out in the field, and the Feds can probably find him faster."

They radioed out the information to Bobby and exhorted him to call on backup if it they needed him. "Don't worry," said Bobby. "I'm not about to get into a parapowered fight with anyone. I leave that to you heavy hitters. Faith, babe?"

"Yes?"

"I love you."

"I love you, too. Be careful."

"God, I've got a headache," grumbled Lionheart. "I don't know how Bobby does this stuff."

"I've got one too," said Faith. "I don't recommend traveling by Steel Soldier Airlines. I think I've got some aspirin in my locker. Want me to get it?"

Lionheart stood up and stretched, arching his back like a cat. "I need to get away from all this paperwork. I'll come with you."

He loped after Faith down the hall. She could feel the heat washing off his furry form and smell his musk in the air. It took all her willpower not to whirl around and throw herself at him. She loved her husband without question, but this was pure animal lust, and it begged and pleaded for satisfaction. She ducked into the locker room and splashed some cold water on her face. She wished she could take a cold shower instead. For that matter, she wished she could pull Lionheart into it with her. She needed to get out and away from him before the temptation grew too great to bear.

Aspirin tablets in hand, Faith returned to the hall and found Lionheart there, leaning against the wall. She stepped up to him, took one of his hands, and dropped two tablets into it. His gentle claws scratched against her palm and made her shiver. She looked up at him to say she hadn't gotten any water, but her gaze locked with his cat eyes, and she was trapped by it.

A low rumble sounded deep in his chest that she'd never heard before and she realized he was *purring*. The sound reverberated through her body to center somewhere beneath her navel. Almost without thinking, Faith reached up an arm, took the muscular Lionheart by the back of his neck, and pulled his face down to hers.

"We shouldn't," he whispered.

"I know," she replied.

A sound of footsteps made Lionheart jump back. A moment later a pale-but-cheerful Javier strolled around the corner. "Why don't you two get a room already?" He opened the door to the men's lockers.

"Hey, Javier, I wasn't expecting to see you at all today," said Lionheart, as if to cover the awkward moment.

Javier shrugged. "It's Wednesday."

~ ~ ~

Momma forbid him to go to bed without a bath, so Harlan got out a pair of clean shorts and a towel and locked himself in the bathroom. He wasn't supposed to lock it, because the small apartment only had the one bathroom, but he wanted a little bit of privacy. He'd had a busy, difficult day and for once didn't mind a hot bath. It would help him unwind.

He grimaced at the state of his ribs, bruised from numerous kicks. His urine had blood in it as well, and he knew it would for at least a day following the almost-professional beating he'd received that afternoon. He didn't care so much. The pain would go away, and soon there would be a reckoning. As the water poured into the tub, he imagined his revenge against the bullies. Torn apart by his bolt guns, burned to ashes, shredded by the great sawblade of his robot, they would die in painful, brilliant ways.

The images aroused Harlan. Even though he knew it was wrong, he reached down and stroked himself. The visions of blood, death, and fire transformed into pictures of Gretchen, and Harlan's hand moved faster. He wondered what it would be like to kiss her, to touch her breasts, and that secret place between her legs. His muscles clenched and he squeezed his eyes shut against sudden tears as he shot his load against the wall beside the tub.

Masturbation always left him feeling triumphant. If Momma knew, she'd be horrified. It thrilled him to have one more secret from her. He took some toilet paper and wiped up the evidence of his self-abuse, keeping his secret. The odor of his spunk made his stomach heave as he dropped the waste into the toilet and what little dinner he'd eaten came back up in a rush. He shook with weakness as he closed and flushed the toilet.

Harlan sank into the hot tub. He took the bar of soap and scrubbed himself, and didn't mind the sting when the suds got into his eyes. It kept him alert.

A gentle but urgent tap at the door startled him. "Harlan," whispered Reggie. "You got to let me in."

"Can't you hold it, Reggie? I just got in the tub."

"No," she said. "Harlan, you ain't supposed to lock this door."

"I wanted some privacy. I still do. Go away, Reggie."

Reggie was silent and for a minute, Harlan thought maybe she really did leave. But then, he heard the scratching of a key in the lock. Reggie must have gone to get the bathroom key off Momma's dresser.

"Reggie!" cried Harlan. He yanked the shower curtain across just in time as the door opened and Reggie stepped into the bathroom. "Just be quick, okay?"

"I don't have to go potty," said Reggie. "I needed to tell you that Momma took your books and tools and threw them down the trash."

"She what?" Harlan shot up to his feet, but slipped in the tub. He grabbed the shower curtain for support, and it tore free of the rings to crumple into the soapy water.

"Shhh," warned Reggie. "I wasn't supposed to tell. When she wasn't lookin', I hid a couple in my room, but I'm awful a-scared if she finds out."

Harlan ignored Reggie and shoved past her. He barreled out into the hall naked just in time to see his mother leave through the front door with a cardboard box. He didn't think about modesty, or embarrassment—only that she was taking his books away.

"No!" He ran after Momma. "Those are mine! You don't touch them!"

She slammed the door in his face.

He wrestled with the knob, his hands still slick with soap, and finally flung it open.

Momma threw book after book into the garbage chute. "Momma, don't! Please! I'll do anything!" He ran after her. Up and down the hall, people cracked open their doors to watch the latest domestic dispute coming out of Apartment 32. When they saw Harlan's nakedness, more than one jeer and catcall echoed in his ears. *Don't worry, boy, that other one will drop someday. Lookin' good, kid. Mommy, that boy ain't got no clothes on.*

Harlan closed his hands on *The Marvelous Inventions of Nikola Tesla* and struggled with his mother for a moment for it. Then she backhanded him across the face. He flew backwards and sprawled on the filthy carpeting.

"You bet your sorry ass you'll do anything," cried Momma. "No more of this nonsense. From now on, the only books you're gonna read are schoolbooks. Instead of a screwdriver, you're gonna use a pencil. Now you get your black ass back into the apartment before I whip the skin right off you."

"Damn," said someone nearby.

Harlan watched as Momma tipped the rest of the box into the garbage. He knew he could get into the trash bins and find his books again, mixed in with dirty diapers and rotten food, but it still felt like he was watching her strip away his life.

He tasted blood on his lip where she'd struck him, but he didn't care. He stood and trudged back to the apartment where Reggie stood wide-eyed and trembling.

"What books did you save, Reg?"

She sniffled and showed Harlan a biography of Thomas Edison and a book about aircraft carriers.

"Keep them safe for me," said Harlan. "Momma will throw them away if she finds them in my room."

"I'm s-sorry I didn't get more of them," she whimpered.

Harlan smiled at her, surprised that he meant it. "You did your best. I owe you for trying. Someday I'll pay you back." He walked to his room and stopped by the door. He could hear Momma coming back and only had a moment to turn back to Reggie. "Whatever happens, Reggie, I'll try to look out for you."

With that, he went into his room and closed the door. And waited.

~ ~ ~

There was no sign of Sundancer as Tommy and John took their seats at the game. "She must not be back from Iowa yet," said John. "It's not like Gloria to miss a ball game."

"True," said Tommy. Despite his earlier laughter with John, he was once again feeling the rift between them that he couldn't bridge no matter how hard he tried. He couldn't understandI love you how someone could be incapable of love. He vowed to try harder to get John to open up.

"Stop it," Tommy muttered aloud. "You're going about this all wrong."

"What was that?" called John over the roar of the crowd. He was using a fat marker to sign programs and other things pushed at him. Tommy felt almost invisible with his hair pulled back in a ponytail and a Mets jersey. After awhile, the fans sitting around them recognized him too and they busied him with autograph requests.

Miranda hadn't arrived, but Tommy kept a seat open for her, and John kept Sundancer's clear too. "Where's your friend?" asked John.

"I don't know," admitted Tommy. "I thought she'd be here."

"You should call her. Maybe something came up."

Tommy shrugged. "If she's already on her way, I'll never reach her. Besides, the game's starting." He needed something to take his mind off his feelings for the man beside him, and baseball would fit the bill well enough.

"Hey, boys, how much have I missed?" Sundancer—Gloria, when she was in civilian garb—squeezed along the row of fans to her empty seat. Tommy had seen and admired her *Playboy* spread a few months ago. She wasn't wearing much more than that now: bikini top, cutoff jean shorts, and flip flops. She had her hair pulled back underneath a Mets cap. Tommy realized he'd been hearing wolf whistles and catcalls for a few minutes. It must have been when she entered the section.

The people who'd gotten autographs from John and Tommy came back all over again to get one from Gloria. A lot more men this time, noticed Tommy, and they hung around afterward until Gloria said, "I can't see the game, guys."

In between pitches, she leaned over and recapped what she and Faith had learned in Iowa. Tommy tried to pay attention, but being huddled in close to John was a distraction.

A fan pulled out a Polaroid and started taking pictures of other fans with the heroes. John grinned with his quartzite teeth, his arms wrapped around a couple of kids. He looked like a cheerful stone Santa Claus with them. It made Tommy's chest tighten to see it, and he knew he had to get away. He mumbled that he needed to use the restroom and worked his way back to the stairs and then down to the corridor.

Out on the field, somebody hit a ball and the stands exploded in cheers and applause. People who'd been loitering in the shade of the concourse hurried up steps to see what they'd missed, leaving the corridor more empty than full. Tommy leaned against a wall and put his forehead against his arm. "Shit," he muttered. "Get a hold of yourself. You're spiraling."

"Hey, man, are you okay?"

Tommy looked around to see a pimply, teenaged usher staring at him. He waved the boy away. "Yeah. Too much heat, too much to drink."

The boy pointed down the corridor. "If you're gonna puke, there's a bathroom there."

Tommy nodded. He didn't feel sick, but at least he could splash some water on his face .

It was the middle of an inning, and only a few men were urinating at the trough. He went to a sink and ran it until the tepid water turned cool. He splashed a handful of water across his face and pulled the moisture back through his hair, letting his ponytail down and then retying it.

More cheers echoed outside and the few men in the restroom hurried to finish their business and ran outside, leaving Tommy by himself in blessed solitude. He went over to use one of the urinals opposite the long trough. As he finished, he became aware of a noise: the rhythmic slapping of flesh on flesh. Muffled groans came from the stall beside him, sounds Tommy knew very well.

He bent down and saw two pairs of feet with pants around their ankles below the edge of the stall.

Tommy shut his eyes and listened to the two men fucking beside him. It helped to drive away thoughts of John. He heard one of them gasp and knew it was done. He blushed, embarrassed that he'd eavesdropped on the two lovers, but then realized if they'd been concerned about discovery, they wouldn't have been in a bathroom at Shea Stadium. Still, when the stall door opened, Tommy stared straight ahead at the wall and didn't look as one man hurried from the bathroom.

The other loitered until Tommy glanced back over his shoulder. The man might have been twenty. Slender, tight blond curls, perfect skin, pouty lips. He wore athletic shorts and a tank top that showed off his wiry physique. He stood leaning against the sinks with a dangerous smile. "How you doing, Ponytail?"

Tommy shrugged. He couldn't find the words to say to this beautiful boy.

The boy slid a suggestive finger between his lips. "Twenty bucks," he said.

Tommy's brain went white, like a television being unplugged from the antenna. He'd finally gotten the distraction he was craving. He dug into his pocket and pulled out a fifty. "What can I get for this?"

"Honey, for that you can get anything you want."

Without another word, Tommy took the boy by the hand and led him into a stall.

~~~

Gretchen lay half across Shane's chest, listening to his heartbeat and watching smoke curl up from the cigarette she'd borrowed from him. She'd tried one drag from it and it made her cough and her eyes water. Shane had laughed, but not in an unkind way.

Shane's attentive ministrations had driven memories of Donny's brutality into a dark corner of Gretchen's mind. Lying on his couch, naked with him, she felt safer than ever before in her life. His steady heartbeat under her cheek reassured her that everything would be all right.

"Sorry about your table," she murmured.

"It's okay," he replied. "I never liked it that much anyway."

The first time she came, little spheres of air had imploded away all around her, like someone popping bubble packing. The second time had been far more intense and she must have made a much bigger volume disappear, for it had thundered inside the apartment and the glass-topped coffee table cracked down the middle.

"I didn't know I would do that when I, you know."

"Yeah. I kind of liked it, though. I could get used to it."

Gretchen looked up into Shane's smiling eyes. "Really?"

"Yeah. Do you want to stay here while you're getting set up with a job and stuff?"

"I'd like that, Shane. If it isn't a bother for you or your roommate."

"He won't care. He's barely here as it is. If you'll let me up, I'll leave him a note."

Gretchen crawled up his chest to kiss him. "Whatever you say." She rolled off him and stood. He rooted around, looking for his underwear. While he was bent over, Gretchen couldn't help but snap her towel at his ass. He yelped, got his feet tangled, and wound up giggling on the floor.

Gretchen dressed and spent a few minutes fussing with her hair while Shane wrote the note. He stuck it to the fridge with a magnet shaped like a hamburger.

"Ready to go?" asked Gretchen.

Shane blinked. "You're dressed? You're ready?"

She nodded.

"But you're a girl. You're supposed to take an hour to get ready for anything."

"I did take an hour. Boy, you write slow." Gretchen grinned at him.

Hand in hand, they took the elevator down to the ground floor. Shane led her onto the street. Even though the sun was low in the west, the asphalt felt soft and gooey under Gretchen's feet. Distant thunderheads showed beyond the buildings, but didn't offer any hope of respite.

Gretchen could already feel herself starting to sweat. "Is it always this hot in the summers?"

Shane shook his head. "No, this is a heat wave. Everybody's pretty miserable, and it doesn't help with that Son of Sam guy out on the streets."

"Are we in danger here?" The idea of a serial killer made Gretchen feel very small.

"I don't think so. But just to be safe, we'll be indoors

before it gets late."

"At Just Cause headquarters," added Gretchen.

"Huh?"

She held up the entry passes for display. "Tonight, after we eat. And you're going with me."

"I am?"

"Every superhero needs a sidekick," she said. "I'm learning more and more about my power. I think maybe I could be part of their team, so long as they can help me with my problem."

"With what?"

Gretchen didn't answer immediately. The thought of talking about Donny made her feel a little ill, but Shane had been so kind to her all day that she felt she owed him. "What I did to that guy. With my powers." Tears threatened, but Gretchen forced herself to stay in control. Nobody was making her tell Shane; she wanted to, because she knew she could trust him. "I—I killed him." she said in a rush.

"I may just be a stupid Con Ed guy," said Shane, "but even I can see that somebody messed you up. I'd say he got what he deserved."

Gretchen shook her head. "No, nobody deserves to die like that."

"Easy, girl. I'm on your side here."

"Are you, Shane?"

He squeezed her hand. "Of course I am. You're my cousin's best friend. You've been great company today. You even kind of saved my life. Far as I'm concerned, you're perfect hero material."

Gretchen couldn't speak, but she stood on tiptoes to kiss Shane's cheek.

"You want to go to Just Cause, we'll go there as soon as we're done with dinner," he said.

"Thank you for understanding. Thank you for everything."

Shane beamed.

TWELVE

July 13, 1977, 8:00 PM

"Wish I'd known you were that way, Faith. I'd have made a play for you." Javier grinned around a toothpick he rolled in his lips like a cigarette.

"What do you mean, *that way*?" Faith didn't like the implication in Javier's words.

"A swinger. A player. Giving up tail to more than one *hombre*." His eyes narrowed. "Or whatever Rick is."

"God, you are such an asshole," said Faith, terrified that her near-indiscretion with Lionheart would get back to Bobby somehow.

Javier shrugged. "Maybe you need an asshole to make you feel more like a woman. What's the matter? Bobby can't get it up so much anymore?" Javier pointed at his crotch suggestively. "Still plenty of iron in this. You ought to be flattered by the attention."

"Flattered?" Faith spluttered, so beside herself she couldn't form any more words.

"Least you still got a tight body. All running does wonders for that ass. You want to feel the touch of a specialist in it, you know where to find me." Javier chuckled as he walked away.

A tear of fury squeezed out of one eye as Faith balled her fists. She could have charged him, beaten him to a pulp before he could blink, but all that would accomplish would be to get her removed from active duty and charged with assault using parapowers. The Devereaux Foundation that operated and managed Just Cause didn't tolerate its members brawling with one another or with non-powered opponents . Before taking over the team leadership role, back when Lady Athena still ran the show, Lionheart had lost his temper and attacked the veteran hero Flashpoint. Lionheart was suspended from active duty for six months and Flashpoint had to retire from an active role in Just Cause due to his injuries.

One super-speed-fueled punch would have knocked Javier ass over teakettle, but the momentary satisfaction would pale when Faith had to serve her own suspension or worse. So she swallowed her pride and stalked away, determined not to let a womanizing drug addict get under her skin.

She didn't mean to wind up back in the coordination center with Lionheart, but her angry feet carried her there so she flopped into a chair. To deal with her nervous energy, she grabbed a pen and twirled it through her fingers until it blurred.

"You're making me seasick watching you," said Lionheart.

"Then don't watch me," snapped Faith. Then she felt bad at her outburst. "I'm sorry, that was uncalled for. That asshole Javier has me all twisted up."

Lionheart smiled, showing his pointed teeth. "I couldn't not watch you if I tried. What did he do this time?"

"He came on to me."

"Want me to tear his throat out?"

"Yes, please."

Lionheart pushed his chair back, spread his claws, and started to stand up.

Faith was beside him in a flash. "No, silly."

"I'd have to suspend myself," he said. "On the other hand, I haven't had a vacation in six years. I've got to have a few months accrued by now. I'm thinking someplace warm, with big skies and open fields. Want to go to Kenya?"

Faith laughed. "I can't go to Kenya with you, Rick. I'm married."

He growled in the back of his throat. "I know."

She thought how easy it would be to give herself over to her lust. Maybe they should sleep together, just so they could be over the unrequited attraction. But she knew he would be like a drug; the first time would be hardest, and after that it would get easier and easier. She didn't want to go down that road and lose her husband.

Maybe she was stronger than that, she thought. She took Lionheart's head in her hands. His great paws closed about her wrists and he turned his head to brush hot lips against her palm. It sent shivers all the way down her spine and made a muscle in her ass twitch. "Oh, God," she moaned as she buried her fingers in his soft mane.

"Rick, you there?" Bobby's voice from the radio made Faith jump.

Lionheart shook himself and picked up the microphone. "Yeah, Bobby. Go ahead."

"The Feds kicked down the door into Clemens' apartment. I guess they don't believe in warrants when it comes to dangerous parahumans."

"Did you catch Gumm?"

"No, but she was definitely here. There's a bag with Elizabeth Hague's name on it. Wasn't that the girl Faith interviewed?"

Faith nodded. Lionheart confirmed it to Bobby.

"Listen, we might have just missed them, within minutes. The goddamn shower's still dripping. Towel is damp and there were long blonde hairs in the drain."

"You're a regular Steve McGarrett," said Lionheart. "Are you sure it was our fugitive?"

"The Feds think so, and I have to say there's too much circumstantial evidence here when you combine it with what Faith found out. There's a note here, presumably written by Clemens to his roommate, saying his girlfriend will be staying with them for a few days until she finds work and a place of her own."

"Damn, she moves fast. Any idea where the two went?"

"No. Kojak and Crocker are knocking on doors, but nobody's seen anything. Shit, most everybody around here's watching TV by this time of night."

"Long as you're looking around, did they cook anything? Fresh takeout cartons?"

"I thought of that too. Either they did dishes right after they ate and already put them away, or they didn't eat here."

"Maybe they're at a nearby restaurant."

"Sure, there are only about three hundred in walking distance, and that doesn't take into account if they took a cab or hopped on a subway."

"And you don't want to bring in a bunch of uniformed cops and tip them off if they're nearby." Lionheart scratched at his mane. Static electricity popped off it in the dry air.

"Right. The Feds are probably going to wait here to see if they come back. I think I've done about all I can do to help. Besides, I kind of think I'm cramping their style. You know, by expecting them to follow the law and shit."

Lionheart snorted. "Feds. Okay, you may as well come back in." He glanced at Faith and shrugged. "It's Wednesday, and people are already starting to show up. Wouldn't be right to have a party without our Master of Ceremonies in attendance."

"Ha ha ha." Bobby sounded anything but amused. "I'm on my way. Set some earplugs out for me."

~ ~ ~

Harlan sat on his bed, dressed only in a pair of ratty old shorts he used as pajamas. The heat in his room was stifling, even with the window open. Droplets of sweat congealed on his skin and trickled down his chest and sides. Legs folded beneath him, he stared without seeing out at the distant clouds and occasional streaks of lightning leaping between them.

In his hands, he held the only tool Momma had left him, because he'd had it hidden. It was an old Swiss Army knife, the first tool he'd ever owned. Irlene had given it to him as a Christmas present when he was ten. He kept it under the corner of his mattress. Sometimes, when he'd have bad dreams, he'd reach down, feel the cool plastic shell, and know things would be all right.

The knife was a beacon of sanity that penetrated the dull, thick fog in his brain to keep his mind from whirling with barely-repressed fury and creative energy. The very act of destruction seemed to fuel his thoughts, but after Momma destroyed everything he'd worked for at home, as he cradled the knife, he felt composed.

The day's events seemed to have been pushing him toward a major life change, like a baby about to emerge from the womb. Perhaps this trauma of his lost books was just one more in a series of birthing pains. Fate was making him sever ties to his past—first the carousel he had made for Reggie, then Gonsalvo, losing Gretchen, and now his books.

Put away childish things, he thought; perhaps today he would become a man. Lightning flared again in the distance, a bright questing tendril from the heavens to the Earth. It awakened something in Harlan, vitalized him. He took a deep, cleansing breath and blew it out, feeling an abnormal sense of peace and joy fill him.

He got up from his bed and went to his open window. Great clouds towered in the distance like the engines of the Earth, sparking with power. Down below on the street, people performed their intricate ballet of errands, games, and socializing. Harlan shook his head in sadness. It was all well and good to see the organization, but it was from chaos and disorder that society evolved. Like Harlan had taken his broken bicycle and built something newer and better, society's potential for improvement was vast.

Something—or someone—just needed to break it first.

Harlan left his room and went to look in on Reggie. She slept on top of her sheets in a thin cotton nightgown. Her hair was pulled into clumps so Momma could style it in the morning and she clutched her stuffed elephant like a raggedy security blanket. He listened to her soft, rhythmic snores. She was at peace; nothing ever bothered Reggie. Even in the middle of the crisis Momma had caused, Reggie had kept a cool head and saved some of Harlan's prized possessions.

He reached out and touched her cheek with a tenderness he didn't know he'd possessed. She moaned and murmured something in her sleep but didn't awaken. Something about her vulnerability moved him, and he made a promise that somehow, some way, he would always look after her.

In the new world, the one he would create, she'd have a real elephant if she wanted it.

He wished he knew more about love and affection. Perhaps he could find Gretchen and she could teach him. He didn't know where she was now, but sooner or later she'd be at Just Cause, and Harlan would find her there. Until then, he touched Reggie's cheek once more and stole out of the room.

Momma had fallen asleep in front of the television, as usual. She sat in her recliner, feet up, a drink at her elbow. On the flickering screen, Grizzly Adams talked to his bear. Every time Harlan noticed that show, the man was talking to his stupid bear. Harlan couldn't understand the appeal. Most shows that masqueraded as entertainment mystified him. Maybe someday there would be something worth watching. In the meantime, television was as effective an opiate for the masses as religion was. He'd read something about that in a book by Karl Marx, who had some interesting ideas even if most of them were still over Harlan's head.

Momma's head was tilted back and her mouth open. She either snored or gurgled in the back of her throat. Harlan stared at her, reaching deep into his soul to see if he felt the least bit of compassion for the woman who'd birthed him. No. He hated her. She'd taken everything he cared about and ruined it: his tools, his books, Gretchen. She'd never loved him, or understood him. She hadn't even tried. He was never good enough for her. He closed his eyes. A tiny voice in his mind begged him to reconsider his choices, but he squashed it like a bug underfoot. He'd never been one to listen to his conscience, anyway.

With one swift, decisive motion, he drew the blade out of his Swiss Army knife and slit Momma's throat.

~ ~ ~

The boy left the bathroom ahead of Tommy, which suited him just fine. He'd gotten what he'd needed, and the boy's name didn't fall in the realm of need-to-know information. He had been pliant and willing to please Tommy for his fifty dollars, and Tommy could still taste the boy's sweet skin on his lips. He fixed his hair and tied it back again into a neat ponytail. A splash of cool water on the back of his sweaty neck helped to rejuvenate him.

He overheard another sound of flesh on flesh outside the door, but instead of the noises of lovemaking, this was the timbre of fists beating in anger. He was tempted to stay hidden in the bathroom, but Tommy couldn't help but remember his tirade from earlier in the day.

"You're a goddamn superhero," he said aloud to his reflection in the spotty mirror. "It's about fucking time you acted like one." He straightened up, took a deep breath, and kicked open the bathroom door.

Four burly men stinking of beer had the curly-haired boy up against the wall. Two held him while a third, wearing a *Skoal* t-shirt, pounded him in the gut. The fourth exhorted them on from under a trucker hat, shouting words like *homo* and *faggot*. A few onlookers stood nearby watching, but like those who'd observed the murder of Kitty Genovese, weren't willing to get involved.

Tommy's ire rose with the speed of a tornado. Blasts of wind down the corridor sent dust and trash whirling. "What is this?" he growled, breezes spiraling around him like flowing armor.

The bullies let go of the boy, who sank to the floor blubbering and bleeding from a broken nose. Trucker Hat, the one with the big mouth, wasn't fazed at all.

"What're you, the faggot's boyfriend?" Trucker Hat challenged. "You fuckin' homos come in here like you own the place, pullin' each others' dicks in the restroom, while decent folks are just here to watch the game."

"Then go watch the game," said Tommy.

"You fuckin' sissy boy," yelled Trucker Hat. "You and your boyfriend oughtta be locked up! It ain't right what you're doin'. It's against Jesus."

"I'm sure he'd approve of you four bull dykes ganging up on one helpless boy," said Tommy, loud enough to be heard above the crowd noise. "Maybe later you can have a nice circle jerk to celebrate."

"Oh, now you're gonna get it, homo," Trucker Hat said. "Come on, guys." He took a deep breath as if in preparation to exhort them to do their worst, but no words issued forth. A look of confusion crossed his face, which melded into one of terror. The man clawed at his throat and his face, making only the slightest gasping noise.

The man's companions gaped at him in surprise. "Joey?" asked one who was missing a front tooth. "You okay?"

Tommy concentrated, using his power to keep the air in Trucker Hat's lungs despite the man's repeated attempts to exhale. He wasn't going to kill him, but he was going to teach the loudmouthed bigot a lesson.

A hard blow crashed into the side of Tommy's head. He lost his grip on the air in Trucker Hat and the man collapsed, gasping for breath. Stars danced before Tommy's eyes and he staggered. "Take that, you faggot!"

"Hit him again, Rick!" cried Skoal T-Shirt.

"Gonna fuck you up," said the man with the huge beer gut, and prepared to punch Tommy again.

Tommy had been training with the best in the world for years. These amateur thugs had nothing to bring against him. He shook off the effects of the blow and offered a specialty blow of his own.

A concentrated blast of air struck Beer Gut in his prominent belly, lifting the man up and away to skid down the concourse, shedding bits of clothing and skin. Tommy whirled and hit Skoal T-Shirt the same way, flinging him into a cement pillar. The man groaned and sank into a pile.

"That's him, that's Tornado!" called one of the onlookers. "Get them, Tornado!" Several of the others started to cheer.

Gap Tooth took a hesitant step toward Tommy. Tommy called up winds to swirl around the man, buffeting him this way and that, spinning him around until his eyes crossed and he fell. Vomit leaked from the corner of his mouth.

Tommy gestured at Trucker Hat, the loudmouth of the bunch, with a distinct come-hither motion. The man's nerve failed and he fled. "You better run," Tommy called after him. "Because this faggot is about to beat your ass some more."

The onlookers applauded and hooted their approval, but then the stands exploded in cheers when somebody hit a deep ball and most of the people milling around hurried back out to see what was going on.

Satisfied he wouldn't have any more trouble from the men, Tommy turned his attention to the injured boy. "You're him," mumbled the boy through swollen lips. "Tornado. I didn't recognize you before."

"Hush," said Tommy.

"I'd have done you for free," said the boy. "If you want your fifty back, you can have it."

"None of that nonsense, now." Tommy helped the boy to his feet. "Look at you. Those assholes really did a number on you. A real crime for a face like yours."

"I'm not anything special. Just another whore."

Tommy put a finger to the boy's lips. "Tonight you were mine, and that made you special to me. Are you going to be okay?"

The boy nodded. "I been beat up before by professionals. Those guys were amateurs."

Tommy laughed. "That they were. What's your name?"

"Moondoggie."

"What?"

"Marvin." The boy blushed. "But everyone calls me Moondoggie."

Tommy squeezed his hand. "Look me up sometime." He walked away from beautiful Moondoggie and returned to his seat. He found it much easier to face John and Gloria after the skirmish in the concourse below.

"Where've you been?" asked John.

"Jesus, what happened to your face?" added Sundancer. She reached out to touch Tommy's cheekbone, which felt bruised and swollen.

"Bathroom," said Tommy. "Some guy opened the door into my face. Accidents happen."

John shrugged. "You look awfully happy considering that."

Tommy smiled. "I'm having a good evening."

~~~

Gretchen couldn't believe how tall the World Trade Center towers were. To her small-town eyes, even a ten-story building stretched to unimaginable heights. "I bet there isn't even enough air to breathe that high up," she said.

Shane let out a laugh. "It's not even half a mile."

"It looks like it goes on forever," said Gretchen, craning her head back to look at the skyscraper in the waning sunlight. The top floors gleamed orange while the lower floors were gray and shadowed. They could have taken a subway beneath the monstrous towers, but Gretchen wanted to see them from the outside, so they'd gotten off one stop early and walked, hand-in-hand, toward the building that housed Just Cause headquarters.

The proprietor of the Greek café where they'd dined had fawned over her like she was a movie star. Shane had whispered that the heavyset woman had been trying to set him up with all her daughters and nieces forever, less to bring him into the huge family than to see him happy and married. The food had been wonderful. Gretchen had liked the spanakopita and baklava, which were almost as much fun to say as to eat.

And now, with a full belly and Shane's callused fingers wrapped around her own, Gretchen stared up at the towering building. Somewhere up there, she hoped she would find answers to what her powers meant.

"Ready?" asked Shane.

Gretchen squeezed his hand. "Yeah, I think so."

They walked across the plaza toward the tower that housed Just Cause. Other partygoers were drifting in from various directions to coagulate around the tower's main entrance. A couple of large bouncers waited at the door, checking people as they reached the head of the line. More often than not, they told would-be attendees to take a hike. Every once in awhile, they'd allow someone they deemed hip enough past the doors where another bouncer would escort the guest to the elevators and presumably up to the team's headquarters.

"Wow, they're really tight on security," muttered Shane. "And we're really under-dressed. They might not let us in even with your passes."

They watched as the doorman gave a man in a glistening white disco suit the heave-ho, while admitting a young woman in full Indian garb complete with beaded headdress and moccasins.

"Maybe we should go back and change," said Shane. He looked at his plain white t-shirt and jeans in dismay. Gretchen wasn't dressed any fancier, wearing cutoff jean shorts and a tank top.

The bouncers seemed to be admitting more people who were dressed in provocative or bizarre fashions than those who dressed for dancing or partying. It gave Gretchen an idea. "Do you have a pocketknife or something?"

"Sure. What's up?"

"Take your shirt off." Gretchen dug in her pocket for her lipstick.

Shane shrugged and pulled the shirt over his head. Gretchen took the lipstick and drew a heart over one of his nipples. Then she loaded up her lips with the color, pursed them together, and pressed a well-defined kiss mark on his taut belly, just over his belt line. "There," she said with satisfaction. "That ought to get you in, pass or not."

Shane snickered. "I look like a male hooker."

"You look delicious," said Gretchen.

"What about you?"

172

Gretchen took Shane's pocketknife and carefully cut around her cutoffs until they more resembled a denim bikini than shorts. She handed Shane the passes and cut out the pockets. She cut her underwear up each side and pulled it out of her cutoffs. With a sigh, she balled it up and tossed it away. She slit down the front of her tank top and retied the loose halves in a few strategic locations. Then she cut her bra straps and pulled it free, tossing it after her cut-up panties. She cut a strip from Shane's t-shirt, put eye-holes in it, and tied it around her head like a mask. "There, how's that?"

Shane was speechless as he looked her up and down like a child with a new toy.

Gretchen laughed and blushed. "I can't believe I just did this, but it ought to get us in the door, passes or not."

"You look astonishing," said Shane as if his tongue had swelled. "What should I do with this?" He held up the remains of his t-shirt.

Gretchen shrugged, and then laughed as Shane balled it up and tossed it after her discarded clothing. "Let's go get in line."

She felt a lot less self-conscious once they were among the crowd. Several women wore far less; indeed, one seemed to be wearing only string bikini briefs, pasties, and a large snake that coiled around her torso.

They reached the front of the line and the bouncers looked them over. "We have passes," said Gretchen. Shane dug them out of his pocket and showed them off.

The larger bouncer took them and examined them in detail, looking for anything out of place. His eyes went from passes to Gretchen and Shane, who put on their best smiles. The bouncer handed their passes back and yelled over his shoulder, "Gordie! VIPs."

The smaller guy with the mustache rushed up to the doors from inside the Trade Center. "Right this way, sir and ma'am."

The bouncer unclipped the velvet rope. As she passed through the doors, Gretchen imagined a giant was swallowing her up.

She just hoped she wouldn't be chewed up and spit out in pieces.

THIRTEEN

July 13, 1977, 9:00 PM

The Trammps pounded on the expensive speakers set up by the disc jockey. Each thump of the bass drum added to Faith's throbbing headache. The aspirin she'd taken had done very little to alleviate the pain. In spite of her general dislike of the party scene, she was nursing a tumbler of rum and Coke—heavy on the Coke. The sides of the glass sweated in the hot, humid air of the dance party in the Just Cause offices and dampened her glove. Maybe as many as two hundred people were crammed into the conference room, lobby, and side offices. Furniture had been stacked out in the hall to make room for dancers. At some point, the disc jockey and his crew had arrived, wiring speakers into the rooms and setting up multicolored flashing lights for atmosphere. A bartender had set up shop in a corner and mixed drinks for cash. The music played, people danced, drank, or made out with each other in the darker corners of the room. Being among the celebrities of Just Cause was a great aphrodisiac to many, and Faith had walked in on couples—or threesomes or even once an orgy—making love in the back offices or bathrooms.

She hated Wednesday nights.

Back when it was just the heroes getting together and playing poker, she enjoyed the camaraderie. It was fun. It was quiet. It didn't smell like sweating bodies, spilled alcohol, cigarettes, and pot.

She wondered where Bobby was. He might be lurking two floors up in the administrative offices—close enough to be able to say he was there but far enough away that the blasts of noise from the sound system wouldn't drive his ultrasensitive hearing crazy. She thought maybe she ought to seek him out, but then she caught Lionheart's eye. He smiled at her in a way that made her shiver. He raised the hand that wasn't wrapped around a large stein of the thick German beer he preferred and motioned for her to come closer. She approached him.

"Hey," she said, keeping her voice quiet enough so only he could hear it.

He bent down and whispered in her ear, hot breath tickling her neck. She almost hoped he was going to proposition her, because she felt ready to accept it, but instead he said, "Irlene looks like she's about to get into trouble. You take her, I'll take Javier."

Faith turned to look and saw that Irlene was engaged in close conversation with Javier. She swayed on her feet and had to keep drifting up into the air a few inches to keep from falling, which Javier found quite amusing. His gaze kept dropping to Irlene's tight body underneath her form-fitting raspberry-and-cream costume. There was no mistaking his intentions. "Jesus Christ, doesn't he ever quit?"

Lionheart and Faith pushed through the crowd. Faith took Irlene by the elbow and led her under protest toward a wall while Lionheart took the simpler expedient of smacking Javier's head.

"Whuh-whazza matter?" slurred Irlene.

"The matter is you're drunk and about to be another notch on Javier's bedpost," said Faith. "Listen, the man has no shame and no self-control. He could have any number of diseases. Do you really want to let him near you?"

"Diseases? He's got th' clap or somethin'?"

"I don't know," said Faith. "And I hope you never find out. He may be a superhero, but he's also a scumbag and I don't want to see you getting dirtied up by him. Fair enough?"

"Oh-kay," said Irlene. She looked down at her empty glass. "Mebbe I need another drink."

"You better slow down," said Faith.

Irlene glared at her. "I don' need another mother. One's enough. I can take care of myself."

"I hope so," murmured Faith as Irlene shrank down and flitted over the crowd.

Someone pulled at her elbow. She turned to see a slender blonde girl in a denim bikini, cotton mask, and cut-up tank top. A wiry, shirtless young man stood behind her with a heart drawn on his chest in lipstick. Something about the girl looked familiar despite her makeshift mask.

"Ms., uh, Pony Girl? I need to talk to you."

She had a Midwestern accent, like she'd just stepped off the bus from Hicktown, USA. Faith's eyes widened. Not Hicktown; Dyersville. "Are you Gretchen Gumm?"

The girl looked behind her at the young man, who shrugged. "Y-yes. How did you know that?" She put her hands to her mouth in surprise. "Can you read minds?"

Faith laughed. It was such a surprising, innocent thing to hear. "No, I can't, but I've been looking for you. Will you come with me so we can talk somewhere quieter?"

"I guess so."

The young man, certainly Shane Clemens, stuck to Gretchen as Faith led them back to the stairs to the upstairs offices. The bouncer guarding the stairs let them through without a fuss.

"Bobby, are you up here?" Faith spoke in a normal tone; Bobby would hear her even if she whispered.

"In the boardroom," he said.

Faith led Gretchen and Shane to the room where Lane Devereaux handled Just Cause business on a day-to-day basis. Bobby sat in one of the large, overstuffed chairs, his feet up on the table, reading a copy of Time magazine. He straightened up as Faith and the others walked into the room. "Bobby, I'd like to introduce you to Gretchen Gumm. And you would be Shane Clemens, sir?"

"Yes," said the mystified young man.

"I'm Robert Thompson, also called Audio. I'm the administrator of Just Cause," said Bobby. "What in the world are you doing here? We've been combing the city looking for you."

Gretchen sounded surprised as she pulled the mask off her face. "For me?"

"You're the subject of a federal investigation," said Bobby. "You're in a whole lot of trouble, young lady."

Gretchen started to cry. "I didn't mean to kill him. He just wouldn't stop breathing on me."

Faith put a hand on her shoulder. "Easy, Gretchen. Nobody's accusing you of anything right now."

"Maybe she should have, like, a lawyer?" asked Shane.

All the lights in the room shut off, plunging them into darkness. The faint thumping music from two floors down ceased. Gretchen squealed in fear. A few of the overhead lights flickered back on, with a red bulb illuminated over the door. "That's emergency building power," said Faith. "What just happened? Did we blow a fuse or something?"

"Worse than that," said Shane quietly. He was standing by the windows looking out over the city. It looked *wrong*.

New York had gone dark.

~~~

Blood sluiced down Momma's chest, soaking her blouse and the afghan she had folded over her lap despite the heat in the apartment. She thrashed but Harlan held her shoulders down, keeping her helpless. After what seemed like eternity but couldn't have been more than a minute or two, her struggles subsided and blood stopped leaking from the large cut he'd made across her throat.

Harlan looked at the blood on his hands. It sickened him, not because of the terrible thing he'd just done, but because it was unclean. Death was messy, stinky, sticky business up close and personal. He thought perhaps if he were inside his armor, he wouldn't mind it so much. Then he could just hose off the remnants when he was finished.

He went to the bathroom to scrub his hands and arms. While standing at the sink, washing away the blood from his knife, he stared at his reflection. A certain hardness showed on his face where before he'd seen nothing but vestigial baby softness. He was becoming a man, he thought. No, he'd already become a man from his deeds today. He smiled, proud of his accomplishments, and then the bathroom plunged into darkness.

He thought perhaps Momma hadn't paid the electric bill. Then he glanced outside and what he saw stole his breath away.

The city had gone black: no streetlights, no building lights. Only car headlights and strange, bright speckles in the sky. Harlan gasped as he realized he was seeing stars for the first time in his life. They were so beautiful that tears came to his eyes.

He became aware of noises down on the street below. People shouting and screaming, glass breaking. As his eyes adjusted to the darkness, Harlan could see dark shapes moving in and out of the corner liquor store. Someone tossed a rock through a window of the appliance store and soon people began to help themselves to the inventory there as well. Bright light flared as a fire started in a parked car.

Anarchy, thought Harlan with glee. No, that wasn't quite right. He tried again. Chaos. Better, but still not the feeling he sought. Destruction, he realized at last. As much as he wished for it, here he believed he was witnessing the collapse of society.

He stood; he could help in his own, special way.

He had an obligation first. He went into Reggie's room and shook her awake.

"Harlan? I was sleepin'," she mumbled .

"Get up, Reggie. We have to leave."

"Why?" She made no move to get out of her bed, a dark shadow on the lighter shadows of her sheets.

"The power's gone. Bad people are outside stealing things and setting fires. We can't stay here in case they set the building on fire."

She sniffled and he knew she was moments from tears. "Where's Momma?"

"She's outside somewhere, acting just like everyone else." Harlan put his arm around Reggie's shoulders and felt them quaking with sobs. "You got to be strong, Reggie. I'll take you someplace safe." He handed her the stuffed elephant. "Get your shoes on."

They found her sandals in the dark. Reggie squeezed her elephant with one hand and held onto Harlan with the other. "I can't see nothin'," she whispered as they moved through the dark apartment.

Harlan hoped the power wouldn't come back on while they were inside. It wouldn't do any good at all for Reggie to see Momma sitting dead under her blood-soaked afghan. Fortunately, it stayed dark all the way down the stairs and out of the building.

On the street, chaos reigned. People looted stores, fought one another over choice items, or caused wanton destruction. The economy had been in a slump and the poorer folks had really felt the pressure. With this blackout, they acted out their aggression and anxiety the way mobs have since the beginnings of civilization: by rioting.

Reggie shrank close beside him. "Harlan, I'm a-scared. Why ain't there any policemen?"

"Because they don't care what we do here." Harlan tensed as a figure loomed out of the darkness at them. Two loud reports sounded even over the yelling of the looters. The man before them crumpled and fell to the pavement. A boy only three or four years older than Harlan brandished a Saturday Night Special at them.

"Don't touch my shit." He bent to collect the items that had spilled beside the wounded looter: two cartons of cigarettes. The boy stuffed them into his pants and ran, leaving his victim behind.

Reggie began to cry in earnest, and Harlan hurried her down the street toward the junkyard. It wasn't safe to be where desirable goods could be found and looted. The man who'd fallen before them sold his life for twenty packs of cigarettes, and Harlan intended that his life would never go for so little.

More fires flared up as he and Reggie ran. Landlords in Harlem were notorious for not keeping their buildings up to safety codes. Now, when it really mattered, people realized their homes were incendiary death traps. But even as fire consumed buildings, residents left to go steal more goods, like Nero fiddling while Rome burned.

The uncontrolled greed displayed by his neighborhood disgusted Harlan.

What was needed, he decided, was a more sophisticated type of destruction.

"Where are we going, Harlan? I'm tired, and I want Momma and Irlene."

"We're going to the junkyard," Harlan said, panting. "You'll be safe there because nobody will come there to steal anything."

Reggie coughed from the smoke. Harlan's throat burned too. They dashed across a street where a small mob was rocking a police car back and forth. The officers within held on for dear life as the car threatened to overturn.

Destruction, thought Harlan with a grim smile. They ain't seen nothing yet.

~~~

The stadium lights went out in between pitches. Hoots and whistles echoed into the darkness. After a few minutes, the jeers turned into mutters of consternation as people realized the lights had also gone out on the skyscrapers.

"We better do something," said John. "We're about to have a problem on our hands with all these people fumbling around in the dark."

Tommy stood up. "I'm going up to the booth to see if they have any generators and a radio."

"Hurry," said Sundancer. "I smell smoke. Real smoke, not cigarettes."

Tommy shook out his hair. He wished he had his costume; he hated flying without it. Winds swirled around him and he lifted away from the seats to flit over the field toward the announcers' booth. People shouted and pointed as he flew through the darkness.

He slipped in through the open windows of the booth. The frantic game announcers were trying to get any of their equipment to work, while a battery-operated radio babbled about a citywide power failure. The announcers looked up in shock as Tommy descended into their midst.

"I'm Tornado of Just Cause," he said. "John Stone and Sundancer are also here. How can we help?"

"Oh, hell, I didn't recognize you," said one announcer. "The radio said Con Ed is completely down. All Five Boroughs are dark."

Tommy gasped. "I thought that wasn't supposed to be possible after '65."

"Do I look like a power guy?" grunted the announcer. "Hotchkiss went down to fire up the emergency generators. It'll give us PA and emergency lightning but not much else."

"How many people you got here tonight?"

"Aw geez, eleven, maybe twelve thousand. Lotta people in the dark."

A few desultory emergency lights lit up around the field. Tommy could see nervous people milling around in the near darkness. New Yorkers weren't used to seeing the stars overhead and looked like they might be suffering a little agoraphobia. "We got PA," shouted a technician.

"We better do something before we have a panic on our hands," said Tommy.

The announcer leaned in close to his microphone. "Uh, ladies and gentlemen, your attention please. We apologize for the inconvenience. The power's out all over. We ask that for your own safety you remain in your seats until it comes back on."

"Jesus Christ, Carl," called a woman's voice. A flame flared into existence as she struck a match and lowered it to a candle. "Are you trying to get these people killed? You're going to cause a panic!"

"But, Jane," began the announcer.

"Don't you *but, Jane* me. You're a fool." She turned to Tommy. "You and your Just Cause yahoos keep people calm for another couple minutes." She turned to hurry up a corridor.

"What are you going to do?" Tommy called after her.

"Keep them calm after that," she yelled back over her shoulder.

"Where's she going?" Tommy asked.

"Back to the loft," said Carl. "That's Jane, the organist."

"Okay, you heard her. Keep these people calm." Tommy flew through the windows, spiraling down until he could pick John's bulky form out of the shadows. Numerous people had cigarette lighters out, and the stands looked like a mirror of the stars overhead.

"What's the word?" Sundancer hovered a few feet over the seats to keep any stray hands from getting a grope on her.

"Power's out across the city," Tommy said.

"Shit, we'd better get back to headquarters," said Sundancer.

John raised a hand. "No. First and foremost we have to protect these people here. If they stampede for the exits, we're going to have folks crushed to death in the dark."

"Uh, ladies and gentlemen," stammered the PA announcer. "We'll have the lights back on just as soon as possible. Just Cause is here to make sure you are safe, so please stay in your seats."

"Shit," repeated Sundancer. "I guess we have to stay here now."

"The organist said to keep people calm for a few minutes," said Tommy. "I don't know how to do that."

"I do," said John. "Gloria, why don't you give the people a little light show? Take their minds off the darkness."

"Well, for one thing, I don't have my costume. These clothes will burn off in seconds," argued Sundancer.

"Glo," said Tommy. "You were just in *Playboy*. Half the people in this stadium have probably seen you naked already."

"Oh, that's true. I guess it's different though when you can see them looking back at you." Nevertheless, she flew out over the field and hovered somewhere over second base. A glow limned around her and people turned to look, murmuring. As she brightened, she spun around, leaving a trail of light behind her like a human comet. Her clothing burned away to leave her nude, showing off her taut dancer's body, which had let her claim the title of Miss March. Some people averted their eyes and hid the eyes of their children. Others stared unabashedly at her beauty.

Organ music swelled from the stadium PA. It was something familiar, bright and upbeat, and Tommy looked around as fans nodded and grinned at each other. People got the joke immediately and many started to sing along. *Dashing through the snow... in a one horse open sleigh...*

As Christmas music blared from the speakers, Sundancer performed her own intricate aerial ballet, spinning and flitting about like a campfire spark. Tommy and John grinned at each other and bellowed *Jingle Bells* like a couple of fools. For the moment, Tommy could forget about his unrequited feelings, his disenchantment with his job, and his recent behavior.

Instead, he sang Christmas carols in a darkened stadium in July.

~ ~ ~

"Tell me what happened," said Pony Girl. "Start at the beginning."

"Don't you guys have to, I don't know, do something about the power being out?" asked Gretchen. She hadn't really thought as far as what to do once she actually made it to Just Cause, and now that she was confronted by the heroes, she felt very small indeed.

"I'm sure this is just a temporary brownout," said Bobby.

"I hate to tell you this," said Shane, "but temporary brownouts only happen in sections. A citywide power failure like this…" He whistled. "This is a crisis. Trust me, I work for Con Ed. This isn't supposed to even be possible."

"I'll tell you what," said Bobby. "You let me ask my questions here and I won't have you arrested for aiding and abetting. Then when I'm done, we can talk about the power."

"You're going to have people stranded in elevators, trapped in subways," said Shane.

"Shane," interrupted Gretchen. "Please stop. Let me speak my piece."

"Hold on," said Pony Girl. She turned to Shane. "Is it really going to be as bad as that?"

He stared back at the superhero, unflinching under her gaze. "Probably worse."

Pony Girl whispered something to Bobby and then slipped out of the room in a flash, leaving papers flapping in her wake.

"All right," said Bobby. "We're looking into it, but let's get back to you, Ms. Gumm. Tell me why you're here exactly."

Gretchen reached for Shane's hand and squeezed it to comfort herself. "I kind of… something bad happened, and I don't know what else to do."

"Go on."

"There was this boy. And he was hurting me. He wouldn't stop. He wouldn't stop breathing on me." Her tears flowed unchecked. "I just wanted him to stop breathing on me. And something bad happened, and I know it was my fault. I came here so you guys could help me or something."

"Had you ever displayed any abilities before that point?"

"No! I swear I never even had any idea!"

"Well, here's the problem. We've got a dead body clearly killed by parahuman abilities, and the law looks very poorly upon that."

"But he attacked me! He… he r-raped me!" Saying it made her feel ill, but at the same time the admission gave her strength, like she'd named a demon.

"Easy, Ms. Gumm," said Bobby. "I believe you, and understand why it happened. Stress is often the primary factor in manifestation of parahuman abilities. Yours just happens to be inherently more dangerous than most. The most important thing right now is for you to learn to control that ability before anyone else comes to harm." He paused. "Has anyone else come to harm?"

"N-no," sniffled Gretchen. "There was a man who tried to mug me, but I didn't hurt him. Oh, I blew up a rat."

"A rat?"

"She was protecting me," said Shane. "We were in the sewer."

"I'm sorry, how exactly do you fit into all this?" Bobby's attention turned to Shane.

"My cousin asked me to meet Gretchen here when she got to New York. She's been with me all day. She helped me with some work underground and popped a rat that mistook my face for a steak."

Bobby raised an eyebrow at that. "So you've learned some control already? Impressive in such a short time."

"It wasn't like that," said Gretchen. "It was more like a reflex. I didn't have time to think. The power feels kind of like it has a mind of its own." She shuddered. "It scares me."

"Well," said Bobby. "We'll do what we can to help you with controlling it, but there's still the question of the death to answer. Self-defense or not, the Feds take a very dim view of using parahuman abilities to commit any crime, and murder is especially severe."

"But I didn't murder him!" cried Gretchen. "I didn't know it would happen!"

"You did the right thing coming here, to your credit. Mr. Devereaux has a couple of outstanding attorneys on retainer, but given the nature of the crime, defending you will be tricky business."

"What do you mean?" Shane sat up a little straighter. "Isn't self-defense still okay?"

"Sometimes," hedged Bobby. "But it's going to be tough to defend you as a rape victim. A prosecutor has a good chance to convince a jury you were asking for it."

"What?" Gretchen leaped to her feet. The power launched out, eager to squish Bobby head like a balloon, and she had to force it aside to shatter a decorative vase behind him. "You think I wanted this?"

"Of course not. I wouldn't wish that upon anyone, but it's the reality of the court system. And the Feds have already made up their minds you're the bad guy here.

You're lucky to have come here before they found you."

"Oh God," whimpered Gretchen. "I don't want to go to jail. I didn't know it would happen!" She burrowed into Shane's arms.

"Easy. Nobody's going to jail yet. You did the right thing by coming here. I have to take you into custody, but I promise you that Just Cause will do everything we can to help you." Bobby stood and walked around his desk. "You're free to go, Mr. Clemens, but please don't leave town in case we need to speak to you."

Shane shook his head. "I'll stay here with Gretchen."

"That's up to you."

Pony Girl burst back into the office. She looked flustered and concerned. "Bobby, things have gotten bad in town. We're needed."

Bobby turned to Gretchen and Shane. "I'm going to have Javelin keep an eye on the two of you. I trust we'll have no problems?"

Gretchen shook her head.

"No, sir," said Shane.

Bobby nodded and then hurried out of the office after Pony Girl.

FOURTEEN

July 13, 1977, 10:00 PM

"All right, everyone, listen up," called Bobby over the murmurs of the crowd. "This party is officially over. We've got a city-wide emergency to deal with. Power is out across all the Five Boroughs. We've got reports of fires and looting all over the city. The elevators aren't working, so if you want to leave, you've got a whole lot of stairs to go down. You're welcome to stay as guests of Just Cause, but understand it will be as refugees, not party guests." Bobby gave the crowd a stern look. "Bar's closed, and I'm detailing security to make sure it stays that way. Just Cause, join me in the conference room."

The heroes moved from the crowd to the conference room. Faith sat beside Bobby and watched as the other heroes arranged themselves about the table.

"Things have gone to shit, make no mistake about it," said Bobby. "The entire city's going berserk. The cops and fire brigades are stuck in gridlocked traffic with the signals down. We're going to have to pick up the slack. I've got to ask each of you to do some difficult things." His eyes were shadowed, as if exhaustion was already taking its toll. "Rick, I need you here in Manhattan."

189

"Got it," said Lionheart.

"Steel, you've got Staten Island by yourself. I realize that's a huge area, but you're the fastest flier we've got."

"AFFIRMATIVE."

"Irlene, you stay with Faith. You guys will handle Harlem and The Bronx. Stay together. That's probably the most dangerous part of town. Faith, I need you to deliver radios to Tommy, Gloria, and John. They're at Shea Stadium or else they're trying to get back here. I want Tommy and John to cover Queens and Gloria to handle Brooklyn."

"What about me?" Javier looked unenthusiastic about an emergency deployment.

"You're on guard duty. We have the parahuman fugitive from Iowa in-house, and I need someone to keep an eye on her."

Javier snorted. "Wait, I'm a fucking babysitter?"

"You're in no shape to deploy," said Bobby. "But you'll back up Rick here in Manhattan if he needs it." He looked across the table at the rest of the team. "I'll stay here and try to coordinate. Make sure you all have radios. Save lives first, then property if you can. Pace yourselves. There is no backup or relief. And for the love of God, be careful."

The team filed out of the conference room. Faith hung back long enough to bestow a deep kiss upon her husband. "I love you," she whispered to him.

"I love you too. Jesus, I'm really scared about this. It hasn't been half an hour yet and things have regressed into anarchy."

Faith squeezed his hand, and then followed the others out into the lobby. Lionheart followed Steel to the landing deck. He'd changed into his duty outfit of pirate-style boots, waist sash, and loose-fitting trousers, eschewing a shirt in favor of increased freedom of movement. The Soldier could lower him to the ground, saving valuable time. He looked back once, meeting Faith's gaze with his own. Unspoken words traversed the distance between them in that moment before he and the Steel Soldier went over the side.

Faith shook herself. Now was not the time to get caught up in her feelings for the tawny team leader. She rushed into the locker rooms and retrieved spare costumes for Tommy and Gloria. "Can you shrink these, and me?" she asked Irlene. "It would be quicker for you to fly me to the ground like the Soldier did Rick."

"I wish I had some coffee. I think I'm a little drunk." Nevertheless, Irlene raised a hand. The world grew to towering heights over Faith. She didn't feel any different, but staring up at Irlene was like standing beside a raspberry-colored skyscraper. Irlene's truck-sized hand descended with such astonishing speed that Faith stumbled. At her small size, she tripped and hit the ground before she even reacted to the fall. It didn't hurt in the least, like she was too small to be injured.

"Are you okay?" roared Irlene as her gargantuan hand closed about Faith.

"Yes." Faith hoped her tiny voice would carry over the distance. "This is really weird."

"Okay, hang on." Irlene's grip was gentle, and Faith found plenty of purchase in the threads of the giant gloves. The world swirled around Faith as Irlene flew off the open deck and spiraled downward toward the dark plaza below. The shadows of Manhattan felt sinister to Faith. Great hulking buildings loomed over her like tangible fear.

Without lights to give her a sense of perspective, Faith became disoriented. When Irlene touched the ground, the shock jarred her so much her teeth clacked together. Irlene set her onto the cement and stepped back. A moment later, Faith returned to her original size.

Irlene bent over and vomited into a nearby flowerbed.

"Jesus," said Faith. "Are you all right?"

Irlene wiped her mouth with a shaking hand. "I feel a little better." She burped. "Too much to drink."

"You need to watch yourself. You're just a kid."

The younger girl shrugged. "Did I carry you down okay?"

"That was the strangest thing I've ever experienced," said Faith. "And I was at Woodstock." She watched as a slow, steady trickle of exhausted folks left the Trade Center. Many of them gasped from the exertion of descending dozens of flights of stairs.

A spark shot off into the sky, heading south, the Steel Soldier headed for Staten Island. A moment later, a bike roared and Lionheart rolled up next to them on his Harley. "Be careful, you two," he said. His eyes reflected starlight as they looked straight at Faith.

"You too," she said and turned to Irlene. "Let's go."

~~~

Harlan led Reggie through the darkened streets, which were punctuated by numerous fires. The flames backlit looters as they rushed in and out of buildings with armloads of stolen merchandise. At one point, Harlan saw somebody crash a car right through a storefront to knock down the security gates.

Reggie staggered on behind him, her elephant clutched to her chest and tears running unabated down her dirty face. "Harlan," she gasped. "I'm so tired. Where's Momma and Irlene?"

"We're almost there, Reg." He pointed down the street. Past a couple burning cars on a block mostly empty of people because the tenements were uninhabited, the junkyard was a shadowy haven. "You'll be safe there."

They continued down the street without anyone hassling them. Harlan showed Reggie his secret entrance. He was careful to disengage his security measures; after all Reggie had done for him, it wouldn't be right for his oversight to allow her to be killed.

After all, he'd promised to protect her.

Darkness bathed the junkyard. Only the stars overhead showed where the piles of crushed cars ended and the sky began. Reggie shrank against him. "It's scary here."

"Don't worry," he said. "I've got a generator stashed here. I can give you some light, but not too much because I don't want anyone to come bother you."

He took her to his Volkswagen Bus-turned-workshop. He shook out a blanket thrown onto a haphazard pile of shredded tires that he sometimes used as a cot. "You can lie down here. I have to take care of some things and then I'll be back for you."

"Are you going to find Momma?"

"I'll try." Harlan fired up the small generator he'd built from a Datsun motor. A pair of headlights hanging from the van's roof began to glow. For the first time since leaving the house, Harlan could see the hollow look in Reggie's eyes.

"Want to see what I built?" he asked.

Reggie nodded and yawned. Harlan went to his giant robot and pulled away the tarpaulins covering it. Like some great movie monster of old, the machine hunched down, folded in on itself, a chrysalis.

He unhooked it from the maintenance bank of batteries and bustled around it, sealing panels and ports with the aid of a flashlight from his tools. In spite of her exhaustion, Reggie watched him work with interest. "What is it?"

"My giant robot." Harlan struggled and sweated over a recalcitrant fuel cutoff valve.

"What's it called?"

Harlan paused. "Destroyer," he said at last. It felt like the right name. If he'd had a bottle handy, he'd have smashed it across the suit's torso in a christening.

"It looks scary." Reggie popped a thumb into her mouth.

"It looks that way to keep people from messing with me," said Harlan. "It's to keep me safe while I'm inside it."

"Oh. Are you going to use it to look for Momma?"

"Yes." Harlan finished his exterior checks just in time; his flashlight was dying.

No reason to wait any longer. "Wait here for me. I'll be back, okay?"

"Okay."

"Now this is really important, Reg. You have to stay inside this van, because I'm going to turn on my security systems when I leave."

"What's secur'ty?"

"It'll make sure nobody bothers you while I'm gone, but you have to stay in the van or else you might get hurt."

She huddled down onto the blanket inside the workshop and stared wide-eyed at him. "Okay."

Harlan climbed up the exterior ladder over the lower semi cab that housed the engines and hydraulics to operate the heavy, articulated legs. A turntable salvaged from a crawler crane separated the upper cab, from which dangled the four arms. Harlan's questing fingers and toes found the familiar handholds even in the darkness. He perched on a narrow ledge and swung open the access door into the cockpit. A few lights blinked slow and regular to inform him the systems were standing by.

He pulled shut the door and dogged it tight with a lever handle from an industrial freezer. Even before he settled into the command chair, he started flipping a row of activation switches. Power systems. Hydraulics. Weapons. Environmental.

Cool, refreshing air from the scrubber system blew in Harlan's face as he slipped his legs into the suit's control sleeves and pulled a helmet down over his head. A tiny slide projector sent on-board data onto his visor so he didn't have to look away from the video screens. The suit had no windows; windows could be breached. Nothing but layer upon layer of armor would be between Harlan and the outside world.

He grasped the joysticks, feeling the suit rumbling to life under his tutelage. All data showed systems nominal. The suit quivered like a racehorse before the bell as it awaited Harlan's final command to make it operational. He thumbed the starter and two powerful Diesel engines roared to life beneath his feet.

The noise was staggering. He put *soundproofing* at the top of his list of improvements. The belt around his waist and hips supported enough of his weight that he could move his legs within the control sleeves. He engaged the twin clutches and flexed his legs. The suit rewarded him by lurching upward into a standing position, the stacked semi cabs supported by the heavy hydraulic legs.

He took a tentative step and the suit mimicked his movement, shifting forward several feet. Harlan laughed and moved the joysticks. The suit's arms raised, lowered, and flexed, first as a unit and then each on their own.

The motion-sensitive cameras spotted Reggie and zoomed in on her. She clutched her elephant wide-eyed, but she didn't look as afraid of the suit as she had the rioting outside.

He raised the suit's grasping claw and waved at Reggie. She pulled her thumb out of her mouth long enough to wave back. Harlan smiled and thumbed on his external speakers.

"STAY HERE, REG. I'LL BE BACK SOON."

~~~

Sundancer lit up the inside of Shea Stadium like her namesake, twirling in the air like a ballerina. Tommy used gentle puffs of air to encourage fans to work their way out of the seats. When folks tarried too long, maybe to get one more eyeful of Sundancer's lithe, nude form, John provided less-subtle encouragement by bellowing at them in his stentorian tones.

"Hey, you guys," called Sundancer toward the Mets players who loitered in the dugout. "You could at least comp my tickets for the free show!"

"Far as I'm concerned, you can have free tickets for life," shouted Joe Torre from the bench, to much laughter.

Tommy saw Faith and the new girl Irlene arrive at the stadium entrance. John waved at them and bellowed for them to come on inside, as Sundancer couldn't safely leave without plunging the stadium back into darkness.

The five heroes congregated at the pitcher's mound.

"How bad is it?" asked John as Faith passed out the radios and handed costumes to Tommy and Sundancer.

"Bad," she said. "The entire city's gone dark. Nobody knows anything. Phones are sporadic and we can't get through to Con Ed. What we do know is we've got people looting and rioting all over town."

"And starting fires too," said Irlene.

"Christ," said Tommy. "Why would people do that?"

"People are assholes," said Sundancer. She pulled on her white and yellow fireproof leotard without modesty. After spending a good half hour floating naked over the crowd at Shea Stadium, she had nothing to hide.

"It's getting worse," said Faith. "Somebody took a shot at me while I was running. Obviously, he missed, but it's chaos out there. Cops can't get around because of traffic jams."

"Which leaves us where?" Tommy shucked out of his shorts and gratefully pulled on his costume. He felt weird using his powers without the cape billowing around him.

"Under-staffed," said Faith. "Tommy, you and John stay here in Queens. Gloria, head to Brooklyn. Do what you can. Check in with Bobby."

"Wait, that's it? We've got Queens? What the hell are the two of us supposed to do with a whole borough?" Tommy gaped at her.

Faith shrugged. "Your job. Be a hero." She looked worried. "And we'll see you later."

"Where are you going?" From the sound of John's voice, he'd also picked up on Faith's concern.

"Harlem." She sped out of the stadium with Irlene following close behind.

"Jesus Christ," said Sundancer. Over the smell of stale popcorn and the grass of the outfield, all of them could smell the greasy soot of burning structures in the air. She flared up to brilliance. "Good luck, you guys." Tommy felt heat wash across his face as she went incandescent and hurtled into the night sky like a living meteor.

John watched her fly away, and then turned to Tommy. "I'll probably have to stay in the immediate vicinity. I'm just not quick enough to cover a lot of territory."

Tommy snapped his fingers. "Subways. There will be people trapped in them. You'd be best at getting them out."

"Good idea," said John. "But I'll be out of radio contact underground."

"Well, just be sure to pop your head up once in awhile to check in," said Tommy. He darted in like a hummingbird and brushed his lips against John's cold stone cheek. In the darkness, nobody would see. "Be careful, my friend."

John spluttered, surprised. "What was that for?"

"For luck," said Tommy. His cape inflated like a parachute and the winds lifted him up and out of the stadium.

He circled once, looking for spots indicative of trouble. A few fires stood out in the darkness, but none looked very large and fire crews were already battling two. Tommy's powers weren't very effective at controlling or stopping fires. Wind tended to worsen a conflagration.

Looters, on the other hand, he could handle. He descended upon a block rife with broken storefronts. Shadowy figures rushed into the buildings and emerged with whatever treasures they found within.

Tommy floated over the intersection, high enough not

to be struck by any passing vehicles, raised his hands, and concentrated.

Air pressure built in a column around him. Breezes swirled around his wrists and ankles. He forced the wind up the street. It gathered speed as it pushed outward from him, picking up accumulated grit and soot from weeks without rain. He increased the wind speed by gradual steps until a veritable gale tore up the street, sandblasting parked cars and people alike.

Looters shrieked and ran for cover. Tommy drifted along the street, pushing the wind before him like a snowplow. When he saw potential looters running into a shop, he used a concentrated air burst to knock them off their feet.

"Go home," he shouted at people. "Stop destroying your neighborhood!"

Anyone who yelled back at him received a blast of air to the face, often sending them head over heels. Tommy had a lot of frustrations to work out and it felt good to cut loose with his powers. He swept the entire street clean of dust and debris, drifting back and forth to target any diehard looters. He knew the anarchy would start up again as soon as he flew away, but for a few minutes he felt he was doing some good by protecting this one stretch of street.

Since saving the whole city was beyond his abilities, he thought perhaps he could save one store, one life. That made him think of Miranda. She was the only person he knew who lived in Queens. He'd already made a difference in her life.

Maybe he could again.

~~~

Shane held Gretchen as she sniffled. The exhaustion of the day had finally caught up with her and her emotions were running wild.

"I'm sorry," she said. "I'm not usually so weepy."

"It's all right," said Shane. "You've had a rough day."

"You're so sweet." She tilted her head back to kiss him. As their lips parted, she felt the day's stresses melt away.

"I'd tell you to get a room, but it looks like you already did," said an accented voice.

Gretchen jumped and spun around to see a leering Javelin leaning up against the doorjamb with his helmet tucked under one arm. "Don't stop on my account," he said. "I like to watch."

Disgusted at Javelin's lewd behavior, Gretchen leaned away from Shane. If she'd been back home, working the Diner, she'd have told him off like any other rude customer. But she didn't feel like she could do that here, so she stayed quiet.

Javelin laughed. "I'm just playing with you." He strode into the room. Despite his bravado and attitude, Gretchen could see he wasn't feeling well at all. His skin had the pallor of sickness beneath the natural tan and his eyes were bloodshot . As he passed by Gretchen and Shane, she could smell the stink of alcohol on him even though he didn't act at all like he'd been drinking. She knew people like that back in Dyersville, who'd spent so many years drinking that they seemed to sweat alcohol like they really had pickled their insides.

He flopped into a chair and threw his booted feet up onto the tabletop, marring the surface with his armor plating. "So," he said. "You're the big bad parahuman killer Bobby told me about." He sniffed in disdain. "I thought you'd be taller."

"Now wait just a goddamn minute," began Shane.

"What are you going to do, pretty boy?" asked Javelin.

Gretchen put a hand on Shane's chest. "Leave it. He's just an asshole."

Javelin smiled and held out his hands. "Guilty as charged. I guess I'm stuck watching you while the rest of the team is out saving the city. I'm Javier."

"Gretchen. He's Shane."

"They tell me you killed some guy back in Iowa." Javier inspected one of his armored gauntlets.

Shane bristled. "You're not being very sensitive."

Javier looked at him. "Fuck you and your sensitivity. So this asshole, did he deserve it?"

Gretchen shuddered at the memory, but somehow Javier's rough speech and dispassionate attitude lent her a new reserve of strength. "Yeah he did." She felt ready to take him on in an argument.

"Good." Javier slipped off the gauntlet and pulled a small toolkit from his belt.

"Good?" repeated Gretchen. "You approve?"

Javier popped a plate off his gauntlet with a screwdriver and started to fuss with some of the intricate machinery and electronics underneath. "I got no problem with one less asshole in the world."

"What is that you're working on?" asked Gretchen.

"Technical," said Javier.

"I see," said Gretchen in her best frosty tone, but it didn't encourage the hero to expound further so she changed she subject. "What's it like, being in Just Cause?"

Javier set the glove down and leaned back as he considered the question. "Boring as shit," he said at last. "The parties are good, and you get laid a lot, but besides that there just isn't much to do."

"What do you mean? You're superheroes. Don't you go out and fight crime?"

Javier snorted. "It's been years since we had any parahuman criminals. Except you, of course, and you aren't exactly worth calling out the entire team for."

"I'm not a criminal!" Gretchen felt her cheeks grow hot.

"You killed a guy. That's murder. Still a crime the last time I checked."

The power yammered at Gretchen, begging to be let loose upon the man in the burnished armor. She forced it back down. "I was being raped," she growled through clenched teeth. Javier had her mad enough to spit nails, as her father liked to say.

Javier shrugged. "You already said he was an asshole. Good that he's dead. Doesn't change the fact that you broke the law. That's why you're here."

"Why are you here?" Shane asked Javier. "You said it's boring. You've got sharp technical skills. You could probably make a mint in the private sector."

Javier grinned. "In the private sector, I'd be just another engineer. Sure, I'd be rich, but foxy young girls don't get all juicy over engineers. Here, I'm like a movie star. I'm famous. We all are."

"That's it?" Gretchen was incredulous. "You've got powers and all you do is use them for sex? That's the stupidest thing I ever heard. What a waste."

Javier shrugged. "I busted up a drug deal this morning. Got to stay sharp in case anything ever gets out of hand."

"Well, I guess that's something," said Gretchen.

"Then I went back to my place and had a threesome. It's the price of stardom." His face clouded. "Bitches ripped me off while I was sleeping."

Gretchen shook her head. Javier lived in a different reality from her. She doubted she'd ever qualify to be a superhero, but she told herself that if she ever did, she'd act like one.

FIFTEEN

July 13, 1977, 11:00 PM

Harlem was like a war zone.

After a few minutes, Faith and Irlene realized they couldn't stop every looter or douse every fire. At first, Irlene would shrink looters down to the size of G.I. Joe dolls, which was enough to keep all but the most motivated thieves from continuing. She assured Faith it wore off after several hours.

Faith had appropriated a hefty socket wrench and used it to open fire hydrants near burning buildings or cars. With Irlene's help in shrinking heavy items and then returning them to normal size, Faith could direct the outflows towards the blazes.

Eventually, though, there were too many people in the streets and too many fires burning for the two heroes to do much more than just save those in immediate danger. Whether it was Irlene flying a shrunken family to safety through a fourth-floor window or Faith scouting out a tenement block to search for more trapped victims, they were running themselves ragged.

Finally, Irlene couldn't do it anymore, and she sank down onto a rooftop sobbing. Faith put her arm around the frazzled, exhausted teenager and tried to console her. The four years' age difference between them felt like a vast gulf to Faith.

"I don't even know if my family's okay," Irlene said between sobs.

"How far away are they?" Faith stroked the girl's hair.

"I don't even know what street we're on," cried Irlene.

Faith told her the last street sign she remembered seeing.

"Maybe a mile, mile and a half." Irlene wiped her eyes. She'd already discarded the raspberry-colored mask as impractical, complaining it interfered with her vision.

Faith pulled out her radio. "Then there's no reason we can't go check on them. We've been running at top speed for close to two hours now. I'm calling a break."

Irlene sniffled. "I thought that's what we were doing up here."

Faith shook her head. "Bobby, are you there?"

"Yeah, babe. How are you guys doing out there?"

"It's bad, Bobby, really bad. I don't know how much of this side of town will even be left by the morning."

"Things are bad all over. People are acting like animals. I'm afraid of what the death count will be when this is all over."

"Listen, we're going to go check in on Imp's family. We're not far from them."

"Ten-four. Hey, what's that noise?"

Faith stopped and listened. She heard the crackle of flames, people shouting on the street below, and glass breaking. "Just normal rioting sounds, if there is such a thing."

"No, beneath that. Deep, almost subsonic. Rhythmic. It almost sounds like—"

Faith still couldn't hear what Bobby was describing. "Like what?"

"Like Godzilla," said Bobby.

Faith didn't laugh. Over the years, she'd learned to trust

Bobby's parahuman hearing without question. "I wish you were here so you could pinpoint it."

"I wish we were both in Aruba," said Bobby. "It's getting louder. Or closer. If I can hear it over your radio, it's got to be close enough you could hear it any second."

Just then, Faith felt a vibration in the building's rooftop that tickled the gravel against her ass. It repeated, accompanied by a low thud.

"I'll call you back," she said and tucked away the radio.

"What is it?" Irlene leaned in close.

"Do you feel that?"

"Yeah."

It came around a corner like a Detroit engineer's fevered nightmare. People on the streets screamed at the twenty-five-foot-tall fire-breathing monstrosity. One woman dropped an armful of looted clothes, turned, and ran face-first into an overturned car to fall unconscious beside it. Other people ran past her to save themselves. A dog ran out, yipping and barking at the giant until a heavy mechanical foot stomped the animal into pulp.

Faith stared at the behemoth in frank disbelief. Her brain tried to resolve what she could see in the reflection of street fires. Four massive articulated legs carried two huge Peterbilt semi-tractor cabs stacked atop each other. Two arms lay flat against one cab while two others spread out to foment destruction. One arm rang like a bell with a huge rotary saw blade. It screamed and threw a cascade of sparks as the machine sliced the roof off a car and the heads off its occupants. The other featured huge hydraulic claws that snipped off streetlamps as if they were tulip stems. Every few steps, it released a blast of liquid fire to set a car or building on fire. Headlights ringed the upper cab and displayed the results of the machine's destructive path.

A burning man leaped from an ignited car and rolled on the ground, screaming in pain. Overturned cars, buildings going up in flames, and people screaming in fear, panic, and pain all competed for Faith's attention.

"Jesus," whispered Faith. She realized Irlene stood beside her, staring with equal shock down at the hellish intruder below. "Can you you shrink it down?"

"Oh, hell no," said Irlene. "It's too big. Look at it. I don't want to get anywhere near that thing." The machine used its huge pincer to reach up and pull down a darkened rooftop sign for Wendell's, bulbs shattering amid the wire frame and glass raining down onto the pavement. It flung the sign across the street through the unbroken panes of a diner and then sprayed the front of the building with more napalm. More screams erupted from within the diner as those who'd sought shelter there were crushed or burned.

Faith grabbed her radio again. "Bobby, come in. Oh God, are you there?"

"Faith? What's the matter?"

"It's some kind of giant machine. It's destroying Harlem. I don't think we can take it down. We need help. Send everyone."

"Everyone?" With a roar of hydraulics and Diesel engines, the behemoth hurled a telephone pole like a spear. It smashed through the side of a three-story building and out the roof to burst open a water tank in an explosion of mist and debris.

"Yes, everyone!" screamed Faith into the radio. "Get us some fucking backup!" She was shaking in fear. The machine punched a tenement building and knocked the entire brick facade down about its ankles. People cried out amid the wreckage as bricks rained down onto them.

"I'm dispatching them now. Where are you exactly?"

"Just follow the fires," said Faith, and shoved her radio into her belt. She turned to Irlene, who had curled up into a fetal position on the rooftop. She hauled the frightened girl to her feet. "Irlene, don't freak out on me now. I need you, girl. You've got to save people. Forget the machine, forget the buildings and cars and fires. You've got to save lives. You're perfect for that job."

"Why, what are you going to do?"

"I'm going to try and stop it."

~ ~ ~

Harlan floated in a glorious rapture of destruction as he guided the suit down the street. Outside, people screamed like panicked ants and buildings crumbled under his onslaught, but Harlan only heard the roar of the Diesels and the hiss of hydraulics. Blasts of flame ignited stunted trees, parked cars, and storefronts, but Harlan was cool in air-conditioned comfort.

The suit felt like an extension of his body. He moved his legs and it walked. He reached for things with his right hand and the great claws closed around them. Pulling a trigger rewarded him with a burst of his junkyard-made napalm from the pressurized tanks below him. The saw blade on his left hand sliced through brick and metal like a hot knife through butter.

The more he tested the suit's capabilities, the less he felt he was wearing it. He was leaving behind the pupa of his defenseless, powerless self and giving birth to his true nature. He was Destroyer, and the screams of the fallen were like a fanfare announcing his arrival into the world.

He reached down with his claw, crunched it into the side of some kind of small imported car, and heaved. Destroyer threatened to overbalance and he had to widen his stance, but the four legs held him firm. The car's tires came off the ground and he hefted it up to show the horrified onlookers. Before he could hurl it into them, the sheet metal failed and the car smashed to the pavement. No matter, he thought with glee. He braced three of his legs and booted it with the fourth. It didn't sail like a football, which Harlan would have loved, but it did flip into the side of the Korean grocery store, pinning several people beneath it.

He hosed them all down with napalm for good measure. If they'd had any sense, they'd have run away long ago. Now they were getting what they deserved, just like the whole neighborhood. Urban renewal, Destroyer-style.

He sauntered across the street, pure attitude on four legs, and sliced through a streetlamp with his buzzsaw. It made a satisfying crash when it fell and an even more satisfying crunch when he crushed it underfoot.

Harlan giggled. He couldn't ever remember having this much fun in his life. If only Gretchen could see him now, wouldn't she be impressed. She could be his Fay Wray and he could be King Kong. Except in Harlan's story, the giant monster would bring down the whole city.

Something on his main monitor gave him pause. A figure stood in the middle of the street, facing him without running away. He touched a couple switches to activate the servomotors and focused a pair of searchlights from an old police car.

It was Pony Girl of Just Cause, and she was in his road. Soot and sweat stained her face and costume, and she looked like she'd already had a hell of a fight without his help. Instead of fleeing like any intelligent being, she stood her ground.

It would have been so easy to just unlimber the bolt guns and turn her into so much hamburger, but Harlan's curiosity was piqued. He flipped on the external microphones.

"Hey, is there somebody inside that thing?" she called.

The question caught Harlan off guard. He'd expected empty threats and demands. He activated his own microphone. It processed his voice through a vocoder and several effects pedals he'd found in the wreckage of a van that had once belonged to a band called Shrew Tamers, according to the garish paint on the side. "YES," he said. Destroyer's speakers gave his voice a delicious baritone that shook dust from cracks in building walls.

Pony Girl put her hands on her hips. "Huh," she said. "Okay, I want you to shut off your engine or whatever, and I'm going to need to see your license and registration."

"You... what?" Harlan blinked in confusion. "I don't have one."

"Operating a vehicle without a license is a crime," said Pony Girl. "So is vandalism, arson, and littering." She pointed at him. "And murder." She nodded toward the car Harlan had swiped aside. She hadn't made any attempt to help those people. What kind of hero was she, anyway? A smart one, Harlan realized. She knew those people were beyond help, and so she'd ignored them. Here was an opponent who would be worth his mettle, willing to sacrifice the little people for her own greater good.

She was going to be dangerous.

"Now we can do this the easy way or the hard way," she called.

"What's the easy way?"

Pony Girl's smile was devoid of any humor. "You cooperate."

"No way!" Harlan hated how emotional he sounded, even despite the vocoder effects. Surely, she could see he was just a kid. And she was in Just Cause, the greatest superhero team in history. What chance did he have against them if they brought their full might to bear against Destroyer?

"Last chance," said Pony Girl. "Then we peel you right out of that ugly monstrosity."

Her last word galvanized Harlan. Monstrosity? Ugly? Destroyer was his greatest achievement!

"You and what army? All I see is you." He touched a control and the arms bearing the bolt guns took on primary control functions. He lowered them and pointed them at her. "And all you are is dead meat, hero."

The bolt guns chattered and blasted chunks of pavement high into the air, but Pony Girl was already gone. Harlan glanced from screen to screen. Destroyer had some awkward blind spots and insufficient lighting for such dark conditions. Already Harlan was adding things to his list of improvements. 360-degree vision. Radar. Infrared detection.

Pony Girl popped up from behind a car and hurled a rock at him. Her arm blurred with super speed and Destroyer rang with the impact. A monitor screen went dark.

Harlan reacted fast, triggering a blast of napalm that turned Pony Girl's cover into a raging inferno.

"COME ON!" He banged Destroyer's arms together.

And it was on.

~~~

Tommy drifted through the streets of Queens, helping people and stopping looters when he could. It seemed like the whole city had freaked out. He wondered if the rest of the world would follow suit. As long as he'd lived in New York, it seemed as the Big Apple went, so did the nation, and as America went, so did the world.

Perhaps it was the pervasive feeling of disenchantment in America that had led to the bizarre antisocial behavior of the denizens of her premiere city. People couldn't afford gas, couldn't afford food, couldn't find work. No wonder they were looting.

Tommy blasted air at the feet of a fleeing thief laden with cartons of cigarettes. Packs of Camels and Marlboros scattered in the wind. "Go home," said Tommy. "There are people out here far more dangerous than me."

The boy's eyes widened as he took in Tommy's flowing cape and hair. He nodded and said, "Yes, sir." Then, as Tommy flew away, he looked back to see the boy retrieving his spilled cigarettes.

Nothing ever changes, thought Tommy. He started to look for a phone book. Every pay phone he came across had been vandalized, with the phone book ripped out. He wondered if any of the looted stores along the streets had directories, but it would be his luck to be mistaken for a looter and shot by police. Tommy had several parahuman abilities, but being bulletproof was not one of them.

He swooped down to scoop a pedestrian clear as a car jumped the curb and crashed right through the front window of a liquor store. The young man he'd rescued yelled in fright and beat at Tommy's hands as they held him. Fed up, he dropped the fellow from several feet up. The young man bounced off the roof of a Chevrolet and rolled onto the street, bellowing in angry pain. "You're welcome," hissed Tommy. He turned and vented his anger against the two looters who'd crashed the store, blasting their bottles into shards around them until they could only cower in fear.

He grabbed a young man laden with a record player and smashed him up against a brick wall. The record player fell to the ground in pieces. "Stop it," yelled Tommy as he punched the man in the face over and over. "Stop destroying everything!"

The young man held up his hands and blubbered through split lips and a bloodied nose. "Doan hit me no mo', man, I'm sorry!"

Appalled at himself, Tommy dropped the man and fled, slipping up and over several blocks. He couldn't do it anymore. Watching these people he was supposed to be protecting as they acted like some brainless herd of frightened cattle made him feel like throwing up.

He crashed down to a bench by a bus stop, his blood pounding in his ears and cold sweat seemed to seep from every pore. In the distance, he could hear a cacophony of destruction: glass breaking, sirens, and angry shouts. He dug his fists into his ears against it. How could he fight an entire city?

When he looked up, he saw a phone booth across the street with an intact directory dangling from its braided steel cord. He blinked at it, not quite daring to believe his luck had changed. Shadows stole through the darkness nearby, but none stopped to look at him as he pulled out a small flashlight from his belt and thumbed through the K section of the white pages.

Kovacs... Kovchenko... Kovnesky! There were fewer listings than he'd hoped and only one M. Kovnesky.

Bobby's voice from the radio interrupted his thoughts. "All Just Cause members converge on Harlem at your best speed. Pony Girl and Imp have encountered a significant threat and need immediate backup."

Tommy couldn't believe his ears. The phrase *significant threat* meant an opponent of parahuman caliber. His eyes widened as the meaning sank in past the disillusioned fog in his brain.

A parahuman opponent.

Purpose flowed back into Tommy like someone had turned on a tap. He looked down at the page clutched in his fingers. Miranda would have to wait. He tore the page free from the book and shoved it into his belt.

"This is Tornado, responding from Queens," he said into the radio. Other voices echoed his: Sundancer's, the Steel Soldier's, even that of a desultory Javelin. He didn't hear John respond, but he was probably underground where the radios didn't reach. Lionheart said he was busy with a large building fire and attendant rescues. Bobby cleared him to continue.

Glorious winds filled Tommy's cape and bore him aloft. He spun around once as he rose to get his bearings. Long Island was a dark blotch against the distant Jersey shoreline, peppered with stray fires and headlights. He spun up the winds to the speed of his namesake and hurtled across the river, heading north towards Harlem, where most of the fires were concentrated.

He spiraled once over town, but Faith's opponent was easy to spot from overhead. It was some kind of gigantic humanoid machine, standing amid a veritable inferno of burning buildings. It twisted around, waving multiple arms in a futile attempt to hit a red blur that wove around and underneath it.

"Jesus," said Tommy as the machine lumbered against a building and collapsed the brick construction. He bent at the waist, dropping into a screaming power dive with a column of compressed air ahead of him like a battering ram. His stomach flip-flopped and his vision grew spotty as he closed on the mechanical behemoth at incredible speeds.

He barely dodged the recoil of air against the machine. If it had hit him, he'd have been splattered across the sky like a bug on a windshield. The force of his compressed wind staggered the monstrosity, which looked like its builder had cobbled it together from wrecked vehicles. It splayed its huge feet and kept its balance.

Tommy slowed his rushing pace to really look at the creation for the first time. He'd given it his best, hardest shot, and hadn't done worse than crack a couple of headlights.

The machine reached down to rip a bus stop bench from the sidewalk and hurled it at Tommy. He dodged the missile easily enough, but there was no mistaking murderous intent.

"Shit, we're in trouble," he murmured.

~~~

Bobby's call to action came across Javier's helmet radio. Gretchen could hear the underlying panic in his voice. The Puerto Rican didn't look up from his tinkering.

"Aren't you going to acknowledge that?" asked Gretchen.

"Nope. I'm busy guarding a dangerous parahuman criminal." A sour look crossed his face, as if he'd burped up a little vomit. "Besides, I'm still way too fucking hung over."

"You are a sorry excuse for a superhero," said Shane. "I can't believe I used to look up to you guys. You're a bunch of drunks and addicts."

"Not everyone. Mostly just me. But here, if it'll make you happy …" He picked up his helmet and reached inside to touch a switch. "Javelin, acknowledging." He set the helmet back down beside him and got to work once more.

Gretchen shook her head in sadness. How were people like this going to help her?

Bobby burst into the room. "What are you doing?" he asked Javier, incredulous at the man's disinterested demeanor.

"Guarding." Javier gave Bobby a canny smile.

"I need you out there. Faith's facing down some kind of giant monster machine by herself."

Javier held up his dissected glove as evidence. "I'm kind of in pieces here. Not really in any shape to battle robots or whatever it is."

"Goddamn it, Javier." Bobby stalked around the table. "Get off your ass and go help my wife!"

"What, Ricky's too busy?"

Bobby grabbed Javier by the shoulders and threw him backwards out of his chair. Shane leaped to his feet. The power in Gretchen begged to be set free again but she held it back.

"You son of a bitch," growled Bobby. "You get your ass out of here right now. If you don't go back up your teammates, I'll throw your ass out of here for good."

"You wouldn't dare." Javier rubbed the back of his head where it had bounced off the wall.

"Want to try me?"

Without another word, Javier collected his disassembled gauntlet and left the conference room.

"God, what an asshole. I don't know why you even put up with him," said Shane.

Bobby flung himself into a chair and massaged his temples. "I don't either."

"How bad is it out there?" asked Gretchen.

"Bad," said Bobby. "People are rioting and looting and setting fires everywhere."

"Maybe I could help," said Gretchen.

Bobby shook his head. "It's safer for you here."

"No, I'm serious." She turned to Shane. "Can I borrow your lighter?"

He handed it to her. It was a scarred Zippo with a faded American flag painted on one side. Gretchen spun the wheel and locked it on. The tiny flame flickered in the darkness. She set the lighter down on the tabletop and raised her hand, concentrating.

The power leaped out to form a perfect bubble of nothingness around the flame, which simply winked out. Gretchen focused on the vacuum, and instead of releasing it, shrank it down to nothing, preventing it from making a miniature sonic boom.

She turned with a proud smile for Bobby. "I can put fires out."

Bobby shook his head. "That's great, and it would be useful, but I can't let you out of here. You're a murder suspect. Devereaux would have my ass."

"Then send someone out with me," said Gretchen. "I want to help. I want to do something to help people instead of hurting them."

"I can't, I'm sorry. I don't have anyone left," said Bobby. "I've got a goddamned giant robot tearing up Harlem in the middle of this blackout. We're spread too thin."

"Harlem?" Shane looked worried. "That's my area. I know a lot of people there."

A harried-looking young man in a sweat-stained button-down shirt hurried into the room and passed Bobby a folded note. He opened it and read it. Lines of consternation appeared on his brow. He nodded at the messenger, who left as quickly as he'd arrived.

"What's the matter?" asked Gretchen.

Bobby stood and took a deep breath. "Change of plans. You want to help? I'm going to let you help."

"You are? Why?"

"The Federal agents hunting you are returning here any minute. If they know I've been sheltering you without notifying them that we took you into custody, they can arrest me for obstructing an official investigation."

"Jesus," said Shane. "They'd do that?"

"In a heartbeat," said Bobby. "The FBI has never liked Just Cause ever since we came out of hiding in the Fifties. Any chance they get to make us look bad, or worse yet, shut us down, they'll take it. And I spent the afternoon with these two guys. They're scumbags. They've already made up their minds about you, Ms. Gumm. You'd be lucky only to be arrested. Guys like that tend to shoot first and ask questions later."

"Wh-what should I do?" Gretchen felt her momentary bravado evaporate in the face of government agents who only saw her as a murderer.

Bobby appeared to come to a decision of some sort. "Come with me. If you're going to be out in the field representing Just Cause, we can't have you looking like that. You either," he added as he looked at Shane's shirtless torso.

"Wait, what are you doing?" asked Shane as he and Gretchen hurried after Bobby to the team locker rooms.

"I'm trying to keep your girlfriend out of prison," said Bobby. "We've got to get the public's opinion on her side. If she's out there fighting fires and saving lives, it'll be very hard for the Feds to quietly put her away."

"I don't understand," said Gretchen.

Bobby thrust some coveralls like he wore at her and Shane. "Congratulations, you two. I'm officially inducting you into Just Cause."

SIXTEEN

July 14, 1977, 12:00 AM

Faith danced away from the machine's chattering guns. She'd discovered that they fired not bullets, but heavy bolts that tended to leave large, ragged holes in whatever they struck. Whoever had built the machine had optimized it for combat.

She ducked behind a parked car for a few seconds to catch her breath. She'd lost her radio and had no idea where Irlene was, or if anyone else was coming to her aid.

"COME OUT, COME OUT, WHEREVER YOU ARE," taunted the machine's driver.

Faith looked around for something, anything to use as a weapon against the machine she'd begun to think of as a walking tank. She'd never before felt so helpless against an opponent. Her super-speed, normally so formidable against mundane opponents, was rendered useless against this armored behemoth.

"EENY, MEENY, MINY, MO," said the driver. The buzzsaw ripped downward through the car in front of the one Faith hid behind. She yelped as hot sparks showered her and burned tiny holes in her costume.

"CATCH A TIGER BY HIS TOE." Napalm splashed across the car to the rear. The palpable heat made her gasp for breath.

She didn't wait for him to finish taunting her, and made a dangerous rush across the street, darting between the walking tank's legs where it couldn't shoot at her.

Faith's heart hammered in pure terror. She had no idea how to battle an opponent like this. When she and the rest of Just Cause trained, they bantered with each other and sparred a little. It had been years since any of them had to fight a parahuman opponent.

In a blur of gray, yellow, and blue, Tommy flashed past the walking tank. A powerful gust of wind staggered the machine but failed to topple it. "Are you okay?" he called to Faith.

"Just singed," she shouted over the din. "Watch it!"

The tank's upper section rotated around to bring the bolt guns to bear on Tommy and Faith. He went one way, she the other.

The Volkswagen Beetle beside Faith vanished. She flinched at the unexpected disappearance, but then an intense, raspberry-colored hummingbird whirled about her head.

"Pick it up," screamed a six-inch-tall Irlene, trying to be heard over the sounds of destruction. Faith looked down to see a football-sized car near her feet. "Throw it," urged Irlene.

Faith realized what the girl wanted to accomplish and bent to pick up the tiny automobile. It had a nice heft to it and fit in her hand. She hurled it at the machine as the bolt guns tracked around to her.

Irlene returned the car to return to its normal size as it spun through the air. In a heartbeat, it became a sizable missile, but as it gained size and mass, it shed momentum, and the tank's driver whirled the buzzsaw arm around to deflect the small car into the second story of a nearby building.

The saw blade didn't survive the impact. The housing bent and the blade shattered at the tank's arm. Tommy tried to press the advantage by buffeting it with powerful winds, but the driver splayed the tank's legs and kept it upright.

"That was good. One arm down," said Faith over the noise. "Can you shrink another car?"

"No, all the others are too big for my powers," cried Irlene.

"Go find some more," said Faith. "We need more firepower."

Brilliant light from overhead defined everything on the street in sharp relief. "More firepower, coming right up," called Sundancer as she circled once overhead.

The machine stopped moving for a moment, its arms hanging like they'd been disconnected in a mechanical impression of surprise. Then Sundancer cut loose with a beam of radiant energy against the tank's armor and the machine backed up several steps, arms raised to protect itself.

The wash of heat from Sundancer's attack made Faith scamper back several yards. She squinted into the glare and wondered what she could do to help. Tommy circled overhead and used the massive rising heat from the machine as an engine to form a powerful, swirling dust devil in the middle of the street. He steered it like a remote control toy, smashing it again and again into the tank.

Faith glanced around her and realized she was right in front of a hardware store. Broken glass littered the front sidewalk and most of the window displays were empty. She ducked inside, found a large adjustable crescent wrench and hurried back outside again.

If nothing else, she'd try to take apart that tank piece by piece.

Javelin flew in, firing a steady barrage of particle beams from one hand. Faith realized that his other hand wasn't even armored. She stood well away from the team's heavy hitters as they brought the full force of their offensive abilities to bear against the walking tank.

The machine's thick armor soaked up a lot of punishment, but the steady assault by the parahumans was taking a toll. The engine noise had become arrhythmic and strained. A hydraulic line burst in a shower of blood-colored fluid and left one of the machine's legs dragging and inert.

The heroes pressed their advantage, and that brought them trouble. An innocuous servo angled outward with a mirror on its end. The tank driver thrust it into Sundancer's energy beam. It melted in the directed radiance, but not before reflecting some back at her. She shrieked and covered her eyes. Her hair became ash and her skin boiled with blisters.

Tommy rushed to cushion her fall but flew too close to the tank. The damaged arm, having once wielded the saw blade, still functioned well enough to knock Tommy hard across the street where he crashed into an awning. It collapsed around him like an undignified net.

As Javier descended to check on Sundancer, Faith hurried to help free Tommy. The tide of battle had turned in only a few seconds.

"I'M GONNA MESS YOU ALL UP." The tank took a step toward Javier and Sundancer.

"I'm okay," mumbled Tommy through the fabric. "I'll be out in a second."

Faith turned and ran back to interpose herself between the tank and her teammates. "That's far enough," she shouted. "I've got a wrench and I'm not afraid to use it."

~ ~ ~

Harlan gasped for air in the sweltering confines of Destroyer's cabin. That bitch with the sunbeam had fried or overheated half the suit's systems. He'd been fortunate to think of the trick with the mirror. Otherwise he might have only had seconds to live.

Then the guy in the inferior armor had shot out a hydraulic line with some kind of beam and left Destroyer limping. The man flew faster than Harlan's bolt guns could track, and if he went on a full offensive, Harlan was in trouble unless he got lucky.

Overall, he was very pleased at how Destroyer had handled the world's premiere superteam. Pony Girl had presented almost no threat, although the trick she and Irlene had pulled with the car caught him off guard and cost him the saw. Tornado had proved ineffective as well; he may as well have been using a hair dryer on Destroyer for all the good his air powers did.

Pony Girl stood before him, challenging him with, of all things, a crescent wrench. Harlan would have laughed in her face if Destroyer wasn't in such rough shape already. He was starting to think about how to escape back to the junkyard.

But first, he had to deal with the annoyance before him. He lowered the bolt guns at her. "LEAVE." The vocoder sounded staticky and distorted in his ears.

Pony Girl shook her head. "I'm going to take you apart piece by piece unless you surrender right now."

"THAT'S HARDLY A THREAT FROM WHERE I'M STANDING," said Harlan.

An unfamiliar shriek over the cabin speakers made him check all his monitors. Less than half of them still worked. He'd address that fragility in the Destroyer Mark II suit.

"Maybe I'm not that imposing," said Pony Girl, "but he is."

With a blast of blue flame and exhaust, the Steel Soldier settled to the street. Delta wings sprouted from the android's back. In its left hand, it held a multi-barreled machine gun with a cartridge feed running from an ammunition box on its torso. Its right arm had been replaced by a four-inch cannon with a long, rifled barrel.

Both weapons were pointed directly at Harlan.

"You are in so much trouble," said Pony Girl.

"CEASE ALL OFFENSIVE ACTIONS, SHUT DOWN YOUR SYSTEMS, AND EXIT THE VEHICLE," said the Soldier at top amplification.

Harlan winced at the noise and incipient threat of the cannon's gaping maw. He stared unabashed at the Soldier. He ached to get a look at its technical specifications, to dig around inside it and find out what made it tick.

Harlan fired his napalm, igniting a long strip along the street and torching the remaining parked cars. He hoped to confuse the robot long enough to get a telling shot at it from the bolt guns.

The Soldier's cannon fired, making an odd chuffing sound. Harlan's ears popped and he became disoriented as his screens lost their vertical or horizontal holds. He felt an impact, then another, and Destroyer fell backward with noisy debris raining down upon the cabin. His engines stalled and sparks shot through the cabin as most of the electronics failed.

Harlan realized Destroyer had fallen back into a building, which had crumbled atop him. A hole the size of a dinner plate poked through the cabin wall. The Soldier's cannon round had blasted right between Harlan's legs. The control sleeves had warped, and he was trapped.

The temperature rose. He realized his napalm had spilled and ignited, and if he couldn't get out, he was going to die. His one remaining monitor screen showed wreckage shifting as the Soldier dug through to get to him.

Harlan wouldn't accept rescue under those circumstances. He still had hydraulic power in the pincer arm, and one bolt gun. As the Soldier moved into range, Harlan worked his controls with feverish desperation. The pincer lashed out to close on the Solder's cannon barrel, crimping it to uselessness. Then with his last power, Harlan fired the rest of his bolt magazine point blank into the Soldier's torso.

The Soldier twitched and danced in Destroyer's grasp as the bolts chewed into and through the android's chest plastron. Sparks flew and the light in the robot's eyes died. Even in his grim situation, Harlan had to smile; he'd beaten yet another top-level superhero.

He turned his attention to trying to extricate his legs from Destroyer's control sleeves. They'd become bent, either from an impact or the Steel Soldier's shell, and Harlan didn't have enough purchase to yank either of them free.

The cabin temperature was so hot from the burning fuel that Harlan couldn't breathe. Perspiration lent him lubrication, and he got one leg to slip free. The other wouldn't budge at all, and he began to wonder whether he'd die from suffocation, heat, or fire first.

Cool air blew in through the hole in the cab. Harlan gasped at it. A bird-sized figure in raspberry and cream darted through the hole and Harlan groaned.

Why did it have to be Irlene?

"Harlan?" she squeaked in surprise. "What on Earth are you doing in here?"

"Go away," he shouted. "I'm busy."

Irlene ignored him. She grew in size and reached for him.

"Leave me alone," he cried.

"There's a building on top of you and a fire all around," she said as she took his hand. "The only way out of here is through that hole."

The cabin loomed larger and larger around Harlan until a gargantuan Irlene lifted him. She carried him the way Reggie did her stuffed elephant. Harlan struggled in her grasp but to no avail. She passed him into a waiting blue-gloved hand that poked through the hole. Harlan looked up into the colossal face of Tornado and knew he'd failed.

~ ~ ~

The doll-sized boy struggled in Tommy's grasp as he flew up and away from the burning building. Fire now engulfed the machine the boy had been piloting, and it was almost too bright to look upon.

He kept tight hold on the boy to keep him from wriggling free as he dropped down to the ground where Faith and Javier were tending to Sundancer. "I'm fine," said Gloria, but with her uncontrollable shivering it was clear she was going into shock.

"We need to get her to a hospital," said Faith. "Those burns look bad."

"What about the Soldier?" asked Javier.

"I can get him," said Irlene.

"Be careful," said Tommy. "That fire's really hot, and there are all kinds of weird air currents from it. You could get slammed into a wall or the ground at any moment."

Irlene shrugged. Tears ran unchecked down her face. "I have to try," she said. "That's my little brother you're holding."

"What?" Tommy tried to ask for clarification but Irlene had already flown off toward the inferno where the Steel Soldier was trapped. He glared down at the boy struggling in his grasp. It was hard to see in the darkness and flickering firelight, but there might be a family resemblance to Irlene. "Settle down, you," said Tommy. "You're in unbelievable trouble."

Something in the burning building exploded, sending chunks of brick flying in all directions. Faith took a step toward the building, crying, "Irlene!"

The diminutive heroine flew out of the flames, shrunken down to only two feet tall. She held the toy-sized Steel Soldier cradled in her arms as she made a beeline for the other heroes.

"Are you all right?" Faith ran to meet her.

Irlene nodded and set the Soldier down on the pavement. She turned toward Tommy and glared at his prisoner. The fire in her gaze was as bright as the burning building. "Harlan... oh, Harlan, what have you done?"

The boy stopped struggling in Tommy's grip. He stared up at his older sister with fierce pride all over his tiny face. Whatever he said wasn't audible over the noise of the burning building.

"Bring him back to size," said Tommy.

Irlene complied.

Tommy squeezed the boy's arm with an iron grip. "Your name's Harlan, right?"

Harlan nodded.

"You're in enough trouble without running away, Harlan, and you can't run fast or far enough we can't catch you."

Harlan sniffed. "Whatever."

Tommy looked over to where Faith bent over Sundancer while Javelin struggled with the heavily damaged Soldier. "What the hell did you do?"

"Nothing that shouldn't have been done years ago," said Harlan. "Somebody ought to have taken a flamethrower to this town long before me."

Tommy gaped in astonishment. The boy had just admitted his acts, without even being officially arrested or advised of his rights. "You did all this with that hunk of metal?"

"Destroyer," said Harlan. "I built it all myself, because I'm smart. Smarter than you."

"Tangling with Just Cause wasn't too smart, kid."

"The only one who challenged me was your robot."

"Tornado," said Pony Girl. "You and Javelin keep hold of the prisoner. Imp and I are going to get Sundancer to the hospital. We'll be back in a few minutes. I'll report in and get Bobby to send some black-and-whites out here."

"Better get a fire brigade too, if you can find one," said Javelin. "That building's a loss, and I don't know what we can to do stop it spreading."

Irlene shrank herself and Sundancer. Faith picked up the injured hero and sped away, cutting a tunnel of slipstream through the smoky air.

Harlan struggled a little in Tommy's grasp. Tommy buffeted him with strong breezes. "Knock it off, you." He turned to Javier. "How's the Soldier?"

"I think he's dead." Javier had removed his remaining gauntlet and had some tools from his portable kit out. The Soldier's perforated chest armor sat discarded to one side. Tommy couldn't make heads or tails of the wiring and components within the android's torso, but even he could see how much damage the kid had done.

Harlan giggled.

Javier stood and pulled his gauntlet on. He stalked over to Harlan and put the muzzle of his particle beam cannon under the boy's chin before Tommy realized what he was doing. "I say we grease this little fucker right now. Nobody takes out my teammates and walks away."

Harlan glared back at him in defiance. "Your robot shoulda been made better. Who built it, you?"

Tommy pushed Javier's hand aside. "He'll pay for his crimes."

"He's a fucking juvenile," shouted Javier. "They won't do shit to him. How many people did you kill tonight, pendejo? How many homes did you destroy?"

Harlan merely smiled. His psychopathy chilled Tommy to the bone. The kid didn't care a whit about anyone except himself. "I am sorry about your robot. It was the only one of all you worth a damn."

Two police cars screeched around a corner, lights flashing and sirens blaring. A fire truck followed in their wake. Their sudden appearance distracted Javier enough that Tommy was able to yank Harlan away before the furious Puerto Rican hero could blow the boy's head off.

"Listen to me, you little shit," said Tommy. "You have no idea just how bad things are going to get for you. You'd better straighten up as of right now and just maybe you won't get sent to federal prison." He bent down and whispered in the boy's ear. "You know what they do to little boys like you in prison? Want me to show you? I got nothing to lose right now." To illustrate his point, he squeezed Harlan's ass.

Harlan's tough attitude evaporated. "Hey," he said. "Hey, I can fix your robot. Make it like new. Better, even."

Javier laughed. "What's the matter, punk? Got the spirit of Jesus in you all of a sudden?"

"I don't want to go to jail," said Harlan. "Can't we work something out?"

"Too late for that," said Tommy as the cops pulled up and got out. "You're going to jail no matter what, kid."

"Hey, at least talk it over with your boss. I can fix your robot. You know I can. You seen what I built. All I need is tools and a place to work!"

Tommy pushed Harlan to the police. "You don't have anything to bargain with, kid. After that rampage you're lucky we even left you alive."

"I can fix it!" screamed Harlan.

Tommy felt Javier at his elbow. He looked over his shoulder.

"Maybe we ought to think it over," said Javier. "Otherwise the Soldier's dead and gone."

"You sure?" Tommy couldn't believe it; Javier's eyes were shiny with tears. Did the team's biggest cynic have the capability to feel something for someone?

Javier nodded. "We got to do something. He's one of us, you know?"

Tommy called to the cops. "Hold on, officers."

~~~

"The federal agents are on their way up, so you've only got about a minute. There's only one elevator functioning while we're on emergency power," said Bobby to Gretchen and Shane. "Go down five floors and listen for the elevator to go by. Once it does, call it and ride it down. I'll do my best to make sure the Feds aren't on it." He pushed a radio into her hands. "Don't call unless it's an absolute emergency. The Feds will know something is funny. If you have to, call yourself, um, Extinguisher."

"But what am I supposed to do?" Gretchen cinched the belt around her waist. She'd rolled up the cuffs on her legs and wrists once again. Only tall, strapping men must have worn the stupid things.

Bobby shrugged. "Put out fires. Save lives. Be a hero." He pointed at the stairwell. "Now get out of here before we're all busted."

Hand in hand, Gretchen and Shane ran for the stairs. Only dim red emergency lighting lit each floor's door, and they had to descend more by feel than by sight. When they had come down five floors, both of them were dripping with sweat and Gretchen felt like her legs had turned to jelly.

The lobby was deserted and very dark. A single emergency light shone like a baleful, crimson eye over the elevators. Gretchen led Shane out from the stairs toward that light.

"Shit," he muttered.

"What's the matter?"

"I just don't like this. The dark."

"It was dark in the sewer," Gretchen said.

"Yeah, but there you're only ten feet below the surface. Up here, it's like being stranded. Hundreds of feet up and nowhere to go."

Gretchen play-punched him in the arm. "You big scaredy cat. Don't worry, I'll protect you from any boogeymen." She stood on tiptoes and kissed him.

With a rumbling rattle, the elevator passed their floor. Looking upward, she wondered if the Feds would sniff her out. She squeezed Shane's hand and thumbed the call button.

They shrank back into the shadows and waited. In a few minutes, the car arrived with a ringing bell and the doors slid open. No Feds jumped out with guns at the ready. The car was empty.

"Let's go," she said, and pulled Shane after her.

They rode down for what felt like an eternity. She hoped nobody was waiting for them at the bottom of the building. When the doors slid apart, she saw only the darkened lobby and a few security guards ushering people out.

Nobody paid them any attention in the red-tinged darkness of emergency lighting. They headed out onto the plaza. Traffic jammed up all around them as people fought to get home with no traffic signals. The noise of engines and horns was deafening.

"Where should we go?" Gretchen had to lean close to Shane to hear his reply.

"Pick a direction," he said.

She pointed.

"North it is."

They advanced up the road, searching for opportunities for her to use her ability. There wasn't much looting in this part of Manhattan because there weren't many retailers. After a few minutes, they happened upon a solitary car fire.

"Okay, here goes nothing." Gretchen pushed up her sleeves and raised her arms.

The power leaped out, eager and capricious. She let it start in the middle of the car and grow outward as a bubble until it enveloped the whole vehicle. The flames snuffed out in only a couple seconds and Gretchen's bubble filled with smoke. Shaking under the strain of concentration, she shrank the bubble down, letting in the air a little at a time. Finally she relaxed and slumped against Shane.

The fire stayed out.

"Wow," he said. "That was crazy."

"It's harder than I thought," gasped Gretchen. "It's so much easier to let the bubble burst." She took a deep, shuddering breath.

"Are you all right?" Shane looked down into her eyes, concern washing over the contours of his face.

"Yeah, I think so," she said. "Let's go find another one."

As they progressed further north through Manhattan, Gretchen learned a few tricks through trial and error. For smaller fires, she created a regular vacuum bubble beside them, which imploded. The resulting blast of air displacement blew out the flames like someone puffing out a candle. Larger fires required more effort and sometimes took several bubbles to take out.

After her third car fire, Gretchen was exhausted and slumped against Shane. "It's been a long day," she said through a yawn. "Can we rest?"

"Of course we can," he said. "You're the hero here. I'm just along for the ride." They sat on a bus stop bench.

She smiled. "You're my sidekick."

He returned the smile. "Maybe I should have short pants on instead."

A prowling police cruiser slowed and the spotlight shone on them, highlighting their Just Cause coveralls in sharp relief. "Everything okay, folks?"

Shane raised a hand. "We're fine. Just catching a breather," he replied.

The officer in the car didn't reply. Perhaps he was looking at their matching coveralls, or listening to his radio. Gretchen hoped he wasn't calling for backup or something.

"Okay, have a good night. And be careful. There are some dangerous people out on the streets tonight."

"Thanks, officer," said Shane.

The cruiser pulled away from the curb to resume its slow prowl.

"I think we better move on," Gretchen said. "That was too close for comfort."

"Are you sure you're up for it?"

She nodded. "Someone's bound to need help more than I need sleep."

SEVENTEEN

July 14, 1977, 1:00 AM

Faith and Irlene returned from checking Sundancer into the hospital to find Tommy engaged in a full-on shouting match with a cop. Firefighters battled the burning building, hampered by the presence of accelerants from the walking tank. Irlene's brother sat sullenly in the back seat of a police car, watching the argument concerning his disposition. Oblivious to everyone and everything else, Javier knelt in the street beside the Steel Soldier and tried to coax life back into the mangled android.

"What's going on?" Faith pushed in between Tommy and the officer.

"This yokel is trying to claim custody of the kid," said Tommy.

"Yokel?" shouted the cop. "This kid committed arson and murder! Our turf, so he's our perp."

"We caught him," said Tommy. "He was driving a machine that caused untold property damage and took parahuman powers to bring down. He sent one of our teammates to the hospital and another might as well be dead. Our collar."

"Look," said Faith. "As ranking member of Just Cause, it's my call. We've already got the Feds here in town looking for one parahuman criminal. You want me to tell them the New York Police Department isn't going to give up another one into our custody?"

"But—" The officer's bluster began to crack with Faith facing him down.

"And I'm sure you don't have anything more important to do tonight than hang around here hassling us about one juvenile."

"Yes, but—"

"So if you'll remand him to our custody, we won't have to make a report to your chief about your unwillingness to cooperate."

The cop sighed. "All right, you can have him. Less paperwork for us at any rate."

"Thanks so much," said Faith with a sweet smile. She turned to Irlene. "Can you shrink down both him and the Soldier so we can bring them both back to headquarters?"

The girl nodded. "I need to go tell Momma what happened."

Faith shook her head. "Not yet. I'm sorry, but this is too important for you to run home when we need your shrinking ability. I promise, as soon as we've got Harlan and the Soldier squared away, we'll cut you loose."

More tears tracked down Irlene's face but she nodded.

The heroes crossed town to reconvene at headquarters. Irlene had shrunk down the Soldier and her brother to make it easier to transport them. Once they arrived and she restored them to their original size, Bobby cleared her to notify her mother of Harlan's arrest by Just Cause. Like a magenta hummingbird, she flitted out of the building toward the war zone that was Harlem.

Faith's heartbeat rose when she saw Agents Simmons and Stull were back in headquarters again, sipping coffee and discussing their investigation while poring over a large map of the city. She pulled Bobby aside to speak with him.

"Where are they?" She made a point not to mention Gretchen or Shane's names, just to be safe.

"They're out," said Bobby. A dark blush colored his cheeks.

"Out?" repeated Faith. "Out where?"

"Out. Fighting fires," he said. "I inducted them onto the team."

Faith's mouth dropped open. "You what?"

Bobby shrugged. "She wanted to help, and she can put out fires with her power. I wasn't going to let her go, but those two assholes came back and I didn't want them to know we're holding out on them."

"So you let two federal fugitives just walk away?" Faith couldn't believe her own ears. This wasn't the responsible Bobby she knew. "I mean, I don't want to turn her over to them either, but this could mean your job. It could get you sent to prison yourself."

Bobby folded his arms. Faith could tell he felt conflicted. "These aren't normal circumstances," he said at last. "City-wide power failure, riots, goddamn children torching tenements with giant robots." His face grew hard. "I need to use whatever resources I have available in this crisis, and if that means I deputize a fugitive, so be it."

Faith threw her arms around him and kissed him. She knew how worried he'd been about her in the battle with Harlan's tank; being unable to participate in parahuman combat meant Bobby spent a lot of time worrying about her and the others.

"Any word from Rick or John?" she asked.

"John's working through the subways, helping stranded riders to get out of the tunnels. Rick's somewhere here in Manhattan. Last he checked in, he was tying a looter to a street light."

Faith burst out laughing.

"Tell me about Gloria and the Soldier."

"Gloria's got some second- and third-degree burns on her face and chest from her own power reflecting back at her. She was in shock but the hospital got her stabilized. We'll know more by morning."

"It's already morning," said Bobby.

"Christ, don't I know it." Faith yawned. "As far as the Soldier goes, Javier thinks he's dead. The kid says he can fix him."

"Do you think he can?"

Faith shuddered. "You should have seen that thing he built. It's all burned up now, but besides the Soldier it was the most advanced thing I've ever seen. And it looked like he built it out of spare parts and junk," she added. "If anyone can fix the Soldier, I'd put my money on that kid. He must be some kind of engineering savant."

Bobby shot her a sharp look. "Do you think he's a parahuman?"

"Like superhuman engineering skill?"

"More like superhuman intelligence."

"That would make him really dangerous," said Faith. "I hope it's not true."

"H-hello?" A hoarse, nervous voice came over the radio. "P-Pony Girl? Anyone?"

"Who is that?" asked Bobby.

"Sounds like Irlene." Faith picked up her radio. "Pony Girl here. Go ahead."

"It's my momma," said the girl. "She been killed dead."

~ ~ ~

The Steel Soldier was like nothing Harlan had ever seen, or even imagined before. The android was complex all the way down to a microscopic level, filled with components for purposes Harlan couldn't begin to comprehend.

The mechanical lab in which the Soldier's remains sat was a marvel of engineering. As Javelin watched him like a hawk, Harlan familiarized himself with some of the high-tech tools and devices. His brain soaked up data like a sponge, taking mental snapshots of everything he saw, redrawing schematics, and gaining deeper understanding.

He saw with pride how much damage his bolt gun had done to the Soldier's torso. He was a force to be reckoned with, he thought. Wearing a device like a bicycle helmet with multiple magnification lenses and articulated lights, he worked to disconnect the Soldier's weapons systems before tackling the damaged torso section.

A hand encased in bronze armor closed around his arm. Harlan looked to see Javelin glaring at him. "Hey, what the fuck are you doing?"

"Disconnecting the weapons," explained Harlan as if to a child. "Then the boot jets. You want one of them to accidentally fire while I'm working?"

"Ain't never happened before."

"Has your android ever been this damaged before?"

Javelin didn't have a response for that.

Harlan adjusted his lights and lenses and bent over the Soldier's arm. As he disconnected the cannon, he began to understand the basic construction method. The Soldier hadn't been built like a machine, but like an organic being. It had a steel skeleton, hydraulic muscles, a circulatory system to deliver power where it was needed, and a nervous system to transmit data and instructions to and from the central brain.

"Amazing," he whispered. He could build a new Destroyer suit with this kind of technology. It could take years, but in the end, he'd have a suit that was like a second skin.

"That the kid?" asked a rough voice.

"Yeah that's the little prick," said Javelin. "Burned down half of Harlem."

Harlan looked up to see Javier speaking with a white guy in a dark gray suit who stank of coffee and cigarettes.

"Christ," said the man as if commenting on the weather. "How old are you?"

Harlan looked back at the Soldier. "Thirteen. What do you want? I'm busy."

"Special Agent Simmons, FBI." The agent extended a hand to Harlan, who looked at it with disinterest. "I understand your sister is part of Just Cause."

"So?"

Agent Simmons cleared his throat. "You're in a lot of trouble, kid, make no mistake about it. On the other hand, the government might be able to intervene on your behalf. If, say, you were to cooperate with us."

"Hold on," said Javelin. "You're not thinking about cutting a deal with this little punk, are you?"

"Stay out of this, hero. This isn't your concern."

"The fuck it isn't," said Javelin. "He could have killed Sundancer. He might have killed the Steel Soldier. How many civilians died under his guns tonight? How many people has he left homeless?" Javelin grabbed hold of Harlan's shoulder and spun him around to hiss in his face. "What's your death toll, *cabron*?"

Harlan spat in the Puerto Rican man's face.

Javelin raised his gauntlet, ready to blast the smirk off Harlan's face.

The sound of a hammer cocking was loud in the tense silence. "Back away from the boy." Agent Simmons had his nine millimeter clutched in both hands and aimed at Javelin's head. "Give me a reason."

"I didn't mean nothing by it," said Javelin with a forced laugh. He shoved Harlan as he stalked away. "Get back to work fixing my teammate."

Harlan returned to the Soldier and began isolating circuits and rerouting conduits as he surveyed the damage. He had an idea for a component he could install. It wouldn't be complex or difficult to build from the tools at hand.

It would ensure that in the future, Harlan would never have trouble with the Soldier again.

"You're out of control, Javelin. This will be in my report."

"Ah, fuck it. I'm just the team babysitter," said Javelin. "First that girl, and now this little shit."

Agent Simmons took a step toward him. "What girl?"

Javelin shrugged, but Harlan noticed a vein throbbing in his temple. He'd said something he wasn't supposed to and the agent had seen it as well. "Just some kid," mumbled the hero.

"Was it Gretchen Gumm? Did you find her and not report to us?" Agent Simmons' face turned thunderous.

"Hey, I know a Gretchen," said Harlan. "I got her passes to get in here from my sister."

Simmons' eyes widened. He yanked a piece of paper from within his coat and shoved it in Harlan's face. "Is this her?"

Harlan nodded. "She's nice. Why are you looking for her?"

Simmons grinned in triumph at Javelin, who wouldn't meet his gaze. "She's wanted for murder."

Harlan's heart leaped and swelled. He and Gretchen had far more in common than he'd ever realized.

Truly, they belonged together.

"Maybe I can help you find her," said Harlan. "She knows me."

"Maybe so," said Simmons. He turned to point at Javelin. "You guys, though, are in a shitload of trouble."

Javelin sighed. "So what else is new?"

Pony Girl burst into the lab. "I need to speak to Harlan."

Agent Simmons folded his arms and set his jaw. "So talk."

"Privately," she said. Harlan could tell she was upset about something. He suspected perhaps they'd found Momma at last. He wasn't worried; he had his story straight.

"So you can let this one slip through your fingers too? I don't think so. As soon as I can get a court order, this kid is going to be in my custody." He shook his head. "I can't trust Just Cause with a prisoner anymore. Not that I ever did."

Pony Girl rounded on Javelin, furious. "What did you tell him, you addled son of a bitch?"

Javelin tried to stammer an excuse but Pony Girl shook her head. "No, I don't have time for your bullshit now." She turned to Harlan. "Harlan, I'm sorry. There's been an accident. Your mother is dead and your younger sister is missing."

As he made his lip quiver and tears spill forth, Harlan thought how proud Gretchen would be if she knew.

~ ~ ~

Sporadic fires and headlights in the shadows below looked like the city dwellers were trying to recreate the majesty of the skies above. It was beautiful and terrible at the same time.

Dark New York spread out beneath Tommy as he cruised back toward Queens, where Miranda lived. He felt guilty that he hadn't been able to check on her since the catastrophe started and he hoped that she was all right.

"Tornado, come in." The crackle of Bobby's voice on his radio disturbed his reverie. He halted his flight to float a couple hundred feet in the air. His cape fluttered gently in a warm breeze.

"Go ahead, Bobby."

"Listen, uh…"

Tommy blinked at Bobby's hesitancy. One thing the man had always been was definitive in his decision-making. It made him a strong administrator and coordinator for a team generally filled with self-important hotheads.

"What is it?"

"We've had some bad luck. Irlene found her mother murdered in their apartment."

"Jesus. Do you think that kid did it?"

"We don't know, but the younger sister is missing to boot. Irlene's a mess. She needs someone with a cool head to help her out right now, and that's you."

Tommy shut his eyes. "You can't send Faith? I was going to check in on someone."

"No, I really can't. We've got those Federal agents breathing down our necks after something Javelin said and Faith is the only one who can help me with this."

"Shit. All right, what's the address?" Miranda would have to wait once more.

Bobby relayed the address. Tommy realized it wasn't far from where they'd battled Harlan's tank. He acknowledged, turned, and headed for Harlem.

Although it galled him to do so, Tommy ignored the looters as he flew past them, making a beeline for the Washingtons' apartment.

He found Irlene on the roof of the tenement. She stank of smoke, sweat, and vomit, and her face was puffy from crying. He floated down beside her. "Hey," he said in as soothing a tone as possible.

She looked back at him with eyes far too old for a face so young. It broke Tommy's heart that she'd lost her innocence her first day on the job. "I got here and the door was open," she whispered. "I thought Momma was asleep in the chair, but when I lit a candle I saw." She retched.

Tommy touched her shoulder. She flung herself into his arms and sobbed against his chest, pouring out all the unfairness of the world against him. "God, I'm sorry, so sorry," he whispered into her hair.

It felt like an eternity passed there on the rooftop until Irlene had cried all the tears she could. Chest hitching, she pushed herself away from Tommy. "Momma's dead," she said in a hollow voice. "But I didn't see Reggie nowhere. I can't go back there to look. Please, can you see if she's down there?"

241

"I'll look," said Tommy. "How old is she?"

She sniffled. "S-six. Look for a white stuffed elephant. She don't go nowhere without it."

"All right. Wait here for me, okay?"

Irlene nodded, and Tommy went over the side of the building and dropped lightly onto the fire escape outside their window. He pulled his flashlight from his belt and shined it into the room that must have been Harlan's. The bookshelves were bare, as was the desk. A few scattered tools and forgotten parts gleamed in the yellow beam. It seemed far too empty for the boy who'd built a tank out of spare parts.

"Reggie?" called Tommy. "It's me, Tornado, of Just Cause. Irlene sent me to come find you. Are you here?" He listened for any noise, but heard only the background sounds of looters. He'd almost come to tune out the cacophony over the past few hours.

He moved into the apartment, careful to keep his cape from snagging on anything. The next bedroom had two twin beds. One side of the room displayed posters of disco bands, while the other had pieces of paper taped up, each bearing a child's crayon scribbles. He shone the light back and forth, looking for any sign of either Reggie or the white elephant, but found nothing, even when he bent down to look beneath the beds. The closet proved fruitless.

A quick check of the mother's bedroom revealed nothing either. There was nothing left to do but check the living room and kitchen.

The coppery stench of blood floated thick in the air of the living room, made worse from the stifling heat. Flies buzzed around, brushing their legs against Tommy's face before dive-bombing back into the feast that had been laid out for them. Tommy gritted his teeth and brought the light up. Mrs. Washington's corpse wore an apron of drying blood, which started at her neck and ended in a tacky puddle at her feet. Her bulbous eyes gazed at the ceiling in an eternal question of why, and her mouth hung slack at the jaw in an accompanying silent scream.

Bile rose in Tommy's own throat and he spat into the corner. He was no detective, but he knew enough not to touch anything. The front door still stood open, but Tommy didn't want to leave that way. He went back through the apartment to Harlan's room, and left via the fire escape.

Irlene huddled on the roof, leaning against a vent chimney, her knees drawn tight up against her chest. Tommy knelt down beside her. "I didn't find Reggie or a stuffed elephant," he said. "She may have left before it happened."

"Why would she leave? And where would she go? She's six, for God's sake!"

"We should ask Harlan. He might know. He also might know what happened." Tommy paused, not really wanting to bring up the next thing, but knew he had to ask. "Irlene, do you think your brother might have killed your mother?"

"I don't know. I really don't know anymore. He never liked her. Never really liked any of us, although I guess he got on all right with Reggie. But to k-kill her? I don't know that I can believe that. He was so cheerful this afternoon when I gave him those passes."

"Passes?"

"For Just Cause. He said it was to impress a girl."

"Irlene, we need to go question him."

"I just don't want to believe that he could have done that to Momma."

"He built a machine for no other reason than to destroy the city and kill people," said Tommy. "I don't think we have any idea what he's capable of. But if he knows where your sister is, we've got to find out before it's too late." He held out a hand to her.

Irlene nodded and stood, wiping her eyes. "Okay, let's go."

~ ~ ~

A feminine voice came across Gretchen's radio. "Extinguisher, come in."

"Hey, isn't that you?" asked Shane.

Gretchen yawned. "Was it? I didn't hear it. God, Shane, I'm so tired, I could sleep for a week."

"Me too," he said. "I don't think I could even get it up right now. Well, maybe," he amended.

Even in the darkness, Shane still found things to make her laugh. She'd already decided to make a concerted effort to get closer to him once things settled down in her life somewhat. She pulled the radio from her pocket and looked at it, not knowing which button to push until Shane showed her. "This is, uh, Extinguisher, uh, over."

"It's Pony Girl," said the voice over the radio. "I don't have long to talk because we're very busy here now. There's a fugitive on the loose and the, um, the Federal agents are coordinating a search for her now."

Gretchen looked at Shane in confusion. "I don't understand. Is she talking about me?"

Shane nodded slowly. "I think I know what's going on. Ask her if the agents have updated information about her recent location."

Gretchen carefully relayed that question to Pony Girl.

"Affirmative. Their information is recent to within the last hour."

As she finally understood what Pony Girl was trying to tell her, she gasped in shock.

"Over and out. Tell her over and out," said Shane.

"Extinguisher, over and out." Gretchen felt numb. She turned to Shane. "They know. They know I was there. Shane, they're going to catch me in spite of everything." Her hands began to shake.

"No, they're not," retorted Shane. "You stop that right now. Pony Girl gave you the best warning she could. It's up to us not to waste it. The Feds might know you were in Just Cause headquarters, but they can't have any idea where you've gone since then. They don't even know if you're on foot or in a car. Not that getting out of Manhattan would be easy right now with all the traffic signals down."

"So what should we do?" Panic thudded into Gretchen's mind like a bale of hay hitting a barn floor. It made her jump at shadows, and with shadows everywhere she looked, she thought her heart might just explode.

Shane took her head in his hands and kissed her hard.

Her fluttering hands found resting spots against the back of his head. Her racing pulse changed subtly from fear to excitement as their tongues caressed each other. "God," she said in between kisses. "How do you do that?"

"It's all in the wrist," he said, and she laughed.

"Ain't that sweet," said a harsh new voice. "Gimme your dough."

Gretchen and Shane spun around to see a short black-haired man in the shadows. He had a shiny blue steel pistol pointed at them. Shane's protective hand tightened around Gretchen's waist.

"What're you, deaf? Gimme your fuckin' dough."

"Look, buddy," said Shane.

"I ain't your buddy. I'm the guy with the gun. Now make with the cash already before I put a fresh hole in your head."

Gretchen felt the power swell in her breast. She knew she could stop the man in an instant, the way she'd stopped the rat; the way she'd stopped Donny. "No," she whispered aloud. "I won't do that."

"I'm gonna count to ten," said the man. "And then I start shootin'. One… nine…"

"Listen," said Gretchen. "We're with Just Cause. You don't want to mess around with us, okay? You could get hurt."

The man sputtered out a wheezy laugh with a smell that suggested a three pack a day habit. "You ain't in no Just Cause."

"Check the coveralls." Shane turned so the Just Cause patch on the breast would be a little easier to see in the sporadic light.

"Fuck you." The man raised his gun.

Her power leaped out, but she was ready for it. She focused it around the man's hand and the gun. A crash of thunder echoed from the walls of surrounding buildings. The man yelped and dropped the gun, wringing a hand that Gretchen could see was swollen and bruised even in the darkness. Even though her ears rang from the booming of her own power, she raised her hands toward the man. "Get lost, punk, or I'll do it again."

The man needed no further encouragement. He turned and ran off into the darkness.

Shane bent and picked up the gun. He fussed with it until he popped open the cylinder. "Loaded," he said, "and look at this." He showed Gretchen where the pistol's hammer had crushed the back of one bullet. "This one had your name on it. Or mine. Lucky it misfired."

"It didn't misfire," she said. "I put a bubble around it. The gun couldn't fire in a vacuum. Gunpowder needs oxygen to explode, doesn't it?"

He nodded. "I guess so."

"We'd better go."

"What about this?" He held up the pistol.

Gretchen shrugged. "I don't think we should leave it here. Should you just throw it in the trash?"

"No, some crazy bag lady might get hold of it and start shooting commuters or something."

"Keep it, then."

Shane dropped it into the pocket of his coveralls.

"Be careful. Don't accidentally shoot off anything you might need later." Using her power to protect them had made her feel confident and strong, and she could feel it resonate in her personality.

He laughed. "Sure thing, Extinguisher. Good name, that."

The crackle of the radio interrupted them once more. "Anyone? Is anyone there?" The unfamiliar voice sounded rough and ragged, as if the speaker was in great pain. "It's Rick. I'm trapped in a burning building. Heavy beam on my legs. Off Hudson and Franklin."

"Hey, that's not far from us," said Shane. "You think that's somebody from Just Cause?"

"I don't know any Rick," said Gretchen, "but if we're close, well, I'm pretty good at putting out fires. And he needs help."

"Gotta be a good mile or more from here. You up for a run? I don't think we'll be able to catch a cab under these circumstances."

Gretchen smiled. "I was in track in high school."

Shane's smile was much more wry than hers. "I should have quit smoking."

They ran.

EIGHTEEN

July 14, 1977, 2:00 AM

Faith found herself trying to mediate an argument between Agent Simmons and Bobby. Bobby held the position that in things relating to parahumans, Just Cause was the expert agency by default and necessity. The team's government benefactors would back him in his decision that Gretchen's abilities would be more useful in quelling the fires than under lock and key. "I've got two heroes down for the count," said Bobby. "I'm short on parahuman resources already. You want to go tell the Mayor of New York that Just Cause had to let his constituency go up in smoke because you assholes are looking to make a name for yourselves?"

"She's a murderer," yelled Simmons.

"There's strong evidence to suggest self-defense came into play."

"Bullshit. You fucking Carter liberals would rather hold hands and sing Kumbaya around the fire than see justice served."

"Justice served at gunpoint isn't justice, it's fascism," said Bobby.

Simmons came halfway out of his seat and so did Faith, ready to defend her husband if necessary. Bobby and Simmons glared at each other, neither willing to back down.

Lionheart's plea for help crackled across the radio. "Bobby," said Faith. "I can get there quickest."

"Go," he said. "I'll monitor from here."

She didn't kiss him before she left. Under other circumstances she would have, but she didn't want to embarrass him in front of Simmons. Instead of waiting on the slow, temperamental elevator, she spun her way down the stairs at a hundred miles per hour, blowing past floors as if they were frames in a motion picture and startling one couple making out on the landing of the 40th floor. She staggered a little as she hit the plaza; her eyes still spun from her spiraling downward race.

Pouring on the speed, she raced north toward the intersection Rick had identified. She vaulted over cars in the jammed intersections, outracing the angry shouts that followed in her wake. She saw the glow of the fire a moment before she skidded to a halt on the pavement. It was the first time since the power had gone out that she could see anything clearly in the darkness.

It was a medium-sized textile factory, according to the aluminum sign over the front doors. Two fire crews were already on the scene, spraying water down onto the building's roof from their extension ladders. Hoses crisscrossed the road and Faith had to take careful steps to avoid tripping over any of them.

"Pony Girl, thank God," said a breathless voice. She spun to see that lanky boy who'd been with Gretchen. Shane, she recalled. He looked odd in the same Just Cause-issue coveralls that Bobby wore on duty. Soot and exhaustion covered his face.

"Shane? Where's Gretchen?"

A deep booming implosion answered her question. A globular area of flames vanished from one corner of the factory, only to reignite a moment later. A small figure backlit by the fire slumped in defeat. "It's no good," Gretchen cried. "Every time I take some out, it just catches again."

"This place is full of chemicals," he said. "Dyes and stuff. Lubricants for the machines. It's a goddamn tinderbox. Firemen said they'll be lucky to keep it from spreading to adjacent buildings."

"Lionheart's trapped in there," said Faith.

"Look at it, for God's sake!" Shane said. "It's an inferno in there. Unless you're fireproof, you're not going to get through a wall of flames to go look for him."

Faith whipped out her radio. "Lionheart, it's Pony Girl. We're here and we're coming in to get you."

She strained to hear Rick's faint "Hurry," over the radio.

"He's still alive. I've got to get inside that building. I can find him faster than anybody else." An idea occurred to her. "Gretchen, how good can you control your power?"

Gretchen shrugged. "Okay, I guess."

"Can you make your vacuum in a tube shape?"

"I think so. Why?"

"I'm going to run through it."

Despite protests from Shane, Gretchen, and the fire commander, Faith insisted that it was the only way for her to get into the building to find her trapped teammate. Nobody knew for sure what would happen to her in the second or so she'd be exposed to Gretchen's vacuum, but Faith knew they had to try.

Once more, Gretchen struggled with her power until she'd forced a tube of nothingness into the fire, letting Faith see all the way through the collapsing wall to the building interior. With lots of open space inside, there wasn't as much fire and she thought she'd be all right. She patted Gretchen. "Hold it just like that for a few seconds."

Before she dared think it over, she dashed through the empty space.

Air blew from her lungs and out her ass in the second it took to pass through the vacuum. She had the oddest sensation of her saliva boiling in her mouth without burning. Passing back into the scalding air made her gasp, but with no air in her lungs, it felt like she'd had the wind knocked out of her. She staggered and fell to her knees, trying to draw breath with a confused diaphragm. The tangible heat washed over her like a physical assault. As air started to find its way back into her lungs, she looked around.

The walls and some of the ceiling were burning. Vats of chemical dyes and bolts of fabric made bright, hot flames in fuming pinks, blues, and greens. Paint peeled and blackened off the machinery as grease and dust made billows of black smoke. Faith coughed, remembered her radio, and held it to her lips. "I'm in," she said. "Lionheart, where are you?"

She raced through the building, dodging around burning support beams and the chemical hot spots, which made the fire dance like a living creature from the air currents. After what felt like hours but probably only took a few seconds, she found him. An interior building, perhaps an elevated supervisor's office, had collapsed and trapped both his legs under a heavy wooden beam.

Rick coughed. "My hero," he said as Faith knelt down beside him. The flames were getting very close to him. He had a blackened two-by-four in one hand that he kept using to push away burning pieces.

"I'm going to get you out of here," she said. Working as fast as she ever had, she found enough debris to lever the heavy beam up with a piece of pipe that she wielded like a pry bar. Rick roared in pain as the pile atop him shifted, but the beam moved when Faith lent her weight to the pipe. Rick dug his fingertip claws into the floor and pulled, his muscles standing out in sharp relief under his golden fur. Then he popped free. The pile shifted and threatened to engulf Faith, but Rick pulled her to safety as well, and the two heroes lay entwined in each others' arms as the factory burned around them.

With a rumble, part of the factory roof caved in. Faith ran, leading a limping and gasping Rick across the floor. "Elevator shaft," he said.

They found a shaft with water running down its walls from the fire hoses outside. Rick was in obvious pain and couldn't put his full weight on one leg. With Faith's help, he climbed up onto the top of the elevator. For the moment, they would be safe in its steel confines. Faith grabbed her radio. "We're in a safe place right now. Elevator shaft. We need to rest before we get out. We're both kind of beat up."

Unmindful of the pools of sooty water, they sank to the roof of the elevator beneath them.

~~~

Never before had Harlan had access to tools or a facility like the one in Just Cause headquarters. He itched to get a peek inside that whatever engineering wonderland had first built the highly-advanced Steel Soldier.

He didn't want to make a sentient suit, but he wouldn't mind stealing all the secrets he could. Over the past two hours he'd learned so much about the internal systems of the Soldier, his brain felt like a coil of overstuffed sausages. He was already desperate to start applying some of that knowledge, but he knew he'd never work with secondhand junk parts again. A project such as the Destroyer Mark II armor deserved nothing less than state-of-the-art components. That meant money, and Harlan already had some ideas on how he could obtain some and make more.

Before he could do that, he had to ensure the Soldier wouldn't trouble him in the future. As Javelin dozed while pretending to watch him, Harlan installed a switch that he could trigger either through a radio signal or a sound broadcast. Said switch would dump fuel gases into the Soldier's battery compartment and trigger its internal capacitors. Harlan smiled as he tightened the connections on the switch. The Soldier would only continue to function as long as Harlan permitted it to.

He replaced a frayed cable, found the spot where it connected and when he plugged it in, the Soldier's eyes flickered and unintelligible garble issued from its speaker.

Javelin sat up. "What was that?"

"Progress," said Harlan.

Agent Simmons came back into the workshop. His face was red and veins stood out in his neck as if he'd been shouting. He sat on the workbench beside Harlan and put a hand on his shoulder. "Son," he began, with the awkwardness of a man destined never to have any children of his own. "I want you to know that I'm very sorry for the loss of your mother, and that the government is going to take care of you."

Javelin snorted from across the room.

Harlan made his lip quiver a little. "I miss my momma." He tried to sound small and pitiable.

"My partner is trying to get a judge roused right now," said Simmons. "That judge will sign an order remanding you to our custody so we can take you away from these so-called heroes."

"I don't like them." Harlan, fine-tuned an adjustment on the Soldier's electronic brain. "They're mean."

Javelin laughed. "Mean? We're a hell of a lot better than you deserve. As many people died in your rampage tonight, I guarantee you'll be tried as an adult. You know what they do to sweet young boys in prison?"

"That's enough," said Simmons.

"You better learn to love cock," said Javelin, "because it's gonna be a real sausage fest."

"That's enough!" Simmons' face darkened again. "Nobody's going to prison."

"He's lying to you," said Javelin. "He's a government stooge. Lying is in his job description."

"You got a hell of a big mouth," Simmons said. "Somebody ought to stick his boot in it."

"You think you got the stones, *hombre?*"

"RRRRR…" said the Soldier. Javelin and Simmons both stopped in their argument. The Soldier's eye lights flickered. With the hum of numerous tiny servomotors, one of the focusing lenses opened, then shut, and then returned to partway open.

Harlan made another adjustment. The Soldier made a noise like a cassette tape in rewind, and the eye lights went out. Harlan growled under his breath and reached for the tin snips. He cut a small piece of sheet metal and with a soldering gun, bridged two sections that had been physically connected before the Soldier's encounter with Destroyer's bolt gun.

The eye lights lit once more. "REBOOT COMMENCING," said the Soldier in its normal tone of voice. "DIAGNOSTICS… POWER SYSTEM AT THREE PERCENT AND FALLING… WRITING SHORT-TERM MEMORY TO ARCHIVE… MOTIVE SYSTEMS AT TWENTY PERCENT OPERATION… SENSORS AT FIFTY-FIVE PERCENT… FUEL RESERVES AT ZERO PERCENT… SUSPENDING DAMAGE CONTROL OPERATIONS PENDING POWER INPUT. STANDBY. STANDBY. STANDB—"

The Soldier's lights went out.

"Is it dead?" Simmons bent down to look closely at the Soldier's smooth skull-shaped head.

"No," said Harlan in satisfaction. "It just needs electricity. Plug it in once the grid's back online. It's got its own damage control. It should be able to handle most of its own repairs." He didn't mention his own special addition to the Soldier's innards. The way he'd tied it into the Soldier's very core, he doubted the android would even detect it.

"Well I'll be flipped," said Simmons. "You're some kind of a savant, kid."

"What happens next?" Harlan yawned. The lengthy, stressful day had taken its toll on him.

"We wait to hear from a judge," said Simmons. "And then I take you out of here."

Harlan rested his head on the table and closed his eyes. "Suits me just fine."

~ ~ ~

One of the Just Cause house security guards stood watch outside the workshop where Irlene's brother was trying to fix the Steel Soldier. He nodded to Tommy and Irlene and stood aside to let them pass.

The Soldier's disassembled carcass lay on a workbench with only a solitary blinking light indicating any function at all. Javier dozed in a chair in the corner while Harlan had his head down on his folded arms. Agent Simmons stared at them, stone-faced, drinking coffee that might have been hot hours ago. "What do you want?" he asked.

"I need to talk to my brother," said Irlene. Her voice had taken in a hard edge that worried Tommy. He hoped she wasn't going to become a grim-faced antihero type. Just Cause always seemed to have one or two members like that, who were driven more by anger and a desire for revenge than by a need to help people.

At the moment, Tommy realized with surprise, that anger-driven antihero was him.

"Don't take him anywhere," Simmons said. "Soon as we get the signed paper over here, we will be taking custody of your prisoner."

"He's ours until then," Tommy said. "So why don't you go polish your badge or something?"

"I'm not going anywhere. You got stuff to say to him, you can say it in front of me."

Irlene shrank the agent down to the size of a plastic army man. She muffled his indignant yells with an overturned styrofoam coffee cup. "We don't have time for The Man's bullshit," she said. "Harlan, wake up."

Harlan stirred and looked up blearily. "What?"

"Harlan, you know about Momma, right? They told you?"

"She's dead," he said. "Yeah, I know."

"Listen. Reggie's missing. Do you have any idea where she is?"

"Yeah I do. When the power went out, I went to talk to Momma but she was gone. I bet she was out there looting like everyone else. People were yelling and breaking glass and setting fires and I didn't think it was safe in that firetrap of an apartment. So I went to wake up Reggie and took her someplace safe."

"You took her? Out into the streets? Jesus Christ, Harlan, you could have been killed."

Harlan shrugged. "You'd rather we stayed and got killed by whoever killed Momma?"

"Harlan," said Tommy. "Enough of this. Where is your sister?"

"Someplace safe. I already told you."

"You didn't tell us anything," Irlene said. "Stop jerking our chains and tell us."

"What's in it for me?"

Irlene's mouth dropped open in shock.

Tommy shook his head in disgust. "You're trying to use your little sister's safety as a bargaining chip for your own skin? That's pretty low, kid."

"You all keep saying how much trouble I'm in," Harlan said. "I'm just trying to get some good will on my side, however I can do it."

Irlene grabbed Harlan by his collar and dragged him off his stool. He yelped in surprise as she pulled him in close to her. "Where's Reggie? Where's my little sister?"

Tommy didn't stop her. Once he might have, but the events of the day had brought out the cynic in him. A noise made him turn.

Agent Stull stood framed in the doorway, an envelope clutched in his hand. "Let the boy go," he said. "I've got a court order right here remanding him into the custody of the United States Government."

"Let him go, Irlene," said Tommy. "If he wants his sister to be lost or taken, that's his call. The Feds sure aren't going to help."

Harlan's confident demeanor showed some cracks. "Of course they will. Won't you?"

"Certainly," said Stull.

"See?" Harlan sounded vindicated.

"He's lying," Tommy said. "How many times have adults lied to you? You ought to know not to trust anyone over thirty."

"You can shut up now or I'll charge you with interfering with a federal investigation," Stull said.

"Speaking of federal charges, you better free the other suit before he suffocates under there," said Tommy.

Irlene grew Simmons back to his original size. The inverted coffee cup perched ludicrously on his head before he shook it free.

"Assaulting a federal officer," he yelled. "I'll have your ass for this!"

"Honey, you couldn't handle my ass," said Irlene, and shook it at him.

Tommy blasted wind through the room, sending small parts flying. "Enough!"

Javier awakened from all of the shouting. "Christ. What the fuck? Where are they going?"

"They're taking Harlan," said Tommy.

"Wait, what about the Soldier? He's still in pieces."

"Your robot is fine," Harlan said. "It just needs power."

The agents hurried Harlan toward the door. Irlene started after them but Tommy held her back. "He's not going to help us," he said. "He doesn't need to now. We'll find your sister some other way."

Harlan stuck his head back in the door for just a moment. "The junkyard," he said quickly. "Make sure nothing happens to her, or else." Then he disappeared with the agents, and it was like he'd never been there at all.

"What junkyard?" asked Javier.

Irlene's face brightened. "There's this place he used to hang out. Probably still does. Maybe it's where he built that tank thing. I know where it is. Follow me!"

"Come on," said Tommy to Javier. "We'll need your light."

"I'm beat, man. I got nothing left," said Javier.

Tommy punched him in the face.

Javier flew backward to land in a heap against the wall. "Motherfucker! Twice in one day!" He rubbed his lips and scowled at the blood he saw there.

"For once in your sorry-ass life, act like a hero worthy of this team," shouted Tommy.

Javier's eyes widened and Tommy thought he might be about to fire a particle beam from his gauntlet. Then Javier wilted.

"All right, all right. Jesus Christ. Taking orders from a goddamn faggot."

"Get a move on." Tommy shoved the Puerto Rican ahead of him.

~~~

Gretchen's world had shrunk until it only contained the building before her, the fire, and Shane. When he wasn't helping the fire crews with hoses or shoving onlookers back, he floated into Gretchen's tunnel vision to bring her a cup of coffee and a doughnut, or to see if she was all right, or to just squeeze her hand in passing.

For her own part, Gretchen was using her two-day-old power like a master. She blew out small sections of fire near where the hoses sprayed and held the vacuum bubbles for a minute or two until the water within them froze solid. When she released the vacuum, the sections were slower to reignite or even stayed out altogether. She and the firefighters working in tandem had managed to gain ground, and flames no longer threatened to leap to the next building.

Every few minutes, she would open that tunnel once more in the hope that Pony Girl and Lionheart would get out. They'd radioed in more than half an hour ago. Lionheart had sustained injuries from being pinned. He said he could heal given time, but couldn't leave the building until more of the fire was out. He and an exhausted Faith had holed up in an elevator shaft. They were resting there to conserve their strength should they need to move with urgency. Firefighters had a hose on the spot where they thought the shaft might be in the hopes that they could keep the area from burning and cooking the heroes alive in a steel oven.

So much power usage and stress had left Gretchen feeling like a worn-out, empty shell. Suddenly someone was shaking her. She was lying on the hard ground with her cheek resting on warm, damp pavement.

"Gretchen? Come on, girl, wake up."

Shane had one of her hands in his and was rubbing her wrist.

She couldn't quite make her lips work the way they should have. She realized it was because her entire face had gone numb, like when she'd had her wisdom teeth removed. "Wha' happened?"

"You fainted," said Shane.

A young firefighter with a bushy mustache checked her pulse. "She's exhausted," he said to Shane, and then looked down at Gretchen. "I know you're a superhero and all, but you're not going to do anybody any good if you kill yourself. Take a break. You've helped out a lot. Let us fight on for awhile."

Gretchen nodded. The pavement felt at least as comfortable as her bed back in Dyersville. She realized she might never get to return there and a tear squeezed from one eye. Shane flopped down beside her, wiped out as well.

They hadn't rested for more than a couple minutes when with a rumbling roar, part of the burning building collapsed. Firefighters shouted as they ran to avoid tumbling debris. Gretchen found herself sitting upright, trying to decide how to use her power to help. Flames hissed and crackled amid the pile of debris.

"Pony Girl!" She fumbled for her radio. "Pony Girl? Lionheart? It's Gret—uh, Extinguisher. Are you okay?"

The radio crackled and then she heard Pony Girl's voice. "We're fine, but a big pile of debris fell beside the shaft. We're stuck in here at the moment. What happened? It sounded like the building came down on top of us."

"That's, uh, that's pretty close to what happened. It looks like one whole corner of the building collapsed."

A firefighter atop one of the ladders yelled down to the one manning the pump at the truck. He turned and called to Gretchen and Shane. "Half the roof's collapsed. I can see the elevator shaft but there's no way to get to it now."

Gretchen relayed that information to Pony Girl.

"Oh." A world of disappointment and fear was conveyed in that single word.

"We'll keep on fighting the fire," said Gretchen, knowing how lame it sounded.

"I know you will. We'll wait here. It's not like we can go anywhere else anyway."

"Can't anyone else on Just Cause get you out?"

"Not really. The only one powerful enough to get to us here and fly us out is in pieces back at headquarters."

"Oh," said Gretchen, crestfallen.

"Just tell them to keep the water coming. It's keeping the temperature tolerable in here, and we're not suffocating from smoke."

"I'll do that. Hey, uh, I wanted to tell you thanks for believing me."

"My pleasure, Extinguisher. I'm glad to have met you. No matter what anyone else might say, you're a good person."

"Th-thanks."

"Pony Girl, signing off for now. Get this fire out so we can all go home and go to bed."

"Okay."

Shane poked her shoulder. "You're supposed to say Roger that or over and out or something."

Gretchen shrugged. "She knows what I meant. I'm not part of this world. Jesus, Shane, I'm just a girl from a small town in Iowa. What am I doing here?"

He squeezed her arm. "I'm glad you are here. Otherwise I never would have met you."

She smiled through her exhaustion. "Same here."

She looked up at the burning building. Somewhere deep in its bowels was a woman who'd laid her reputation on the line for her.

She intended to make sure it hadn't been a wasted effort.

NINETEEN

July 14, 1977, 3:00 AM

"Well, that's it, I guess," said Faith. She set her radio onto the roof of the elevator car where it wouldn't be doused by the water running down the side of the shaft. "We're stuck."

Lionheart closed his eyes and leaned back. "Super." He sounded exhausted.

"How's your leg?"

He didn't open his eyes. "It hurts. I think I may have broken something."

"Dammit, Rick, why didn't you say something before now?" Faith began to examine his leg, paying close attention to his foot and ankle where the swelling seemed to be the worst.

"Would it have made any difference?" He winced when she moved his foot up.

"I don't think it's broken, but you've got a bad sprain here. You're not going to be kicking any training dummies for awhile."

"I always thought those bastards would get the better of me someday."

Despite their dire circumstances, she laughed. "I'm sure you'll be up and at them in no time."

He opened his eyes. They sparkled like stars in the near darkness of the shaft. "But, doctor, will I ever play the piano again?"

Faith smiled into the darkness. "Of course you will, stupid."

"You're a wonderful doctor. I never could play the piano."

Faith punched him gently in the shoulder. "Wise-ass."

"Faith, I'm glad you're here."

"I'm not, Rick."

"You know what I mean." He raised himself up on his elbows.

She slumped down beside him. "Yeah, I do."

Outside, the sounds of burning intensified as the fire found a new source of fuel. They could hear timbers falling from the roof to crash against the cement floor. Faith could see a faint, flickering orange glow above, where flames tore into the upper level of the building.

"Rick, do you think we're going to die here?"

"Of course not. We're superheroes. We die doing heroic things, not baking to death in an elevator shaft."

She sniffled a little. "I always liked that about you. You can always find a ray of hope even in the darkest moments."

"I'm an optimist."

They listened to the sounds of fire and water for a few minutes.

"I've had a crush on you for a long time." She was glad for the near darkness; it made her admission easier when she couldn't see his face. "I've fantasized about, you know, being with you. What it would be like to get you somewhere alone where nobody would ever know. And now here we are and all I can think about is Bobby."

"I understand, Faith."

"Do you, Rick? What you don't know is how guilty I feel. He's a good man. God, we've been together since I was fifteen. I love him so much, but right now I'm thinking of him because if I don't, I'm going to give in and do something we'll regret." She shivered in spite of the heat.

"It's not any easier for me, having feelings for someone who's not only married, but married to a good friend as well. It's hell working alongside you, knowing how much I want to be with you and that I never will."

Faith realized she could see his face after all. He looked as miserable as she felt. The firelight from above was growing brighter. She could see flames licking at the top of the shaft. Sooner or later, they'd jump to the grease-coated cable, and then the fire could spread downward and throughout the shaft, and they had nowhere to get away from it this time. She leaned her head onto his shoulder. He put his arm around her and they waited for something to happen to them.

"How will we ever get past this? I don't want to hurt Bobby. I hate that I'm hurting you, Rick. I hate that I'm hurting. It's not fair."

"No, it isn't. I'm sorry. I wish I had an answer for you." A loud crash made the elevator shake as something big collapsed outside. "But I think the point is probably moot by now."

"Rick," she said, but couldn't find the right words.

His arm tightened around her shoulders. "It's okay."

Tears ran unchecked down her cheeks. It wasn't fair. She had so much in her life left undone. She'd wanted children. She'd wanted to see Just Cause grow beyond itself. She'd wanted to retire to Arizona like her mother had.

She wanted to see Bobby again.

"It's getting hotter in here," Lionheart said in a soft voice.

She felt so bad for Rick. All these years he'd been in

love with her, and here they were going to die together like some couple out of a romantic novel without ever having connected. And even now, when their fate seemed to be sealed, he held back from her—a true gentleman to the end.

But it didn't have to be that way.

She turned his head with gentle pressure. He could have resisted anyone short of an angry John Stone if he'd chosen to. "It doesn't have to be this way. Not now."

She took his leonine head in her hands, twisting her fingers into his soft mane, and breathed in the delightful scent of his musky fur. Her lips found his.

He pulled away. "Faith, are you sure?"

"Yes."

"My leg," he whispered. "I don't know if I can."

"Hush."

She covered his mouth with hers, and met him part way.

~ ~ ~

"So where are we going?" Harlan asked the two FBI men as the elevator doors closed, taking him away from Just Cause. He hoped it would be forever. "The Pentagon, maybe?"

"Shut up, kid," said the agent with the shaved head.

Harlan stood in the dim emergency lighting of the elevator and lost himself in a happy reverie. He'd seen the future in the design of the Steel Soldier. Not only did he understand it, he already saw ways he could improve upon it. With a real, high tech lab and brand new machined parts instead of rebuilt junk, Harlan would become the foremost inventor of his era. His name would be among the likes of Da Vinci and Tesla, Edison and Fulton.

They reached the lobby and the agents shoved him rudely ahead. "All right, all right," Harlan said.

They took him across the plaza to a parking garage where they located their late model, nondescript sedan by flashlight. The one with the shaved head opened the back door. "Get in," he ordered. Harlan did and the other agent slipped in after him while the bald one climbed in behind the wheel. He started the car and negotiated it through the confines of the garage. Traffic had finally thinned out as people settled in for a long haul without power.

"I'm Agent Simmons and this is Agent Stull," said the one with the hair. "We're with the FBI. You are in one motherfucking load of trouble, kid, and right now we're the only people standing between you and a fucked up prison system that likes to chew up kids like you and spit them out into general population."

"I'm listening." Harlan wasn't the smartest person on the planet when it came to dealing with other people, but even he could tell Simmons was leading up to something.

"The way I see it," said Simmons, "we've got three choices when it comes to you. We could turn you over to a federal prosecutor. We get nice letters of commendation in our files, and you wind up spending the rest of your life toiling away in a lab somewhere to make the world safe for democracy."

"That doesn't sound so bad," said Harlan.

"It's bullshit," said Stull from the front seat. "You're basically chained to your desk. You want to go see movies, date girls? Forget about it. Your ass would belong to the government and it doesn't care about stuff like that."

"Oh. What's the second choice?"

"The second choice is we put a bullet in you and report you killed while trying to escape. Saves us a lot of trouble and probably better for you in the long run than going to work in a government lab." Simmons pulled his sidearm out and placed it against Harlan's forehead. "I could pull this trigger right now, go home and fuck my wife, sleep for ten hours, and get up refreshed and hungry for waffles with strawberry syrup. You get my point? Whether you live or die doesn't matter a bit to me."

Harlan felt his ass muscles twitching, as if they wanted to run away with or without him. He didn't think they'd kill him right away; they wanted something from him. He tried to keep his voice steady. "And the third option?"

"Government pays us pretty well," said Simmons, "but that's not where the real money's at. Government contractors, now, those guys get all the dough. We've got a little business proposition for you. Say that me and Joe here decide to leave our cushy jobs to go into the private sector. Now, Joe's got a good business sense and I can kick down a door to open a new account. All we need is a product. That's where you come in, kid."

"I don't understand." Harlan felt lost.

"We want you to go into business with us," said Stull. "You make the high-tech shit, he sells it, and I run the company. Everyone makes the dough, everyone wins."

"Really?" Harlan couldn't believe his ears. "You'd do that?"

"You got a gift, kid," said Simmons. "I saw that when you fixed that robot. That kind of talent's worth big bucks."

"But what do you do about me now? I'm a prisoner, right?"

"Prisoners escape," said Stull.

"Yeah, we'd be all broken up about it too," said Simmons. "Maybe we'd even retire." Almost as an afterthought, he realized he still had his gun centered on Harlan's forehead. He tucked it away in his shoulder holster once more. "So what do you say? Have we got a deal?"

Harlan considered. Their offer sounded awfully attractive. It would give him the chance and wherewithal to build Destroyer Mark II, and perhaps much later, an opportunity to exact his revenge upon Just Cause. "Sure, sounds good to me."

Stull picked up the radio handset. "Stull, go ahead." The agent must have heard a call for him amid the steady stream of babble.

"Joe, it's Ken back at the office. We just got a tip from an NYPD uniform. He said there are a couple of people in Just Cause uniforms fighting a fire in central Manhattan. He didn't recognize either one, which he thought was odd, and one of them was using some kind of thunder power. Her description matches that of your suspect."

"Copy that," said Stull.

"Son of a bitch, we got her!" Simmons pounded a triumphant fist against the roof of the car.

"Who?" asked Harlan.

"Gretchen Gumm. Didn't you tell me you know her?"

"Yeah, I met her earlier today. But I thought you guys were going to leave the FBI. Why do you care about her?"

"Because we hate goddamn parahumans," said Simmons. "And like it or not, she's a murderer." His voice grew cold and ugly. "And you're going to help us take her down."

"All right," said Harlan. With the prospect of a bright future ahead of him, he wrote off Gretchen. She wasn't his type anyway. Too old. Too skinny. Too white.

"Then here's what we'll do…"

~~~

Tommy felt the knot of anger roiling in his stomach like a bad hot dog. Too much bad shit had gone down in the past day. He was at the end of his emotional rope, and needed something positive to restore his faith in the order of the Universe.

If he, Javier, and Irlene could rescue her younger sister, it would go a long way toward ameliorating that growing sense of nihilism in Tommy's heart.

Without streetlights and landmarks to guide her, Irlene had to circle over Harlem for several minutes until she spotted the junkyard in question. The three heroes spiraled down and hovered over the teetering piles of crushed cars and other junk, unsure how to proceed under such unusual circumstances. What Tommy had thought were headlights of parked cars turned out to be something even more unexpected.

The lights were on.

Reflectors made from highly-polished trash can lids had been attached to poles. Yellowish lights burned at the center of each, illuminating a clearing within the piles. Each light was angled to minimize what could be seen from outside the yard. Within the clearing, they could see bits of machinery and projects that Harlan must have left unfinished.

Javier whistled. "That kid is something else." He looked sidelong at Irlene. "How did you not know he was doing this shit?"

"I guess I never paid enough attention," said Irlene. "None of us did. He hated us."

"Enough to kill your mother?" asked Tommy.

Irlene didn't answer.

"Let's get down there." Javier reduced thrust from his boot jets.

"Hey, wait!" Tommy cried.

Javier set down in the clearing. Bolt guns none of them had noticed swung around and peppered Javier with engine block bolts. Even despite his armor, he crumpled to the ground and stopped moving.

"Shit!" Tommy started to dive down but Irlene held him back.

"Don't," she said. "Who knows what else Harlan set up down there."

"He could be hurt," he said.

"He's wearing armor," said Irlene. "I sure ain't. How about you?"

"No. Can you carry him out?"

"I can't shrink him without getting close, and then I could get shot by those gun things too."

"Then we have to take them out. I'll find them, you shrink them."

Tommy created a small dust devil amid the clearing, keeping it well away from Javier. He spun it faster, picking up extra dirt and small debris until the whirlwind was solid enough to attract the guns' attention. As they fired bolts at the windstorm, Irlene flitted back and forth, shrinking the guns until they were too small to fire their bolt magazines.

Once the defense weapons had stopped firing, Irlene and Tommy darted down to check on their wounded companion. He was unconscious. Because of Javier's burnished armor, Tommy couldn't tell if the man was injured or not.

"Hey, wake up, amigo." He shook Javier.

"Leenie!" cried a juvenile voice. Tommy turned to see a young girl in a thin cotton nightshirt and pigtails running toward Irlene. A stuffed elephant bounced against the girl's side as she ran.

"Reggie!" Irlene flew to her sister so fast she didn't seem to cover the intervening distance. She caught up her sister in a tight embrace. "Oh, thank God."

"I was so scared, Leenie. All the people were yellin' and breakin' stuff and I didn't know where Momma was."

"But what are you doing here, baby doll?"

"Harlan said we had to leave 'cause it wasn't safe to stay home. He brung me here and showed me his robot." She started to cry. "I'm tired, Leenie. I wanna go home. I want Momma."

Irlene cried too. "We can't go home right now," she said. "But you'll come with me. I'll take you someplace safe and I'll stay with you there." She turned to appeal to Tommy.

"Go ahead," he said. "I'm glad she's all right. Get her out of here before something else happens."

Lifting Reggie as if she weighed next to nothing, Irlene floated up into the air. "We're going to fly, okay? I won't drop you, I promise."

Reggie laid her head on Irlene's shoulder. "Okay."

They flew off to the south, back toward Just Cause headquarters and maybe the only safe place left in the city.

"Oooh my head," Javier groaned. "What the fuck happened?"

Tommy loosened Javier's helmet. A round dent like a hailstone mark on a car marred the smooth finish. "You got shot," said Tommy. "This one had your name on it. If you didn't have a helmet on, you'd have been killed."

Javier spat out a glob of phlegmy blood. "Feels like I bit my tongue," he said. "Hurts like a motherfucker."

"At least you can still feel it. Can you stand?"

Javier struggled to his feet. "A little dizzy," he said. "Not as bad as a good coke buzz."

Tommy snorted in disgust. "Can you fly?"

Javier nodded. "Armor systems read functional. Barely, though. Been a rough night. I got enough juice to get home from here."

"Want me to follow you back to be sure?"

Javier hesitated before he answered. "No. You've already done enough for me today. You're a good friend, Tommy. Better than I deserve."

Tommy blushed. "Now that's not true," he said.

Javier held up his hand. "Yeah it is. I'm an asshole, and I know I've got problems. Lots of people have given up on me, but you still hang around. I guess what I'm trying to say is thank you." He held out his un-armored hand.

Tommy grasped it in silence.

"I'm going to try to do better," Javier said. "I promise."

Tommy smiled. He knew the likelihood of Javier following through was remote, but the man didn't need to hear that. "Okay, you fly on home," he said. "Call me if you need me."

Javier nodded and his sardonic grin returned. "I might need your help, amigo, but it'll be a cold day in Hell before I need you, you faggot."

Tommy laughed. "Don't be so sure. I've seen you checking out my ass."

Javier snorted, ignited his boot jets, and flew away.

The radio crackled. "Just Cause, it's John checking in. What's going on up on the surface?"

Tommy grabbed his handset. "Bad things, John. Stay where you're at, I'm coming to you."

~ ~ ~

As tired as she was, Gretchen was too restless to doze. She stared at the fire as it consumed the building despite the fire crews' best efforts. Finally, she slapped her knees in frustration and stood.

"What is it?" asked Shane, whose head had been nodding in slumber a moment before.

"I can't do this. I can't sit by and wait to see if the firemen are going to rescue Pony Girl and Lionheart or pull charred bodies from the wreckage later." She tossed her hair. It felt stringy and greasy to her after spending a couple hours fighting the fire in her own way. "They wouldn't be resting if it were you and me in there. They'd be doing whatever they could to get us out. And so should I."

She marched over to the nearest fire truck. Shane scrambled after her. The firefighter manning the pump controls glanced over his shoulder. "Ma'am, it's not safe here. You need to move back behind the lines."

Gretchen cleared her throat. "I'm with Just Cause, and I'm here to help," she said. "Who's in command of this?"

The fireman turned to look at her and realized who she was. "Oh, right. I remember now. Um, that would be Chief Mancini." He looked around. "That fellow over there by the ladder truck in the red hat."

Gretchen thanked him and jogged across the maze of hoses. Shane followed her and stood behind her as she stopped by the fire chief. "Chief Mancini? I'm the Extinguisher, from Just Cause. I've been trying to help your crews, but my teammates are trapped inside the building, and I want to do more to help."

Chief Mancini was a stocky, muscular Italian with a luxurious salt-and-pepper mustache and an unfiltered cigarette stuck in the corner of his mouth. "You're the young lady who the lads said was shutting down sections of the fire, eh?"

"Yes, that's me."

"I never heard of you before."

"I'm new. But I have powers." She raised her hands and made a tiny bubble of vacuum appear around Mancini's cigarette. It went out with a small popping sound.

Mancini's bushy eyebrows rose up so high that they disappeared beneath the brim of his cap. "So that's how it works, eh? You can put out fires?"

"Well, I can make the air around them disappear. But when I was working earlier, it seemed like every time I put a section out, it would flare up again."

"Problem is there's so much heat in the structure," explained Mancini. "Ambient temperatures are high enough that stuff reignites once air is present again. What we really need is to not only smother the fire, but to draw away heat from it."

"Hey, what if we pulled the fire away from the building? Wouldn't that accomplish the same thing?" asked Shane.

"Who're you?" Mancini lit a match and held it back to his cigarette.

"I'm just an assistant. She's new. They, uh, they assigned me to her."

"To draw the fire away, you'd need some kind of powerful draft, and then you'd risk igniting something else. Bad idea, kid."

"What if I pulled it straight up?" asked Gretchen. "There's nothing up there to burn. Wouldn't it just kind of stop?"

"It might," said the chief. "So long as we could get the building itself cooled down quickly enough. I get what you're thinking. Create a vacuum over the building and the fire gets pulled up to it, right?"

"Something like that," said Gretchen.

"How big a pocket can you create?"

Gretchen chewed on a knuckle, hesitating. "I'm not sure," she said. "I'm really wiped out, but I'm willing to try anything." An idea occurred to her. "I work best when I'm kind of upset or panicked. Scared."

Mancini raised an eyebrow. "If you're not scared of this fire, you should be."

"What about drugs?" asked Shane. "Like a powerful stimulant or something?"

"Come with me." Mancini led them to a rescue truck. He requisitioned a syringe from the kit and showed it to Gretchen. "Adrenaline. This'll kick in your fight-or-flight response. Think that'll do it? I'm against the idea, but this fire's kicking our asses and I don't have high hopes for your friends stuck inside."

Gretchen nodded. She looked up at the burning building. She was going to save Pony Girl with whatever it took. She pulled her collar down to show a thin arm to Mancini. He hollered for a paramedic, who ran over.

"Inject her with this, on my authority," he ordered the medic.

The medic swabbed her arm, knocked the bubbles free of the syringe, and injected the dose.

It only took a few seconds. Gretchen's heart started hammering. She felt like everything was moving too slow and she was too fast in it. Her breath came in short, sharp gasps. "Hold me up!" she hissed to Shane. "I can't... breathe ..."

As red tinged her vision, Gretchen raised her arms. Her hands fluttered at the ends of them like imprisoned birds. A murky, shadowy void started to form in the smoky haze over the building. The power danced in her mind, eager to show itself off. Firefighters paused to watch the strange shape as it grew larger.

"Going to be loud," said Gretchen.

"Jesus, she's right," said Shane. "Like the worst thunder ever."

Mancini got out his bullhorn. "Cover your ears, everyone," he ordered. "All hoses to full pressure. Get ready to soak this beast."

"I can't hold it anymore!"

The void imploded. A wallop of sound shattered windows all around. Wind blasted past them, knocking over men and any equipment not tied down. Gretchen felt like she'd been punched in the chest and head simultaneously, and staggered to her knees. She didn't know where Shane had gone. But as she watched, the fire spiraled upward from the building along with the wind as it filled the vacuum she'd created. Firemen struggled to gain ground in the momentary advantage she'd created for them. She didn't care if she saved or destroyed the building, just that Pony Girl and Lionheart would have a chance to get out alive.

The power spent at last, Gretchen succumbed to exhaustion, and collapsed.

TWENTY

July 14, 1977, 4:00 AM

Faith and Lionheart huddled together in exhaustion. The shaft was growing hotter and hotter and breathing had become difficult. They'd dressed again, because as Faith had said, whether they were rescued or not, it would be better to preserve their dignity.

Sweat matted Lionheart's fur and soaked Faith's costume. The temperature seemed to climb another dozen degrees every couple of minutes. The water running down the shaft was evaporating quickly and it felt like being inside a sauna.

"Rick," said Faith. "Thank you."

"Likewise," he hissed, his tongue lolling out as he tried to cool himself down. "At least now we know."

"Maybe if things were different."

"I know. I understand."

Faith wanted to say something else, but the loudest noise she'd ever heard drove all thoughts from her mind. It was like an explosion multiplied by thunder. If she'd stuck her head inside a jet engine, it would only begin to compare to the decibel level. Too late, she and Lionheart clapped their hands to their ears. The elevator shaft quivered around them and the light from the fire went out as a terrifically powerful wind roared through the shaft.

With a bang and a whistle, one of the elevator cables snapped and Faith avoided its fall only by her superspeed reflexes. Her ears ringing, she groped for Lionheart in the darkness. She found his hand and clutched it. The shaft was still sweltering hot, but now a stream of cooler air brushed past her face.

"Are you all right?" She had to scream just to hear her own voice.

"Yes. Are you?" roared Lionheart.

"Yes."

"What happened?"

"It must have been Gretchen," Faith said.

A rhythmic pounding came from somewhere over their heads. Lionheart picked up a piece of fallen debris and banged it against the wall of the shaft in response.

For a few minutes, Faith and Lionheart sat in tense silence. Then overhead they saw a shower of sparks and heard the shriek of metal upon metal. In a moment, a powerful flashlight beam stabbed down the shaft. "Pony Girl, Lionheart, are you all right?"

"Yes," called Lionheart. "Get us out of here."

The firefighters lowered down a sling on a rope. "You go first," Lionheart said.

Faith was too tired to argue, so she sat herself in the sling and called for them to raise her. The ascent seemed interminable, but at last the strong hands of two young firemen pulled her safely into the basket of a ladder truck, parked far below.

They insisted upon her waiting in the basket while they pulled Lionheart from the shaft. As she leaned against the railing, she looked down at the building below. It still burned, but the fire was much less severe than when she'd first arrived, and the fire crews seemed to be winning the war.

In a few minutes, Lionheart joined her in the basket and the firemen lowered the ladder so they could reach the ground. Faith felt like falling to her knees and kissing the pavement as she stepped from the basket. Instead, she was almost bowled over by a crying Gretchen.

"I'm so happy you're all right," cried Gretchen. "I was so worried."

"Miss, I really think you ought to be resting," a paramedic said to the young woman.

"I know, I will."

More paramedics escorted Faith and Lionheart back with Gretchen to the temporary triage station they'd established across the street. They began to check over the recently rescued heroes.

"I understand we have you to thank for our still being alive," said Lionheart to Gretchen. "Thank you very much. I never thought I'd appreciate breathing the air of New York City as much as I do right now."

Gretchen fidgeted where she sat. After being dosed with a signifcant amount of adrenaline, she was suffering the aftereffects. "I'm just glad you guys are all right."

"Well, I'm going to personally testify on your behalf," said Lionheart. "You deserve more than fair consideration for your actions tonight." He growled at the paramedic poking and prodding him.

The medic went white as a sheet. "I think you're going to need x-rays," he said. "I don't like the way your ankle is swelling, and you may have a broken rib. Maybe two."

"A broken rib?" Faith whirled to face Lionheart. "Why didn't you tell me?"

He smiled weakly. "I didn't want to worry you."

"You asshole."

"My hero," he shot back.

"Pony Girl, Lionheart, or, uh, Extinguisher come in," said Bobby over Gretchen's radio. Faith and Lionheart had lost theirs in the elevator shaft.

Gretchen handed the radio to Faith. "Audio, it's me. We're all alive and okay, although Lionheart is going to need a trip to the hospital."

"Listen, the Feds took the Washington kid. They got a judge to sign off on it."

"Jesus, where did they find one at this time of night?"

"I don't know, but I think they will come after Gretchen next. I overheard them talking about it. And she hasn't exactly kept a low profile."

Faith looked over at Gretchen, who was yawning. "No, I guess she hasn't. Lucky for Lionheart and me though."

"I think you'd better get her back here pretty quick. Imp is back here safe and sound with her sister. Tornado went to go meet John Stone. Javelin's running on emergency power but he's going to see if he can spot the Feds in the area before heading in for a recharge."

"Understood. Pony Girl out." She turned to the paramedic. "You going to clear me and her to leave?"

The medic nodded. "There's really nothing wrong with you that a good solid twelve hours of sleep won't cure."

"Lionheart." Faith didn't know what else to say.

He smiled. "Go. I'll give 'em hell at the hospital."

Faith stood and motioned to Gretchen and Shane. "Let's go, you two."

~~~

Agent Stull shifted the car back into Park. He'd placed it where it would be in shadow as the sun rose. The sky was already brightening to the east. They overlooked the plaza in front of the World Trade Center where they could potentially spot Gretchen on her return to Just Cause headquarters.

"What if she doesn't come back?" asked Harlan.

"Then my hunch is wrong," said Simmons. "But I got a feeling we'll see her pretty soon."

The agents got out of the car. Since he wasn't cuffed or anything, Harlan got out too. These were his new friends;

he didn't even consider running from them. Stull opened the trunk and removed a long case. The simple black shell with non-reflective hinges and hasp made Harlan feel all shivery inside.

"What are you going to do?" he whispered.

"Deal with a parahuman murderer," said Stull. "What do you think?" he asked Simmons.

Simmons pointed to a nearby building of only six stories. "That one," he said without hesitation. "Good angle, clear field of fire."

"Wait, you're going to kill her?" Harlan asked.

Neither agent replied. Stull took a set of two-way radios from the trunk and handed one to Simmons.

"Well, I'm okay with that," Harlan said. "I hate parahumans too." He caught a gleam in the sky and realized they weren't alone. "Give me your keys," he whispered to Stull.

"What? Are you out of your mind?"

"Trust me," hissed Harlan. "Trouble's coming."

Stull looked at Simmons, who shrugged. "He's sharp," said Simmons. "And you don't need the keys up on the rooftop."

Stull handed Harlan the keys. Harlan slipped inside the car and hunkered down in the footwell, taking out his Swiss Army knife and beginning to work on the car's wiring.

With a roar and hot flash of plasma jets, Javelin dropped to the cement by the car. Stull was caught with his hands full but Simmons' gun appeared in his hands like magic. "Hold it right there, hero."

"What's going on, guys?" asked Javelin. "If I didn't know better, I'd say he's got a sniper rifle in that case, and I can't imagine what you might intend to do with one of them. Surely nothing bad, right?"

"Fly away, Javelin. This isn't your problem." Simmons pointed at him.

Javelin's voice sounded like he was grinning behind his helmet visor. "I'm making it my problem. You guys got who you wanted, now get lost already."

"See, that's where you're wrong," said Simmons. "We didn't yet get who we came for. Now you're interfering with a federal investigation. You think you're above the law?"

Harlan worked at a feverish pace, isolating current to one wire and feeding it through the firewall. He'd only get one chance at this, and wasn't sure it would work. Javelin had been flying around a lot and certainly hadn't had time or opportunity to recharge his batteries with the blackout. He must be on reserve power, Harlan reasoned. The Feds wouldn't know that, but to Harlan it meant an opportunity.

He intended to exploit it.

"No, I'm not above the law. And neither are you fascist pukes," said Javelin.

Harlan heard a gun being cocked. "Last chance, spic," said Simmons.

Javelin's voice grew cold. "I hate that term, asshole."

"I will fire upon you, I'm warning you."

"Your peashooter can't get through this armor."

"You're not armored everywhere, spic. Spic spic spickety spic."

Javelin growled. "That's it!"

Harlan twisted the final connection and sat up so he could see. He jammed the key into the ignition, and cranked the starter. The engine turned over once and died, killing itself to fulfill its redesigned mission. A bright light flashed from the front of the car and sparks shot from all over Javelin's armor.

"Motherfucker!" Javelin yelled. He fumbled with his helmet and tore it off.

Simmons stepped forward and smashed Javelin across the jaw with the butt of his gun. The hero dropped like he'd been shot.

"What the fuck did you do?" Stull stared into the window at Harlan.

"I shorted out his armor by turning the engine into a magnetic pulse generator," said Harlan. "It only worked once, but that ought to be enough."

"You what?"

"I knocked out his armor. Your car ain't going to be no good now though." Harlan shrugged. "Sorry."

"It's all right," said Simmons as he approached. "We can always get a replacement. We're government. Nice work, kid."

Harlan swelled with pride. "So what do we do with him?"

"He isn't shit without his armor," said Simmons. "Strip him, bind him, gag him, lock him in the trunk." The two agents proceeded to do exactly that after removing the rest of their gear from the trunk. Harlan watched in glee as they dumped Javelin and shut the lid. These agents did things Harlan would love to do, and they had permission because they worked for the government.

"So what do we do now?" Harlan imagined himself in a suit like that. With a gun. Powerful.

"We stick with the plan," said Simmons. "Joe gets up on the roof. I take cover. You wait here. When the Just Cause types show up, you try to get Gretchen away from them."

"How do I do that?"

"Fuck, kid, you said you knew her. Think of something. Just get her clear from the others and leave the rest to us."

"Okay." Harlan wasn't worried; he knew he'd think of something.

After all, he was brilliant that way.

~~~

The sun was still below the ocean horizon, but the eastern sky was beginning to turn creamy orange. John was a gray shadow against the lightening street as Tommy circled and descended beside him.

"Hey," said John.

"How was it here?" asked Tommy.

"Crazy in the subways. Several were stuck between stations. I had to wrench doors open and lead people through the tunnels. I went through all my flashlight batteries. What's been going on that's so terrible up here in the surface world?"

"Bad things. Rioting and fires. Irlene's little brother is some kind of techno-engineering genius. He built this giant walking tank thing and took it to the streets, burning buildings and tearing things up. He hurt Gloria and seriously damaged the Soldier before we got him."

"Jesus Christ," murmured John. "He's how old?"

"Thirteen. Can you believe that? He kidnapped his youngest sister and may possibly have murdered his mother too."

"Oh no. Please tell me he's in custody."

"He is, but not ours. The Feds chasing Gretchen Gumm claimed custody."

John shook his head. "NYPD won't like that."

"Listen, I've been trying all night to go check on someone. That girl whose life I saved earlier was supposed to meet us at the game. Since she didn't, I really want to go make sure she's all right."

John nodded. "Things seem to have calmed down somewhat. I expect people will go crazy again in a couple hours after the sun is up."

Tommy yawned. "Don't remind me. It's been ages since I pulled an all-nighter." He fumbled through his belt until he found Miranda's address. "You know Queens better than me. This isn't far, is it?"

John squinted at the address in the fading glow from Tommy's flashlight. "Four blocks," he decided. "It should be an apartment."

The two men covered the distance at a brisk pace. The streets sat mostly deserted as the looters had retreated ahead of the sun. John's heavy steps echoed off the brownstone buildings and those few storefronts that hadn't yet been broken by looters, rioters, or vandals. Tommy blew the feet out from under one enterprising young man who labored under an armful of stereo equipment that he was liberating.

"Tommy." John's tone was reproachful.

"I'm just sick of them. All of them. People are assholes, John. They don't appreciate us or what we do for them. They don't appreciate our suffering on their behalf."

"You've had a rough day. As soon as we check on your friend, I think you'd better get some real rest."

Tommy shrugged. The exhaustion seemed to have solidified into his very bones, as if helping to support him. "Yeah, I will," he said, unsure if he was lying to his best friend or not.

"Here, this is it." John pointed to a building that looked like all the others on the street.

A hand-lettered sign was taped to the security door: Electric lock not working. Please do not shut. Thanks!

"Some people are far too trusting." Tommy pushed the door open past the rock someone had set to prop it from closing. He shined his flashlight briefly across the mailboxes in the entryway and spotted *M. Kovnesky* on one.

"I'll wait here," said John. "I don't trust the floors in these older buildings."

Tommy went up to the third floor, hovering to keep his footsteps from disturbing anyone who might be sleeping. When he got to Miranda's door, he hesitated. He didn't want to disturb her if she was asleep, but his concern overrode common sense. He rapped his knuckles on the wooden door. "Miranda?" He couldn't detect the sound of anyone stirring within, so he checked the doorknob.

It was unlocked.

He turned it and pushed. No chain was latched and the door swung open into the darkened apartment. "Miranda? It's Tommy. Are you here?"

He moved inside. His dimming flashlight showed the clean apartment of someone obsessed with neatness, loaded with feminine touches: frilly curtains, houseplants, a Raggedy-Ann doll perched jauntily on a rocking chair in one corner. The air was perfumed, and the polished coffee table gleamed even in the dim light. "Miranda?"

He glanced into the bathroom. Spotless. Tommy liked to keep his own place clean, but Miranda took it to an entirely new level. Even her towels hung perfectly, like something in a four star hotel.

He found her in the bedroom. She lay on the bed in a chaste cotton nightgown. A faint acrid smell hung in the room, giving a sour tinge to the omnipresent perfume. Even in the stuffy heat of the air, Tommy felt a chill. "Miranda?" he asked once more, with fading hope. He cautiously touched her wrist. No pulse. Cool skin. On her nightstand, he saw an empty drinking glass beside an empty bottle of sleeping pills. Beneath them sat a folded piece of paper with the word Tommy written across it in flowing cursive.

With shaking hands, he pulled the paper free and shone his light on it.

You were wrong. I'm sorry. I wish you hadn't saved me.

Tears of impotent rage rushed down his cheeks. He felt like a vise was squeezing his chest. Tommy's heart pounded. The walls closed in on him. He needed to be free. He drew his power into himself, a tight angry ball of concentration. Then with a primal scream of fury, he flung it outward.

A blast of compressed wind exploded out from him and shattered the wall into dust. He stood for a moment, too wound up to be astonished. Then he flung himself out into the smoky sky with only his rage to propel him onward.

He heard John's surprised bellow of "Tommy?" waft up after him, but pretended he hadn't as he flew away.

~~~

Gretchen staggered and nearly fell. Only Shane's arm around her waist kept her from tumbling to the sidewalk. "I'm sorry," she said. "I'm so tired."

"Me too," said Shane.

"Are you all right?" asked Pony Girl. She was escorting the two of them back to the safety of Just Cause headquarters. Despite the difficult events of the day, she'd explained that it was still probably one of the safest places in the city.

Gretchen nodded. "I'm fine. Really done in, though. I'm so tired that even the curb is beginning to look soft and inviting."

Pony Girl laughed. "Well, I'm sorry we have to walk, at any rate."

Firefighters and police at the textile factory fire had offered them a ride, but Pony Girl had refused. She wouldn't hear of one of them acting as a taxi service under such dire circumstances.

Unfortunately, the few real taxis still on the streets wouldn't stop for them. Gretchen could understand why. The three of them were filthy. Soot had mixed with water and sweat to make a fine layer of black mud that stained their clothes, skin, and hair. Pony Girl's costume was torn and her skin scratched. Gretchen wouldn't have stopped for them either.

She'd reached that stage of exhaustion where she had a semblance of fresh energy. Although she trudged and staggered, her mind felt clear and sharp. Instead of yammering at her, the power was blessedly silent. She felt she had mastered it at last.

"Hey, Pony Girl?" she asked.

"Please, call me Faith."

"Faith, then. I was thinking. You know how Audio, er, Bobby said he was making us part of Just Cause?"

"Yes?"

"Well, did he mean it?"

"I'm sure he did, Gretchen. He doesn't make decisions lightly."

"Good. Because I think I'd really like to stay part of it. The team, I mean."

"Are you sure?"

"I've had so many things happen in the past couple of days. Everything's moving so fast. I never even imagined myself with parapowers. Now that I have them, it felt really good to use them to help people instead of hurting them."

"That's good to hear."

"You guys have been so wonderful to me." Gretchen squeezed Shane's hand. "All of you. I want to stay here in New York. I want to return the favor."

Pony Girl smiled. "It's not always like this, you know. Most of the time it's really boring. Occasionally we bust a mugger or drug dealer but besides that, it's a lot of boring celebrity stuff. Autographs, parties, opening shopping centers." Her smile grew wistful. "Being a superhero doesn't mean what it used to."

"Except days like today. Well, yesterday," added Gretchen, since the sky was brightening. It felt like she had arrived in New York weeks ago.

They rounded the last corner and strolled onto the large plaza before the Twin Towers. Even though the sun hadn't yet come up over the horizon, the very top floors glistened in the early morning light.

"What does it look like to see the sun rise from the top floor?" she asked Shane.

"I don't know," he said. "I've never been up that high for sunrise."

"Can we go soon?"

"You bet."

"It's amazing," said Pony Girl. "Worth getting up well before the sun."

"Or staying up all night," added Shane with a yawn. "Christ, I could sleep for a day and a half."

"We've got rooms at headquarters. You're welcome to stay."

"Thanks," he said. "I'll catch a couple hours of sleep, but Con Ed is going to need every hand they can get to bring power back to this city."

Pony Girl squeezed his arm. "You're every bit as much a hero as anyone on the team."

He grinned.

"Gretchen," said a voice.

They all turned to see Harlan Washington standing by a bench.

TWENTY-ONE

July 14, 1977, 5:00 AM

"Harlan!" said Faith in shock. She looked around but saw no sign of the Federal agents. She wondered if he had somehow escaped from them. If so, given his recent history of violence, she wouldn't be surprised if they might already be dead. Regardless, he was a threat not yet contained and she had to do something, despite the weariness making her arms and legs leaden. She started forward.

A bullet cracked off the cement near her feet.

Faith froze. The shot had come from somewhere above her and to the right. A glance confirmed a shooter on a nearby rooftop. She saw the rising sun glint off his scope. It had to be one of the agents. "What is this?"

"We're just after Gretchen," said Harlan. "Release her and we'll let you go."

"She's not our prisoner," said Faith.

"I knew it!" cried Agent Simmons. Faith turned her head to see him flanking the group on the left. His pistol was out and aimed at her. She was fast, but even she couldn't outrun a bullet. If he fired, she might dodge it, but that was a dicey proposition at best. "You goddamn superheroes and your liberal agendas. You're going to let her go, aren't you? She's a murderer!"

"She's a victim," said Faith. "And according to the law, she's also innocent until proven guilty." Her voice lowered. "Unless you intend to take that law into your own hands, Agent Simmons."

"Stop talking about me like I'm not here!" Gretchen yelled.

"Gretchen, I realize you're upset, but will you please shut up?" asked Faith. "There's a sniper up there and he could shoot any of us at any moment."

"Gretchen," called Harlan. "Come on, just walk away from them and come here. You know me. I made that carousel for you."

Faith clenched her teeth. "Simmons, why's that kid free? What did you promise him?"

Simmons laughed. "Nothing that concerns you. You're harboring a fugitive, Pony Girl. Far as I'm concerned, that voids your rights. Now you release Gumm into my custody or else we're going to have a problem."

"We already have a problem," said Faith. "You and your partner up there on the roof. What's he going to do, shoot us? You're so gung-ho about going after a murderer. Are you ready to become one?"

"Don't push me to find out. Now get your hands up."

Faith hesitated. Her eyes flicked downward at super speed. Her radio was right there on her belt, only inches away from her hand. If she was fast enough... "I'm unarmed," she said. "Never carried a gun. There's no finesse in one."

"It's amazing what people will do when you're holding one, though," said Simmons. "Hands up, hero."

"Do as he says," Faith said to Shane and Gretchen. "Trust me." As her own hands came up, her left hand flicked to her radio. She hoped the motion would be so fast that neither Simmons nor his partner on the rooftop would see it. Her thumb found the Send switch and locked it on.

No bullet smashed into her. Simmons didn't seem to notice the small traitorous act. Even Harlan, who Faith now knew was working alongside the Federal agents, didn't respond to her motion. Now she just had to stall until someone could come and help.

Just then, she realized that the night's events had decimated Just Cause. A citywide blackout and one psychopathic thirteen-year-old had humbled and defeated the world's greatest superheroes.

There might not be anyone left to come to their aid.

~ ~ ~

Harlan stared at Pony Girl and Gretchen. Hatred washed through his system, flushing uncertainty and doubt away. Pony Girl had helped take down Destroyer; he owed revenge against her. He didn't know how or when he would exact it, but he would have plenty of time to plan and resources to implement it.

Harlan's attention turned to Gretchen. Her lithe form filled the smudged Just Cause coveralls in a nice way. He still felt great attraction toward her. If only he could turn her, she would still be a good ally. Maybe she could teach him all the intricacies of sex, one great mystery about which he had yet to learn anything substantial. But then he remembered she'd been holding hands with the Con Ed guy. She'd made a choice, and it wasn't Harlan.

Her loss.

His attraction to her crumbled as he realized she'd probably been fucked by that asshole. She was no better than the whores who worked the street corners in Harlan's neighborhood.

Perhaps after Destroyer's rampage, they might take their business elsewhere. Harlan knew that he'd begun to effect the change in society he so desired. All he needed was more time and another suit.

A stray thought of Reggie crossed his mind. Irlene must have found her by now in Harlan's junkyard. He wondered if his security systems had gotten any of the superheroes. He doubted it; they'd been designed to defend against those on foot, not those who could fly. He'd never repeat that mistake again, he told himself. He didn't need the junkyard lab anymore. The Feds would give him a real workshop, with legitimate tools.

He considered that Reggie was safe for the moment with Irlene. Just Cause wouldn't harm her just to get back at Harlan, but he didn't think that would last long. His first action once this standoff was over would be to rescue his little sister and bring her with him to a new safe place. He'd raise her the best he could, take care of her needs, and ensure she would be safe.

And she, of course, would be grateful.

"All right," ordered Agent Simmons. "Ms. Gumm, step away from the others and come here."

"I'll stay here, thanks," she said. "I think I'm safer in Just Cause custody."

"You think?" mocked Harlan in derision. "What would you know about thinking, you stupid bitch?"

Gretchen's mouth dropped open in surprise.

"I can't believe I even liked you," said Harlan. "We would have been great together, and then you had to go get involved with some… some power guy."

"I can't believe I'm hearing this," said Gretchen. "You're just a kid, Harlan."

Harlan bristled. "I'm more of a man already than most guys will ever be. Him included."

"Shut up, kid," ordered Simmons. "Last warning, Gumm. Walk away from Pony Girl and surrender."

"Or else what?" called Pony Girl. "You going to start shooting at us right here in the shadow of our own headquarters? Gun us down here in the plaza?"

"If I have to," said Simmons. "I'm representing the federal government here, and you're breaking the law."

A distant flash of blue and white caught Harlan's eye. It wasn't a cloud or puff of smoke floating in the breeze. It moved with a purpose. He gasped as he remembered what Pony Girl had just said. She wasn't just talking; she was giving directions.

"Oh shit! Incoming!" screamed Harlan.

~~~

Tommy headed out toward the sea. He wanted to just cut loose, start a real tornado or something. He was so upset he felt he could easily launch a hurricane if he tried hard enough.

How could everything have gone so wrong in a single day? His hopes of love with John had been dashed. A woman who could have become his friend had died by her own hand, and with her dying words chastised Tommy for having the gall to save her life.

He squeezed his eyes shut against the sun as it pushed up past the horizon; he didn't wish to see the city below, burned and broken at the hands of its own residents. What was wrong with people that they were so quick to turn on each other? Were they inherently savage, no better than beasts, without morals or creeds?

No. He wouldn't believe that. There was still hope; there had to be.

And yet, over the flapping of his cape in the breeze of his passage, he fancied he heard Miranda's voice, shouting at him, accusing him of his failures from Beyond.

Then he realized the voice was coming from his radio. Still angry at himself, at Miranda, at the world, he was tempted to ignore it. Or better yet, he could hurl the offending device into the sea and be done with it.

He pulled the radio from his belt and looked at it in distaste, ready to pitch it away, and perhaps likewise to pitch away Just Cause with it. He couldn't keep being a hero when he no longer believed in those ideals.

"You going to start shooting at us right here in the shadow of our own headquarters? Gun us down here in the plaza?" The voice on the radio was Faith's, he realized. She was in trouble.

He didn't hesitate. He wheeled about and poured on the speed, blasting toward the World Trade Center plaza on a sheet of hurricane-force wind.

As Tommy approached his destination, he caught a glint of sunlight on glass and motion from a spot on a rooftop where none should be. He flipped sideways in his headlong flight just as he saw a muzzle flash.

Pain hit him like a fist to the ribs, knocking the breath from him. It radiated outward like fire spreading across a fuel spill. He'd been shot!

The sniper wouldn't get a second chance. Tommy recognized Agent Stull as he closed with the rooftop. The pain in his side forgotten, Tommy blew the rifle out of Stull's hands with a precise blast of high-pressure wind. Stull staggered and went for his sidearm.

Tommy was having none of it. Repercussions be damned. He blew Stull right off the roof. The agent yelled as he spun out into open air, and yet still retained enough presence of mind to squeeze one shot off at Tommy from his pistol, which missed.

Tommy created a downdraft, the kind that hurtled jets down hundreds of feet in seconds, and used it to pound Stull into the plaza with the force of a small meteorite.

He'd never killed before, and he searched his soul for any feeling of remorse or contrition and found none.

Black spots started to tinge his vision. Tommy looked down to see his blue and white costume had gone crimson as blood pumped from his body with each beat of his ice-cold heart. He grew dizzy and the plaza spiraled up to meet him as with his last energy he slowed his plummet to wafting down like a dead leaf before succumbing to the darkness.

~~~

At Harlan's warning, Gretchen saw the federal agent covering them stiffen. Despite her weariness, she started to call on her power once more to defend her and those she cared about. Then a gunshot rang out from overhead and Shane tackled her, knocking the wind out of her.

Gretchen gasped like a fish out of water, trying to regroup herself enough to use her power.

Pony Girl never hesitated. The moment the agent's attention was overhead, she charged at him. She staggered on burned and blistered feet, but even limping, Pony Girl was faster than everybody.

Harlan flung a fistful of shiny things at the ground. From her vantage point on the cement, Gretchen could see they were nuts and ball bearings. She had no breath with which to warn Pony Girl.

The speedster stepped on one and lost her footing. She skidded across the cement, shedding bits of skin and costume as she bounced to a stop.

Gretchen gasped as Shane held her tighter. "Get off," she said. Shane rolled to one side and she sat up, ready to stop the agent from shooting Pony Girl while she was down.

Except his gun wasn't pointed at the speedster on the ground; it was pointed right at Gretchen. The look on his face said it all. She was going to die at his hands.

A body hit the cement hard enough to crack it. Chunks of flesh and bone scattered outward from the point of impact. The agent staggered back in shock and disgust, and then horror as he recognized his erstwhile partner.

Tornado slumped down to the plaza from overhead, his costume bloodstained from a wound in his side.

Shane grabbed Gretchen's arm. "Run, while you can," he said.

Gretchen had no intention of running away. She'd spent far too much time running the last few days. It was time to stand and fight. "Go help Tornado," she said. "I'm the only one left to stop that guy."

"Oh goddamn, goddamn!" Madness tinged the remaining agent's blood-spattered face. He backed away, his gun hanging forgotten at his side.

Harlan grabbed Gretchen's arm. "I got her," he said.

"Get off me!" she screamed, and flung him aside.

A Swiss Army Knife appeared in his hand. He unfolded the blade. "Kill you! I'll fucking kill you!"

And then he was small, the size of a Barbie doll. Imp dropped from the sky and slammed a heavy trash can upside down over him. "I'm sorry, Harlan," she cried.

Galvanized into action, the federal agent raised his gun again and pointed it at Shane, whose back was turned as he knelt down beside Tornado.

"No!" Thunder roared between Gretchen and Shane as she used her power to pull herself toward him faster than even Pony Girl could run. The blast of air flung her across the intervening space and slumped against him just as the agent fired. She raised her hand, letting the power loose one last time and imploded the agent like the rat in the sewer. The instant vacuum rent and tore him to shreds.

Gretchen smiled at Shane. "It's okay," she said. Her voice sounded strange in her ears, breathy and bubbly at the same time. "I stopped him."

Shane gasped. His arms went around her as the world spun. She couldn't feel them. She couldn't feel any pain.

She couldn't feel anything.

"Oh God! Gretchen!"

She found it hard to reply. She couldn't seem to draw enough breath. "I'm sorry… Shane. I would have… loved to be… your girlfriend."

The world got brighter and whiter and Shane called her name over and over from many miles away.

TWENTY-TWO

July 14, 1977, 6:00 AM

Faith hobbled through headquarters on her turned ankle with the help of a crutch. She'd cried a little for Gretchen, but she was too exhausted to grieve for the girl she'd barely known who died protecting her friend. She'd given a statement to the police to explain the injuries to her teammates and the two dead federal agents. At least, she thought she had. She was so tired she really had no idea what she'd told them. Whatever it was, they seemed satisfied enough not to press further.

Lionheart returned to headquarters with his ribs taped up. He stayed a discreet distance from Faith, for which she was grateful. Instead of the warm afterglow of lovemaking or the excitement of a shared secret, she was wracked with guilt.

She checked in on Shane. Bobby had set him up in a small side office where he could rest and recuperate, telling him to take as long as he needed. He sat at the table, his head pillowed on his folded arms, and slept. Her heart went out to him. He'd taken Gretchen's death particularly hard. From what Faith gathered, the two had become close over the course of the day, and she'd sacrificed herself to save his life.

"How's he doing?" Faith turned to see Bobby standing in the hall.

"He's asleep," she replied. "Poor guy." She took a deep breath. "Bobby, I'm sorry I screwed things up tonight. First that horrible kid with his machine burning down Harlem and then Gretchen and the Feds. I've left a hell of a mess to clean up and I'll do whatever it takes to make sure things are right."

"It's a mess, that's for sure. Dead federal agents attract the wrong sort of attention from the government. So do thirteen-year-old psychopaths. It's bad enough we've still got Son of Sam running loose out there somewhere. New York gets enough bad press without stuff like this going on." Bobby sighed. "It's only going to get worse from here."

"What's going to happen to Harlan?"

"NYPD has arrested him and charged him with murder, criminal vandalism, arson, aiding and abetting, and pretty much everything else they can think of to keep him locked down. Irlene's legally of age to be his guardian. I think we can count on her to keep him within the penal system as long as possible. The DA will certainly try to prosecute him as an adult. If they can prove he killed his mother, they might just manage it too. Most likely he'll go to juvenile hall." He leaned against the wall. "I think we'll see him again someday. That frightens me."

"God, I hope not." Faith moved to embrace Bobby.

He pulled away.

"I'm disappointed in you, Faith."

"What?"

He sighed. "I can hear through walls. Nor am I blind. I know what's going on." He turned to look at her. His face was a study in pain and dismay. "I can smell him on you."

Bobby turned and walked away, leaving Faith behind. Tears ran unchecked down her cheeks. If she'd had anything in her stomach, she'd have thrown it up as a wave of nausea overcame her. She only hoped that somehow, someday, Bobby might forgive her. She promised herself to do whatever it took to regain his trust and love again.

She hoped he would give her that chance.

~ ~ ~

Irlene looked at Harlan with a mixture of sadness and contempt in her eyes. He stared back at her, feeling nothing but revulsion for the bitch unworthy of sharing his genes. He sat at a table in an interrogation room at a police station. A uniformed officer stood watch outside the locked door. Harlan knew others probably sat behind the one-way glass so they could smart off about him.

Someday, they would pay.

"You've made a mess of everything, Harlan. I can forgive a lot of things, but not this."

"I don't want your forgiveness." He yawned. The lengthy day had caught up with him at last and he was ready to sleep and didn't care whether it was in a cell or on the street. "I just want to sleep."

"Goddammit, Harlan! Momma is dead! Doesn't that mean anything to you?"

He didn't feel that deserved a reply.

Irlene stormed around the room. He could tell he'd hit her buttons and that gave him a surge of pleasure. She didn't know how to deal with a brick wall. If he answered, she'd try to play mind games with him.

Harlan could play mind games too.

"I'm taking custody of Reggie. I'll see to it she's raised properly, safely, and far away from people like you."

"She's my sister too. You can't change that."

Irlene raised her head high. "Actually, I can. After I walk out of here, I'm signing a form to make you a ward of the state. You are no longer part of my family, Harlan. From now on, it's just me and Reggie. You don't belong with us. I won't look back."

Again, Harlan replied with only his silence. Deep inside, he seethed at her. He didn't care if he ever saw her again, but she was taking away Reggie, for whom he felt something besides distaste and hate. He couldn't allow that. It might not be something he could change at the moment, but in the future he would take Reggie back. And then he'd take his revenge. He'd take down the team that had ruined his life.

Irlene sighed and went to the door. "Let me out. I'm done here."

Harlan waited until she was almost out of the room, and then called after her. "In five years at the most I'll be out. Five years, Irlene. That's your head start. You and the rest of Just Cause. Mark it on your calendars."

Irlene didn't reply to him, and Harlan knew with glee that he'd delivered the worst blow of all.

~ ~ ~

Tommy lay in the post-op recovery room, pumped full of drugs and plasma and who-knows-what. His body hurt all over, centered around a dull ache in his side. He had a vague memory of being shot. He wondered if he still had all his parts more or less intact. He stirred a little and discovered a whole new world of pain that had been waiting for him.

"Hey," said a familiar voice. "Are you awake?"

Tommy struggled to open his eyes. The lights were dimmed. Only one of every three was lit. A grayish blur beside him resolved into John Stone. Tommy tried to smile and discovered that even his lips hurt. "Hey," he managed.

"If you weren't lying there fresh out of surgery, I'd kick your ass," said John. "You're lucky to be alive."

"Hurts to be alive," mumbled Tommy.

"Well, it would hurt me if you were dead," said John. "Dammit, Tommy, you're my best friend. I hate seeing you in pain." His sigh sounded like steam escaping from a radiator. "I also hate knowing I'm part of the cause."

"It's okay."

"No, it's not," John said. He reached out and touched Tommy's hand, careful not to bruise it with his great stone fingers. "I'm sorry about today, and I'm sorry about your friend."

Tommy shut his eyes. "Miranda. Her name was Miranda. I saved her life yesterday."

"You saved mine too, puto."

That unexpected voice made Tommy open his eyes once more. Javier stood at the foot of his bed. He looked tired but cheerful. A large, colorful bruise decorated one cheekbone. "What are you doing here?"

"Hello to you too, and I'm fine, thanks for asking. That asshole kid did something to my armor and then that Fed introduced me to the butt of his pistol." He held out a bouquet of flowers. "These are for you. Queers are into frilly shit like this, right?"

Tommy smiled. His face hurt all over again, but he didn't mind it so much. "Yes, we dig the frilly shit."

Javier set the bouquet on a side table. "Good, because I ain't going to return them."

"Thank you, Javi."

"Hey, only my girlfriends get to call me that," he said.

John's fingers tapping gently on his arm made a sound like river ice breaking up.

"All right, I guess you can call me Javi too. Just don't let it get around, okay? People are going to think I've gone all soft and shit."

"I'm done being soft," said Tommy. "Tornado died today. From now on, I'll be Stormcloud."

"So what, you're gonna change your name? Change your costume? It don't change who you are underneath it.

You're still one of the good guys. You're a hero, you asshole, whether you like it or not."

"I could say the same about you... asshole." Tommy managed a ghost of a smile and closed his eyes. He was very tired.

As he drifted back under once more, he heard Javier's voice say, "I'm glad you're going to be okay, *amigo.*"

ABOUT THE AUTHOR

Ian Thomas Healy dabbles in many different genres. He's a nine-time participant and winner of National Novel Writing Month and is also the creator of the *Writing Better Action Through Cinematic Techniques* workshop, which helps writers to improve their action scenes.

When not writing, which is rare, he enjoys watching hockey, reading comic books (and serious books, too), and living in the great state of Colorado, which he shares with his wife, children, house-pets, and approximately five million other people.

Ian is on Twitter as @ianthealy
Ian is on Facebook as Author Ian Thomas Healy
www.ianthealy.com

~~~

ABOUT THE COVER ARTIST

Jeff Hebert is the creator of the HeroMachine online character portrait creator. He splits time between Austin, Texas and Durango, Colorado pursuing his lifetime dream of drawing super-heroes all day while not wearing pants.